BRYANT & MAY
The Bleeding Heart

www.transworldbooks.co.uk

BRYANT & MAY
The Bleeding Heart

CHRISTOPHER FOWLER

Doubleday

LONDON · TORONTO · SYDNEY · AUCKLAND · JOHANNESBURG

TRANSWORLD PUBLISHERS
61–63 Uxbridge Road, London W5 5SA
A Random House Group Company
www.transworldbooks.co.uk

First published in Great Britain
in 2014 by Doubleday
an imprint of Transworld Publishers

A CIP catalogue record for this book
is available from the British Library.

ISBN 9780857522030

Addresses for Random House Group Ltd companies outside the UK
can be found at: www.randomhouse.co.uk
The Random House Group Ltd Reg. No. 954009

The Random House Group Limited supports the Forest Stewardship Council® (FSC®),
the leading international forest-certification organisation. Our books
carrying the FSC label are printed on FSC®-certified paper. FSC is the only
forest-certification scheme supported by the leading environmental organisations,
including Greenpeace. Our paper procurement policy can be found
at www.randomhouse.co.uk/environment

Typeset in 11/13pt Sabon by
Kestrel Data, Exeter, Devon.
Printed and bound in Great Britain by
Clays Ltd, Bungay, Suffolk.

2 4 6 8 10 9 7 5 3 1

MIX
Paper from
responsible sources
FSC® C016897

For Sally Chapman

Done with the work of breathing; done
With all the world; the mad race run
Through to the end; the golden goal
Attained – and found to be hole!

Ambrose Bierce

ACKNOWLEDGEMENTS

I think there are probably two secrets to the longevity of a detective series. The first is that you must get the balance right between freshness and familiarity. The second is knowing that there's someone who trusts you enough to let you keep doing it. I write on many other subjects, but keep coming back to Bryant & May because I have some incredible support for my rather odd ideas. Plus, they're ridiculously good fun to write.

On the support front, I'd especially like to send a hurrah to my agent, Mandy Little, for grace under pressure and endless notes over the retsina in Daphne's, Camden Town. And to Simon Taylor, my editor, for his ridiculously cheery enthusiasm, and for the lunch we had in Bleeding Heart Yard that inspired this book. Huge thanks also to Kate Green and Kate Samano, for PR and proofing.

Jan, you're a London freak who's more curious about the city than anyone I've ever met. Stalky, you know way too much about my books. Pete, you never complain that I'm writing when I should be behaving like a normal person. And readers, I salute you for sharing ideas and posting them so regularly on my website. As always, the strangest facts in this novel are the truest, particularly those in Chapter Sixteen. St George's Gardens and the rest of the places mentioned here are real. You can discover more background to the book at www.christopherfowler.co.uk.

Peculiar Crimes Unit
The Old Warehouse
231 Caledonian Road
London N1 9RB

STAFF ROSTER FOR MONDAY 8 JULY

Raymond Land, Unit Chief
Arthur Bryant, Senior Detective
John May, Senior Detective
Janice Longbright, Detective Sergeant
Dan Banbury, Crime Scene Manager/InfoTech
Giles Kershaw, Forensic Pathologist
Jack Renfield, Sergeant
Meera Mangeshkar, Detective Constable
Colin Bimsley, Detective Constable
Crippen, staff cat

PRIVATE & PERSONAL MEMO – DO NOT FORWARD OR COPY

From Raymond Land to All Staff:

So, it's a new beginning for us. I'm sure we're all going to find it very exciting, although I'd much prefer it if we didn't.

This is the unit's first week under City of London jurisdiction. Even though the PCU's coverage extends far outside the Square Mile, we are now part of their workforce and they will come down on us like a ton of bricks if we break their rules. Would it be too much to ask that you don't upset them for the first few weeks? This means no weird stuff. Try to behave normally for once. Keep regular hours. Avoid provocative behaviour. Don't be imaginative. Play it strictly by the book and keep your paperwork up to date. And if anyone from the City of London calls, don't give them your opinions on anything. If you're in any doubt, refer them to me. In fact, it's probably better that you don't talk to them at all.

The City of London Police headquarters is in Love Lane, behind the Barbican, so they have no reason to come over here to King's Cross. Let's try to keep it that way. I don't want them seeing how we operate and thinking we're a bunch of amateurs. I've tried pointing out that some of us are older than the trees they've got round their building and deserve respect, but they still talk to me as if I was born yesterday.

As you know, one of the PCU's key remits is *to prevent or cause to cease any acts of violent disorder committed in the public areas of the city*, but luckily for us this is very loosely defined in our terms of contract. Let me tell you how the new system is going to work.

Investigations will be referred from CoL HQ in all but the most extreme circumstances (i.e. acts of terrorism and serious fraud, which are handled by separate divisions). They will only commence once we have received full clearance to proceed from our Public Liaison Officer. From then, every step will be documented and approved by me.

What this means – and I'm talking especially to you, Arthur – is that I don't want you running around like a superannuated Harry Potter spreading insurrection, holding meetings with fake spiritualists and causing things to explode. I'm absolutely determined that the next major investigation we undertake will not end up with anyone having to gallop through a cemetery at midnight.

We're going to start solving crimes the proper way, by sitting at desks and working things out with bits of paper, and going home while there's still something decent on the telly. By the way, you'll notice that I've dropped the 'Acting' part from my job title. After fifteen years of trying to escape from you lot I've resigned myself to the fact that they'll probably carry me out of the PCU feet first. This doesn't mean that I wouldn't rather be somewhere else. If I had to choose between this rundown doss-house and a nice little sinecure in Somerset, I wouldn't think twice.

OK, general housekeeping. There seem to be kittens everywhere.

Will somebody please find homes for them and take Crippen to the vet before she decides to have any more? I counted nine but there may be others. Also, the towel rail in the second-floor toilet is electrified, something to do with a damaged heating element. Unfortunately it has to remain in use as the first-floor loo is still blocked, thanks to Mr Bryant's experiments with a cooked ham the size and shape of a human head. Just be careful when you've got wet hands, that's all.

The CoL is sticking us with an intern for two weeks. Try to be nice to him. That means no showing him how the handcuffs work and 'losing' the key, or sending him along to autopsies. Don't make him cry on his first day.

The new face-recognition system is being installed in the ground-floor hallway as an added security measure. Dan informs me that to activate it you just need to stand before the screen and press the red button. And in Mr Bryant's case, try taking your balaclava off first.

As you can tell, British summertime has arrived, so water is pouring through the third-floor roof extension whenever it rains, i.e. all the time. If you're going to leave anything in the evidence room that you don't want ruined, wrap it in a Tesco bag. Remember we're professionals. Apart from that, we're open for business as usual. Good luck, ladies and gentlemen, and may God have mercy on your souls.

1

DEAD OF NIGHT

For a teenager who had never been outside of London, Romain Curtis knew a lot about astronomy. His knowledge seemed pointless in a city where the night sky was usually barricaded behind an immense lid of low sulphurous cloud. When he looked up between the buildings, all he could see was a wash of reflected saffron light. But behind this he sensed the glimmering tracery of constellations, and could point to them with the certainty of a sailor.

Unfortunately it was a talent that impressed no one, least of all the girls from the Cromwell Estate in Bloomsbury, where he lived with his mother. Shirone Estanza was no different, and had stared blankly at him when he offered to name the stars, but she still pursued him. She was physically unlike most of the girls he had hung out with – shorter and rowdily brash – but she seemed like a lot of fun. She changed the colour of her nails every week (tonight, acid green) and wore the tightest skirts he'd ever seen. But he was still finding his feet with girls, and couldn't be sure if he even liked them, or if they liked him.

Romain appeared younger than his fifteen years. He

had his father's flat nose and wide forehead, but never appeared intimidating because he was rail-thin. He read voraciously, preferred heavy metal to hip-hop, and wanted to study textile design at Central St Martins. He saw movies about angry West Indian kids on council estates and failed to recognize anything of himself in the characters. His father had told him to be his own man, to keep close with his mates, to stay fit and fight back, pointless advice from a warehouseman who spent his days borrowing money from girlfriends, shuttling between the pub and the fixed-odds terminals in betting shops.

For a kid with hardly any money, London is a city of closed doors. Astronomy was a free hobby. Romain could go to museums and libraries, and sit in parks on clear evenings, using the app on his mobile to identify constellations. Tonight, Shirone had insisted on paying for their drinks in the Gunmakers, a pub she could enter without being carded because one of her brother's best mates ran the bar. Although Romain had nowhere to take her now, it was a warm, muggy night, and as he had been running wild in the neighbourhood since he was old enough to stand, he knew every dark and secret space for miles around. Leading her down Wakefield Street into the narrow gloom of Henrietta Mews, he reached the closed iron gates of St George's Gardens and stopped, turning to her.

Shirone had folded her arms and was offering a defiant jut of the jaw. 'If you think I'm going in there you've got another think coming.'

'What's wrong?' Romain asked innocently. 'There's never anyone in here.'

'Been inside with a lot of girls, have you?'

'No, what I mean is it's dead quiet and calm, all grass and trees an' that, and sometimes it's dark enough to see the stars.'

'You gonna start naming 'em all again?'

'No, I just fancied a sit-down with you. Look.' He swung a long leg over the black iron railings and stepped lightly down inside. 'It's easy. You need a hand over?'

'I can manage.' A moment later she had joined him and was looking around. 'That's nice, innit? You didn't say we was going to a graveyard.' She pointed to the stone circle of sarcophagi that rose between the paths like sacrificial altars, and the broken line of verdigris-topped headstones leaning against the back wall, under the shade of the plane trees. She had been in the little park many times but had never really taken much notice of the graves before. By day most of them were lost in the shadows.

'It's a garden; it's not used for burials no more, not for ages.' Romain ushered her past the headstones, towards a grassy area between the stone memorials. Tall buildings hemmed the park in on all sides. Here, at the backs of several blocks of flats, sheltered by the dense canopy of branches, they moved unobserved. Even the pale nimbus of the moon was lost from view. He dropped to the neatly clipped lawn and pulled out his mobile. She sat more gingerly, wary of ground that felt perpetually damp, even after a few days of dry weather.

'I got this tracking app that shows you the position of the planets,' he said, tilting the light to her. 'See?'

'How old are these graves?' asked Shirone, twisting about. She was wearing stretch jeans and very high heels, and sitting on grass of any kind was a tentative activity at best.

'About three hundred years, maybe more.' He returned his attention to the phone. 'See, Ursa Major is right overhead. In Greek mythology Callisto got turned into a bear and was almost shot with an arrow by her son. He was turned into a bear too. Ursa Minor. It's supposed to be the only constellation that never sinks below the horizon.'

'Yeah, whatever.'

Something ticked down from a nearby tree: a bird

releasing a twig, perhaps. Shirone looked as if she was about to spring to her feet. She had no problem pushing her way through a gang of ten classmates but more than three trees in the same place bothered her.

Romain pulled a battered joint from his jacket pocket and dug for his lighter. 'I used to come here when I was little, for picnics and that.' Perhaps it was best not to go on about the cemetery, he decided, as it would ruin his chances with her tonight, but he hadn't been able to think of anywhere else they could go. He dragged on the roll-up and tried to pass it to her, but she pushed his hand away. A single car broke the silence, heading south. The little park's greenery insulated it from surrounding sounds.

'I used to see you around all the time,' said Shirone, 'but you never said nothing. I didn't think you liked me.'

'It wasn't that, I just didn't know what to say. You was always with your brothers.'

'Yeah. They'd kill me if they found out I was here.'

'Why?'

'You're joking, right? They're Italian. I'm just half-Italian.' She laid herself back on the grass. 'It's weird being in here at night. Like we're in the country. What's that park in New York?'

'Central Park.'

'Yeah. My dad's got pictures. It's really big, right, but you can see buildings all around it.'

'I s'pose it was planned that way. Like a garden.'

'Yeah, but this . . .' She gestured vaguely around the green. 'It's not, is it? It just got sort of left behind. I mean, it was here first, and everything else got built around it. Like it's the original land, and everything else is just—'

He stopped her with a kiss. He wanted to take it slowly but there was something wonderful about her that he wanted to capture in his mouth. She tasted of mint and lemons; she had chewed the garnishes in her drink.

She broke off and turned her head. He thought he had

made the wrong move, but then she raised a hand and said, 'Listen.'

There was somebody else in the grounds. He heard a scrape, a crack of wood, a grunt, a displacement of earth, a cascade of small stones. He pushed himself up from the ground and looked about. On the far side of the park there was a shuffle of movement, a black-on-grey shape that folded, rose and folded again. It almost looked as if something was coming out of one of the graves. It made him think of a Lucio Fulci zombie film, one of those once-forbidden Italian B-movies that now looked so cheesy on YouTube.

What if Shirone's thuggish brothers had followed them in? She was fifteen years old, and he was lying on top of her beneath a pall of dope smoke.

'Get off me,' she whispered, 'someone's here. Let's go.'

Reluctantly, Romain rose. To get back to the railings they had to pass whoever was watching. Shirone grabbed the sleeve of his shirt and made him keep up with her.

The curve of the path took them near the wall, the graves and the bushes. As they drew closer, the rowans shook abruptly and violently, scattering leaves and twigs. He could see a figure now, tall and angular, swaying drunkenly. 'Oi, mate,' Romain called, 'what you doin' there?'

Before any answer came Shirone ran forward and began shouting something about perverts, angry at being followed. A moment later, her shout turned into a scream.

It was hard for Romain to recall the exact order of events after that. Shirone stumbled into the torn-up earth, twisting her ankle in the gap between the ground and the opened coffin. Romain tried to grab her and failed, knocked aside by the onlooker who had reached out an arm towards him. At some point he remembered seeing the raised lid, the muddy pit, a sliver of moonlight on the empty polished casket.

He saw the man standing above him, middle-aged, with greying hair and occluded eyes, clearly and irrevocably dead, dressed in his best black business suit, his arm still rising, the claw of his right hand extended as if to clutch at the living. Then the moon was unveiled from the clouds, highlighting his silvered pupils, his distended marbling flesh. The arm had risen high to point into the night sky, as if to transmit some dire warning.

Romain could not believe what he was seeing. It was as if all the horror films he had been allowed to stay up late for as a child had rolled into one and come suddenly true. There, in the pale patch of moonlight, a cadaver had risen from the grave and was lurching stiffly through the penumbral gloom. The only way it could be any cooler would be if—

And then that happened too. The corpse spoke to him. He heard its grunted command and followed its pointing hand. And there in the night above him lay the answer.

As a luxurious sense of panic began to burn through his stoned mellowness, Romain's senses registered everything at once: the overpowering smell of decay; the body lurching towards him from the grave with its outstretched arm; the putrid sighing of breath. Shirone was still yelling loudly enough to wake the dead single-handedly, and now there was a bright square of bathroom light shining between the branches of the trees, high above the wall against which the row of ancient headstones leaned, in the little park where no one had stirred from beneath the ground in the last three hundred years.

The body tottered forward and landed face down in the earth. Suddenly Romain's excitement seemed absurd, and all he could think of now was that he had been tricked and had missed his best chance with Shirone, and that even if they remained friends after this she would never let him touch her again, because a stupid reanimated corpse had spoiled it all.

He glanced back at the dead body, inelegantly sprawled in the dirt, and grabbed Shirone's hand, which only made her scream more fiercely, so he let it go. She ran for the gate and virtually vaulted it. He followed her out on to the street, but then decided to go back, angered by his flight from something so strange and exciting.

'Wait here a sec,' he told her. He needed to take another look.

2

CEMETERIES AND GRAVEYARDS

St George's Gardens looked smaller and friendlier in the misted warm start to the following day. Euterpe, the Muse of Instrumental Music, stood with her arms folded in a small circular bed of vivid geraniums, her stonework a little the worse for wear. A granite obelisk rose between weathered tombstones, chill to the touch even after three days of warmth. Here, Anna, the favourite daughter of Richard Cromwell, the second Lord Protector of England, lay beneath a modest tomb of worn slabs, unloved and overlooked by all except the ladies of the Bloomsbury in Bloom Society, who tended the graves and freshened the flowers because they had time on their hands and preferred cultural tranquillity to the push and bellow of London streets.

The burial ground was indeed three centuries old, and had exits into three different roads, yet it suffered from the peculiar indifference of Londoners towards their green spaces, remaining virtually invisible to those who passed it. An awkward shape and of no fixed purpose, it led nowhere and did nothing except provide a green lacuna in the grey-brown landscape. Luckily, even an oasis as forgotten as this had its guardian angels.

One of them was at the graveside now. Jackie Quinten was a natural nurturer, a tender of graves and planter of daffodils who rode an orange hand-painted bicycle around Bloomsbury and always kept several packets of seeds and a trowel in her wicker basket. Unable to improve the temperament of her sour-spirited husband in the years before he expired, she had taken to ameliorating the city. But as she pushed her bicycle through St George's Gardens at 8.15 a.m., she was surprised to find a green nylon tent erected between the pathway and the far wall. Surely homeless people weren't living in the little park now?

As she studied it in puzzlement, one flap of the tent opened and a sandy, cropped head poked out. 'Sorry, love, this is off-limits to the public,' it said in an accent Jackie nailed somewhere between South London and Kent.

'Mr Banbury?' she enquired. 'We've met before, I think.' She squinted, venturing a little closer. 'I'm a friend of the gardens. I mean I work here as a volunteer. I know Mr Bryant, your boss.'

'Ah,' said Dan Banbury non-committally, his eyes darting about. 'He's not with you, is he?'

'Why no, I haven't seen him since – let me see, something to do with a disappearing pub. He was looking for a murderer.'

'He's always looking for a murderer. He's supposed to be here. I told him eight o'clock. He only lives up the road in Harrison Street. You'd think he could manage that.'

'Yes, I heard he'd moved into the neighbourhood,' said Jackie, glancing about. 'Has something happened?' She indicated the tent.

Banbury thought for a moment. If he lied, she would hear about it soon enough on the news, and he didn't like to undermine public confidence. 'We're not really sure yet,' he said finally. 'I'm hoping it's just some kind of a bad-taste joke. Are you here a lot?'

'Most days. It's a shortcut for me.'

'When did you last come through?'

'Last night, at about seven o'clock.'

'Did you see anything unusual here?'

'What do you mean by unusual? Sometimes there are some very thin students practising juggling and fire-eating, but that's not unusual, is it? Not these days.'

'Undesirables hanging about,' said Banbury.

'Oh no, this is a nice quiet neighbourhood.' Jackie noticed that Banbury had pulled the tent-flap tightly shut behind him and closed the Velcro fastening.

A crackle of static brought an absurdly young police constable out from the prickly clutches of a holly bush. He listened to his headset and called across. 'He's on his way, sir.'

'There used to be junkies and drunks,' she continued, 'but they were moved away when the gardens were restored. Now the gates are locked at dusk, although the railings are low enough for anyone to climb over if they had a mind for it. It may not look like it has much to offer, but there's a lot of history buried beneath this little patch of land.' She looked up as an elegantly dressed man with neatly combed silver hair and an overcoat of navy wool marched towards them.

'Ah,' said Jackie, hastily turning her bicycle, 'I think I'd better make myself scarce. That's Mr Bryant's partner, isn't it? I'm sure he doesn't like people getting in his way when he's trying to work.'

Mrs Quinten knew that whenever John May appeared, Arthur Bryant could not be far behind, and he would not appreciate finding her here. He sensed that she wanted to mother him and feed him up, and wriggled out of her clutches like a fractious cat whenever he could. Guiltily, she walked her bicycle away.

'I'm glad you're here at least, John,' said Banbury, looking down at the tent. 'But I'm afraid it's a bit of a waste of time.'

'No sign of Arthur?' May checked that the grass was fine for his carefully polished black toecaps and stepped on to it.

'No, and it's probably for the best. He might be tempted to make more of this than is necessary.' Banbury ushered May into the tent, where a small battery-operated LED lamp had been set up. A neat square of turf had been removed and placed in a clear plastic bag.

May found himself looking down at a new cherry-wood casket with brass handles, spattered with nuggets of earth.

'OK, take a look at this,' said Banbury, kneeling down and pulling up its lid with a grunt. 'You might want to breathe through your mouth.'

Inside was the corpse of a middle-aged white man in a black business suit and white shirt collar. The odd thing was that he was lying face down at the wrong end of his final resting place.

'I already turned him over once and had a good look, but I wanted you to see how he was found,' said Banbury.

'Somebody dug him up and dropped him when they were disturbed. So it's an act of vandalism?'

'You would have thought so, wouldn't you, but it's not quite as clear-cut as it appears,' Banbury replied. 'A couple of teenagers found him last night. They'd come to the gardens after the pubs shut to get high and fool around, and saw movement over here. They were sitting about twenty yards away in that direction.' He pointed back to the flattened grass. 'When they came over, the boy swore he saw this bloke walk out of his grave. On the way out they bumped into a Community Support Officer coming off duty and told him what had happened. Quick as a flash he did the wrong thing: smelled dope, carried out a very officious stop and search and found a stubbed-out fatty in the boy's pocket. Usually around here the beat cops let them go with a ticking-off, but this one was a by-the-book merchant. Eventually he took them back to the park to check out their story, saw the body and then ran them in under suspicion. He said he had misgivings because the lad was wearing some kind of satanic death-metal T-shirt, but this isn't Arkansas, we don't bang kids up for having lousy taste in clothes. I was in the office when the call came in and whipped over to take a look. Apparently I was the only bloke still working in the area at that time. I didn't think there was much point in getting you up until daybreak.'

'So they were stoned and dug him up. Did you find a shovel?'

Banbury scratched his nose and left behind a dab of London clay. 'That's the thing. I'm pretty sure they didn't do it. They had no dirt on their clothes and she was in high heels. We haven't found any kind of digging implement. It hasn't rained for three days and the rest of the ground's pretty hard, but this plot is soft and fresh. British law requires thirty inches of soil between casket and surface, but this was buried shallower. The earth's very loosely packed under the turf. Besides, if it was them, why would they own up to it? It's bloody hard work getting one of these out of the ground.'

'And getting it open, I imagine.'

'Contrary to popular belief, caskets aren't usually made airtight because of the cost.' Banbury showed May the dark piping that ran around the edge of the wood. 'You can have a gasket installed that provides an extra seal, but the normal practice is a compromise, a rubber lip around the top that makes it tough to open from the outside without a specialized tool. Not like the old days, when they used to add a double lining of nails to deter bodysnatchers. You don't need nails any more. Imagine trying to get the lid off a sealed jam jar without any kind of a lever. And I really don't think these teens would have had one.'

Much as he was loath to, May knelt and studied the body. 'His position is odd.'

'Yes, I thought that. It's as if he stood up in the casket and then fell forward.'

'You don't suppose . . .' May was reluctant to voice his thoughts.

'He was buried alive?' Banbury laughed. 'That's the sort of thing Mr Bryant would come up with. I suppose he's in the exact position he'd be if he climbed out, then collapsed forward. And the lid would have been easier to push off from the inside, because the two sides of the gasket aren't of equal width, favouring a shove from within rather than an external pull. But no.'

'Why not?'

'First of all he's been dead for a couple of days at least – Giles will be able to tell you more about that – and even if by some miracle he had still been alive he wouldn't have had much room for leverage.' Banbury rose and stretched. 'This isn't my area though. We need a body man. I left a message for Giles an hour ago. He was away for the weekend grouse-shooting with his wife's nobby friends, but he's supposed to be back mid-morning.'

'It can't have been grouse. That doesn't start until August. The Glorious Twelfth and all that.'

'All right, maybe polo then. Something upper-class-twittish.'

'How are we on prints?' May had noted the white dust on the coffin.

'Interesting. Nothing at all on the lid. Doesn't look to me like anyone touched it. There's a mess of bootprints in the vicinity, but the grass has been trodden flat around here for a long time. The park gets a fair bit of foot traffic on a sunny day. People come in to eat their sandwiches.

Something else, though. The boy seems to think they interrupted some kind of satanic ritual.'

'Why would he think that?'

'He didn't explain himself very coherently, just said something about it looking like a scene from a horror film. I think he was quite taken with the idea. The Community Support geezer put it down to him being stoned, although he clearly doesn't know the difference between dope and pills. You know how some kids are when they get a mind for such things, a fascination with the paranormal is almost a rite of passage for them.'

'Arthur never grew out of his. Speaking of which . . .' He cocked his head to one side and listened. Someone was whistling 'Oh Happy the Lily' from Gilbert and Sullivan's *Ruddigore* very badly indeed. May stuck his head out of the tent and saw a figure ambling towards them down the path, the steel-tipped heels of his scuffed brown Oxfords clicking on the gravel, their rhythm punctuated by the thump of an ancient Malacca walking stick. The remnants of Bryant's hair had entered the new day without the benefit of a comb and thrust out horizontally from above his ears, lending him the appearance of a barn owl.

At this point it might be worth pointing out that if you're looking for the steely grip of deductive logic, you may wish to find some other narrative that doesn't involve Mr Arthur Bryant. While it would be hard to find a gentleman more connected to the world, it isn't the world of today. Rather, the world he inhabits is one largely filled with what could loosely be described as 'alternatives', consisting mainly of fringe activists, shamans, shams and spiritualists, astronomers and astrologers, witches both black and white, artists of every hue from watercolour to con, banned scientists, barred medics, socially inept academics, Bedlamites, barkers, fibbers, *flâneurs*, dowsers, duckers, divers and drunks. Many of the names in his grubby old Rolodex have gone on to greatness, although some have gone to jail and a few to pieces. Between them, they consistently provide a service not available to any other section of the British police network. They offer up their ideas without boundaries, guile, manners or any thought of payment. They want to help, and Mr Bryant is just the man to let them.

'You're not answering your phone,' said May irritably.

'No, I've put it somewhere and haven't narrowed down the list of possibilities yet.'

'Have you checked your pockets?'

Bryant made a theatrical show of thrusting his hands into his ratty overcoat, and pulled out a small black kitten. 'Another one,' he said absently. 'They seem to be everywhere.' He gently tucked the mewling furball into his waistcoat.

'I was about to give up on you. We're almost finished here.'

'Actually, I was here shortly after it happened.'

'How did you even know about it?' asked Banbury, nettled. He knew there was little likelihood of Bryant spotting the case registration online.

'The old-fashioned way, Dan. I looked out of the window. I don't sleep well, especially after I've had a slice of Alma's cabinet pudding just before bedtime. I can just see that patch of pavement back there, and clocked that something odd was going on.'

'What, all the way from your bedroom?'

'I've got a view straight between the houses, if you stand on a stool. My long sight's perfectly functional, although I can't identify anything smaller than a battle-ship under five hundred yards. I came down and talked to the fake plod, then took a shufti while he ran them in. I thought it was a good idea to get them off the street while I had a look around.' He loosened his immense sea-green scarf a little in deference to the already warm morning. 'I wouldn't close this up just yet. I was struck by a couple of peculiarities.'

'What do you mean?' asked May, stepping back to allow him access to the tent. Bryant waved away the offer of another look.

'The first thing that bothered me was the state of the body,' he said. 'It's only recently been buried. The rest of the corpses in here have been underground for centuries, so what's this one doing here? Do you know the difference between a graveyard and a cemetery?'

'I didn't know there was one.'

'Oh yes, most definitely. It's a matter of geography. Cemeteries aren't attached to churches. Their plots can be sold to the general public. There are strict rules governing their upkeep. Graveyards belong to churches and most have hardly been used at all since the nineteenth century. But this space is rather special.'

May had scanned a brief history of the site, helpfully printed on a board at the entrance, but knew that his partner would have a more idiosyncratic viewpoint. 'In what way?' he asked.

'St George's Gardens was the first burial place in London that didn't have its own church. Founded during the reign of Queen Anne, it received the headless remains of ten martyred Jacobites who'd been hanged, drawn and quartered in 1745, one of whom was due to be married on the day of his execution. So it had a certain amount of notoriety. Somebody still leaves a floral tribute here every July the thirtieth in commemoration.' Bryant poked about for his pipe and dug it out, lighting the remains of his last smoke.

'This is all very interesting, Mr Bryant—' Banbury began.

'And that notoriety extended into a scandal,' Bryant continued. 'This is the birthplace of bodysnatchers.'

'Oh dear Lord,' Banbury muttered, mentally passing his hand over his face.

'I'm afraid it's true. The coffins were buried very close to the surface – as indeed was this chap's, by the look of it – and in 1777 the gravedigger and his assistant were arraigned for stealing the corpse of one Jane Sainsbury. They tied her up and popped her into a sack, but were caught just up the road in King's Cross. They served six months in jail after being whipped from Holborn to Seven Dials, about half a mile by my reckoning. That's an awful lot of whipping.'

'And this matters—?'

'Certainly it does, because in 1977, on the two-hundredth anniversary of the disinterment, it happened again to one Anthony Dickenson, but this time no one was ever arrested.'

'You see,' said May, exasperated, 'this is what you always do, Arthur, you try to connect entirely separate events to form a pattern where none exists.'

'I didn't say it was a pattern. It's a precedent.' Bryant sucked noisily at the pipe, then peered into the barrel.

Banbury had had enough. 'Right,' he said, 'that's it. I'm trying to work here. I need to . . .' But he found himself at a sudden loss, not quite sure what he needed to do at all.

'I said there were a couple of peculiarities,' said Bryant. 'Far be it from me to belabour the obvious, but did neither of you notice that he had no headstone? Somebody pulled up the temporary one and threw it over there.' He waved his pipe at a small wood marker lying almost hidden in the longer grass. 'I imagine it had been placed on top of the grave in readiness for the headstone setting. Thomas Edward Wallace, aged forty-seven, buried three days ago. And another thing: there were no flowers. You'd think someone buried that recently would have had tributes stacked around his plot, but there's nothing. Let's put out a call for witnesses while we find out who buried him here and why.'

'Mr Bryant, this isn't really our sort of thing,' Banbury began.

Bryant had donned his bottle-thick glasses to read the marker. He stared down crossly like a tortoise with indigestion. 'Oh, I think it is,' he replied. 'This is a public sanctuary, a place provided for peaceful reflection. If people can't feel safe here, it's our job to find out why not.'

3

THE HANGED MAN

Rosa Lysandrou was a virtuous, decent woman who knew that the world was a wicked place and that life was short, ugly and disappointing. Most of the time sin and ill fortune surrounded her, seeping into her bones like damp and dragging at her limbs until she sometimes longed for the release that eternal sleep would bring. On other days she cheered up a bit and went to bingo.

Today a vaporous sun was glinting through the crimson and emerald stained-glass windows of the chapel in the Camley Street Coroner's Office, and there were even a few sickly-looking birds singing in the trees that lined the Victorian graveyard of St Pancras Old Church. Her sister was coming to visit, and would bring a number of large, heavy cakes. Her favourite soap serial was on. The only thing that could possibly spoil her day was a visit from—

There was a sharp knock at the front door. When she opened it, she found *him* standing there.

'Ah, there you are,' said Arthur Bryant, lowering his walking stick. 'I thought I could see you lurking behind the glass.' He took in her shapeless black dress and Birkenstocks. 'You're looking particularly pious today.'

'I've been praying for your soul,' Rosa replied.

'Oh, I think it's a bit late for that. I've never been one for a single religion. I don't care for anything that narrows the outlook.' Bryant removed his beaten-up Dorfman Pacific homburg and entered the foyer. 'I prefer the words of William Blake: "The road to excess leads to the palace of wisdom."'

'It leads to the Devil.'

'Ah yes, the Devil. Satan, a corruption of Saturn, the Destroyer. A creation of the Church, and so often a resident within it, one finds.'

'You are English. You find it easy to doubt and mock.' Rosa stepped aside with resignation.

'Doubt, yes; mock, never. My parents were both raised Church of England. But my line of descent has no call upon me. My beliefs were established by what I read and absorbed as a child.

'Kind hearts are more than coronets,
And simple faith than Norman blood.

'Tennyson. Can Giles come out to play?'

Rosa knew when she was defeated. She led the way to the mortuary, where Giles Kershaw was one-finger typing his notes into an electronic tablet. 'I thought I might get a visit from you this morning,' he said, rising to find another stool. 'The body's only been here half an hour. I should have known when I saw your name on the report that this wouldn't be straightforward.'

Dan Banbury had apparently suggested that his colleague should examine the body before having it re-interred. 'Why does he want me to look at it?' Kershaw asked. 'A cause of death must have already been decided.'

'Oh, we thought nobody would mind,' said Bryant, picking up a resin model of a human head and tilting it until its brain fell out.

'You mean you thought nobody would find out. Can you put that down?'

'We haven't got permission from the next of kin for a re-examination because we haven't located them yet.'

'What's the story then?' asked Giles. 'Somebody just dug him up and dumped him when they were disturbed?'

'The kids in the park thought he'd come out of the grave to get them. The boy's positive he saw the corpse walk, although he'd been smoking a little weed. I don't know what we've got here. We're checking the local undertakers to find out how and why he was buried there, but who knows what evidence might be lost in the meantime?'

'There isn't a need to find any evidence, is there?' Kershaw pointed out. 'There's no case. Evidence of what? What are you going to look for?'

'That's what I thought you could tell me. I'm intrigued, aren't you? The blue world turns, empires rise and fall, we live and die and nobody really knows anything. Wouldn't you like a few answers before heading off into eternal darkness?'

'You really are the most obtuse man.' Kershaw ran his fingers through his glamorous blond hair and looked down at the detective, relenting a little. Bryant looked as if he was on a planet with a heavier gravity than anyone else. He appeared to be squashed and shrinking. It was hard to stay annoyed with him for long. 'Well, I suppose in the light of my initial examination there might be something.'

'Oh, so you've already taken a look?' Bryant was triumphant, knowing that Kershaw's curiosity would get the better of him.

'I thought it would make a nice change to have the unit send me a death from natural causes. Myocardial infarction perhaps, probably brought on by stress, trans-fatty acids, alcohol and cigarettes, the usual depressing urban workaholic scenario.'

'How long has he been dead?'

'Skin marbling has only just started. The veins appear closer to the surface after about five days, so less than that. Not much gaseous inflation either, which at first seems surprising, except that Dan tells me the temperature of the earth in the gardens is low because the site is in almost permanent shadow, as well as being affected by the local water table. Water keeps the clay cold. He did a soil test.'

'Of course he did.'

'Besides, bodies don't decay at the same rate because of any number of factors. I was going to take a peep inside him and check out the state of his heart, but as it seems you hadn't cleared permission I'm rather glad I didn't do so. There's supposed to be a full post-mortem carried out by the local hospital mortuary and an NHS pathologist in cases of sudden death, but this doesn't appear to have been the case.'

'What do you mean, sudden death? Why not?'

'Incompetence on behalf of the doctor, I should imagine. Because there *was* something rather special.'

'What?'

'Well, take a look at this.' Kershaw headed for one of the steel drawers that held his pending workload and pulled it out, sliding down the grey metallic covering that hooded the body's facial features. 'It would help if I knew something about his family. All I've been given so far is his age and name.'

'Sorry about that,' said Bryant. 'We got it off his marker. John will find out where he came from.'

'There's this crescent-shaped contusion, here. It's hard to see even in this light but if you look very carefully . . .' Kershaw shone a pencil torch across Wallace's pale forehead. 'Just on the crown, there.'

'It looks like a tiny dent.'

'Yes, the blood's been raised to the surface but it didn't bruise.'

'So it was done before he died, perhaps when he collapsed.'

'That's the obvious supposition. Except that according to Dan the mark could correspond with something on the lid of the casket. I asked him to take some shots of the interior. Beneath the satin layer there are a couple of small bolts holding the brass nameplate to the outside of the lid, and the dent is a possible match.'

'You're saying he tried to sit up suddenly inside the coffin and banged his head?'

'Don't put words in my mouth. That's just one scenario. I'm merely pointing out the coincidence.'

'It would mean he was buried alive.'

'Not necessarily. He could have been violently jostled in the casket, although funeral homes are very careful about such things. Resurrections have occurred in the past, although with far less frequency than most people imagine, maybe once or twice in a decade. But he wasn't buried deeply, and the earth wasn't tamped down . . .'

'His grave-marker had been thrown into the bushes, Giles. That suggests someone removed it to disinter him.'

'How do you know when that occurred? Perhaps the marker hadn't been set in place yet. I need more information before I can give you an accurate verdict – not that I actually need to make one, because presumably he already has a death certificate.'

'I don't know,' said Bryant. 'We don't know who buried him, or how it was even possible.'

'What do you mean?'

'Nobody's been interred in St George's Gardens for centuries. How did Thomas Wallace end up in there? Come on, you've had the body for a full half-hour, didn't you get anything else?'

'He was kitted out in a very nice Gieves and Hawkes suit and I didn't want to mess up the stitching – it had been sewn on to him – so I just unbuttoned his jacket and opened his shirt. I didn't have to go into his heart to see the likelihood of adipose tissue, but I did open his shirt a bit further.' He leaned forward and carefully loosened the collar. A slender grey line ran around Wallace's neck, a whipmark of a bruise.

'He's been strangled,' said Bryant.

'No, not strangled, hanged. There's no disruption of the cervical vertebrae, but these diagonal markings don't run around the full circumference of the neck, suggesting that the method of suspension pulled up and away from the body at the back. That's how you can tell the difference between a hanging and strangulation. The marks of the ligature are too narrow for a rope. I'd say some kind of fine-woven fabric.'

'So he killed himself. What with?'

'A necktie would do the job nicely.' He sounded like a chef suggesting the addition of an egg to a recipe.

'You don't think he went into a coma, and somehow came back to life due to medical misdiagnosis?'

'It doesn't seem very likely. I've never heard of such a thing, but I suppose you could consult an expert on the appearance and diagnosis of death. All I know is that you've got a hanged man.'

'Who killed himself and therefore wasn't eligible for a Christian burial.'

'I think you'll find the Church has softened on that ruling, especially if anyone in the family was active in the parish.'

'But it could explain why he was granted interment rights within the former cemetery, and why no one left flowers.'

'Wouldn't it be quicker to ask someone rather than trying to work it out for yourself?'

'Obviously, but I need the mental exercise.' Bryant sucked at his false teeth, thinking. 'It still doesn't help us determine what happened. Dan thinks he might have some shovel-marks in the extruded clay around the coffin but it's impossible to tell whether they were made putting him in or digging him up. A hanged man comes back to life and frightens off the people who were trying to resurrect him? It doesn't make sense.'

'I see what you mean,' Kershaw agreed. 'It sounds like something you'd find in a pack of tarot cards. Or a Robert Louis Stevenson novel. Certainly not London in the twenty-first century.'

'That's the thing about the backstreets of Bloomsbury. They've barely changed in hundreds of years. They'll probably be the same long after . . .'

'What's the matter?' asked Kershaw. 'You've gone quite pale. You'd better sit down for a minute.'

Bryant looked as if he'd swallowed a bar of soap. 'It's nothing,' he said. A most peculiar feeling had swept over him. It was as if he'd just looked down into the ground and seen himself. 'I think somebody just walked over my grave.'

While Detective Sergeant Janice Longbright was waiting to hear back from the four funeral homes listed as operational in the Bloomsbury and Holborn areas, she dug sultanas out of Arthur Bryant's optical drive with a pastry fork. She had no idea how they had managed to get in there but they had wrecked the damned thing, and now she was unable to eject her disk. She had been forced to upload CCTV footage to DVDs and run them the old-fashioned way, because whenever she tried running files on Dan's trial shareware they kept vanishing: an OS update glitch, according to May; a ghost in the machine, according to Bryant. On his computer screen a dead wasp was stuck in a smear of blackcurrant jam, and she could barely bring herself to touch the keyboard, as it had been serving as a table mat for the last few years. There were peas all over the desk. Who had peas for lunch?

She looked around the room jointly shared by her bosses and couldn't help noticing how appropriately it reflected the occupants. John May's half was gracefully arranged with an ergonomic seat and a tasteful modern Spanish armchair finished in grey felt. His desk was orderly to the point of OCD. Those few files he had not yet been able to digitally transfer were priority-coded and alphabetized. There was no paperwork; he used Cloud storage. A stylish red table lamp with an exposed filament painted a warm ellipse across his pale ash shelves, where a few treasured paperbacks shared space with some blue Venetian wine glasses and a set of white china coffee cups.

She glanced over at Bryant's side.

To start with, there was half a cow's head lying on his desk. Its skull had been split lengthwise and placed inside a torn Primark shopping bag. A pool of black blood had hardened over a 1973 copy of *Exchange & Mart* and dripped into his top drawer, which appeared to be full of soil and bits of mushrooms. There was a cricket bat with a lot of nails hammered into it, his beloved Tibetan skull, which still reeked after all these years, an empty ant farm filled with murky water and dead frogs, a pen-holder containing a stick of crimson sealing wax, a length of what appeared to be dynamite fuse, several lethal-looking scalpels with their blades left unsheathed and pointing up and a Pelham Puppet of a skeleton from circa 1959. On the opposite corner was a tottering pile of battered books that included *Cross-Stitching in the Time of Edward the Confessor, Hungarian–British Trade Fairs of the 1950s, The International Handbook of Underwater Acoustics, Across Europe with a Kangaroo, The Complete Works of Edward Bulwer-Lytton in Braille, Churchill's Favourite Engineering Problems, Recreating Renaissance Masterpieces with Cheese* and *Bombproofing for Beginners*. There was also a sock. Half a mildewed sardine and tomato sandwich lay on the windowsill, being nibbled by a small black kitten with wild yellow eyes. To Bryant these were the liminal accompaniments to his thoughts. To everyone else they were a health hazard.

Longbright lifted the kitten off and put it in a paper-filled cardboard box with the others, only to find that several had managed to climb out. Sighing, she went off to answer the door buzzer, but was beaten to it by Banbury. The new intern had probably arrived. That was all she needed today, a sleepy-faced youth to follow her around tweeting sarcastic comments while she was trying to get on with her work.

The good news was that she had been able to get all charges dropped against the upset teenagers from St George's Gardens. She felt sorry for the boy, Romain Curtis, because he seemed sensitive and shaken, while the girl had shrugged off the entire incident and asked if she could get compensation for missing school in the form of some lunch money.

Longbright checked her phone and saw that Raymond Land had summoned everyone to the common room at 12.00 p.m. He only ever did that when he was upset about something.

'Isn't the old man back yet?' asked Banbury, sticking his head around the door. 'What do you want done with your intern?'

'Arthur went to see Giles,' replied Longbright. Apart from May and Land, she was the only other member of the unit who ever dared to refer to Bryant by his first name. It was a right she had earned. 'As for your intern, you might as well give him to me.'

'It's not a he.' Banbury opened the door wider. 'This is Amanda Roseberry.'

Longbright was far from dowdy. In the summer months she switched to a tight black T-shirt and the occasional low-cut summer dress that could make passers-by walk into oncoming traffic. But in walked a self-assured and absurdly opulent blonde with upswept tresses, keen grey eyes, a relaxed smile and a miniscule waistline. Amanda Roseberry held out her hand like a princess.

'I've just finished a twenty-three-day intensive at the Peel Centre,' she explained in clear received pronunciation. 'Radio Operation and Driving Skills. I'm waiting to be placed somewhere in serious crime. I wanted to intern here for absolutely ages but was told you weren't taking anyone.'

'No,' Longbright admitted. Bryant hated the idea of having trainees running around under his feet while he was trying to think. 'How did you even find us?' News of their operations was generally disallowed at the Met, although certain officers tagged their movements, waiting for them to slip up.

'You moved from Metropolitan jurisdiction to City of London and I was able to transfer here by applying directly through Orion Banks.'

Longbright racked her brain but came up with nothing. 'Is that an observatory?'

Roseberry laughed. It was the sound of wind chimes in cherry trees. 'No, she's the City of London Public Liaison Officer. She went to my old school. She said she'd speak to you.'

'Well, she hasn't, at least to my knowledge. Never mind. Get your coat off while I find you a desk, then make yourself useful.'

'How shall I do that?' Roseberry smiled sweetly. She had only been here two minutes and the smile was already becoming unnerving.

'Can you make tea?' Longbright asked, suddenly aware how patronizing the question sounded.

'Well – I suppose so.'

'It's a good way of ingratiating yourself around here.'

'I hope I won't need to "ingratiate" myself.' She made

a little air-quotes gesture around the word. 'I had the highest pass-mark of my class.'

'Trust me,' said Longbright, 'brewing a decent cuppa will stand you in good stead. There's a lot they don't teach you up at Hendon. You can show off your operational skills later. Come with me.'

'There seem to be kittens everywhere,' Roseberry said as Longbright ushered her from the room. 'There were half a dozen on the stairs as I came in.'

'Yes, there are nine or ten of them. Don't worry about it. You'll have to duck under a few ladders around here, too, so I hope you're not superstitious.'

'No, but I have allergies. I'll need to take some medication if the cats are to stay.'

If they're to stay? thought Longbright. 'We're trying to find them homes. Tea-making lesson, you, right now.' As she pushed the girl out of the door, she began to wonder what else the day would bring.

4

THE NEW BROOM

'A new-found respectability, that's what I thought we'd get,' said Raymond Land, fussily lining up the pens on his desk. 'City of London jurisdiction over the Met? It had to be a good idea. City nicks have their own bars. You can go for a quiet drink without an Old Bailey defence brief tailing you to see if his strategies are working. And they do lovely breakfasts. Lower crime rate, too, except around those huge new nightclubs they've opened by Smithfield Market. And nice uniforms with proper county helmets, and height restrictions. Grace and order. What a pleasant change, I thought. But now it looks like they're going to micromanage us. It's going to be tougher than ever to get any kind of autonomy for the unit.'

'I know you, Raymond,' said John May, turning from the murky window in Land's office. Outside, the traffic was at its usual standstill. 'You thought it would be a cushy number. The City of London Police were always considered to be nothing more than glorified security guards. Given the tiny residential population inside the Square Mile, all they had to do was plod around a bunch of empty buildings and turn off the odd faulty alarm.

They never saw a living soul from midnight until the tubes started again the next morning. Well, it's not like that any more. I heard they were about to be incorporated into the Met until the terrorist bombings changed the game. Then they had to deal with the so-called Ring of Steel until number-plate recognition and National Mobile Phone Register technology came in. But now that the licensing laws have changed, the Square Mile is getting to be as rowdy as the West End. And it's where the bulk of the city's major fraud takes place. Their CID seriously punches above its weight. The CoL regulars have their hands full. We'll have to take on everything else.'

'You misunderstand me, John. I don't mind a bit of supervision, but *this*' – he lowered his voice and wagged a forefinger at the door – 'this isn't what I had in mind at all. I haven't the faintest idea what she's on about. God knows what Arthur will make of her.'

'Who?' May suddenly understood to whom Land was referring. 'You mean the new Public Liaison Officer? Isn't she some kind of ex-marketing guru?'

'She wants to modernize the unit, and I don't think she'll have much time for your partner. She wants hard-nosed young go-getters, not some old fossil creeping around museums on a walking stick. We're going to have to buck our ideas up. Ssh, I think I can hear her. We'd better go in before there's trouble. Apparently she's a stickler for timekeeping. For heaven's sake don't mention this . . . disinterment business, or whatever it is.' Land rose and made a hopeless attempt at straightening his tie. Since his wife left him he had been coming to work in unironed shirts and the occasional mismatched socks. The other morning he had had shaving cream behind both ears. In an odd way, it made him fit in for the first time.

Together, the detective and the unit chief headed for the common room. The others were already seated before a large whiteboard. Longbright had agreed to let the intern attend the briefing, which would bring the personnel total to ten when Bryant arrived, give or take a few cats. The mewling black furballs were rolling and scratching between the chairs, getting under everyone's feet.

The City of London's new Public Liaison Officer entered with a look of ill-supressed distaste on her face, probably because she had put her hand on one of Bryant's mildewed petri dishes, and was trying to wipe off something brown and gelatinous that appeared to have stained the heel of her palm. From her glossy jet fringe, protractor-perfect, through tiny pearl stud earrings to patent black shoes, via her tailored grey cotton suit and tightly buttoned black shirt, Orion Banks's look suited an advertising agency more than a public service unit. She could not have been unaware of this – and perhaps that was the plan; she wanted to make them conscious of outward appearances.

Longbright was no stranger to the wilder excesses of fashion, but drew the line at co-ordinated monochromes. Jack Renfield glanced back at the flowery, fragrant intern, then forward to the styled-up liaison officer, shifting uncomfortably in his seat. He had the nervous look of a man suddenly surrounded by too many women.

'Are we all here?' Banks asked, checking her list.

'There's just Mr Bryant to come,' said Land. 'He's always late.'

'That's not really acceptable, I'm afraid. Ah, Mr Bryant, you're just in time.'

Arthur had slipped into the back of the room. He had made an effort, doing up the top button of his shirt and tightening his tie in a look that could only be described as 'Grandfather of the accused photographed outside Old Bailey'. Flicking a cat from the only remaining chair, he seated himself and began emptying his pockets on to the floor in front of him.

'When we have your full attention perhaps we can start?' asked Banks.

'Oh, you go right ahead, don't wait for me,' said Bryant. 'I've lost a bag of pear drops.'

'I'm sorry, we don't know who you are,' said Colin Bimsley, raising his hand as if he was requesting a bathroom break.

'It's all right, Mr Bimsley, you can put your hand down, you're not at school now,' said Banks testily. 'You should have found an e-intro on your laptops about this meeting.'

'We don't have laptops,' said Meera Mangeshkar.

Banks ignored her. 'Read it and you'll see I've objectivized an agenda for an informal intra-communicational face session. I'm Orion Banks, and I'm here to discuss administrative flexibility and workforce incentivization, bringing you up to speed on the public-interface components of your skill sets.'

Everyone stared blankly back at her.

'You're probably aware that the CoL's consultants are running a top-down initiative recommending parallel management contingencies in which this unit will be upgraded to offer a more blue-sky approach to what we shall be terming, for the sake of argument, functional modular processing.'

She attempted to make eye contact with each of them in turn, as she had been taught in her match-and-mirror behavioural patterning course. Jack Renfield was staring fascinatedly at the ceiling. Colin Bimsley had seen something out of the window. Meera Mangeshkar had become hypnotized by the ends of her hair. The intern was taking frantic notes. Banks decided to soldier on. 'Hopefully,' she said, 'with enough ambient management alignment we can generate more interactive asset innovation.'

Bryant tapped at his hearing aid. 'I'm sorry,' he said loudly, 'I think this thing's on the blink. I can see your lips moving but all I can hear is rubbish.'

'Ah, of course. I was warned – informed, rather – that

some of you had . . . how can I put this? Exceeded your optimal efficiency timelines.'

'What?' asked Bryant, screwing up his face as if listening to someone speaking Swahili.

'You're of a more senior sensibility than I'm used to,' said Banks, attempting clarity but looking as if she was speaking through a pane of glass. 'It makes the transactional process more challenging. Well, I think we can still get on-message as far as strategic programming, don't you? We can monitor the system in a more holistic manner, perhaps via one-on-one encounters.' She checked her tablet. 'I'm sure I can find a window.'

'Young lady,' Bryant piped up. 'I'm old but I'm not stupid. I appreciate that you may hold an MBA in Advanced Gibberish but that won't help when you're stuck on the roof of a suspect's apartment at two in the morning and you need to go to the toilet.'

Banks raised her chin and lowered her eyelids to an angle that was just enough to be really annoying. 'This isn't about the practicalities of real-time assignment,' she explained. 'It's about synchronizing capabilities and transitional organization options. Taking into account logistical contingencies—'

'I think Mr Bryant would like you to speak a tad more plainly,' said May. 'If you don't he'll simply turn off his hearing aid. Maybe I can translate for you. You're not happy with what you see here.'

'Most certainly not.'

'And you'd like to change things.'

'I'd like to oversee a paradigm shift, yes.'

'Then perhaps you could be honest and tell us what you think is wrong.'

Banks started to speak, stopped and began again. 'There needs to be some administrative reprogramming that's more responsive and forward-looking in terms of—'

'What is it you don't like?' May interrupted. 'In plain, simple English.'

Banks sighed. 'I fell through a hole in the stairs,' she said, regarding her laddered tights. 'Then I electrocuted myself in the toilet. Half of the lights are out and the rest are making a funny noise. There are two men, both answering to the name of Dave, who are sitting in the corner of the second-floor operations room boiling a kettle on a primus stove. Could somebody tell me what they are doing there?'

'The Daves are handling the building repairs,' Land explained. 'They were meant to finish several weeks ago but . . . they didn't,' he ended lamely. 'They're very nice, and sometimes they chip in with bits of advice.'

'I'll have to speak to them myself about possible breaches of security.' Banks tapped at her tablet, making a note. 'There's something very wrong with your plumbing. I don't think it meets European health and safety standards. If the public were to see—'

'That's just it,' said Land, 'they don't see. This unit is only accountable to the general public insofar as it is here to protect them. And we have to work in a way that we see fit.'

'Fit?' said Banks, her eyes widening. 'Is it fit to have cats running all over the building? None of the computers are password-protected. Your filing system is incomprehensible. I have no idea what anyone is working on or how anyone gets assigned cases. The door to the evidence room has no lock on it. There's a fortune teller in a glass case at the top of the stairs and a dead squirrel on the landing.'

'About our caseload,' said Bryant slowly and patiently, as if talking to an upset child. 'We only handle serious crimes, but sometimes that definition is debatable. For instance, last night a teenager saw a corpse rise out of a grave just down the road from here. Obviously that's impossible, but we don't know what we're dealing with yet. It could have been a practical joke or something more sinister. Nobody knows what we're working on until John and I decide whether the case is suitable.'

'But how do you define that?' Banks was visibly struggling with the vagueness of it all.

'We ask if it meets our criteria. In the advent of a suspicious death it used to be that the Met – or in your case the City of London Police – would call in a Home Office forensic pathologist. Now it's fielded to us. If we think the situation is unique enough to cause public distress or a loss of trust in government bodies, we take it on. First and foremost we're police officers, but among our number there are also creative and academic freethinkers. And although it may appear that you have wandered into a building full of mad people, we consistently achieve the kind of results that regular policing units can't match. This is because we're not required to meet the same targets. Do you understand now?'

Banks nodded dumbly, but Bryant could see she was far from happy. She had been prepared to confront old-school working practices, but found herself inside an analogue world of Victorian throwbacks. How on earth were these people allowed to operate untouched? What magical incantation protected them from the bracing forces of modernization? Were there other pockets of cobwebbed antiquity scattered throughout the City of London, protected by hereditary peers and sorely awaiting a new broom? She resolved to take a look, after she had dealt with these Cro-Magnons. 'And that is your total caseload at the moment? A graveyard prank?'

'It's our first day,' said Land plaintively.

'I want a total press blackout on this,' she warned. 'Nothing gets out; nothing is leaked. The CoL Police have worked very hard to be taken seriously, and I will not have our efforts undermined. Is that understood?'

'So we're to continue looking into this "prank"?' asked May, seeking confirmation.

Banks considered the question. 'You honestly think it falls within the remit?'

'Without a doubt. The park is a public space. At the very least, this was a criminal offence and an act designed to cause outrage.'

'Very well. But no more courting the press. I know that in the past you had connections with someone at *Hard News*. As far as I'm concerned, from now on you're a stealth agency. I'll decide what gets leaked on a case-by-case basis. And make sure this thing is wrapped up by the middle of the week.' She held up a hand. 'Wait. Explain something to me.'

'If I can.'

'Your job titles.' She flicked a painted nail between Bryant and May. 'You're both just detectives. Your sergeants never made inspector. Didn't any of you ever put in for promotion?'

'We made a collective decision,' May explained. 'We didn't want to come off the street. None of us wanted to end up stuck behind desks fielding emails and organizing PowerPoint presentations. You lose touch with what's happening in the real world.' There was rebuke in his voice. He softened it a little. 'It's one of the hardest things to do: halting your promotion progress; but we managed it as a group.'

'Fine,' said Banks, 'but remember this. The old ways can't stay in place for ever. *I'm* the new broom.'

Once the meeting was over, May laid a friendly hand on his partner's arm. 'I have to say that you handled that with a degree of sensitivity for once,' he said.

'I am trying,' Bryant answered as they walked back to their own office. 'It's not Banks's fault, poor love. She's been insulated by all that jargon. Once she sees that there's a simpler way to get results, she'll come around. She might even turn out to be an ally.'

'What makes you say that?'

'I suspect she has the potential for peculiarity. She's just a little too tightly wound at the moment. It'll be interesting to see what happens when we start disobeying her orders. She'll either have a meltdown or she'll come around to our way of thinking. Let's get to work.'

They passed Meera Mangeshkar, who had been studying the new intern with annoyance. 'You couldn't take your eyes off her all through the meeting,' she hissed at Colin Bimsley. 'You were making a right fool of yourself.'

Bimsley grinned. 'It's nice to have a fresh face around the place,' he said. 'Maybe I'll ask her out for a drink.'

Mangeshkar released a hoot of derision. 'She's out of your league, pal. You'd be punching above your weight. Look at her, all teeth and cheekbones. She can probably trace her family back to the Magna Carta, not as far as Brixton nick.' She knew Bimsley came from a long line of coppers, boxers and prison wardens.

'I'm not working class any more,' he said, 'I'm lower middle. I use three types of oil in my kitchen. Admittedly one of them is WD40, but that counts, doesn't it? We all move up over time; it's like karma. Anyway, if I make a fool of myself, so what? What do you care? You never give me a tumble. You don't want to go out with me, but you don't want me going out with anyone else. How does that work?'

'She's interning here. It's inappropriate.' Mangeshkar scowled. 'And she's too young. And her legs are too long.'

'Ah! Now we get to the truth,' said Bimsley. 'You're jealous. Admit it. You think she's too good for me just because she's tall and posh.'

'What, and I'm short and common? Is that what you're saying?'

'Amazing as it sounds, this isn't about you, Meera. And I never said you were too good for me.' Colin had had enough. He was tired of being told what he could and couldn't do. No woman had the right to be that prescriptive unless she was going out with him, and Meera had always turned him down.

'Go on then, ask her on a date. See if I care. You'll only be hurting yourself because she'll laugh right in your face.'

'Meera, if there's one thing I've learned from you, it's how to handle rejection.'

'Really? I haven't seen any evidence of that. I virtually had to take out a restraining order on you.'

'Yeah, I kept giving you another chance, didn't I? Well, not any more. Besides, if she turns me down I won't have been rejected. According to Orion Banks, I'll just have exceeded my core competency.'

'Fine. But – but – just don't say I didn't warn you.' Mangeshkar made a smile in the air and pointed at him. 'Laugh. In. Your. Face. Remember that.' She stalked away, not entirely sure that she had won the argument.

5

CORPSES AND CONSTELLATIONS

Bryant had a routine. Builders' tea, never café latte. Paperwork, never computer screens. Scribbled sketches, illegible addenda, manuals and manuscripts, ink stains and gnawed pencil stubs. A pipeful of something grown under his desk and dried out on the bathroom radiator whenever he could sneak it in. This was how he liked to work, seated opposite the same familiar friendly face, surrounded by the bookmarks of his soul.

'Dan says that the casket has a rubber skirt running all the way around the inside that effectively seals it shut,' said May. 'He reckons it was either pushed open from the inside or unsealed from outside – there's no damage to it.'

Bryant worried at a nail as he tried to decipher a note. His hands were a disgrace. 'I want to see the boy, Romain Curtis.'

'He already made a statement last night.'

'You mean this thing?' Bryant rattled a thin sheet of paper before his partner's eyes. 'I asked them to send me over a copy but I might as well not have bothered. There's hardly anything on it. Look, four lines. The idiot who ran them in didn't ask any proper questions and failed to make a verbatim report. He didn't take them seriously. I need to talk to the lad myself. If he's adamant that Wallace got to his feet, it means he was somehow buried alive.'

'What, he fought his way out and then someone strangled him?'

'No, Giles is sure the ligature mark was made earlier. And that he was hanged.'

'So a hanged man rises from a grave and then drops dead. That isn't a case, it's a scene from a Hammer horror film.'

'But it's a scene that happened. Dan measured sight-lines from Curtis's position to the grave – it's feasible that under the night lamps he really saw what was happening. But there's nowhere near enough data to draw any conclusions yet. We need to talk to the undertaker, the family, everyone. Why is it taking so long?'

'Because Raymond has to vet everything through Banks, and she still hasn't cleared us to go ahead. What a case to start with.' May pushed his fingers through his silver hair. 'Anyway, why would the City of London let us take it on in the first place? It's not even in their jurisdiction.'

'Don't you get it?' said Bryant. 'It'll be just like it's always been. We're going to be given the stuff nobody else wants. Batted back and forth, a dead letter office, a dumping ground. And perhaps that's not a bad thing.'

'What do you mean?'

'If we can keep Orion Banks on our side, they'll leave us alone. And that's when we function best.' Bryant offered up a disconcertingly hopeful smile.

'Then let's find out if we've got a murder on our hands, or whether a dead man really came back to life,' said May.

'Good,' Bryant agreed. 'You can start by getting the boy back. I want to interview him by myself. You're too friendly-looking. I need to wrong-foot him by acting like a weird old man.'

'*Acting*?' said May.

*

Romain Curtis arrived an hour later, having been fished out of a physics class by Renfield. The boy was at the awkward age when height outstripped strength and a quick mind was compromised by inexperience. He wore regulation school trousers topped with an immense black and yellow T-shirt that had a design of the solar system across it. His rolling walk and two-setting clipper cut gave him a little edge, but there was nothing threatening about him.

When ushered into the detectives' room he appeared uncomfortable in his own body, not knowing what to do with his large but oddly delicate hands. Settling himself in the ratty ochre armchair opposite Bryant's desk, Romain found himself facing what appeared to be a very old monkey in a giant's overcoat. He waited to be told what to do.

Bryant set down the page he was holding and peered at the lad. 'Well now,' he said, 'it seems you were a witness to something pretty unusual, even for around here, so you'll have to excuse the pretend-policeman who took your statement. He's more used to dealing with phonejacking and household disturbances. I imagine you completely threw him.'

'He wasn't interested, man.'

'I can tell that. He barely bothered to take down your statement. Of course he'd have been more inclined to believe you if you hadn't been smoking dope.'

Romain had spotted the healthy marijuana plant that grew under Bryant's desk, and was clearly distracted by it.

'Oh, *that*,' said Bryant airily. 'It's for my arthritis. A medical prescription, entirely legal. I'm the law and I say so. Look, I know that a little grass can relax you, but it won't make you see things that aren't there. Therefore you may find me a tad more receptive to your story than

56

some over-zealous nitwit looking for someone to arrest. Because judging by this' – he waved the page again – 'I get the feeling that you didn't tell the officer everything.'

'No point,' Romain mumbled, looking down at his red Converse trainers. 'He wouldn't have believed me.'

'Why not? What did you see? Start from when your lady friend – Shirone, is it? – first heard a noise in St George's Gardens.'

'We was – were – sitting on the grass and that.'

'Doing what?'

'Nothing, man, hanging out.'

'Stargazing?'

'What?'

'Your T-shirt. The solar system.'

Romain pulled at his shirt as if seeing it for the first time. 'Oh, yeah, it's a kind of hobby.'

'Make the shirt yourself?'

'Yeah. I got the dyes and pattern-cuts at home. I make them for friends. I'm hoping to go to St Martins.'

'They specialize in fashion design, don't they?' London's famous college of art had recently moved into the old customs houses at the back of King's Cross Station.

'Yeah, textiles.'

'Have you told your friends at school?'

'No, man. They'd take the piss.'

'So, an astronomer, a designer. You have hidden depths, Mr Curtis.' His voice softened. As alien as the lad was, he was likeable. 'There you were lying on the grass, smoking a little weed, thinking about the immensity of the universe – you don't take anything stronger, do you?'

'Than weed? No. I've seen what that does.'

'Good, right answer. There's a purposefulness of ambition about you. What happened after Miss Estanza heard a noise?'

'She got up and acted a little freaked, and I went to see what the damage was. We was – were – in the middle of the park, and the noise was kind of to our left near the trees. There's a high wall at the back, then flats.'

'Was it cloudy or clear?'

'A bit of both. I was pointing out the stars to her.'

'So you went over towards the shadows, and then what?'

'I saw him, standing up in the grave, trying to walk towards me.'

'Standing in the grave or beside it, behind it?'

'In the grave, I think. He must have been right in the damn coffin.'

'*Must* have been.'

'It was dark over there, under the cover of the branches; I can't remember exactly. His legs moved and his right arm went up, and he pointed at the sky behind me. I turned around to look at what he was pointing at. Then I heard him speak.'

'Wait, he spoke to you?'

'Yeah, in this kind of raspy voice. He said, "Ursa Minor".'

'He pointed out a constellation of stars?'

'Yeah. But he was wrong. It's a mistake everyone makes.'

'What do you mean?'

'It was the Plough. Ursa Major. It has seven stars, just like its little brother, but there's a difference. Ursa Minor has a saucepan shape, the same as the bigger constellation, but it starts with Polaris, the North Star.'

'Forgetting for a moment that we're talking about a dead man, why do you think he wanted to impart this information to you?'

Romain hesitated, started, then stopped again. 'You're gonna think—'

'Forget what you think I might think,' said Bryant. 'Tell me what you thought at that moment.'

'Just when I looked up, there was a shooting star. I suppose I thought he was trying to tell me he came from there. You know, like an alien. I thought he'd come from space.'

'But now you don't.'

'No, of course not. That part was definitely the dope.'

'Well, I'm glad we agree on that. How much had you had to drink?'

'A few lagers.'

'Feeling the effects?'

'Yeah, a little.'

'Think it messed with your perception?'

'I don't know. Maybe.'

'Pity you didn't take a picture, put it on Facebook.'

'Yeah.'

'Then what happened?'

'I could smell him. He smelled really rank and was still wobbling about and that, and Shirone was yelling at me, all twisted out, and the lights started going on in the flats overlooking the park so we legged it.'

'Into the hands of our wonderful quasi-legal system.' Bryant sat so far back in his chair that for a moment Romain thought he was about to vanish beneath the desk. 'Well,' he said finally, bouncing back up, 'that's quite a story. Anything to add?'

'No, man. That's it.'

'I think we'll let you go now.'

'Is that it?'

'Probably. You seem like a bright lad. You've got a game plan for your future. I can't imagine that you'd want to waste our valuable time by making up such a ridiculous story.'

'I seen a lot of crazy stuff around here, man. You keep it to yourself. That's the only way to stay safe.'

'You saw what you saw. It's up to us to interpret it. We'll be speaking to your lady friend, just to corroborate the circumstances, nothing more. Please feel free to take a ginger biscuit on your way out.'

Shrugging, puzzled, Romain rose and took his leave, pausing at the door. 'Aren't you going to ask me to call you if I think of anything else?'

'No, Mr Curtis, it's not a television show,' said Bryant, returning his attention to his desk paperwork. 'Good luck with St Martins.'

Half an hour later, Longbright was able to speak with Shirone Estanza to confirm Romain Curtis's story. The girl was less focused about the night's events and more prone to exaggeration, but she agreed with their rough order. Crucially, she also thought she had heard the cadaver speak, although she had not understood what it said. There was, however, one detail on which her testimony differed. 'He went back into the park,' she said. 'After we came out, Romain ran back in.'

'Did he tell you why?' asked Longbright.

'No.'

'How long was he gone?'

'Not long, probably less than a minute.'

'Did he say anything when he came back?'

'I asked him what he did and he said "nothing".'

'Constellations and corpses,' said Bryant later, reading Longbright's computer screen over her shoulder. 'There must be a perfectly simple explanation.'

'If there is,' sighed Longbright, 'it'll be the first time. What's happening at the site?'

'There's still a crime scene tent over it. Until Banks approves a full investigation, our hands are tied.'

'So we've just conducted two interviews that weren't signed off.'

'It would seem so, yes,' said Bryant lightly. 'Our first open challenge to Ms Banks.'

6

ETERNAL REST

Romain Curtis wasn't sure it was a good idea to see Shirone again – having a girl go into a screaming fit on what was basically a first date had put him off – but when he came home from school that afternoon she was sitting on one of the brightly painted swings in the children's playground in front of the flats, waiting for him.

'The cops called me in, too,' she said. 'Why do I feel like we did something wrong?'

'They're trying to figure out what happened,' said Romain, anxious to get inside and crash through his homework.

'Where did you go? When you left me outside the park and went back.'

'I just wanted another look. We left so quick—'

'And what did you see?'

'Did you tell them I went back?'

'I said you were only gone for a minute.'

'If I tell you then two of us will know, and if they pull you in again you'll have to lie, so it's better that I don't, OK?'

'Come on, Romain. I've lived in your street all my life. We should stick together.'

He sighed. 'Nothing happened. I wanted to see who was there but the dead guy in the suit was lying face down in the dirt. I didn't even touch him. I came straight back to find you.'

'OK.' She could tell he was missing something out. He dug out his door keys and turned to leave. She knew he still didn't trust her, and wanted to make up for the interrupted evening. 'Listen, the Fly Rebels are at the Scala tonight,' she said, jumping to her feet and following him. 'Me and some mates are going.'

'Does that include your brothers?'

'Old-school soul? Not their kind of thing.'

Romain had a pretty good idea what their kind of thing was; it involved violently disputing territorial rights with the Indian gang that ran Drummond Street near Euston Station. It didn't seem likely they'd stay out of trouble for long, and it was best to keep away from them.

'So, are you coming tonight or what?' asked Shirone.

'I have a pile of schoolwork to do.'

'It's early. Do it now and we can meet up later.'

He'd meant to say no, to stick to his promise and study. But after the previous night's fiasco part of him still itched to have a little fun. 'OK,' he said. 'What time?'

'Ten thirty.'

'I'll have to see that I can get out.'

'The first drink's free before eleven. I'll call for you.' Shirone lifted herself off the swing and turned to allow him a good look at her body. 'Maybe we can pick up where we left off. Only I'm not going near the gardens this time.'

'That's OK. They still got a police guard in there anyway.'

'Why?'

Romain shrugged. 'I guess they haven't reburied the dead guy yet. Hey, don't look now but there's your boyfriend.'

A tall, stooped teen with very black hair was passing on his way to the next block. He was dressed in a long leather coat with a silver skull painted on the back. 'Don't let him see me,' Shirone pleaded. 'Martin's always hanging around somewhere. He's too intense.'

'You want me to say something?'

'No, he's harmless, just annoying.'

'You're never going to get away very far from him,' said Romain. 'We grew up here and most of us will probably die here.'

'Not me,' said Shirone. 'I'm going to get out as soon as I can.'

'Me too,' Romain agreed. 'I got big plans.' He had the whole thing worked out in his head. He just wasn't sure if he wanted to share it with anyone yet. There was an unspoken truth among some of the Cromwell Estate's kids that if you wanted to leave, you were betraying those who stayed behind. The best thing to do was just disappear one day.

Jackie Quinten had a hand-knitted look. Like a generation of English ladies from the Home Counties, she at first seemed maternal and matronly, but there was a steeliness in her. And like the plants in St George's Gardens, she was bred to withstand the most severe urban conditions and outlast virtually everything else.

She was shown into the PCU's interview room by the intern, Amanda Roseberry, who had asked to sit in on the conversation. Bryant preferred to conduct such sessions in his office, but decided to try and play by the rules for a few days, especially as Roseberry seemed to be on friendly terms with the City of London Public Liaison Officer. At least Banks had now greenlit their interview sessions, even though she had no idea that they'd already started behind her back.

'I've been tending the gardens for seven years,' Mrs

Quinten explained. 'We've never had any trouble. Bloomsbury has more squares and gardens than anywhere else
in Central London, and people are grateful that they're
there. They used to be known as "open-air sitting rooms
for the poor", you know. Virginia Woolf used to walk
among the graves to plan her novels.'

'I don't understand why someone could still be buried
there in the present day, if the original graveyard was
closed in 1885.' Bryant had a huge photography book
of London burial grounds open on his desk, and was
defacing the relevant pages with notes.

'Well, it was intended to serve as a burial ground for
the parishes of St George the Martyr, Holborn, and St
George's, Bloomsbury, but the parishes were combined
and others were allowed to use the site.'

'Other churches, you mean?'

'Mainly funeral homes. You know what London's like;
nothing is ever straightforward. Because two churches
had used the ground it was considered to be non-
denominational, and after 1885 a few of the local funeral
parlours continued to have dispensations to bury clients
there in exceptional circumstances, but very few ever did.
I think only one of them still does, John Wells and Sons
in Lamb's Conduit Street. They've been around since the
beginning of the nineteenth century, and they're still in
the same place.'

'When was the last time it was used as a graveyard before Mr Wallace?'

'About five years ago. And that was just for a funerary
urn, I believe.'

'Doesn't it strike you as odd that Mr Wallace was
buried there?'

'Not really. He was placed in a fairly inaccessible corner
of the gardens set aside for the remaining interments. I
assume he had left a specific request in his will. Either that
or he inherited the plot – they can be willed forward, so

it would have already been paid for. Why, what happened there?'

'Somebody dug out his casket last night,' said Bryant, scribbling another note on a photograph.

'Oh my goodness.'

'Has there ever been any vandalism of the graves?'

'Not at all. People barely notice they're there. A high proportion of the gardens and squares in London have headstones in them somewhere. I think most of us consider it quite picturesque.'

Bryant consulted his notes. They were still awaiting approval to interview the directors of the funeral parlour. 'What do you know about Wells and Sons?'

'Apparently it's a very respectable, upmarket establishment. They've buried prime ministers and admirals, and even minor members of royalty.'

'Well, if you think of anything unusual . . .'

'I'll tell you, of course. Or you could always pop round, Arthur. We could have a nice meal together.'

Bryant bridled at the memory of a particularly emetic kidney casserole. 'Thanks, I'll bear it in mind the next time I'm very, very hungry,' he said hastily, and ushered Quinten out.

Amanda Roseberry was waiting for him when he returned. 'Can I just say this?' she offered in a tone that suggested nothing would stop her. 'That interview wasn't, strictly speaking, conducted in the manner we're trained to follow?' She spoke with a rising inflection, a habit Bryant had noticed was rife among young women of a certain class.

'That's because I don't follow any prescribed pattern,' he replied, gathering his notes. 'It's not an exact science.'

'But you know her, you clearly have some kind of history – how can you be sure that's not unbalancing the impartiality of the interview?'

'Miss Roseberry,' said Bryant patiently, 'this city is a collection of tribal villages and, as in any tribe, there are some active and highly visible members and some who are never seen, either because they have something to hide or because they need someone else to speak for them. Over time, the visible ones become familiar to us and prove useful. And because we know them well, we know when they're exaggerating or omitting information, so in many ways we get a better reading from them than we ever could from complete strangers. Over forty million people pass through King's Cross Station every year, and a great many of them are visitors, which is why we need a few friendly faces, contacts on the ground like Mrs Quinten. If she remembers something more, I'm sure she'll call us. In fact, I can't imagine anything stopping her.'

'But why not start with people who knew the dead man?'

'Because I don't yet have permission to start questioning a grieving family who probably have nothing to do with this. And because Mrs Quinten was the nearest and easiest to deal with.'

Roseberry said nothing, but he could tell she did not approve. Bryant studied her and softened. He saw a pretty girl with a hairslide and expensive knee-boots and an air of entitlement, and thought about the years ahead of her. Either the realities of the job would leave her with a more sanguine attitude, or she would become disillusioned and give up. Whichever path she chose, there would be a series of unavoidable rude awakenings, and the last thing she needed right now was an annoying old man telling her how things had always been done in the past. Bryant was a firm believer in the power of history, but also understood that the future lay in the hands of the young.

He returned to his office and eased himself behind his desk, his head filled with visions of London's dead. *I'll join them soon enough myself,* he thought, *but I'd counted on eternal rest, not being disturbed by the living – or something even worse, waking up alive.*

'Stop that,' said May, walking in. 'I've seen that look on your face before, like a tortoise with a liver complaint. You're getting maudlin. Come on, grab your coat; we've got a lead. We've an appointment with Thomas Wallace's widow in twenty minutes, number twenty-seven, March-mont Street, right on our doorstep if you're up to walking. Banks just came through with full approval to go ahead. You might be right about her after all.'

7

THE PRICE OF FAILURE

Bryant stopped before the grey-brick Victorian terrace and stared up above the ground-floor stripped-brick coffee shops. Plastic signs had been replaced with artisanal blackboards touting today's specials. 'These used to be slums when I was a nipper,' he said. 'I suppose they go for a million apiece now. The bookies and bucket shops have all become organic bakeries. Look at that, "Gluten-Free Dairy". What does it even mean?'

'Bloomsbury has become a fancy neighbourhood once again,' said May. 'The high-end publishers are moving back in. Remember when it wasn't safe for a copper to walk down here at night? Apparently Thomas Wallace grew up in this street and never left.' He rang the doorbell and stepped back. 'His wife didn't want to stay in the city, but he wanted his son to be in London. There can't be many of the old families left now.'

The door was opened by a small, tidy woman with the brisk air of someone who was not to be trifled with. It was clear from the look on Mrs Wallace's face that she wished a great wind would come along and blow the detectives off her front step. Her auburn hair had been knotted in a severe bun that made her look impatient and cross.

'We're sorry to intrude at this difficult time, Mrs Wallace,' May began. 'We need to ask you questions about your husband.'

'Yes, someone called Sergeant Renfield warned me you'd be stopping by,' she said. 'I'm not going to be of much use to you.'

'Don't worry, we'll try not to detain you for more than a few minutes.'

She held the door, barely allowing them enough room to enter. May could sense the widow's hostility. They entered a gloomy narrow hallway lined with monochrome photographs of empty beaches and wild moorlands. Although the house was in a smart corner of Bloomsbury, the rooms were more penumbral and claustrophobic than in any Midlands sink estate. As he climbed around a pair of bicycles and was ushered into a bleak grey sitting room, May marvelled at the power of a desirable postcode.

Bryant shot his partner a look. The room was furnished with a pair of uncomfortable-looking Swedish armchairs. An old oak table was covered in paperwork. 'I'm trying to sort out Thomas's documents,' said Mrs Wallace wearily. 'His insurance, his bank statements, I don't know where any of it is.' In the corner, her teenaged son – for there could be no mistaking the resemblance – had the lank black hair and kohl-rimmed eyes of what used to be called an emo but was now indie. May attempted to update his partner with a guide to teen tribes, but they changed too fast to keep track. The boy was sprawled sideways across a leather sofa, texting on his mobile, and barely bothered to look up at his mother's visitors.

'I'm Vanessa; this is my son, Martin,' said Mrs Wallace. 'Martin, at least sit up while there are others in the room. You'll have to ignore him – he's at the age where nothing is of interest unless it directly affects him. Hormones.'

The sallow-faced boy was in his mid-teens, his legs

angled awkwardly, his fringe falling over his eyes in a deliberate attempt to hide them. 'The school has given him the rest of the week off,' Mrs Wallace explained. 'The loss of his father has affected him terribly.'

'No it hasn't,' said Martin, barely lifting his eyes from the screen. 'I'll still go to school.'

'Why don't you go and make yourself something to eat while I talk to—'

'John May,' said May, offering a conciliatory smile. 'And this is my partner, Arthur Bryant.'

'I'm not hungry,' said Martin. 'I want to stay and listen.'

'I don't think that's a good idea.'

'It's OK; I'm not going to embarrass you, if that's what you're worried about. Anyway, you're the one who always gets upset.'

'I don't think that's true.'

'Well, it *is* true.' Martin stabbed at the phone, concentrating harder than ever. May sized up the situation. It was easy to see why the boy and his mother were at odds with one another. The rival for their affections had vanished, leaving nothing to separate them. By killing himself, Thomas Wallace had let them both down. He had proved that their love and loyalty were not reasons enough to remain alive. Now they were stuck with each other, united only in grief and confusion.

May remained standing because no one had invited him to have a seat. Bryant plonked himself on one of the chairs, not so much sitting as falling wearily off his walking stick.

'I know you already spoke to an officer, but this call is slightly different,' May explained, handing her his PCU card, an old-fashioned habit that he found put people more at ease. 'Mr Bryant and I head up a specialist unit that takes a unique approach to policing. It's about trying to understand unusual situations, and making sure that they don't happen again.'

'It's not going to happen again, is it, 'cause he's dead,' said Martin angrily.

'You might want to show a little more respect in front of police officers, sonny,' said Bryant, who did not enjoy children until they were mature enough to stop hating everyone over twenty. 'Mrs Wallace, I understand you've been briefed about the events of last night.'

'Yes, but I have no idea why something like this should have happened. He hadn't long been – I mean, my husband was found dead on Wednesday and was buried on Friday morning.'

'That was fast.'

'Well, there were certain – circumstances. There was no church service to arrange. He took his own life.'

'Mum,' said Martin.

'Well, he did. There's no use pretending anything else, is there? I was asked to formally identify him. The local police recorded his position and appearance, and inter-viewed us to try and establish his state of mind. I think they also talked to his work colleagues. There was an external examination by a pathologist the same day, and he seemed satisfied enough to allow a death certificate. My husband wasn't religious, but he had specified where he wanted to be buried.'

'Isn't that rather an unusual request?' asked May.

'Not in his case. Thomas was exact about everything.' She made it sound like his curse and her burden. 'His family used to own property in Bloomsbury, and both he and his father had a special dispensation to be interred in St George's Gardens if they so wished. As it turned out, his father died overseas, but Thomas's final wish was honoured. The funeral director was most accommodating.'

'How did he die?' asked Bryant.

'I'm sure you must already have this written down somewhere,' said Mrs Wallace, looking about herself as if trying to decide an escape route. 'I found him hanged on the back of our bedroom door. The doctor was called, then the police. They're required to notify you in cases of suicide, apparently.'

'Indeed,' said May. 'I assume you spoke to the doctor to ascertain the . . . uh, circumstances of his demise?'

'There was hardly anything to ascertain, was there? It appears that he showered and dressed for work, then went back upstairs and hanged himself. He left a note. I suppose you want to see it.' She walked over to the sideboard drawer, gathered up a single slip of white notepaper and all but threw it at him. It read simply: 'Vanessa, Martin – I'm sorry for the pain I will cause you both by this action, all my love, Thomas.'

'Not exactly one of the greatest farewell letters in history, is it?' she said. Her tone was acid.

'He didn't have anything left to say to you,' said Martin, adding to the atmosphere of rancour.

'It's his handwriting, just in case you were wondering,' said Mrs Wallace.

'Perhaps you could tell us a little more about your husband's state of mind,' May asked.

'Thomas had been diagnosed as bipolar some years before. He suffered from extremely debilitating bouts of depression. He was a partner in a small law firm in the City, handling a vintage wine merchant, some finance companies, an auction house. Things hadn't been going well for a while. There was one particular client who had been giving him a lot of problems. That hardly explains why he should choose to take his own life, but I'm given to understand that such tragedies are rarely explicable.'

'I can explain it,' said Martin. 'He was shit scared.'

'Martin,' Mrs Wallace hissed, clapping her hands together. 'Can you *please* go and do something useful elsewhere?'

The boy remained where he was, still staring at the

screen of his mobile, a model of carefully studied self-absorption. 'I'm not leaving,' he said. 'You can't make me.'

'Do you have any theory of your own—' May began.

'Well, of course I have an idea. Two of the partners had been let go, the practice was about to declare bankruptcy, most of Thomas's key clients had left, but even so he was in a perfectly good mood—'

'That's not true,' Martin cut in. 'He was worried sick about money. He worried about everything. The doctor always said—'

'He wasn't worried, it was just you saying that he was all the time,' Mrs Wallace interrupted. 'If you hadn't kept on at him about his job – for God's sake, put that bloody phone down for five minutes.'

May knew he needed to break up the pair of them, or their testimony would be of no use to him. Mrs Wallace seemed to intend this as the final word on the subject, but Bryant had not yet had his say.

'Perhaps we can go back to the morning of the suicide,' he requested.

Mrs Wallace gave a sharp little sigh of impatience. 'We have a house just outside Windsor. I'd been down there the night before. Martin was here with his father—'

'I never go to Windsor,' Martin interrupted. 'It's full of disgusting old Tories down there. *She's* the only one who likes it.'

Mrs Wallace ignored him. 'I came up to town early to do some shopping and walked into our bedroom. Thomas was hanging from the back of the door. He'd been dead for about an hour. Martin was still fast asleep in his room. I'm sure there's a very detailed report you can read.'

'I prefer to form my own impression,' said Bryant. 'Was it readily apparent to you how he died?'

'Well of course. He had kicked over a footstool and strangled himself with his Old Harrovian tie.'

'So there was no evidence of—'

'Oh, please don't say "foul play",' she snapped. 'It's bad enough that you have to come here just when we're trying to put the whole ghastly business behind us.'

'He kicked over a stool and didn't wake up your son?'

'I'm a heavy sleeper,' said Martin.

'Teenagers always seem to have the capacity to sleep through anything,' said Mrs Wallace, a little more gently. 'Martin's studying for his examinations next year. He's brilliant with technology. He may appear untouched by all of this but it's having a terrible effect on him. He's very sensitive. I suppose I'm more sanguine about such things. Thomas left his financial affairs in a terrible state. I'm dreading the thought of his accountant finding irregularities.'

'Why?' asked Bryant. 'Are there likely to be?'

'Well, you hear about people being left in awful situations by their husbands, that's all.'

'Where was his office?'

'In that funny building in the City, what's it called . . .'

'Number One Poultry,' said Martin. 'He could have jumped off the roof garden of the Coq d'Argent, that's what all the fashionable suicides do these days.'

May was dumbfounded. It was true that a number of bankers had thrown themselves from the garden of the building's rooftop restaurant since the recession, but he was shocked by Martin's callous attitude towards his father. He was about to move on from the subject when Bryant picked it up.

'Why do you think he didn't?'

'What, jump from the roof of his office? I don't suppose it occurred to him,' said Mrs Wallace. 'Too untidy.' It was probably just the anger of bewilderment, but she sounded cruel. 'He slept badly. He probably would have been awake all night worrying. He did that a lot.'

'Forgive me, but your relationship with your husband sounds strained.'

'You could say that. He wasn't a strong man. He took everything to heart. As I say, he was about to be fired.'

'Why?'

'He lost a very big account, some kind of brokerage. They terminated their contract because of him. It was Thomas's own fault, he admitted that himself. He lost the firm a fortune and only had himself to blame.'

'We're investigating the doctor's verdict on your husband's death,' said May, 'because my partner thinks he may have been wrongly declared dead when he was actually in a vegetative state, which would explain why he was able to briefly return to life on Sunday night.'

That shut Mrs Wallace up. He hated to do it, but it was the only way to make them work together. It was better that the mother and son both hated him.

'You mean he wasn't dead?' Martin asked. 'But I thought you said someone dug him up. There's some girl at school who knows what happened and she's online saying that—'

'There is an outside chance that he was still alive. If that proves to be the case, there may be cause to pursue a prosecution.'

'That damned doctor,' said Mrs Wallace with venom. 'He was in such a bloody rush, doing too many things at once, taking *phone calls*, barely bothering to look at my husband.'

'While we're waiting for a more detailed medical report on Mr Wallace's condition at the time of interment, I want to talk to a couple of his colleagues,' said May.

'What on earth for?'

'They might be able to shed further light on his state of mind.'

'He wanted to get out,' said Martin.

'That's a lie. We were happy together. We had our differences but we were a happy family.' Mrs Wallace sat down with an air of defeat. 'We were a happy family,' she said again, as if trying to convince herself.

'Nevertheless, I'd like to have a quiet word with someone who was close to him at work.'

'Thomas didn't get on with the senior partners. He never socialized with them. He was closer to his clients.' She reached over to a notepad – the same one, it seemed, that her husband's suicide note had been torn from – and after thinking for a moment, jotted down a telephone number. 'You might be better off talking to this gentleman,' she said. 'A man called Krishna Jhadav – I don't know if I've spelled that right. He runs the brokerage, the account my husband was looking after until Mr Jhadav pulled it away from him. The pair of them were quite close. They played golf together at least once a month.'

'I had to sit through a disgusting dinner while they talked about industrial waste,' said Martin. 'The guy was a total scumbag, obviously on the take from other companies, like all of his capitalist pals.'

'My husband paid the price of failure,' said Mrs Wallace. 'What I'd like to know is why somebody decided to compound that price by vandalizing his final resting place.'

'It crossed my mind that someone might have had an objection to him being buried in a public park,' said Bryant.

'It has been some kind of graveyard for centuries. Nobody seemed to mind.'

'Was there a shovel?' asked Martin, genuinely interested.

'I suppose there should have been,' May admitted, 'but we haven't turned one up. We have a colleague examining CCTV footage, but the nearest cameras may not be able to show us anything.'

'Why not?'

'It's summer. The trees are in full leaf, and around here

that's a problem. Unless they're cut back all the time they obscure some of the cameras. And the council's tree cutters are out on strike at the moment.'

'So neither of you have any other theory as to why my husband's grave was attacked, or what he was doing . . .' She looked for a moment as if she might break, but rallied. 'What his body was doing,' she corrected. 'I mean, he *was* dead.'

'That is the supposition,' said Bryant carefully.

'Well, he's not *really* likely to have come back to life. Even for a moment, surely?' She looked from one to the other.

'Well, *I* don't think so—' began May.

Bryant cleared his throat. 'There were cases outlined in Dr Heinrich Kornmann's book *De Miraculis Mortuorum* of the pulse and heartbeat lowering to such an extent that they become undetectable and a deathlike state was induced,' he mused. May glared a warning at him.

'Surely you're not suggesting that a modern doctor could fail to notice such a thing?' Mrs Wallace was outraged.

'They can't be expected to be conversant with the state of *Scheintod*, or death trance, also referred to as the Counterfeit of Death,' said Bryant. 'It's extremely rare and generally involves undiagnosed epilepsy, but I think at this stage we have to consider all possible—'

'We have to go,' said May, seizing his partner's arm. 'Please allow us to offer our most sincere condolences for your loss, and be assured that we'll contact you as soon as we have any further information.'

'For all the good it will do,' Vanessa Wallace muttered, utterly lost. She was looking down at the profusion of paperwork, her hand at her mouth. Her son had finally set down his mobile and was staring angrily out of the garden window. The only sound in the bare room was the ticking of a 1930s carriage clock, but when May looked more carefully he saw that it was a cheap reproduction, the gilt too bright, the tick without weight.

It's time to leave them in peace, he thought, giving a nod to each in turn. *This is a house where grief will live for a long time yet.*

'I can't believe you did that,' he said as soon as they got outside. 'The poor woman just lost her husband and you're going on about undetectable heartbeats and the possibility of him waking up in his coffin. Do you understand that other people have feelings, even if you don't?'

'Oh, come off it,' Bryant replied indignantly. 'Even you were surprised when the lad made that crack about jumping off the restaurant roof. And she's not remotely sorry for him, she's angered by his weakness and by the parlous state in which he left his finances.'

'Thomas Wallace was about to be given the boot for losing his firm's biggest account. It seems pretty clear-cut to me that he died and his grave was vandalized by kids, unless you think there's something else worth investigating.'

Bryant was pursuing his own train of thought. 'We need to see if he had any enemies. Someone might have thought it was a good idea to desecrate his grave, just to hurt his wife. See what you can find out.'

'What are you going to do?' asked May.

'I'm going to the Tower of London,' said Bryant. 'I've been urgently summoned by the Raven Master.'

8

CRY CORPSE

The Tower of London had changed since he was last there. The visitors' entrance had been moved to a different spot and there was a new café near by. These days the White Tower looked so much smaller, hemmed in as it was by the shimmering steel and glass cliffs of the business district.

There was a time in the not-too-distant past when Bryant remembered standing in the centre of Tower Green and imagining himself present at the execution of Anne Boleyn, for the simple reason that there had been nothing to bisect the horizon. Although views possessed intangible values and the sightlines to St Paul's Cathedral remained protected, the frontline of financial London had gradually advanced around the Tower. Since 1066 the old fortress, protected by a moat and a river, had accrued purposes to become a complex of mismatched buildings set within the concentric rings of its defensive walls. It had been a palace, a prison, a residence, an armoury, a treasure house, a menagerie, a mint – and was now a box to tick off the bucket list, another World Heritage site to trot through in a couple of hours, squeezed in between a ride in the London Eye and a West End musical.

The Tower was a place no true Londoner ever really thought about; it was just *there*, over to the east and down at the waterline, barely visible behind nests of scaffolding and the accretion of ugly red rooftops, a bank of Gormenghastian dwellings that housed the Yeoman Warders, who were required to be home each night before the 700-year-old Ceremony of the Keys. If it had been founded upon a hill like other castles, the Tower would still have looked down upon the city. Instead, the city had risen volcanically above it, and how paradoxical it was that England's most potent monument should now sit beneath its people, awaiting their attendance.

Bryant was shown in through a narrow causeway separated out from the tourist trail. The site was closing now, and the last few visitors were making their way towards the exit. Since the beginning of the sixteenth century, twelve Yeoman Warders had been kept here to guard the palace. In typically English confusion, their duties were different from the Yeoman of the Guard, the ceremonial bodyguards who were still required to search the cellars of the Palace of Westminster prior to the State Opening of Parliament. The Warders, or Beefeaters, dressed in thistle, rose and shamrock, in maroon and gold stripe for state occasions, but during the day they wore simplified uniforms of navy and red, and spent their time entertaining tourists with stories. They were men – and one woman – of maturity and gravity; a minimum of twenty-two years' distinguished service in the armed forces was required before a new member could be appointed.

Bryant had known Matthew Condright since the Falklands War, but had seen little of him. The Warders gave their lives over to the Tower, and Condright had remained a steadfast royalist whose duty came before all other concerns. At least, it had until a problem had arisen involving the hounding of a fellow soldier, and then he had asked for Bryant's help in finding the culprits. Today he had turned to his old friend once more.

Condright received him in his tied accommodation, a cosy home he shared with his wife under the battlements of the castle keep. His sideburns and shovel beard seemed to mark him as a Warder even out of uniform. He shook Bryant's hand warmly, but ushered him from the door and into an outside passage almost immediately. 'I'm sorry, I can't talk in front of Hannah,' he said, 'although she knows – God, they all know – and that's why I called you. Bloody useful that you're under the City of London now, because we can't allow outsiders to get hold of this. It's a matter of national importance, and nobody can know. If it got out, I hate to think—'

'Why don't you start at the beginning?' said Bryant impatiently. 'Nobody's dead, are they?'

'No, nothing like that – something far stranger, if you can believe it. I can barely believe it myself. You probably know that I'm the Raven Master here.'

'I did read something about it, yes.'

'They've gone. All seven of them. Hugine, Erin, Merlin, Munin, Rocky, Pearl and Porsha. Vanished into thin air. I know it doesn't seem possible.'

'Wait, the Tower ravens have all disappeared? Doesn't that mean that England will fall?'

'Bloody hell, Arthur, let's start with the practical part first, eh? They're one of our star attractions, and they've been nicked.'

'There's method in my madness, Matthew; indulge me for a moment.'

'All right.' Condright sighed. 'The legend says that the ravens must never leave the Tower because it's tied to the Crown of England, but these days we think that was a romantic myth created by the Victorians.'

'I thought there was a history of English kings associated with ravens dating back to the time of Charles the Second.'

'I believe there is, but the legend can only be dated as far back as 1955. Forget the history for a moment. What I need to know is where they've gone and who took them. I'm about to lose my job over this. Can you imagine what would happen if the news got out? There would be an international scandal. The Crown Jewels are housed here. What if they're not safe either?'

'When did you become aware that the ravens were missing?'

'On Friday morning. I went down to feed them – they're kept in overnight.'

'Can we go and see the cage?'

'Of course.'

Bryant and Condright set off across the uneven cobbles of the walkway leading from Henry III's Watergate to the Lanthorn Tower. They made an incongruous pair; Condright towered over the detective. He stopped before a low metal cage covered by a large black tarpaulin.

'They're natural carnivores. I feed them raw meat from Smithfield Market, and biscuits soaked in blood,' he explained. 'Nobody could have got in to steal them, because the building is locked up tight every night.'

'The Ceremony of the Keys.'

'And the birds always pass the night inside this cage.'

'How do they get in?'

'There's a flap at the back. They always come in for their food. We don't let visitors feed them.'

'Who else has the key to the cage?'

'That's the thing. Only me. Nobody else.'

'Could someone have borrowed it from you and copied it?'

'No. It never leaves the chain inside my coat. And the only time I take this off is to go to bed.'

'So – your wife.'

'No, Arthur. She never touches my clothes. I take care of them myself. She knows that my livelihood is tied to the performance of my duties.'

Bryant crouched down and lifted the edge of the tarpaulin. Beneath it were the black steel struts and wire mesh of the empty cage. 'What happens to the birds during the day?'

'They're free to roam about during visitors' hours but their wings have been clipped, so it's impossible for them to fly away.'

'Could somebody have walked out with them?'

'Not possible. Have you seen how big they are? The visitors' bags are carefully checked, and besides, the birds are noisy and will attack strangers if approached. They're vicious, raucous buggers. I'm at a complete loss.'

'There has to be a symbolic purpose to the theft,' said Bryant. 'They're not valuable, are they?'

'They're the symbol of England, Arthur. At least, that's what they've come to stand for. We've covered the cage for now and posted a sign saying it's closed for renovation, but in a couple of days people are going to start asking why they haven't seen any birds hopping about on the green. You have to keep this to yourself. Don't let anyone outside the unit know what you've been asked to investigate. My head will be on the block if they're not found quickly.' It was an unfortunate turn of phrase, given the setting.

'I don't suppose someone's pulling your leg, are they?' asked Bryant. 'This couldn't be some kind of elaborate practical joke?'

'I wish it was,' said Condright. 'We're trying to buy some replacements right now, but so far we haven't found good matches. To me, each bird has a distinctive personality, although the public can't see the differences between them.' He helped Bryant to his feet. 'Well, what do you think?'

'I can see why it was done but not how, or by whom. Tell me, who else knows about this?'

'We've informed a select few, but it would be disastrous if any details reached the press – they'd turn us into a laughing stock.'

'We should be able to keep a lid on it,' Bryant agreed, 'but I'll still have to clear the investigation with my superior at the City of London. I can't wait to see her face when I tell her about this.'

When Bryant got back to the unit and informed his partner, John May laughed so hard that he nearly choked on the piece of cheesecake he was eating.

'Where did you get that from?' Bryant demanded to know.

'The new intern went out and bought cakes for everyone,' said May, dusting crumbs from his suit jacket. 'So England will fall unless you find who swiped the ravens? Are you sure you didn't fall asleep reading an Agatha Christie?'

'All right, have your laugh, but look at it from his point of view. Matthew has been entrusted with the safekeeping of one of London's best-known traditions. Someone's out to get him. Someone from his past, someone he encountered in active service for his country, who knows? The Warders aren't immune to scandal, you know. Back in 2009 two of the Yeomen were dismissed for bullying the only female Warder. One was reinstated, but it tarnished the reputations of them all. They work as a team in the service of the Queen. It's a very serious matter.'

'OK,' said May, holding up a hand. 'I'm going to let you deal with this one. If I were you, I'd check their meat supplier. From what I remember, those birds are the size of Alsatians and ferocious. If somebody made off with them, they would have to be drugged first and smuggled out in . . . I don't know, the false bottom of a holdall or something.'

'You'd need seven very big holdalls. Strictly speaking, there are six ravens and one in reserve, like a volleyball team.'

May tried to stifle another laugh, as he had no desire to spit cake crumbs over the office. 'Fine,' he said. 'You do what you have to do, Arthur. I'm going to carry on checking CCTV footage with Dan, looking for a way that Thomas Wallace might have risen from the grave. And if you think of it, you might ask Raymond when we're going to get assigned a nice normal murder case again.'

'Not every investigation starts with a body found in a canal or a railway siding,' said Bryant indignantly. 'According to my latest copy of the *Police Gazette*, London's murder rate is at a forty-three-year low and dropping. Last year there were only half a dozen gun deaths in a metropolis of nearly eight million people. We're living in one of the safest cities on the planet. That's a welcome bit of news for the good citizens of London but it's bloody boring for those of us who make a living from bad tidings. You and I are going to get fewer cases that involve gruesome slaughters and more that involve cats stuck up trees.'

'I suppose that's true,' said May. 'Most of the really big crimes take place on the other side of computer screens now, shifting dodgy mineral deposits from the Congo to Russia.'

'I'm too old to retrain for investigating anything like that. Besides, I like a proper crime, something that involves a blackjack or a garrotting, or a humiliated colonel trying to offload a crate of black-market nylons.'

'Fine,' said May, 'you carry on pretending it's 1953 and I'll try to make sure that we still have jobs to go to in the present day, shall I?'

Bryant opened a page of his 1932 Arthur Mee *Children's*

Encyclopaedia and pointed to a sinister photograph of a raven casting a great dark shadow on the English landscape. 'The ravens aren't just the symbol of England, John, they're also a sign of death. If you see them flying overhead, someone will die. It's because their cry sounds like "Corpse! Corpse!" And although the idea of the loss of the ravens preceding the fall of England is recent, it's an extension of a much older myth. There have been royal animals at the Tower since at least 1213. As late as 1882 the three great sights of London were meant to be the lions at the Tower, the tombs of Westminster Abbey and Bedlam. If ever a lion died, it was thought that the sovereign would also perish. The animals are fertility symbols, of course, a nod to London's pagan past.'

'I don't see what any of that's got to do with someone nicking a bunch of fancy crows,' said May.

'Oh, that I had your gift of eloquence,' said Bryant sarcastically. 'Those "fancy crows" weren't killed by some mindless vandal; they were spirited away without leaving a trace. This was an emblematic act of treason, a warning.'

'A warning of what?' asked May.

'I would have thought it obvious,' Bryant replied. 'The fall of England. It's not a theft – it's a signal to begin.'

9

GIRLS AND BOYS

Romain Curtis felt as if he'd been given a second chance.

Even though he had managed to frighten the life out of Shirone the night before, she had waited for him to come home just so that she could invite him to the local club. With its curved white entrance and three huge portholes, the Scala resembled a boat as much as a building, thrust out on a pavement promontory into the swirling flow of King's Cross traffic. The former arthouse cinema was just ten minutes' walk from the Cromwell Estate.

Shirone met him in the courtyard below the flats. She wore a lurid purple T-shirt and black tights that accentuated her long legs, and had done something complicated to the colour and curl of her hair that he was clearly meant to notice. She had been given comps because her brother occasionally worked at the club as a bouncer, although he was mercifully absent tonight. The Scala was so loud and crowded that it defied movement or conversation, so they drank and danced, and drank some more without speaking. Shirone went to the bar because Romain looked too young to get served, and she knew the staff. The dancers pushed them steadily back, until they found themselves pressed against one of the gigantic bass speakers. Above the black and red auditorium spun a matrix of green lasers, disorienting the clubbers just enough to ensure that nobody thought about leaving.

Between sets they came out to the stairwell between the ground floor and the mezzanine, where it was cooler. 'You're a funny one,' said Shirone, sitting herself on a step. 'You don't hang out with the others, do you? Half of your class is in there.'

'We haven't got a lot in common,' Romain admitted, seating himself beside her. He was in a good mood tonight, and felt like talking. 'When I leave school I want to have a career, not a job. If I'm going to do that it means saving some cash and not going out so much.'

'Yeah, but you don't talk to them at school either.'

'So what? Nobody in my family ever made anything of themselves. My mum wants me to have the chances she never had. I've got a lot of interests. My old man was a pattern cutter. I made this T-shirt today, see? I'd be good in fashion design but I can't tell anyone at school, can I, 'cause they'd only take the piss.'

'I'm going to be a hairdresser,' said Shirone. 'Get my own salon and nail bar.'

'How are you going to get the money together?'

'I don't know. Borrow some from my brothers.'

'But you know where they get their money from. That would be well troubling for you.'

'It's my family, Romain. My brother got us in here tonight. We saved twenty quid. Does that make us criminals?'

'You know what I mean.' Romain did not want to say anything that would spoil the evening. 'Come on,' he said, pulling her to her feet. 'I'll buy you a drink. I've got enough money for that, at least.'

They returned to the crowded ground-floor bar and let the pounding bass resonate through their bodies, and soon it seemed that there was no difference between them, nothing to worry about, nothing to be aware of except the music and the night. Romain was happy. It felt as if the whole of London was dancing.

DS Janice Longbright – she could not remember a time when the formal prefix had not existed – looked over at her colleague, lightly snoring in the corner of her sofa. It had just turned midnight, and he had somehow managed to doze off in the middle of a dim and deafening film involving Tom Cruise and an army of aliens. Jack Renfield had spent the evening at her apartment twice in the past week, and was already developing habits: ordering noodles from the Great Wall takeaway; leaving his shoes by the front door; chucking his coat into the spare bedroom; emptying his small change into the ceramic bear on the kitchen counter.

The former desk sergeant from Albany Street nick had settled in very well at Longbright's Highgate flat. Habits were reassuring and natural, but she wondered why he had never invited her to visit his place in Vauxhall. She had disliked him intensely when they had first met, but now she was starting to understand him. One of six kids, raised in the roughest part of Bermondsey by a burned-out junkie mother, he'd had his work cut out avoiding jail, let alone getting into the police force. Before they realized that he might prove an asset to the unit, Bryant and May had continually made fun of him. Now he had earned their respect, and they had realized that his blunt by-the-book attitude was the result of never having had any rules to follow. He used a framework of discipline and order to insulate himself from others, and vice versa.

She wondered at him, though. She'd modified her taste in trashy clothes, had invested in a pair of jeans that weren't modelled on 1950s styles, had even taken the kirby grips out of her dyed-blonde hair, but he hadn't said anything about the changes. She was trying for him.

Still, watching his broad strong stomach rising and falling, it was hard not to feel the pleasure of sharing her life with someone decent and true. Renfield had come along only just in time. She'd started to become so independent that she had feared she might never allow another man space in her life. Deciding to let him sleep for another half-hour, she rose and washed the plates as quietly as possible, although it seemed likely that he could sleep through a storm.

As she folded his clothes – he rarely removed his PCU jacket in public – something fell on the floor and rolled under the sofa. She crouched down and felt around, her hand closing over something that felt like a tube of mints. She withdrew her fist and opened it. It was a key ring, a clear plastic stick with a tiny photograph inside. It showed a blonde girl holding a red cardboard love-heart.

So he has a past, she reasoned. *Who doesn't? No big deal.* But as she tipped the key ring to the light, trying to see how pretty the girl was without her reading glasses, she wondered why he kept it in the pocket he usually emptied every night.

She was still squinting at the photograph when he awoke with a start and blinked at her. 'Hi, babe,' he said, struggling upright. 'What's the matter?'

She said nothing, but was not able to hide the key ring quickly enough. He gradually focused on what was in her hand. 'Ah,' he said, and then she knew that he always carried the picture with him.

Romain was definitely woozy-headed, and when he tried to speak his words emerged in a thick slur. He knew what he wanted to say, but the sentences folded up on themselves. Shirone was looking at him oddly, as if he was attempting to speak another language.

He made a mental calculation of how much he'd had to drink.

There were two draught pints in quick succession, then two rounds of cheap shots, taking advantage of the club's Monday-night BOGOF deal. Then another beer. That was it, nothing more, but he felt as if he'd been hit by a truck. Some of the kids in his class had started drinking before they had hit their teens, and took miniatures of vodka into clubs to top up their drinks. They brought home-made cocktails that didn't show up when they passed through the knife arch, ice pops created by using syringes to draw out half their liquid, replacing it with hard liquor before refreezing. Some of the girls kept flasks in their sports bras. Romain had never been that fussed about alcohol. He could only think that tonight the bargirl had made a mistake and mixed him a triple instead of a single, because he was becoming more unsteady by the second.

Shirone was talking to him. He heard the words 'all right' and 'sit down' but then the music took over, filling his head with beats, and the laser contrails juddered past in sharp emerald shards.

Shirone's brothers, Nico and Enrico, had both turned up. What were they doing here? He pushed himself away from the bar and accidentally slammed into one of them. Enrico shoved back hard, then Shirone was angrily shouting in his face and he was lurching off towards the doors at the rear of the auditorium, the lights expanding in rainbow colours all around him.

The street felt cooler but his black T-shirt was soaked in sweat. He stood against the wall, felt his heart pounding against his ribs. Something was not right. When he tried to walk, the road turned into a ship's deck that tipped away from him, sliding left, then right. A car blasted its horn and he lurched into a run, barely making the opposite kerb. *Concentrate*, he told himself, *just watch your feet and keep moving one in front of the other. You can do this.*

The route through the darkened backstreets was as familiar as the layout of his flat. There were never any cars back here. All he had to do was watch out for the local kids, who cruised the empty night corridors waiting to pluck mobiles from the hands of drunken commuters.

His head cleared a little, clouds briefly parting, and he thought of Shirone left behind, probably complaining to her brothers' mates about his behaviour. It seemed unlikely now that they would ever get it on. But he had done nothing wrong. On both nights it had been someone else's fault.

Someone else's fault . . .

He started putting the whole thing together just as he turned into the unlit cobbled road that dog-legged over the railway tracks behind the Scala. Walking past the riveted steel slabs that lined the bridge, he remembered the face at the bar and realized what he had done. He needed to sit down and think it through properly.

St George's Gardens last night.

The Scala tonight.

But why?

He looked down and realized. *You're an idiot,* he told himself. *Why did you have to go back?*

He rose unsteadily to his feet, leaning against the lamp-post. The effort of concentration was his undoing; he didn't hear the vehicle approach, and then he couldn't control his limbs. As he turned and tried to right himself he slipped from the kerb. The vehicle's left-side fender caught his tibia and cracked it, whipping him around. He fell crookedly as the vehicle passed, smacking his head hard on the raised kerbstone.

He felt nothing, but could see from one eye that the gutter beneath him was turning crimson. As he tried to raise himself, the tyres squealed as their direction was reversed. He heard the engine whine and saw the rear wheel approaching fast, and knew then that it would not stop.

'Why do you keep her picture in your jacket?' Longbright tried to sound merely curious, but something terrible had welled inside her, a fear that he was about to lie – or, worse, that he might not even bother.

'I keep her there because I love her and she loves me,' said Renfield blearily. 'Can we go to bed now?'

Longbright did not know what to say. Dumbly, she handed back the key ring and turned away, trying to stay in control of her emotions. As she made to leave the room, she felt the warmth of his calloused hand on her arm.

'She's my daughter, you dummy,' he said. 'Her name is Sennen. We named her after Sennen Cove in Cornwall, where her mother and I first met. She's fifteen and she lives with Angie in Finsbury. She comes to me every second Saturday. At least, she used to.'

Longbright was relieved and angry. 'Why on earth didn't you tell me before? Why do you have to keep everything so damned close to your chest? Why wind me up like that?'

'I'm a bloke, OK? We don't "share" everything. Sometimes we smell weird and make strange noises. We have issues about our daughters, and when it comes to other women, our daughters do too. So we don't talk about them until we're sure.'

'Sure of what?'

'What do you think?'

'Fine, but you could have told me earlier. You nearly got a frying pan round the back of the head.'

Looking at Longbright's hurt expression, Jack knew that she deserved an explanation. 'Sennen's got some behavioural problems,' he said. 'She's smart, precocious, but a bit – unmoored. She doesn't like living with her mother.

She says she wants to be with me, but the court – well, I'm sure you know how that one goes. I'm not the best father in the world. Work has a habit of getting in the way.'

'Jack, I'm sorry.' She turned and let him take her in his arms. 'Maybe I could meet her the next time she comes to see you.'

'Janice, I don't think that's a good idea.'

'Why not? Arthur and John always tell me how good I am with teenagers. You could at least let me try. I can just be your colleague from work.'

'No, she'll know. She's really not ready to share me with anyone.'

'How could she know? I'll just be one of the guys.'

Renfield studied Longbright's astonishing figure doubtfully. At home she toned down her outfits, but she still looked enough like Marilyn Monroe to stand out in any crowd.

'Sennen and her mother are going to be nearby on Wednesday evening, visiting friends,' he began, 'and I said I'd see them because they're in King's Cross, but I really don't think—'

'That's perfect, I'll be there,' said Longbright, giving him a reassuring squeeze. 'It'll be fine, just wait and see. Trust me, Jack. Five minutes at the station. What could possibly go wrong?'

10

REVERSAL

Alma Sorrowbridge knocked again, then gave up waiting and barged into Bryant's bedroom. 'You've slept right through your alarm,' she began, then uttered a cry. Bryant opened one bloodshot eye and glared at her over the top of the duvet.

'Thank the Lord you're alive,' she said. 'For a moment I thought you'd gone to meet your maker.'

Bryant hiked up the collar of his blue and white striped Andy Pandy pyjamas. 'Yes, Alma, amazing as it may seem I appear to have struggled through another night and am likely to survive for yet one more day,' he said. 'Put my tea down over there. I hope you brought biscuits.'

'Ginger and mandarin, I baked them this morning,' she said, setting down her tray.

'Good God, what time did you get up? Why can't you sleep like normal people?'

'So it wasn't you I heard walking about at three o'clock this morning?'

'That's different. I was thinking. You don't need to think to bake.'

'In all the years I've known you, Mr Bryant,' Alma said, 'I've never once seen you cook a meal.'

'That's because you've always got a bucket of something bubbling away on the stove. What would be the point of making more? Go on, bugger off and let me get dressed in peace.'

'You're a very unpleasant man first thing in the morning.'

'I hope to be even more unpleasant in the afternoon. Did you iron my trousers?'

'Yes, but you'll have to buy new ones soon. I could see myself in the seat of your pants.'

'I'm not buying new ones, thank you. Nobody makes turn-ups any more.'

'You could smarten yourself up a bit. You have new bosses now. It's important to stay on top of things.'

'And how am I supposed to do that at my age?' cried Bryant indignantly. 'I'm a funny shape. I'm not fashionable. I'm not technical. I'm not meant to be there. I'm not even meant to be *here*.'

Alma sat on the edge of the bed. Bryant pulled at the duvet, resenting the intrusion. 'You mustn't say that,' she said. 'You're one of God's children and He will not let you go.'

'Why not? Most of my friends are either dead, deaf or living in the wrong part of Kent. The world is for the young. Have you seen television lately? Do you understand a word of it? Perhaps we're just not meant to soldier on indefinitely, did you think of that? We can't all be Cliff Richard.'

'Is this what was keeping you pacing about in the middle of the night?' She looked at him with suspicion welling in her hazel eyes. 'Have you got a new case?'

Bryant scratched his head blearily. 'The night before last a man came back from the grave. And the worst part of it was, he might have been alive in his coffin. Except that he couldn't have been. He had all the regular symptoms of death: gas in his stomach, onset of putrefaction, changing skin tone – he was going rotten, so how could he have risen again? How could he come back from the dead unless he was a zombie? You must know something about voodoo. How does it work?'

'I'm from Antigua, not Haiti. There must be a logical explanation. Didn't you say there's always one?'

'But what if there isn't? What if this time, for some reason beyond our knowing, the laws of science and logic have been upended? Then what do we do?'

'I won't have blasphemy in this house,' said Alma. 'The dead don't come back to life, no matter what those Hollywood films say. If you believed in God you'd have a better understanding of the world.'

'Rubbish, woman. It's man who gives mankind a better understanding of the world, not God.'

'But it's man's interpretation of God's will that makes us better people. You believe in the spirit world and witchcraft and all these crazy things, yet I can't convince you to believe in the power of goodness.'

Bryant emerged from his cocoon far enough to reach the biscuits. He hadn't put his teeth in yet, but he could at least suck one. 'I believe in good and evil, but there's no point in trying to make people believe in something they can't successfully practise.'

'That's not true, and you know it. I'm a good person, Mr Bryant, because I practise what I preach. I don't try to do the impossible. I think if I can save one horrible miserable old sinner and teach him to be nice then I'm doing the work God set out for me.'

'It's not going very well so far, is it?'

'You're better than you used to be.'

'That's true. I don't dry my socks on the lampshade any more.'

'And maybe you're doing God's work, helping to protect us all from unquiet souls.'

'What do you mean, "unquiet souls"?'

'Like this man you say climbed out of his grave. He wasn't at rest. Some people die inside long before their bodies die.'

Bryant sat up. 'But what about the reverse? What if his body died before he did?' He searched about for his trousers. 'A coma. What if he'd been misdiagnosed and his brain was still alive? Alma, you may be on to a winner. I need to consult an expert.'

'I didn't mean anything specific,' Alma protested.

'Maybe your gods are working through you.' He wriggled out of bed, gave her cheek a painful pinch and headed for the bath.

'God singular,' she called after him, 'not gods!' but her words were drowned out by running taps.

'He was dead long before the Emergency Medical Team got to him,' said Giles Kershaw, holding open the door for May. The forensic pathologist always looked as if he should be playing cricket rather than peering into dead bodies. Today he was actually wearing a white cricket jumper. 'They brought him here to UCH and immediately put the incident down as suspicious.'

'Why did they do that?' asked May, following him down the eye-wateringly bright corridor that ran beneath University College Hospital. This was the medical equivalent of a theatre's backstage area, where doctors worked behind the scenes and patients who had not survived their stays awaited collection. 'They couldn't have known that we interviewed him as a witness yesterday.'

'There's a chance they could have. EMTs around the stations get updates on all local incidents.'

'The grave desecration wouldn't have gone down as anything major. I don't think anyone would have known what to put it down as.'

'Well, the medics got the call at just after one thirty

98

a.m. so their thinking is that he was at the Scala nightclub and left at around one fifteen a.m., somewhat the worse for wear.'

'What makes them assume that?'

'There was a club night on, nothing much else happening in the area on a Monday.' He pointed the way ahead. 'Sorry about the walk, it's just down here on the right. He had alcohol and a high dose of MDMA in his system, and was hit by a vehicle in Britannia Street, round the back of the club.'

'Britannia Street. It would have been the logical route to follow if he was taking a short cut back to his mother's flat. I'm presuming the driver left the scene.'

'Yup, and the suspicious part is that the contact marks aren't consistent with a single collision. Legs, one arm and throat crushed.'

'I've seen that from a single collision before.'

'The med team thought it didn't look right,' said Kershaw. 'He was lying half on the pavement but there were no corresponding bruises from the kerbstone underneath him. They thought it was likely that someone had moved the body afterwards. It was called in and a couple of officers made a report. It should be in your inbox by now.'

'Anything stolen?'

Kershaw opened the door to the area ironically nicknamed the Delivery Room, a storage point for bodies that required pathological investigation, and ushered May inside. 'He still had his wallet, keys, mobile and loose change,' he explained. 'The mother doesn't know what else he normally had on him. She's a nurse over at the Killick Street Clinic, says he rarely drank and never took drugs, but that's what they all say. Anything else, you'll have to find out about. I'm just necrology, love.' He led the way over to a stack of white aluminium units and searched the labels. 'Behave yourself in here. UCH medics don't like jokes so it's just as well you left your comedy partner at home. Don't worry, I'm not going to make him suffer the indignity of public display, I just want my prelim.' Kershaw fished inside one of the drawers and pulled out a sheet from the clear plastic envelope attached to its headboard. 'The NHS computer system has been down for repairs again today so I made hard copies. Here you go, Romain Wellington Curtis. Brave middle name, that.'

He unfolded the top sheet and laid it flat. The page showed a line-diagram of a generic male body with different areas shaded in pen. 'As you can see, fractured front right tibia, right patella, fractured right tarsals and metatarsals, *left* ulna and radius, *left*-side fracture on the clavicle and crushed trachea. It may well just have been an accident – you see pedestrians left in all kinds of impossible positions, and for all I know he was so stoned that he could have been lying in the road – but there is another scenario.'

'The vehicle hit him once, spinning him around, he fell, then the driver reversed on to him. So you get the fractures on both sides.'

'Something like that.'

'Any tyre marks?'

'I was hoping we'd get a lift from the trachea but it looks unlikely. The whole thing must have happened very quickly. There was no time for bruising, but the skin was broken so it's possible there are blood spots on the tyres. Perhaps you could locate your driver before it rains? I'd like to bring in a trace-evidence examiner to look for rubber samples but I suppose you're going to tell me there's no money.'

'Not unless the City of London has suddenly raised our budget without telling us.'

'Then I'll run my own check for residue particles, but it won't be as exact. Britannia Street's your beat, isn't it?'

'I know every inch of it. Those half-dozen backstreets are never used by vehicles. The lighting's atrocious and there's no CCTV because there are hardly ever any pedestrians. No private residences, just offices that close their doors at six. It's one of the council's Catch-22 areas.'

'What do you mean?' Kershaw sucked a pen, leaning over his diagram.

'They won't go to the expense of installing infra-red security cameras because nobody uses the street, and it's deliberately underlit so that nobody will venture down it. A nice little money-saver all round. Besides, when they do install CCTVs kids tend to deliberately hang around them, just to look hard.'

'Why don't local gangs use it for drug pick-ups?'

May stuck his hands in his pockets and had a nose around the room. 'Because both ends come out on to brightly lit main thoroughfares, and they're squarely inside the King's Cross Stop and Search Zone. Anyone wanting to use Britannia Street as a drop point would have to pass through a surveillance area in order to get in there – while they're carrying. It's too risky. There was a spate of phone thefts around there a few months back – a couple of kids on bikes snatching mobiles out of office workers' hands, but they were caught.' He wandered over to the map of catchment areas Blu-tacked to the wall beside the department duty roster and various gruesome hygiene posters. 'These backstreets are generally safer than the main thoroughfares around the stations. Temptation occurs in crowds, not in dead zones. Between Euston, St Pancras and King's Cross you've got a complex footfall going in every direction, which makes crimes easier to commit. It wouldn't have been gang-related, either.'

'Why not?'

May tapped a blank-looking area of the map. 'Britannia Street is neutral territory. Gang boundaries don't start until you reach the edges of the estates below Euston

Road. There's nothing worth disputing in these little pockets of office buildings.'

'There's something else. Take a look at this.' Kershaw withdrew a slender grey electronic tablet from his pocket and raised its cover, thumbing through to some photographs. 'I asked the attending officer to let me have his stills. Nobody from Camden associated the death with you guys, otherwise someone would have called Dan out to the scene.'

'He would never have got there in time. He lives too far away.'

'That's what I figured. The EMT had another callout, so it was left to the local team to sort out. Anything odd strike you about this?' He turned the photograph around and showed May. Curtis was on his back, half on the kerbstone, his legs angled awkwardly.

'The clothes,' said May. 'It looks like he's been pulled upright.'

'My thought exactly. Like the driver got out and tried to sit him up. Now why would he do that?'

'Maybe you're right about sticking to necrology, Giles. Despite what Arthur will try to tell you, in cases like this the obvious solution is usually the right one. Curtis realizes he's in a bad state, leaves the club, weaves his way through the darkened backstreets, sits down on the kerb to wait for his head to stop spinning and someone accidentally runs over him. He's already in a seated position so he turns over beneath the wheels and gets the fractures on both sides.'

'I guess that's feasible,' Kershaw admitted. 'It doesn't seem likely that anyone was lying in wait for him.'

'There is another way of looking at it. One of Arthur's favourite tricks is to reverse investigations by starting from the other end. Assume that the likelihood of Romain Curtis being killed just after he'd made a police statement is impossible to conceive as coincidence, a bit of Occam's

Razor. Which would mean his attacker targeted him, waiting for him to leave the club, then followed him until he got his chance.'

'And sitting him upright after?'

'Either he wanted the boy to talk while he was still alive, and tried to clear his airways, or he did it to search through his clothes. Maybe he was looking for something.' May tapped his teeth with a nail, thinking. 'If Curtis was followed from the club by car we'll have the licence plate, because the Congestion Zone camera line is just south of the Scala on Gray's Inn Road. It'll take a couple of hours to get access to the drives, then someone will have to go through all the footage.'

'It's funny having you here without the old man,' said Kershaw. 'I thought he'd jump at the chance. He loves coming down here.'

May's face clouded. 'Something's up with Arthur. I don't know what it is. I told him I was meeting you and he fell silent. Usually he can't resist the opportunity to start poking about among the dead. He seemed all right last week. It's just since yesterday morning.'

'How's his health these days?'

'He had a full medical a few weeks ago. As far as I know his report was adequate, although the doctor gave him the usual warning about giving up his pipe.'

'Maybe it's an intimation of mortality,' said Giles.

'He had his first one of those forty years ago. And he's been around death all through his career. We both have. You know what it's like: you learn to separate it out from your own life.'

'That could be it,' said Giles ominously. 'Perhaps this time he's associated it with himself. You know how certain cases get to people. I've seen pathologists chuck in successful careers because they couldn't handle it any more. You should keep an eye on him for a while and let me know if he gets any worse.'

'How can I keep an eye on him?' said May, exasperated. 'You know what he's like. He's always going off on his own. I have no idea where he is right now.'

If May had known, his fears would have increased.

II

THE LAZARUS COMPLEX

Shirone Estanza sat on the bench outside her school chewing at a fingernail painted with tiny silver stars. Class had already started but she couldn't bring herself to go inside. She still couldn't take it in. How was it possible that Romain was dead? She was no fool; she knew how little she'd meant to him, but in the back of her mind was the feeling that somehow they might have remained friends.

She seemed to be jinxed when it came to boys.

A terrible thought crossed her mind – what were her brothers saying about her? Nico and Enrico hated her talking to anyone. They only cared about themselves. You didn't have to sleep around to be branded a slut, and they didn't want their little sister getting a reputation in case it reflected badly on them. The word was already going around that Romain had been hit by a car, and her brothers both had part-time work driving vans. She could see the law beating a path to her home. She decided to cut classes and go over to Drummond Street, where the boys hung out.

She found Nico outside the Indian bakery, his grey

hood turned up above the collar of an expensive-looking black leather jacket. As he saw her he turned away, continuing to talk into his mobile.

'Oi, I want a word with you,' she began as he held up his hand and dismissed her. She knew he was doing some kind of dodgy deal. He and Enrico were always up to something involving van drivers, little packages and visits to blocks of flats after midnight. She didn't know the details and didn't want to know. She tapped her painted nails on the bakery window, impatiently waiting for him to finish the call.

'What?' he said. 'What you here for?'

'Did you do something to him last night?'

'What, your little mate?' He sucked his teeth in annoyance. 'You think we whacked him?'

'You was there in the club, right?'

'Yeah, and so was, like, a thousand other people. Make some sense. Your batty boy got nothing to do with us. Someone run him over, yeah?'

'That's what they're saying,' said Shirone, standing her ground as Nico's friends ambled over, looking for something to break the monotony of the morning. 'And if I find out anything that makes me think you messed with him, I'll be telling Mum what you and Enrico get up to down here every night, you understand what I'm saying?'

'What, you been shagging him, then? He been in your pants? You wanna try covering yourself up a bit, then blokes won't get the wrong idea.'

She turned and walked away, trying to look confident, but she was shaking with anger, close to tears. *This is a nightmare*, she thought. *Romain, why did you have to bloody die?*

Dr Evrim Ersoy had come to the University College Hospital from the finest teaching college in Istanbul, and was now acting as a consultant on the new exhibition about death at the Wellcome Collection, a museum that displayed medical artefacts and artworks exploring ideas about the connections between medicine, life and art.

He met Arthur Bryant in the elegant café attached to the gallery on Euston Road. Ersoy had glossy, shoulder-length black hair and a carefully trimmed beard that gave him the appearance of a benign Satan. A playful intelligence danced in his eyes; he always seemed on the verge of becoming uncontrollably excited.

'I was surprised to get your call, Arthur,' he said, sliding into the opposite seat armed with tea mugs. 'It's been quite a while. Have you seen the exhibition?'

'No,' Bryant admitted, 'I'm not sure I've got the stomach for it.'

'What? That's not like you. The final grand adventure? I thought it would be right up your street.'

Bryant accepted the mug and leaned forward confidentially. 'It's not much of an adventure, is it, losing everything that's dear to you? Anyway, I see enough of death every day without peering at pieces designed to turn it into a decorative motif, thank you. I don't think they'd tell me anything I don't already know. But you might be able to.'

Ersoy sipped his mint tea. 'How so? What have you got for me?'

'Your speciality is coma patients, isn't it?'

'That's a bit of a simplification. I'm a neurologist. My specialist area is the reticular activating system, yes.'

'What is that, exactly? I think you explained once before but I wasn't listening then.'

Ersoy added a staggering amount of sugar to his mint tea. 'It's a structure consisting of connected nuclei in the brainstem that's responsible for the regulation of sleeping and wakefulness, and the transition between the two states. If either that or the cerebral cortex gets damaged, you have yourself a coma patient. The RAS is a more primitive structure than cerebral tissue or so-called "grey matter". It has a system of acetylcholine-manufacturing neurons arranged in two paths, one rising, one falling – they're what wake you up or keep you asleep.'

'How do you define a coma?'

'Usually more than six hours of unconsciousness. That's to say you're in such a deep sleep that you can't be shaken awake.'

'And how long can it last?'

'Up to about five weeks.' Ersoy dropped yet another sugar cube in his tea. 'But in theory it can last indefinitely. There have been extreme cases where patients have returned after twenty years. The danger is that over long periods of time in a vegetative state, secondary infections kick in. We think coma states originally developed in order to compensate bodies while they repaired themselves, to stop the system from wasting energy. But you don't necessarily come out of it in one piece.'

'All right.' Bryant pressed his hands flat on the table, thinking it through. 'Say I'm a doctor and my patient has been knocked out. How do I know he's in a coma and not merely unconscious?'

'Comas result from a number of conditions. The most common are drug abuse, diseases of the central nervous system, lack of oxygen, car accidents, other traumas, strokes and so on. What do you have in mind?'

'Asphyxiation. A suicide – hanging.'

'That would be lack of oxygen, certainly.'

'What would stop me from thinking my patient is dead?'

Ersoy gave a guttural laugh. 'Well, you wouldn't be a very good doctor if you couldn't tell the difference. But it has been known. First you perform a general examination. Then you check the medical background. History of drugs, other compounding factors. Make sure that he's not in a locked-in state.'

'What's that?'

'Total paralysis except for the eyes. He'd probably be able to move them due to oculocephalic reflex, also known as doll's eye. Psychogenic response isn't repressible. You'd run lots of tests including looking for trauma, doing the blood work, checking levels of sodium, urea, phosphate—'

'Skip the boring details, Evrim. I'm old, I may not live long enough to hear them all.'

Ersoy laughed again. He was a natural chuckler. 'Same old Bryant. There'd need to be a brain scan if a coma was suspected. Or you could pump glucose into a body to try and give it a shock. But if it was certain that this patient of yours had hanged himself, such tests wouldn't be performed, or performed less thoroughly than they should be.'

'If a coma state went undiagnosed, you think my theoretical patient would still be awake inside his own body, thinking and feeling everything?'

'The degree of awareness varies, but yes.'

'All right, one last question, then I'll let you get back to your Mexican death puppets or whatever it is you're sticking in glass cases back there. What happens to my patient's body while he's in a coma?'

'Nothing, so long as he's cared for correctly by the hospital.'

'And if he isn't?'

Ersoy brightened. 'Ah, that's an interesting question. In theory all kinds of terrible things could happen. Bacterial growth in the liquid waste, neurological damage, necrosis—'

'You mean you could start to rot?'

'I suppose so, yes – but we're not talking about academic theory here, are we?'

'I'm afraid not,' Bryant admitted quietly. 'I think I've got someone who returned from the dead, even after his body began to decay. Have you ever heard of such a case?'

The doctor was pensive for a moment. 'You're talking about the Lazarus complex.'

'What's that?'

'The spontaneous return of circulation after all attempts at resuscitation have failed. There have been only some forty cases documented in the whole of medical literature worldwide. There was talk of one such case, a Turkish farmer who had suffered a stroke and impaled himself on a piece of machinery. He was buried and dug his way back to the surface four days later. But by then his neck and shoulders had rotted away because of the bacteria present on the iron spike of the equipment he fell upon.'

'Then you concede it is possible,' said Bryant insistently.

'It was a story, Arthur. Hearsay. From Turks.' Ersoy leaned over and patted the detective's arm. 'If you can find me a documented case, I might be able to make medical history.'

'I think I may have one.'

Ersoy's eyes lit up. 'Can I meet this patient of yours?'

'It wouldn't do you much good. He'd dead now.'

'Then remember what John always tells you. Don't force the facts to fit the theory.'

'I have nothing else to go on, old *kuru fasulye*. Ta for the tea. Try to cut back on your sugar intake.' Bryant rose with some effort and jammed his hat back on his head.

'If I were you, I'd get an expert to check out this doctor's diagnostics,' Ersoy said. 'He could have missed something. There'd have to be an inquiry and a possible criminal prosecution. If your medical man neglected to make the correct diagnostic tests, he'll have buried his patient alive.'

'That's exactly what I think happened,' said Bryant gloomily.

Ersoy studied his old friend. Bryant appeared quite shaken by the thought. 'Are you all right?' he asked. 'You don't look so well.'

'It's just—' Bryant opened his mouth to speak, then thought better of it. 'Nothing. I don't want to tempt fate,' he decided, and abruptly took his leave of the mystified neurologist.

12

LOSSES

John May wondered what he was doing here, poking about in the life of a man who had died by his own hand.

It wasn't as if he had been asked to find Wallace's killer. The others were running checks on vehicles in the Bloomsbury area and Bryant had wandered off to talk to some kind of medical expert, leaving him to interview the client who had supposedly driven their risen corpse to suicide.

Krishna Jhadav was a slender young British Asian with severely cropped hair and a twitchy, intense manner exacerbated by the protuberance of his large eyes. He had agreed to meet May with obvious reluctance, and paced about his minimalist glass box overlooking one corner of Threadneedle Street with the attitude of a cornered animal. He froze when May explained the purpose of his visit, and sat up like a meerkat whenever anyone walked through the open-plan office outside. In these jittery times many people would prefer to meet the law in their own homes rather than have them come to the office.

'I can't have the police turning up on these premises,' he said, glancing out anxiously at his staff. 'Luckily you don't look like an officer. If our staff thought for a moment—' He broke off, fidgeted with his fingers, tried again. 'When you're doing deals at this level, Mr May, anything remotely suggestive of irregularity can upset the equilibrium . . .' He tailed off, realizing perhaps that he was encouraging suspicion.

'I'm just filling in some final details in a case,' said May. 'It's purely routine.' He eyed the brushed aluminium logo on the far wall that read: 'Defluotech Management Systems'. 'What is it you actually do here?'

'We're waste brokers,' Jhadav explained, sliding over a corporate brochure covered in sunflowers, mountains and happy children. 'Let's say your factories produce glycerine or ethanol as a by-product of your production process, or you have catering waste like cooking oils. We broker deals with companies that will remove, recycle or dispose of them. We also take care of ABPs.'

'What are they?'

'Sorry. Animal by-products. They're entire animal bodies, parts of animals, products of animal origin or other products obtained from animals that aren't fit for human consumption. They must be dealt with in accordance with strict regulations designed to prevent harm to human beings, wildlife or the environment. Waste is an increasingly precious commodity. Northern Europe is building generators that recycle garbage, and they've already run low and are having to import it. There's a lot of money to be made.'

An overweight colleague with thinning ginger hair leaned in at the open door. May tick-boxed the bulging shirt, nicotine-stained fingers and red cheeks that marked him as a likely candidate for a stress-related coronary before his forty-fifth birthday. He had an alarmingly high voice. 'Everything all right here, Mr Jhadav?'

'Yes, fine, thank you. This is Mr May, a – friend of Mr Wallace's,' he said. 'Mr May, one of my fellow directors,

Justin Farthingale. Sorry, we won't be long if you need to use the meeting room.'

'I suppose I can come back in a few minutes,' said Farthingale, who seemed suspicious that something might be occurring that didn't directly involve making money for the company. Jhadav was looking more nervous than ever. He glanced helplessly at May as his colleague hovered undecided at the doorway. 'Mr Farthingale, either come in or go out,' said May. 'I'm a police officer. I'm here to ask Mr Jhadav about his relationship with Thomas Wallace.'

'Oh.' Farthingale looked as if he'd just had a trouser accident. 'Perhaps I'd better stay.'

'Thomas Wallace used to represent our firm,' said Jhadav. 'He made quite a packet out of us. It was a very large account for one small law practice to handle.'

'Then why did you go there? Why not pick more heavyweight legal representation?'

'We wanted a more personal level of service,' said Jhadav. 'You can get lost in the larger firms, and they're more expensive. Has Mr Wallace been saying something about us?'

'No, but I'm looking after his concerns. I'm afraid Mr Wallace is dead. He killed himself last week.'

Jhadav didn't appear unduly surprised. 'I'm very sorry to hear that.'

'What exactly did he do for you?'

'We put him in charge of handling our legal issues here in the UK, in Europe, India and the Far East. It was a position of great responsibility.'

'And when did you decide to end the relationship?'

Jhadav studied the neon ceiling panels, anxiously calculating. 'About six weeks ago. We were reaching the end of a two-year contract. It was up for renewal.'

'But you made the decision not to renew?'

'That's right.'

'Why?'

'Honestly? It was a lot of work, and there were certain doubts—'

Farthingale cut in. 'We weren't convinced he could handle it, Mr May. He never filled us with much confidence. He started suffering from panic attacks. They were affecting his behaviour in meetings. There were some slip-ups that cost us a lot of money, and a couple of embarrassing incidents, so we decided to review the arrangement.'

'What kind of incidents?' May pressed.

'He'd make simple mistakes and fly off the handle. Sometimes he became extremely agitated. As I said, he was making good money from the account, although it's fair to say we were demanding clients.'

'Do you think his stress was caused by something in particular?'

'No,' said Jhadav, 'I think he was just that kind of person.'

'Did you ever socialize with him?'

Farthingale seemed keen to take control of the conversation. May sensed the kind of power struggle between partners that marred so many business practices. 'Once or twice,' he said, 'only in the early days.'

Jhadav shot him a look. 'That's not strictly true. We played golf at Sunningdale sometimes. There were the usual dinners, of course. Thomas didn't really enjoy discussing business. He always seemed to have a lot on his mind.'

'When was the last time you spoke to him?'

'About two weeks ago. He came here to return the last of our files. He told me there was a strong likelihood that his practice would go into administration. I think he blamed us for taking away our account.'

'His wife said he'd been troubled for some time.'

'Well, he had personal problems, too . . .' Jhadav wavered for a moment, as if seeking permission to admit something indelicate. 'When he started behaving erratically we ran a background check and discovered he'd been treated for depression several times in the past. He had this thing, this issue, kind of a recurring subject. He'd mention it whenever he'd had a few drinks.'

May patiently waited for him to continue. Jhadav looked mischievous. 'It was sort of an obsession. He said he was worried about being buried alive. He told me that in the event of his death he had arranged for someone to come and dig him up, just to make sure there hadn't been a mistake.'

'There you go, clearly mentally unbalanced,' Farthingale added superfluously, determined to own the tail of the conversation. 'It's all very sad. Some people just can't take the pressure. An old, old story. Perhaps if I could have the meeting room back now?'

'He loved old horror films. He read a lot. Books with titles I couldn't even pronounce. He was kind to others. He was a good boy.'

DS Janice Longbright held the woman's fingers lightly between both hands and waited for her to stop crying. Louisa Curtis sobbed with hardly a sound, her large shoulders rising and falling, her face dropped in shame. 'I'm so sorry,' she said, gently disentangling herself and wiping her eyes with the tissue Longbright had given her. 'It's just – he had so much going for him. Not like some of the other kids around here. Romain was different. He was only a skinny little lad, and got picked on. He wanted to make something of himself. He didn't want to end up like his father.'

They were seated in Louisa Curtis's small, neat lounge, where bright cloths covered the more knocked-about furniture, giving the flat a homely air. 'Where is Mr Curtis?' Longbright asked.

'Gravesend, I think. He got a job down there as a warehouse foreman. He hasn't been around here in a long time. Hasn't seen his son since – well, two years at least.'

Longbright sensed a hidden story. 'Since what?' she asked.

Louisa gave her a plaintive look. 'They argued. Lenny – his father – he wanted him to get a job but Romain had already decided on college.'

'So I was told. Fashion design.'

Louisa gave a sad little laugh. 'Can you believe it? Of course, his father was against it. Too feminine, not the right sort of work for a man. I think he was jealous of Romain having a talent. Lenny ran away from school at fourteen to work on the fairgrounds. He could read the *Sun* and add up, and that was about it. Romain was worried about how much college would cost. He bought himself some old pattern-cutting equipment from the tailor's down the road and made clothes for some of the parents around here, just to earn a bit of money. He was saving hard. He wouldn't let me help him, said, "No, Mum, I'll pay my own way." And now that dream has been taken away. He was my only son.'

'I'm so sorry, Louisa,' said Longbright. 'May I call you that? I can't imagine what you must be going through.'

'You don't have children?' Louisa looked up. 'A handsome woman like you? I feel so sorry for you.'

She's just lost her only son and she feels sorry for me, Longbright thought. 'We're going to find who did this,' she promised. 'We're searching through footage for the car's licence plate right now. There must have been witnesses. We're doing everything we can.' She tried to sound confident. 'Do you have someone who can stay with you tonight?'

'My sister's coming over when she finishes work. I'll be fine.' Straightening her T-shirt, she held out the material to Longbright. 'He made this for me. Look at the stitching. He found a picture of a tiger and copied it on to the front in special dyes, 'cause he knew I liked tigers. He had a very visual eye. He could have really been someone.' Louisa decided that the time for pity was over. She rose and patted herself down. 'I suppose I must get on. Was there anything else I could help you with?'

'Did he have any real enemies? I know boys form allegiances and cliques but I was wondering if there was someone who took a particular dislike to him.'

'No, no one. He didn't have an enemy in the world.' She looked down at Longbright's feet. 'You're wearing high-heeled shoes,' she said. 'Isn't it difficult if you have to run in those things?'

Longbright smiled. 'Most of the time I don't have to. I keep a brick in my handbag and I have a good aim.' She turned her ankle, letting Louisa see the red patent-leather heel. 'I shouldn't be wearing these to work. We all do things that make no sense. It keeps us human. I'll come and see you again, not on business, just to make sure you're all right.'

'I'd like that,' Louisa said.

'But if you do think of anything else—'

'Actually there was one thing, but it seems so unlikely . . .'

'Tell me.'

'When I went to identify him. He was wearing jeans and a pale blue T-shirt.'

'I believe so, yes, something with a brand name. Superdry, I think.'

'He hated Superdry shirts. He went to the club in a black shirt. I'm sure of it. I just saw his back as he went down the stairs, but the light was on and it was definitely black.'

'You think he could have changed it in the club?'

'I don't know. He was very particular about his clothes. He wasn't carrying anything to change into.'

'Thank you,' said Longbright. 'I'll make sure we check it out.'

As she walked away from the flat, Longbright felt a sorrow deeper than any she had felt for a long time. She was upset for Louisa Curtis of course, but comforting the bereaved had been part of her daily routine for years. The melancholia she felt was of a different kind.

She detoured past St George's Gardens. It looked as if the casket had been reinterred, because the police tent had come down. A group of Middle Eastern children were happily playing ball, watched by their mothers. She stood and watched them for a few moments.

Three years earlier, she had undergone a hysterectomy, and the world around her had grown a little greyer. To raise a child – and possibly to lose one – was to feel a connection to the world, even at the expense of unbearable pain.

Recalling Louisa Curtis's attitude as she paced away from the park, Longbright felt as if she had seen too much death in her life. She needed to start living again.

13

COINCIDENCES

At a little after 6.00 p.m. on Tuesday evening, as other office workers were checking the weather and stepping out into the littered streets to head for King's Cross Station, the Peculiar Crimes Unit got permission to step up its hunt for the killer of Romain Curtis. Giles Kershaw's report had helped to change the status of the case.

Time was of the essence. There was a threat of overnight rain in Central London, which meant that vehicles could be cleansed of evidence. In hit-and-run cases, especially when pedestrians ran across roads trying to beat the traffic, it was common for the victim to place a hand on a vehicle, and that meant fingerprints.

Arthur Bryant opened the window a crack and lit his pipe.

'Do you really have to smoke that thing in here?' asked May.

'Gone six, old sock. European law, I'm allowed to in my own home.'

'This isn't your home.'

'It's as good as. Right, do you want to compare notes?'

May squinted at his screen. 'I've got half a dozen

interviews left – Curtis's schoolfriends, some doorstep work with neighbours, trying to find out who he hung around with, whether anyone was out to get him, who saw him at the Scala club. According to Janice, the mother is adamant that he didn't take drugs or drink to excess, so it would be useful to know where he got the MDMA. Then there are the Congestion Zone cameras on vehicles entering Britannia Street – nothing so far, but there are still a few hard drives to check – and another check on the street's office CCTVs to see if they might have picked up anything happening on the pavement outside. We've set up an online callout for witnesses. I had some data back on grave desecrations but there have been no major cases for years. I still have to see Wallace's doctor and talk to his law partners, then I'm pretty much done. What have you got?'

Bryant sucked at his pipe, checking a scrap of paper on which he had made some illegible scribbles. 'I've quite a few people to consult myself: experts on the resurrection of corpses, star constellations, astrology, voodoo, deciphering messages from the dead, the semiotics of Satanism, the works of Edgar Allen Poe and the country's foremost expert on burial techniques.'

May thought for a moment. 'Quite a variance in our methodology.'

'Yes, I would say so.'

'Do you want to explain your thinking at all?'

Bryant looked up with blank blue eyes. 'About what?'

'Why, for example, you need to consult someone about the semiotics of Satanism?'

'Shirts. Romain Curtis was wearing a satanic cult band shirt when he was held up by the comedy-cop on Sunday night. Something called "death metal", I believe. He'd designed it himself. I suspect he merely dressed like a rocker to take the curse off the fact that he was about to train as a fashion designer. Preparing the way with his peers, reassuring them that he wasn't about to lose respect through his choice of profession. But maybe there was something more to it, and he upset someone who took his use of symbols more seriously.'

'OK,' said May slowly. 'And the deciphering-messages-from-the-dead thing?'

'The dead or possibly undead Wallace named Ursa Minor rather than the constellation they could see overhead, Ursa Major. I don't know what that means, but maybe someone else does.'

'And voodoo?'

'Ah. Graveyard visitations, popularity of, in the preparation of spells. Necromancy.' He inscribed the last word with a flourish of his pipe stem.

'I see. I probably wouldn't mention any of that to Raymond at the briefing session.' That was the nice thing about John May; the fact that he refused to criticize his partner's approach, even though he could not bring himself to agree with it. Bryant's methodology was an exercise in disarray, and his peculiarly lateral thought processes defied logical analysis. It was far safer to leave him for a while and only complain when things started burning down.

Although the thought was not voiced by either of them, there was an underlying urgency about the death of Romain Curtis. Every investigation was counted down from its initiating act, and each tick of the minute hand erased evidence, changed stories, obscured culpability. In a city like London, the truth was scuffed away with every footfall.

'All this is assuming we ignore the two most likely scenarios,' May added. 'Those of coincidence. Thomas Wallace committed suicide and was dug up by crazies. Or he was subsequently misdiagnosed, and the boy who witnessed his revival suffered a tragic drunken accident. The events were probably linked by geographical proximity, nothing more.'

'No, something doesn't make sense,' said Bryant. 'Somebody sat the boy up against a lamp-post. A hit-and-run driver wouldn't have done that. It wasn't a burglary. He still had his wallet and mobile. So it must have been a grudge.'

May checked the time. 'The briefing's about to start. Remember—'

'I know, keep it clean, pipe out, no funny stuff.' Bryant sighed. 'My life was never intended to be one long slow descent into respectability. Lead on.'

'Right, you lot, it's time to stir things up a bit,' said Raymond Land, drawing himself up to his full height of five feet seven inches and pacing across the front of the common room. 'I'd like to remind you that we were shifted from Home Office jurisdiction because we caused them so much trouble that they were glad to get rid of us. We've got new bosses now, so I think it's time to re-structure.'

'What does that mean, exactly?' asked Bryant. 'There are only nine of us, not counting the cat and the two Daves. Actually, there's only one Dave this morning.'

'Where's the other one?'

'Apparently he dropped a cistern lid on his foot and got replaced by someone with an entirely unpronounceable name.'

'I don't want you working in your old teams any more,' said Land. 'We should jumble you all up a bit. Colin and Meera are always complaining that they get stuck with stakeouts. Jack always forgets to fill out his team status reports. Nobody ever does what they're told. Even Crippen changed sex behind my back. Well, I want a little order around here from now on.'

'Look, Raymondo, we all enjoy a laugh, especially when it involves you trying to exert your authority,' said Bryant, 'but you're not going to change the way we work.

It's not your fault that we have no respect for you. We all know you got stuck here with us after your transfer application was turned down. We like you – well, some of the others do – but we're never going to be able to take you seriously.'

'We'll see about that,' said Land with determination. 'Right now we're reliant on Orion Banks to feed us cases, but judging from our workload, which amounts to a traffic accident and a case of public affright, we're going to be starved out of existence unless we do something about it. There are plenty of ongoing investigations in the CoL that we could help out on—'

'City crimes? You're talking about a bunch of office thefts and financial scams,' scoffed Renfield. 'It's not our field.'

'It is now,' Land warned. 'I've told Ms Banks that we'll take on anything she deems fit. So I want you to deprioritize the Wallace case, such as it is, and concentrate on whatever she feeds us, quick stuff—'

'Boring stuff,' Janice corrected.

'Yes, perhaps, but they're cases that could raise our performance ratings and secure our future. Which brings me to you, Bryant. For the time being I'd like you to concentrate on this business with the stolen ravens.' Somebody sniggered. 'It's no laughing matter, I assure you. The English Tourist Board is very worried by the implications. Do you know how much revenue visitors add to the British economy? About 115 billion quid per annum. It's hard to believe, but people actually come here for the fun of it. And the Tower of London is our biggest single attraction. It's a symbol of stability, and we cannot afford to have our most venerable institution turned into a laughing stock.'

'Why don't they just get more ravens and forget about it?' Colin shrugged at the others, thinking the question was reasonable.

'They can't just do that,' said Land, as if it was obvious. 'That would defeat the whole point, wouldn't it?'

'Actually, that's exactly what they're doing,' said Bryant.

'Then what *is* the point?' Colin persisted.

'That there's a very serious breach in national protection. Someone's made a mockery of the security system, not once but seven times over. They're trying to show that the nation's most venerable institution is as impenetrable as a tobacconist's shop. So, Bryant, that will be your priority. As for the hit-and-run, unless I hear a good reason why we should waste resources pursuing—'

'I've a good reason,' Bryant interrupted. 'Romain Curtis wasn't alone in St George's Gardens. He was with a girl called Shirone Estanza. She saw Wallace's body as well, and she wasn't stoned. If there's even the slightest possibility that Curtis's death was a consequence of what happened in the park, then she could be at risk and we have to protect her. There are omens here, and superstitions, and premonitions of death. But there's also a real risk from persons unknown. We need to continue the investigation.'

'Fine,' said Land. 'Don't worry about the omens, Mr Bryant, let us handle those. You just concentrate on finding a birdnapper.'

'The bloody cheek – palming me off with missing ravens,' fumed Bryant as he stalked back to his office. 'Raymond might as well have sent me away with a colouring book.'

'He didn't mean it like that,' said May, attempting to sound placatory. 'You can see the awkward position he's in. He needs fast results.'

'And I'm too slow, is that it?'

'No, Arthur, you know that's not the problem. It's your tendency . . .' He hesitated.

Bryant's eyes popped wide. 'What tendency?'

'To get sidetracked.'

'It's the way I work, the way I've always worked. This case is not as straightforward as everyone seems to think it is. There's no obvious causal link between Wallace and the dead boy beyond what he witnessed. We know from the girl that he went back into the park. He saw something there, did something – and it got him killed. Jhadav said Wallace was frightened of being buried alive and he *was*. Somebody wanted to hurt him very badly.'

May threw his hands wide in frustration. 'Can't you see the false assumptions you're making? Wallace was a *suicide*. He hanged himself in his family home. Nobody killed him or rendered him comatose. It has to be coincidence.'

'Another coincidence? Really? They're stacking up, aren't they?' said Bryant. 'At what point do they stop being coincidences?'

'There's no pattern,' May insisted. 'It's like your constellations. We draw lines between the stars and make pictures we'll remember so that we can identify them, but there's no real connection between one star and the next.'

'We've missed something,' Bryant insisted. 'I think Wallace's widow knows more than she's letting on. I think Romain Curtis knew more, too.'

'Romain talked to the police – why didn't he say something?'

'I don't know,' said Bryant, his jaw set. 'But I'm going to find out.'

'You can't.' May dropped his voice. 'Do you want to play into Raymond's hands? Do you want to give him a reason to remove you?'

'*Remove* me? What are you talking about?'

'Orion Banks. She told Land she wants you out. She thinks you belittled her in front of the others.'

Bryant stopped and turned. 'Why didn't she tell me to my face? Why is everyone so scared of speaking their minds all of a sudden? We used to nearly come to blows in the old Mornington Crescent offices. We had fights at least once a week and nobody took offence. It was part of the process of investigation. Longbright once dangled a thief out of the window. I tied a vicar to a chair. Colin used to settle arguments by arm-wrestling Met constables in the Nun & Broken Compass. The losers had pints poured over their heads. Now we're threatened with suspension for sending a sarcastic email.'

'Well, pouring drinks over people and tying them up is not the way we do things any more. You heard Banks, she wants targets met with efficiency and through the prescribed routes. She'll get rid of you if you don't.'

'All right,' said Bryant. 'I'll strike a deal with you all. Do your best on the case for twenty-four hours, and I'll stick with the ravens. If at the end of that time you're no further to closing the case, I'll come back on board and handle things my way. Understand?'

'I'll run it by Raymond,' said May helplessly. 'But he won't like it.'

'Forget the protocol and the office politics,' said Bryant heatedly. 'A young man died. Someone with his entire life ahead of him. Finding out why and stopping anyone else getting hurt – that's the only thing that matters now. I'm going to my balcony to smoke a great deal, and if anyone comes near me during the next half-hour, they will feel the wrath of my tormented soul, is that clear?'

He strode off to light up, and took all the air in the room with him.

14

A SIGN OF DEATH

Jack Renfield and Meera Mangeshkar had ended up on duty together. They were settled on an abandoned sectional sofa outside a block of flats in Hunter Street, Bloomsbury. It was cooler now and smelled of rain. The first fat drops were starting to spatter the pavement around them.

'It makes a change not being teamed with Colin,' said Mangeshkar. 'For once I don't have to put up with him eating fistfuls of chips all night and staring at me like a drugged puppy. I don't know what we're doing here, though.'

'You heard Bryant. Our job is to protect the innocent and identify the guilty.'

'If somebody really decided to take out Curtis because of what he saw, they won't come after the girl. She didn't see anything, and she didn't go back into the park with him. He went alone. She stayed outside on the pavement.'

Renfield grunted, checking the windows of Estanza's flat with his pocket binoculars. At night the terraces of the estate took on a melancholy air, like the runways of an abandoned airfield. 'This is a waste of time,' he said finally. 'No one's going to come after her.'

'How can you be so sure?'

'Gut instinct. I'm a career sergeant.'

'Did you never want to rise higher in the ranks?'

'Nope. I like it just where I am. Never try to rise beyond the level of your own competence.'

'What, this is all you can aspire to?'

'Don't be so bloody rude, Meera. You're not with Colin now. You don't know what you're talking about. When I first met Bryant and May, they made jokes about me to my face. Because of my name.'

'What about your name?'

'You know, the bloke who eats flies in *Dracula*.'

'No, I don't know.'

'They thought I was stupid. In time they came to respect me. I didn't need a different job title to prove my worth.'

'Yeah, but the money – you'd have been better off on a higher grade in the Met.'

Renfield pulled at a clump of sofa foam. 'You can only do things one way in the Met,' he explained. 'You follow the rules. Besides, they agreed to match my salary. They fought for me. I never even had to ask them. Those two—' He shook his head in wonder. 'They pass unnoticed on these streets. John looks like just another retired City gent, but the old man – if you didn't know, you'd think he was senile. Nobody's interested in them; they're invisible. That's why they can get away with what they do. Sports, telly, films, jobs, socializing, it's all about selling to the young in London, who can brag the most and shout the loudest. But those two don't take any notice. They don't care how anyone looks, or where they're from or who their families are. They have different values. That's why I stay. They let me be who I am. Who I want to be.' It was the most he had ever said to Meera, but for the last few months her condescending attitude had been needling him, and Renfield felt he had to say something. Now, though, he was embarrassed.

'Well, at least I'm getting plenty of experience on stakeouts,' said Meera, a little chastened. 'To be honest I prefer the physical stuff. When Bryant starts going on about criminal psychogeography he loses me.'

'Wait.' Renfield suddenly held up a hand. 'Tell me – what do you see over there?'

Mangeshkar looked over to the stilted ground floor of the council block. 'I can't see anything.'

'Second pillar to the left. Just at the edge of it.'

'Is that a person? If it is, he's not moving much.'

'Damn – go, go.'

Shirone Estanza's front door was opening. Suddenly the figure was moving out from behind the pillar towards the silhouette framed in the hallway of her flat. Mangeshkar was faster than Renfield and covered the courtyard in seconds, staying in the shadows. As the sergeant followed, he saw the schoolgirl pull her door shut behind her.

The dark figure was only feet away.

As Mangeshkar burst into the light on the terrace, Shirone Estanza saw her and screamed. Renfield knew they had made their presence known too early. The grey-hooded figure on the walkway had a head start, and Mangeshkar fatally hesitated while she decided what to do about the girl.

She was fast, though. Taking off after her quarry she quickly closed the distance. The pair cut a diagonal path through the estate, over the playground and around the centre flowerbeds. The railings around the edge were intended to be unscaleable.

By the time she reached them, Mangeshkar realized she had lost. There were gates cut into the railings all the way along the perimeter. Too many exits to cover. Feint, run, feint; they played cat and mouse in silence, and the figure slipped away.

She started to radio in a pursuit request, but cut the call. There was not enough to go on: a watching figure, sweatshirt and jeans, dirty white trainers, probably heading into the maelstrom of passengers eddying between the three station terminals. All she could do now was head back to Estanza and reveal why they were there.

She found Renfield attempting to explain what had happened.

'Who was it?' Shirone demanded to know.

'Probably just a local kid who knew you were a friend of Romain Curtis,' said Renfield. 'A rubbernecker checking out where you lived.'

'Why would anybody do that?'

'I guess it kind of makes you a celebrity.'

'That's just great,' said Shirone. 'At school today somebody put a drawing of a band called the Bodysnatchers on Facebook and linked my name in. They all had a good laugh about that. And now I've got a bleeding stalker.'

'All this will go away in a few days,' Renfield assured her. 'These things don't last long.'

'What if he comes back?'

'We'll make sure somebody's posted here. And you should keep your online presence low this week.'

'Why are you here at all?' Shirone asked. 'You think someone's going to try and hurt me because of what happened?'

'We just have to take some extra precautions.'

'That isn't what I asked.'

'Maybe. We don't know. It's better to be safe than sorry.'

'All right, but try to catch him next time, eh?' She went back inside and slammed the door.

Renfield turned to his partner. 'Did you get a good look at him?'

'Only from the back. Slight build, five ten, grey cotton hood, blue Replay jeans, white Adidas trainers. Young enough to move fast. That narrows it down to half the planet.' She pointed back at the front door. 'So now we've got a scared kid to look after.'

'Meera, I don't think she's that scared,' Renfield pointed out. 'Just annoyed.'

As they stood looking back at the flats, a large black bird swooped in and landed on the top of a railing in the children's playground. Its eyes darkly glittered in the lamplight. Renfield squinted at the creature as it flicked out its wings. 'Isn't that a raven?'

'I couldn't tell a raven from a crow,' Mangeshkar admitted. 'You reckon it's one of Bryant's escapees?'

'It had better not be,' said Renfield. 'They're a sign of death. That's all we need right now.'

15

FOWL PLAY

By Wednesday morning it seemed as if the spell of fine summer weather had never happened. At 7.00 a.m. rain pattered, then showered, then hammered down, forming torrents in the gutters, gushing from drainpipes and flooding across the cambers of roads.

Bryant still felt deeply aggrieved. He sat up in bed, thumbing through some old reference volumes, notably *Cryptozoology & Creation Myths, Sheep and Goats' Death Loss Figures for 1952, Victorian Romantic Suicide Ballads* and an exhausting tome entitled *Avian Longevities and their Interpretation under Evolutionary Theories of Senescence.*

There seemed to be a lot of superstitions concerning ravens. Specifically, they were associated with royalty and bereavement. Legend had it that King Arthur turned into one, and a raven circling a house was said to predict the demise of someone within. In Somerset, locals used to tip their hats to ravens in order not to offend them. In many parts of the country they were associated with the Devil. In Yorkshire children were threatened with a giant raven which would carry them off if they were bad. It was said that if a raven's eggs were stolen, a baby would die.

Eventually Bryant rose and shaved. He bypassed the PCU offices in Caledonian Road, making straight for the Rooks & Emeralds Magic Suppliers, Hatton Garden. Trudging through the ward once known as Farringdon Without, he peered from the dripping edge of a half-collapsed umbrella that flapped like a crippled bat, and remembered the tumbledown bookstalls that had lined Farringdon Road for over a century, right up until the last decade. The book market had vanished entirely now, to be replaced by yet more coffee shops and cocktail bars.

Passing down Herbal Hill to Clerkenwell Road, he found himself entirely alone on the narrow pavements. In every other direction the city's great arteries were choked with traffic and pedestrians, but on a rainy morning the hilly backstreets of the Italian quarter were silent and deserted. Elsewhere only scraps and fragments of London's ancient fabric remained, but here, in the very oldest part of the city centre, it was easy to spin back the clock to the late nineteenth century. Once there had been a great convent at this spot, and a stream that marked the dividing line between the city's two police forces. The Hasidic diamond merchants of Hatton Garden were fewer in number now, but the street was still aglow with jewellers' shops, their windows gleaming with amber and amethyst, emerald and sapphire – but mostly the sharp white sparkle of diamonds.

He stopped before a mean black doorway, checked the number on a scrap of paper, then rang the top bell of six. The door buzzed and admitted him to a second door that only opened after the first was shut. The terrace looked like a normal row of Victorian houses from outside, but within were all sorts of surprising security systems. They had been installed to protect the diamond polishers and traders of precious stones from burglaries. The smash-and-grabs of the pre-war years were unheard of now, but elaborate money-laundering swindles still took place occasionally, the most celebrated being the loss of the Congolese 'North Star' diamond in 1997. Hatton Garden was a fortress disguised as terraced housing.

Bryant found himself in a dingy hallway barely wider than his shoulders. Shaking out the umbrella, he left it just inside the door and made his way up the sloping stairs. He could smell damp, leather, cigarettes, cooking – old smells.

The top landing was occupied by two businesses: Messrs Rowland & Goldberg, Necklace-Makers, and the Rooks & Emeralds Magic Suppliers, Proprietor Maurice Weiss, maker and supplier of traditional bird tricks to the magic trade. Bryant was greeted by an immaculately dressed old man in a black satin waistcoat criss-crossed with a silver diamond pattern.

'I've got the kettle on,' said Maurice, holding the door wide. 'Fresh-leaf, none of your teabag rubbish. Come in and make yourself at home.' He lifted a packing case full of playing-card decks from a chair and bade Bryant sit. 'I was surprised to get your call, Arthur. I was beginning to think I'd never see you again.'

'I was just as surprised to find you still in business, Maurice,' said Bryant, eyeing the orderly, overcrowded room with undisguised pleasure.

'We very nearly folded, like most of the magic suppliers, but we've still got the shop down the road – not that it makes much money these days.'

'Then how do you survive?'

'The internet, my dear fellow – a lifeline for us. There are a great number of budding young magicians out there, thank goodness. Not so many professionals now that the variety shows have all gone. There's not much call for a rabbit out of a hat or a flight of doves from the flourish of a lavender glove.'

'Which rather brings me to the purpose of my visit,'

said Bryant. 'Birds, the disappearing of. How big can you go?'

Maurice poked about in a tea caddy. 'What, you mean in physical size? Like could you make a swan disappear? Only by using the sort of special-effects trickery they get up to on television nowadays. Most of the new generation of magicians are more interested in performing flashy stunts like making Ferraris explode. Doves aren't exciting enough for them.'

'Could you make a raven vanish without anyone knowing about it, for instance?'

'What, the common *Corvus corax*?' Maurice thought for a minute. 'It wouldn't be easy. They grow to over two and a half feet in length, and they're heavy. Not quite the size of a writing desk but not far short.'

'Ah, Lewis Carroll,' said Bryant. 'He never intended an answer to his riddle, you know, although he later provided one. He said, "Because it can produce a few notes, though they are very flat; and it is never put with the wrong end in front."'

'They're noisy buggers, too,' said Maurice, warming the pot. 'Making that low guttural rattle, sort of a *toc-toc-toc* sound.'

'Yes, I've been reading up about them. Apparently they're very intelligent, playful but quarrelsome when you get a few of them together.'

'Why do you want to know?'

'I can't tell you that just at the moment. It's a case I'm working on.'

'What a pity. I always liked hearing about your cases. They're not endangered in some way, are they?'

'No, I don't think so. If anything their population seems to be growing. They're pretty much omnivorous.'

'They'd be all right around here, then. All the old diamond shops are going, Arthur. We're getting more and more junk-food outlets and trendy restaurants, so all the rubbish gets left outside. They'd do well scavenging in these streets.' Maurice rattled old grouts into his bin, an expert in the art of tea-making.

'Let's assume for a moment that I needed to make one vanish,' said Bryant. 'What would be the best way to do it?'

'Well, magicians like doves because they're stupid and docile, and you can make them appear out of virtually anything. They're the only bird that can be completely dehydrated, stored in a tiny space, then rehydrated and instantly returned to life with no more damage than a bit of a confused look in their eyes. They're incredibly flexible. Of course, you have to train them carefully. A raven does have one advantage, of course: its colour. We like doves because their white feathers look good against a black suit. But if you could get a raven into a triangle-pouch . . .'

'What's that?'

'It's rather like a purse that hooks on to the inside of, say, a top hat. You release the catch and out comes the bird. The case then folds flat. If you were wearing all black, the raven would blend in nicely. But there's still the size, and it's not a docile bird. It's got a long, sharp beak. I imagine you'd have to stupefy it in some way. I couldn't recommend doing that. You'd have Animal Welfare down on you like a ton of bricks.'

Bryant looked around, noting the catalogued tidiness that signified a man living alone. 'Your wife was Uzbekistani, wasn't she? Dolores.'

'Her stage name.' said Maurice. 'I miss her every morning. Not every evening, though. She was . . .'

'Controlling.'

'I was going to say wonderful. After she died it was a chance to get this place sorted out. On the whole, though, I think I preferred it messy.' He looked around in sadness, then pulled himself together. 'Anyway, a raven.'

'More than one.'

'How many?'

'Seven.'

'Lumme. Perhaps a really good magician could pull it off.'

'How?'

'Hang on, I'll show you. I haven't got a raven, but there's a frozen chicken in the fridge.' Maurice rose and went into the little kitchen off his studio. He emerged a couple of minutes later wearing a black jacket and white gloves. Standing directly in front of Bryant, he circled his hands back and forth as if they were hinged at the heel of each palm. When he parted them, he was now holding a black velvet cloth. Unfolding it like the petals of a rose, he revealed a pallid supermarket chicken that had not been there before. 'You see,' he said, 'it can be done.'

Bryant was delighted. 'You should put that down. Sir Francis Bacon froze to death conducting experiments with frozen chickens. Where did you hide it?'

Maurice set the chicken aside and showed him. 'I wrapped the bird in the cloth then knotted the whole thing to the underside of my right forearm. My prestiges – that's the distracting movements I made with the gloves – they kept you from noticing the lump, black on black, until I was ready to unfold it.'

'Very impressive,' said Bryant. 'I suppose he could have taken them one at a time and transferred them to a larger holdall.'

'Are we talking about the ravens in the Tower?' Maurice asked.

'You're not supposed to know,' said Bryant, who was never less than fabulously indiscreet.

'That's a rum one. They say when the ravens leave, the Crown falls.'

'An old wives' tale, luckily, but bad for public morale. Think it could be done?'

'Yes, but he'd need something like a big black cloak.

Not the sort of outfit you'd see in the street without arous- ing suspicion.'

'Don't worry. I have an idea how that part might have been managed. The executioner.'

'I'm sorry?'

'Just thinking aloud.' Bryant rose to his feet. 'Lovely to see you again, Maurice. You've been a great help.'

As Bryant headed back into the rainy street of diamonds, the elderly magician watched from his upstairs window. He was glad he had chosen not to mention his doctor's gloomy prognosis; Bryant looked as if he had enough troubles of his own. But he couldn't help wondering if he would live to see his old friend again.

16

THE BLEEDING HEART

'Jack and Meera reckon someone was watching the schoolgirl's flat,' said Janice Longbright. 'Unfortunately he got away, but it could be evidence of a link.'

'Did they find any physical proof that she's being stalked?' asked Raymond Land. 'If not, it's not enough. What about the lad?'

While Bryant was studying the teleportation of frozen poultry, Raymond Land had demanded an update on Romain Curtis.

'Some of his schoolfriends were in the Scala with him,' Janice said. 'We've talked to a couple of them. They didn't sound that fond of him, but he didn't seem to have any real enemies. One of them saw him trip up the stairs of the club as he left, said he looked drunk.'

'Hearsay, Janice – come on.'

'Still nothing on where he got the MDMA. The club has a strict no-drugs policy, but you know how well those work.' She flicked through the other pages on her desk. 'The Congestion Zone CCTV hard drives don't show anything unusual. No vehicles hanging around outside the club. It's a one-way street with red no-stop zoning.

Nothing from the office cameras in Britannia Street either. Most are trained on their reception areas. No reliable witnesses so far. The entrance to the club is right on the corner of the crossroads, and the queue to get in runs all the way down one side. There were just too many people milling around for anyone to stand out.'

'Don't you have *anything* positive for me?' asked Land.

'Wallace's client, Krishna Jhadav, surrendered one interesting titbit yesterday – he says Wallace had a morbid fear of premature burial, and had arranged for someone to dig him up if he died suddenly. It suggests that someone either carried out his wish or played a sick joke on him.'

'But the man committed suicide.'

'I know. We're seeing his doctor later to try and work out if anything was missed.'

'Is that it? There must be something else.'

'I'm afraid not. You took Arthur off the case, remember?'

'Please try to see my problem, Janice,' Land pleaded. 'I simply cannot have him running around hiring witch doctors and conducting séances just when we're trying to prove ourselves.'

'You can't make us into something we're not, Raymond.'

'Well, we can't bloody stay as we are.' Land winced and shook a kitten from his foot. 'I wish somebody would get rid of these damned things; they're spreading like coathangers. I need results, Janice, something I can report back.'

'Then get Arthur back on the case,' she said simply.

Bryant was now on his way to Bleeding Heart Yard, just a short walk from Maurice Weiss's studio in Hatton Garden. Stopping outside the tavern by the entrance to the T-shaped courtyard, he leaned on his stick and watched the rain bounce off the cobbles. He knew that the area had long been associated with religion, murder and the black arts, but today he had come to find number 17, the home of Paul McEvoy, a Royal Academy painting restorer who was the country's leading expert on premature burial.

What interested Bryant was the reason behind McEvoy's specialist knowledge. For a while now he had heard rumours in academic circles, but had never been given good reason to check them out. He knew he was breaking Land's rule about not interfering in the Wallace case, but McEvoy's home was just around the corner and, after all, what harm could it do to have a chat in passing?

He had last walked these backstreets in the purgatorial month of February. Dickens had pointed out that here even the snowflakes were covered in soot, 'gone into mourning . . . for the death of the sun'. There was something about the low level of light that muted the shades of brick and concrete, turning homes into prisons. The geography of Farringdon and Clerkenwell matched its weather, being perverse, grey, unsettled and confusing.

The empty roads were never less than atmospheric, and made fertile ground for the creation of dark mythologies. Many stories of murders, hauntings and hangings were associated with the old Smithfield Market, where the bones of slaughtered animals washed down from the butcheries to the riverbank. Bryant found it impossible to pass over the pavements and not be aware of what lay below. He could see the forgotten tributaries of the River Fleet through the drain covers, hear the rushing waters and follow the chain of underground wells from King's Cross down through Farringdon to the river. He caught himself thinking; *There's more death here than life . . .*

McEvoy was waiting at the door to greet him. Wrapped in a maroon quilted dressing gown over a Jamaican kaftan and baggy blue silk trousers, he looked more than a little mad. 'You must be Mr Bryant,' he called. 'Come in from the rain,' and he waved him inside.

Bryant followed his host to the second floor and was ushered into a room that reeked of wet dog, furniture polish and air freshener. In the centre, a polished coffin lay on a trestle table. The copper-coated casket had a number of riveted metal tubes extending from it, to which were attached a system of bells, the whole contraption affixed to hooks in the peeling, bowed ceiling.

'Don't be alarmed,' said McEvoy. 'It's a security coffin. The smallest movement of the corpse's hands, feet or head rings the bells, and the graveyard's nightwatchman comes running.'

'Assuming he hasn't gone to the pub,' said Bryant, walking around the device. 'When was this made?'

'Oh, it's just a facsimile, but it's based on a design from 1829, German manufacture, obviously. Taphephobia was a very powerful thing.'

'Taphephobia?'

'The fear of being buried alive! These things weren't just to stop the living from being trapped below ground,' McEvoy explained. 'They were intended to ward off the resurrection men, too. Digging up the dead to sell their bodies to anatomists was once an integral part of London life. Mind you, that's not really my field. If you wanted to find out about snatching the dead, you'd have to consult a real resurrectionist.'

'There are no such people any more, Mr McEvoy.'

'Aren't there now.' His host rolled beady, knowing eyes at him. 'And you're so sure of this?'

It didn't seem to occur to McEvoy to introduce himself or to ask what his visitor was doing here. He excitedly ran around the coffin, demonstrating the various bell-pulls. 'Of course, there's a modern version that substitutes electronics for the mechanics, but what if the electrical supply is cut? Then what, eh? There was a London Society for the Prevention of Premature Burial, you know. It was formed in 1896 by the spiritualist Arthur Lovell, a rather dubious character by all accounts, but at least he alerted people to the dangers of being buried alive. Before that, of course, there were the waiting mortuaries, special chapels where the dead could be housed in case they woke up. Some of the cadavers were long past their best, so they had to fill the room with flowers to disguise the smell of putrefying flesh. There were plans to construct a *Totenhaus*, or house for the dead, in every German town. They were built in Ansbach, Munich, Frankfurt, Berlin, and spread to Brussels, Prague, Amsterdam, Lisbon, even New York.'

He's completely barking, thought Bryant. *I'll have to humour him until I can get away*. This was what came of finding field experts on the internet. 'I heard you were the right man to ask about premature interment,' he said.

'Absolutely,' McEvoy agreed. 'I began my researches while I was a student in Edinburgh, but the more I learned, the more I feared it might happen to me. It happens all the time, far more frequently than people realize. Misdiagnosed coma states in this day and age, can you believe it? I have a history, you see. It used to be known as lucid hysterical lethargy, but now they call it narcolepsy. I could fall asleep at any time and not wake up for hours, days, years. The heartbeat slows and becomes quite undetectable, even to the finest electronic instruments.'

'Have you ever heard of Thomas Wallace?' Bryant asked.

'No, why, did he come back from the dead?'

'In a manner of speaking.'

McEvoy was barely listening. 'Someone came to see me, wanted to know how to open a coffin, but I said I don't give out that kind of information, be off with you.' He waggled his fingers at the empty air.

'Do you recall who this person was?'

'No, no, I wouldn't let them in – ringing on the doorbell out of the blue. Besides, I was busy.'

'Was it a man or a woman?'

McEvoy ignored the question. 'I've devised various solutions of my own invention, naturally. I wouldn't just rely on a Gutsmuth and Taberger Security Coffin even if it had a filibrated air tube. I have the equipment all prepared and my burial plot already purchased.'

'Why not just be cremated?' asked Bryant, tinkling one of the bells.

'And wake up in flames? No, thank you so very much!' McEvoy tightened the dressing gown about himself. 'I've left strict instructions for my doctor based on tests devised by the great German physicians of the late eighteenth century. There were all kinds of tests to see if the dead were actually alive: blowing pepper into the nostrils, shoving red-hot pokers up the jacksie, slicing the soles of the feet with a razor, tobacco-smoke enemas, galvanic muscle revivers, *Lebensprüfer*—'

'What's that?'

'Metal cones covered in cloth that's saturated in sal ammoniac. They generate an electric current when attached to a body's lower lip and eyelids, I have some here if you'd like to test them—'

'No thanks, I really should be going . . .' Bryant took a step back towards the door.

'I have my own magazine – self-published, obviously,' McEvoy continued. 'WH Smith weren't keen to take it. The latest issue has an interesting article on galvanizing techniques.' He thrust an issue of *The Casket* at the detective. Bryant opened it and found himself looking at graphic photographs of corpses with electrodes clipped to their extremities.

'I'm adapting a device that revives unconscious cows for use with comatose human beings that's not dissimilar to Dr Laborde's Rhythmic Tongue Puller. I tried to hand out some illustrated pamphlets concerning the dangers of premature interment, but I've been banned from distributing them anywhere near the local schools. So lately I've switched tack.' He flipped the page and held it high. 'I've been developing an updated version of Dr Plouviez's patented metabolizing heart acupuncture needles—'

That pulled Bryant up short. 'Wait. I've seen something like that before.'

McEvoy released a sharp bark of a laugh. 'Of course, at the corner just outside, on the tavern sign.' He dragged Bryant to the window and wiped away a patch of condensation. 'There, look.'

On the other side of the courtyard, the pub sign swung in the rainy wind. On it was painted a crimson heart, pierced in five places with silver arrows. 'The Blessed Virgin's heart,' said McEvoy, awed. 'The five sorrowful mysteries of the Rosary. The symbol dates back to before the Reformation. It signifies a compassion too vast for finite conception, the enduring love that led God to give up His only son to the nails and the crucifix, the spear, the burning wrath of the universal destroyer and the loathsome grave-pit beyond, that He might redeem us from the curse of human frailty. But it's also a practical test, you see? If you pierce the heart and it still bleeds, then it means that a corpse may live on and be revived!'

'Er, yes, thank you, I think you've answered all my questions,' said Bryant, backing out. 'It's been very interesting—'

'Don't go!' cried McEvoy. 'Don't you see, it's a sign that you were sent here to me, very possibly by the Virgin Mother herself. We must pray together!'

'I'm not sure that's a very good idea,' said Bryant. 'I'm a practising heathen, I'd put the mockers on any prayers you sent.' With that he headed for the door and launched himself down the unlit stairs.

'Idolater! Sybarite! Denier!' yelled McEvoy from his upstairs window as Bryant beat a hasty retreat across the
rainswept courtyard. 'The final blast of heaven's trumpet
is upon us! *Vento dei venti!* You cannot deny the proof of
the Bleeding Heart!'

17

ABANDONED

John May was worried. Nobody had seen his partner to-day, and he wasn't answering his phone – although that wasn't unusual; it was probably in a washing machine or down the toilet. Over the years he had learned not to worry when Bryant went missing, but Arthur had been in a very odd mood for the last couple of days.

'I called Alma,' said Longbright, coming into May's office. 'She says he left before she got up at seven.'

'Where would he go at that hour? The libraries and archives aren't open.'

'He has his own keys to some of them,' Longbright reminded him. 'They say widowers never sleep beyond dawn.'

'I don't know where you get these old-fashioned sayings from,' said May, irritated. 'I never think of him as a widower. Nathalie died so long ago.'

'He hardly ever mentions her,' said Longbright.

'No, and he doesn't even keep any pictures. I've only ever seen one photograph, although of course I met her several times.'

'What was she like?' Longbright had never been able to form an image of Bryant's wife in her head.

'Small, delicate-featured. But strong-willed and stubborn, just like him. I liked her a lot. They used to fight all the time, but in a constructive way. Arthur says that was the best part. I wonder where he could have got to.'

'Perhaps he's got some personal errands.'

'He has no surviving family members that I'm aware of. Plenty of loopy insomniac friends he might have gone to visit, I suppose.'

'Where would you begin to look?'

'I've no idea. My codebreaking skills aren't up to his contacts book; it's written in Babylonic cuneiform. I always get suspicious when he goes missing. It means he's up to something and doesn't want me to find out.'

'You think he's put himself back on the Wallace case?'

'I'm willing to place a bet on it. If he was dealing with the missing ravens he'd be calling me every five minutes to let me know what he'd discovered.'

'Well, in that case we'll have to cover for him until he turns up,' said Longbright. 'We've done it before, we can do it again.'

'But for how long? We desperately need a break, Janice. Colin and Meera are still wading through interviews, Jack's on Curtis's friends and relatives, Dan's having another look at St George's Gardens. Even the intern's checking local blogs. We've solved serial killings faster than this. Did you talk to Wallace's wife and son again?'

'Neither of them recall Thomas Wallace mentioning he was scared of being buried alive. Perhaps it's something he felt more comfortable discussing with a colleague rather than a member of the family. You know how funny men can be about death.'

'Well, that's it, then,' said May. 'I don't see what else we can do.' He checked his watch. 'Four hours. Raymond wants a breakthrough by five p.m., and at this rate he's not going to get it.'

*

Bryant's day was taking another strange turn.

The London Metropolitan Archives in Northampton Road housed an extraordinary range of documents, images, maps, court rolls, films and books about London. Bryant was so well known there that he had been given his own keys. He was searching the stacks for the legend of the Bleeding Heart.

He vaguely recalled that the courtyard had been named after the tavern that still stood there, but there was some story attached involving a ghost. He would probably not have bothered to look it up, but the LMA was only a few streets away, and as the rain was coming down like stair-rods it made sense to shelter for a few minutes, if only to calm down after his bizarre encounter with McEvoy.

He found the legend easily enough, but there were several contradictory versions. According to Charles Dickens, who had written about it in *Little Dorrit*, a lovelorn young lady had been imprisoned in her bedchamber by a cruel father, and had murmured a love song with the refrain 'Bleeding Heart, Bleeding Heart, bleeding away,' until she died. Unusually for Dickens, it wasn't much of a story.

But there were older sources: a poem set in 1626 described one Alice Hatton, the wife of Sir Christopher Hatton, whose family owned the area around Hatton Garden. Alice summoned the Devil and made a pact with him in return for wealth and social standing. On the Eve of St John at a grand housewarming ball, a tall figure in a black cloak entered at midnight. As a violent storm broke overhead he jigged like a dervish and spirited Alice Hatton away with him, bursting up through the roof. Their *danse macabre* left the tapestries and dinner tables scorched and blackened.

The next day the horrified guests found all that remained of Lady Hatton in the courtyard outside; her heart had been pierced with silver arrows and thrown down beside a pump filled with her blood – and the heart was still bleeding.

It was said that on the night of a full moon, she returned in a white gown to work the pump, trying to wash the blood away, but it continued to gush scarlet, and the ragged hole in her ribcage never healed, for the bleeding heart had been taken out and buried in an unchristian spot.

At this point, Bryant decided he had been sidetracked somewhat from the problem at hand, and took himself off for a Chelsea bun and some tea.

I'm a foolish, selfish old man, he thought, sitting in the empty café beneath the archives, breaking off pieces of bun and soaking them in his mug. *I should be toeing the line, helping John and Janice and the rest of them, instead of going off on these wild-goose chases.*

But he also remembered why he was here.

He had been ten years old when it had happened, on a chill night in early March. His father had been thrown out of the house for drunkenness again, and was sleeping it off in the backyard shed. Young Arthur had tiptoed out to meet up with the kids from the next street, over on the bombed-out waste ground that had once existed beside Aldgate East tube station.

The plot of broken earth and rubble from demolished houses hid a hundred potentially lethal traps, and was naturally a huge draw for adventurous ten-year-olds. He could see the others in his mind's eye but had no recollection of their real names. They were known only by attributes, Fatty and Ginger and Breathless. He was known as Swotty. It was growing dark as they commenced their last game of the night, a complex rule-ridden chase-and-catch competition that involved spies and traitors, blame and punishment, and, being the smallest, he had lost.

The others had grabbed him by his jumper and dragged him across the puddled mud to a half-collapsed brick tunnel, shoving him into the dark. Then they had found a heavy sheet of rusting corrugated iron and wedged it across the tunnel mouth, sealing him inside.

He had not become scared until he realized he could no longer hear their taunts. Shivering in the dank darkness, he waited for them to grow bored with their game and release him. But after a while no sound came from without. He shoved against the iron sheet but it refused to budge. It got colder and darker. This was his first intimation of death; its power crept over him, numbing his limbs and filling his heart with a terrible panic.

He threw himself at the sheet until his shoulder was black with bruises, but still it failed to give more than half an inch. He picked at the rusted edges of the corrugated iron until his nails bled, but could not prise off more than a few small patches.

As the slow minutes passed, the others did not return. All was quiet outside his makeshift tomb. In the distance he heard two men stop to chat on the street, but no one answered when he yelled, and soon they went. He had never cried before, not even when his father had spanked him for coming into the public bar of the Crown & Goose and shaming him in front of his mates, just for saying that Mum said his dinner was getting cold. But now hot tears coursed down his cheeks, and he sat down in the mud to prepare for the terrors that death would bring.

A full two hours later, a policeman tore down the sheeting and released him. The constable had thrown the other boys off the waste ground, refusing to listen to their tangled explanations about punishments and forfeits. But when Bryant's mother missed him the bobby had grown suspicious and returned to search the ground. Young Arthur threw himself at the constable's waist and refused to let go. He wanted a father like this, someone who would come and find him and lead him to safety instead of an unreliable drunk, a failed street photographer who barely even noticed that he had a family.

On that day, Arthur Bryant had sworn that when he grew up he would become an officer of the law, and rescue others in need of protection, others like himself.

He had been left with a horror of abandonment, a deep-rooted dread that surfaced when the stone chill of the grave reached into his heart. He could feel it now, and the only way of dissipating the fear was by saving others.

He was convinced that Romain Curtis had been killed for something he had seen in the churchyard, and resolved not to rest until he discovered what it was.

18

DISTURBED

'He was dead, Mr May. I don't know any other way of putting it. Deceased. I know how to search for signs of clinical death, believe me.'

Thomas Wallace's doctor operated from a small local practice in Marchmont Street, Bloomsbury. May had finally secured an interview with him towards the end of the afternoon. Dr Iain Ferguson was in his mid-thirties but looked creased and older, the way politicians did. He appeared to have been battered by the day's parade of patients and was half asleep at his desk, but on the point of Wallace's demise he was adamant. 'Death used to be defined by the cessation of the heartbeat. Now if there's any doubt we check for brain activity.'

'How do you define brain death?' May asked, looking around the depressing little room filled with warning posters.

'We look for structural damage, a blood clot or hypoxia, hypothermia, overdose, metabolic disturbance. Obviously one has to be more careful in cases of trauma to the regions of the spine, neck and head, but the state is still finite and infallibly diagnosable. He was drug-free and inside the house.'

'Of what relevance is that?'

'Well, if he'd taken morphine, say, and hanged himself from a tree in the middle of winter, there might have been reason for caution when determining the cessation of the heart. At a lower temperature you need less oxygen. The heart can reduce the pulse rate to just a handful of beats per minute. Even EEG readings could conceivably prove false. But Mr Wallace was found in a warm environment. And in the last few decades there have been changes in the criteria for declaring patients brain-dead. There are no mistakes made in this field any more, I can assure you, despite what the tabloids may have you believe. I certainly don't feel the need to stand by the details of the death certificate – to do so would be insulting.'

'A witness says he heard Mr Wallace speak,' said May.

'Then your witness was mistaken. If you want my advice, you should talk to the funeral home, Wells and Sons in Lamb's Conduit Street, a highly reputable family firm. As far as I know they're the only undertakers still with a dispensation to conduct burials in St George's Gardens. They would be able to tell you about post-demise anomalies.'

'What do you mean – anomalies?'

'Corpses have been known to explode quite noisily,' Dr Ferguson explained. 'A build-up of bacterial gases in the gut. It's possible the boy heard something like that and imagined the rest. What happens after the cessation of life is beyond my remit. It's probably better that you get the details from them.'

'Did you ever treat Thomas Wallace for depression?'

A harassed woman knocked and stuck her head around the door. 'Are you going to be very long?' she asked. 'Mr Turner's here to have his – you know.' She grimaced and mimed something unpleasant.

'Just keep him there for a sec,' Dr Ferguson suggested. 'We discussed the possibility of therapy, Mr May, but it was never pursued. Sometimes it's not the doctor's place to voice an opinion.'

'What do you mean?'

'I could see problems in their marriage. I think the father and son were close. The mother felt – thwarted.'

'An odd word to choose.'

'Wives don't like to see weakness. Thomas Wallace was clearly upset about something he could not or would not explain. There's little point in me prescribing treatment if the root of the problem lies somewhere else. I'm not a psychiatrist.' Ferguson stifled a yawn. He looked as if he was testing for a broken jaw. May tried not to yawn as well. 'Forgive me, I've been up for thirty-two hours on the trot. I'm cream-crackered. There's a virus working its way through the Cromwell Estate. From the number of callouts I've been getting in the last couple of days you'd think it was the return of the Black Death, but mostly it's people panicking over ordinary colds. I suppose you realize the residents know.'

'About what?'

'Your miraculous resurrection in St George's. They're wondering why they haven't seen anything about it in the papers. They think you're hiding something. It's always the same with you lot, you go blundering in and leave us to clear up the mess.'

Raymond Land's self-imposed deadline came and went.

He paced the corridors fuming, feeling sidelined and ineffectual, unable to discover why his instructions were being ignored. Everyone seemed to be following agendas set for them by Bryant and May. Whenever he stopped someone to ask why they had failed to appear in the common room, he was presented with strange, and in some cases incomprehensible, explanations. Realizing that the investigation had stalled, he placed his call to Orion Banks and was silently grateful when it was diverted to her voicemail. He was just about to hang up when she suddenly answered, making him jump.

'Mr Land, I assume you're calling to update me with a progress report. As far as I'm aware you have only two minor cases in hand, neither of which is likely to require much attention.'

'Mr Bryant is dealing with the Tower of London, as you know,' said Land carefully, 'and he hasn't provided me with anything yet.'

'Is it your custom to wait until he deigns to show you something?'

'Well, yes,' said Land. Banks made him too nervous to come up with fast excuses.

'But this vandalism in the churchyard – surely it's a fairly simple matter? We're dealing with multi-million-pound cases of fraud over here. I assume you've wrapped that up.'

'No, our team is still out on the beat.'

'What do you mean?'

'What you have to understand, Miss Banks, is that we get our best results when we spend time gaining public trust, and that requires getting to know people at a personal level.'

'So we're to stand by while you organize coffee mornings with the local parishioners, is that it?'

'We're a street force. We work from the ground up.'

'You'll be working from the ground down if I don't get my report first thing tomorrow,' Banks snapped, hanging up.

By 7.00 p.m. Bryant had still not appeared, and the PCU changed shifts. At May's request, Colin Bimsley agreed to visit St George's Gardens on his way home, to check that Thomas Wallace's grave had been properly restored to its former condition. Meanwhile, Meera Mangeshkar arranged to keep watch on the flat where Shirone Estanza lived with her mother.

At 8.00 p.m., Longbright met Sennen Renfield in the Ladykillers Café, King's Cross, where her mother had deposited her. Sennen had dyed the front of her black fringe several different shades of pink, and hid her pale features beneath the stripes as if sheltering under a beach umbrella. What was it, Longbright wondered, that drove teenagers to conceal themselves? Her clumsy attempt at an introduction was met with silence, a sigh, a fidget, a turned-aside head. Renfield shrugged an apology and went to fetch teas, glad of an escape route.

'Sennen – that's a very pretty name,' said Longbright.

'I hate it.'

'You go to school around here, don't you?'

'There's only one decent school, so we all have to go there.'

'You're at the Albany?' Longbright remembered that Romain Curtis was a pupil there. 'Do you like it?'

'The teachers are these old, old women who are all, like, forty.' Sennen stared pointedly into her face.

Longbright was no stranger to the rudeness of teenagers, but was more used to interviewing them in criminal investigations. 'What do you like to do at the weekends?' she asked, trying another tack.

'I don't know. Sleep.'

God, Longbright thought, *it's like pulling teeth*. 'Well, what do you like to do best in London?'

'Nothing.'

'Not even shopping?'

'I'm not interested in shopping. There are more important things to do.'

'I thought you said you liked to sleep.'

'So am I being interrogated then?' Sennen sat back and folded her arms, ready to close off the conversation until her father returned.

Longbright was made of sterner stuff. 'In a way, yes,' she countered. 'That's what we do. Perhaps I should take you into my confidence. Your father might have mentioned that we're conducting an important investigation at the moment. I'm not officially allowed to discuss it, of course, but I can say that it involves a terrible murder. I have a problem. One of our key witnesses is a schoolgirl roughly the same age as you, and we think someone is watching her, possibly stalking her. It's a long time since I was at school. I need to find out if she knows more than she's told us, but I can't really imagine how she thinks. If I could just understand—'

'Well then, how are you two getting along?' asked Jack with lousy timing.

'I was just about to ask Sennen if she'd like to see what detectives do,' said Longbright. 'Maybe she could spend a day at the unit helping us with an investigation.'

'I don't think that would be permissible,' said Jack. 'You wouldn't want to do that, would you, love?'

Sennen was about to reply but something stopped her.

Well well, guess who's suddenly interested in something, thought Longbright, *not that she dares to show it. Too cool for school, this one.* She quickly moved away from the subject, asking Jack a series of deliberately inconsequential questions.

Renfield glanced at his mobile. 'You'd better get off, love, your mother is waiting outside,' he said, rising and giving his daughter an awkward hug. As Longbright rose, she was careful to avoid catching Sennen's eye.

When they reached the door, she briskly turned and shook the girl's hand. 'It was nice to meet you, Sennen,' she said. 'Perhaps our paths will cross again.' She made to leave, then stopped. 'Oh, and if you get the time, think about what we discussed?'

I'll get you, my pretty, she thought, casting a sidelong glance back at the girl's puzzled face as she left.

*

As he walked towards St George's Gardens, Colin Bimsley pictured Amanda Roseberry and felt his heart glow. The young intern was smart, attractive, single and very laid-back. After months of angry sarcasm and only the vaguest grudging pleasantries from Meera, Amanda was a breath of fresh air. He wondered what she would say if he really did ask her out for a drink. He knew Meera was right and that he would be punching above his weight, but surely it was worth a try?

Climbing over the railing, he headed to the far perimeter where Thomas Wallace had been re-interred. It took a minute to find the grave in the gloom. The soil was wet from the day's rainfall, but had been packed down and neatly resown with grass. A sad little bouquet of peonies had been left on the fresh earth.

A dozen further graves were irregularly spaced behind a thicket of bushes, reaching to the railings on the other side of the gardens. Some were so old that lichen and ivy had split the granite headstones and worn away their epitaphs.

Colin had been feeling perpetually tired and fed up of late. He wasn't earning enough to be able to afford a car or move from his poky, cluttered flat. He missed having a steady relationship, but his long working hours put women off. He thought of Roseberry again and decided he would definitely go for it when they next met.

Having checked the gardens, he headed over to Judd Street and queued for a vast lamb kebab covered in crimson chilli sauce. He was just about to take a bite from it when his mobile buzzed.

'Colin, how close are you to St George's?' asked May.

'Only a couple of streets away. I just checked it and everything was fine. Why?'

'Get round there again, fast. A woman overlooking the grounds called in a disturbance. King's Cross routed the call to me. She's still on the line.'

'On my way, boss.' Colin reluctantly threw his kebab tray in the bin and hoofed it. Afterwards, he realized that running into the street and vaulting the railing was a mistake. Beyond the light thrown by the park's spindly lamps, he could see only a vague shape shifting in the leaves. As he approached, he realized that the sound he'd heard was that of a shovel hitting earth.

It was too late to remain unnoticed. They had already seen him coming. Bimsley was a bulky man who dominated most spaces smaller than aerodromes and stadiums. When he attempted to quell his presence the results were absurd, like a rhinoceros performing in ballet shoes. There was nothing to be done except push rowdily ahead into the foliage and make a grab for whoever was standing there.

The sight that confronted him brought him up short: a fresh grave, already half dug out, the shovel sticking out of a mound of soil; a nimble figure, almost certainly male, launching itself away and hopping over the wall behind the plot.

Incredible, Bimsley thought, *I was here only twenty minutes ago.* He followed, but had trouble scrabbling up the brickwork. On the other side was a poorly lit alleyway that led to the Drug Rehabilitation Centre at the end of Heathcote Street. The man in front of him swung nimbly over another railing and landed on a flight of steps above. Bimsley sized up his opponent; he had the agility of youth and was familiar with the area. A moment later he had slammed through the doors of the drug centre.

Bimsley followed and found himself in an empty, bright municipal corridor lined with closed wood-veneer doors. There was an eye-watering smell of disinfectant. He tried the first door and found it locked. He stopped and listened. A faint sway of the far fire door set him off in pursuit once more.

This time he found himself in an unlit stairwell leading up to other floors. Bimsley's spatial awareness diminished in the darkness, and moments later he was clutching the stair-rail, trying to stay on his feet.

There could only be another half-dozen steps to the first landing, but he did not dare to look down. Then he heard the breathing. Someone was standing very close by.

Spinning about, he lashed out hard and caught a stubbled chin. There was a yell, a grab, a tangle of legs as they fell back down the bottom five steps and hit concrete.

Feeling for a jacket collar, he seized it and dragged the protesting man towards the fire doors, hurling him on to the linoleum floor. Under the lights he immediately realized his mistake.

'Don't hurt me,' begged the man, raising a skeletal hand to a parchment-coloured face. He was young but looked old: a recovering heroin addict – a much rarer sight on the Central London streets these days. 'I came here for my prescription but they're shut. It's warm in the stairwell.'

'Did you see anyone go past you?'

'Yeah, some studenty-looking bloke, he ran past just before you come along.'

'Did you see where he went?'

'Out the back. You can get out on to Heathcote Street from there.'

'What did he look like other than "studenty"?'

'I don't know – glasses – it was dark.'

Bimsley helped the man back on to his feet and apologized.

'I'm broke – can you let me have a quid?'

'That won't even buy you a coffee, will it? You need to start asking for two pounds fifty, mate.' Bimsley gave him a couple of pounds and headed out to Heathcote Street.

It was too late – the object of his pursuit could have fled in any direction. He ran back to St George's Gardens and found the disturbed gravesite. The digger had already reached the coffin – it had not been buried as deeply this time – and a corner of the polished lid was exposed.

Then Bimsley realized his mistake. He was not looking at Thomas Wallace's grave at all, but the next one over. A small wooden marker read: 'Elspeth Mary Duncannon "Always In Our Hearts"'. She had died at the age of eighty-seven and had been buried ten days ago.

Someone had been digging up a second plot.

Bimsley wrapped the handle of the dropped shovel in the plastic bag that had held his foil kebab box, then phoned in his findings and headed back to the unit, angry with himself for having let the possible cause of their investigation slip through his fingers.

The figure by the grave had hardly looked human, bouncing, no, *hopping,* over the gravestones – what would he have done to this second grave if he had not been interrupted?

Bimsley recalled an engraving he had seen of Victorian bodysnatchers at work. It had been pinned on the wall behind Bryant's desk.

19

ALONE

'A resurrectionist,' said Bryant. 'Or the modern-day equivalent, at least. In both cases he was either interrupted in his task or got what he came for – perhaps just the thrill of digging up the dead. This is the sort of area in which I shine, Raymondo. You have to put me back on the case.'

It was a little after eight on Thursday morning, and in the last twenty-four hours the investigation had not significantly advanced. Any moment now Orion Banks would start pressuring them all for more results. She wasn't looking to take the case elsewhere. She just wanted to prove that they were incompetent.

'That depends,' said Raymond Land. 'How are you getting on with the ravens?'

'I have an idea how they were smuggled out and why, but I don't have any proof.' Bryant gave him a wide-eyed look that at least contained a vague suggestion of honesty.

'All right,' Land agreed finally, 'I'll bring you back on one condition: that you get something more on those damned birds by the close of play today.'

'I've got an idea about that,' said Bryant, 'but I don't

think I shall tell you what it is. It's a bit of a wig-lifter and you'll only get angry.'

Land watched his top detective unsticking sherbet lemons from his cardigan, which was amateurishly embroidered with shaky outlines of Mithraic temples, a gift from one of his old-biddy admirers. He knew that the unit's hopes were now pinned on this strange old man's thought processes, and his stomach flopped. 'The City of London Police won't co-operate until they've stopped regarding us as a joke,' he warned, 'and we can't get anywhere without Banks. They all know we were once under the jurisdiction of the Met.'

'Ah. I heard that in the bar at Snow Hill, or whichever City nick is closest to the Old Bailey,' replied Bryant, 'some CoL jokers put up a rack of coat pegs at a height of about five foot six, then raised a sign that said "For the use of Met officers and traffic wardens only". The height restriction for City PCs used to be over six feet, didn't it? A bit antagonistic, one feels.'

'They'll do a lot worse than that to us if we screw up, I promise you.'

'Right you are, *meine alte wurst*.' He held up a sherbet lemon covered in grey fluff. 'Do you think these are still edible? I'm off to get some results, then.' Bryant popped the sweet into his mouth and looked about for his coat.

'Do me a favour and take John with you,' said Land. 'He can help you.'

'You're right. I've been working by myself too much lately. We're better as a team. But not just yet. There's something I have to do first. It involves visiting a pub – purely business, you understand.'

'And this is about the theft of the ravens?'

'A theft, yes, but ravens, no – it concerns operettas and dead cats.' He smiled and sauntered from the room.

*

John May and Janice Longbright arrived at the shopfront in Lamb's Conduit Street and looked in the window. An arrangement of faded plastic flowers had been set in a wooden model of a Viking boat that bore the inscription:

> Cattle die,
> Kinsmen die,
> All men are mortal.
> Words of praise
> Will never perish,
> Nor a noble name.

Above, in a tasteful white serif typeface on black marble, it read: 'John Wells & Sons, Founded 1806, Funeral Services'; and below that, painted on diamond-shaped panels of ruby and emerald glass: 'Funerals – Cremations – Embalming – Private Chapel'.

'The Viking saying, it's from the *Hávamál*, the great Eddaic poem from AD 800,' said May.

Longbright gave him a funny look. 'How would you know that?'

May shrugged. 'I've been hanging around with Arthur for a long time.'

They went in and found themselves in a mahogany-panelled room that had absorbed two centuries of salt tears. The man who came out to greet them was clearly in the wrong job; he looked like a camp pork butcher who was too happy in his work.

'Sorry to keep you,' he said, holding out a pudgy hand, 'our embalmer just passed his driving test and we were having a bit of a laugh backstage. We call it backstage because, you know, we can be ourselves back there. My name's Mr Rummage, but call me Ronald, please.' He adjusted huge round tortoiseshell glasses on his nose. 'I think I've got the answers to your questions. Come on back, there might be some chocolate cheesecake left.'

Behind the sombre surroundings of the receiving parlour was a slightly more cheerful room with late-eighties pastel sofas, two computer desks and a tea station. 'That's Andy, our embalmer, in the corner,' said Rummage, indicating a more traditionally cadaverous young man. 'And that's our Betty. She handles the accounts.' Betty looked up from her screen, gave a tentative smile and hastily shrank again. 'William's my partner; he's out seeing a client about floral arrangements. There are only four of us now, down from sixteen at one time. Cholera. Our peak. A tragedy, of course, but a wonderful opportunity to build up the business. Have you got that bit of paper, Betty?' He accepted a page and unfolded it. 'Yes, you see, it's a legacy bequest. Mr Thomas Edward Wallace. There are only six of them left.'

'Six what?' asked Longbright.

'Burial plots. After St George's Gardens stopped being a churchyard it was turned into a public park.'

'Why did it stop?'

'Because the land company went bankrupt. Three funeral firms supplied the churchyard, one in King's Cross, one in Holborn and us, here in Bloomsbury. When the other two went, we were the only ones whose clients still had an entitlement to be interred there. But by then the council had decided to create a public space for local residents, so we agreed not to sell any more plots.'

'When was this?' asked May.

'Nineteen sixty-something. I don't have an exact date. But in the interim, a few more plots had already been sold. We contacted our clients and asked if they would like to be interred elsewhere, and I think three – yes, there you see, three said yes. The others still had families in the area, so we came to an arrangement with the council. They agreed to let the last three be quietly settled in the gardens, near the back wall.'

'So the lady who was buried a week and a half ago—'

'Elspeth Mary Duncannon, she lived in the council flats just over the road, bless her. Emphysema, a lifelong smoker. She'd been virtually bedridden for ten years and didn't really have much quality of life, poor soul. We chose the headstone inscription because there was no immediate family to do it for her.' Rummage pushed his glasses back up his nose. 'And then just a few days later, Mr Wallace. He lived over in Marchmont Street in his father's house, and had been bought the plot by the old man. Funny they went so close together, but that's life, isn't it?'

Elspeth Duncannon, thought May, *almost disinterred like Wallace before her.* 'That means there's just one more person to go,' said May. 'Can you let me have their details?'

'That's easy,' said Mr Rummage. 'It's me. End plot on the left. I'm marked out with lilacs and daffodils; you can't miss it. But don't expect me to fill it any time soon.' He laughed and patted his stomach. 'I've got years left in me yet.'

Arthur Bryant tacked around the raised concrete circle above the traffic, searching for the entrance to the Museum of London. It didn't matter how many times he came here, he could still never locate the way in. Heaven only knew how overseas visitors ever found the place. Like the city it portrayed, it was hidden in plain sight.

Bryant had come to repay a debt, but also to ask some questions. Mr Peregrine Wosthold Merry was an academic who lectured and curated at the museum. He was also an acolyte of Ipsissimus and practitioner of necromantic rites connected to the system of Paradox Philosophy, the process of freeing yourself from the concepts of good and evil, and was said to be a very dangerous man. Bryant had recently been introduced to Mr Merry by his old friend Maggie Armitage; she had provided Bryant with a set of guidelines for dealing with her nemesis. She had even written down the ten most important rules on a scrap of paper:

1. Do not shake his hand.
2. Never come into contact with his person. If he reaches out to touch you, step out of his way.
3. Don't accept anything from him. If he tries to get you to take anything, politely refuse.
4. If he drops anything, do not pick it up. He'll try to trick you.
5. If he looks you in the eye, quickly break contact.
6. If he asks you a question, reveal nothing of yourself or your loved ones. Preferably, try not to say anything at all.
7. Under no circumstances should you be drawn into an argument, or disagree in a manner designed to annoy him.
8. Do not tell him a lie. He'll know and use it against you.
9. Keep your hearing aid slightly turned down. It will screen out anything he might whisper to you.
10. Stay wary and alert the whole time you're in his presence. Don't lose your concentration for even a second.

Of course, when it came to a man like Bryant this was a big collective red rag to a bull. He had met self-mythologizing academics like Mr Merry before, and they had failed to impress him. They got lost in their researches and came to believe in such strange, abstruse concepts that they ended up wrecking themselves and their careers. Even so, Mr Merry struck him as different. There was an aura of genuine menace around him. He was not lost in his own world, but rather looking out for opportunities to involve and absorb others. It seemed to Bryant that he would use those weaker than himself without scruples or compassion, and that alone made him dangerous. It was this quality of arrogant self-belief that united serial killers from Charles Manson to Dennis Nilsen, so Bryant was determined to watch his step.

A receptionist directed him to the rear of the building, where he found the door to a dimly lit, casket-shaped room housing some of the museum's crated, undisplayed items. Mr Merry was there to greet him, calmly waiting. He was as round as Bryant remembered, but still gave the appearance of immense strength. His rainbow-beaded beard was spread across his broad barrel chest, and his thick dyed ponytail hung beneath a black velvet skullcap woven with silver threads. Every finger sported a symbolic tattoo and a large silver ring; every nail was painted glossy black. His crimson tunic was silver-edged and piratical, as were his tall black leather boots. The luxuriant eyebrows might have been painted on to complement his hooded, watchful eyes. He smelled of patchouli oil and tobacco, and something unwholesome. It was as if Judge Dee and Blackbeard had been combined in one man.

'I thought we might meet again,' Mr Merry boomed, suddenly marching towards him with a hand outstretched. Bryant ignored the gesture of greeting and strolled past him, looking into the nearest crate.

'What are you keeping hidden from members of the public?' he asked cheerfully. The game had begun.

'Oh, all sorts of things,' said Mr Merry, mirroring Bryant's casual attitude. 'The history of this great city is full of surprises, as you well know. Civilians can't be allowed to poke about among things they don't understand; they'd quickly get their fingers burned. So it gets crated away where it can't hurt anyone. Can I get you a cup of tea? I know how you English love your tea.'

'No thanks, I just had one,' said Bryant. 'So you're not English?'

'I have no nation, Mr Bryant. I am of the world. Surely

one cup? To buck you up? You're looking rather more tired than when we last met.'

Bryant gave a non-committal grunt.

'Then perhaps a cigarette.' He withdrew a slim silver case and held it out. 'It's all right, they're herbal.' Bryant shook his head. 'Are you here to repay your debt, or to ask another favour?'

'Perhaps both.' He decided to take a chance and explain. It was essential to be exact. 'Two unearthed coffins in the same graveyard, buried a few days apart. No, not a graveyard, a cemetery.'

Mr Merry's eyes unhooded slightly, a sign that his interest was piqued. 'When was this?'

'One first buried eleven days ago, one just under a week ago.'

'Were the bodies removed?'

'One was. The culprit was interrupted before he could open the lid of the second coffin.'

'You say "he". You saw him?'

'One of my men did – not his face, just his form against the street lights.'

'So this was here, in central London.'

'I'd rather not describe the exact circumstances for the moment.'

'You want to understand what this gentleman had planned, of course.'

'There's something else. The boy who witnessed the first disinterment was run down by a car the following night.'

'Did he survive?'

'He did not.'

'I can see your problem. You seek a rational explanation but your mind takes you in another direction, towards black-magic rituals, arcane rites, secret ceremonies.' Mr Merry shifted fussily and sighed, touching his fingers together. 'The truth is likely to be something more mundane: boys vandalizing graves from boredom, either as dares or rites of passage. You know what lads are like without a steadying influence. You seek my counsel, but you already owe me for the last piece of advice I gave you.'

'Perhaps we can find a way to wipe the slate clean.'

Mr Merry narrowed his eyes. 'I'm intrigued as to what drew you back to me, Mr Bryant. After the last time we met, I gained the distinct impression that you were frightened of me.'

'I'm too old to be frightened,' said Bryant, and instantly regretted saying it, for he knew that Mr Merry would read the opposite into the statement.

'I see. So death holds no fear for you.'

Bryant shifted uncomfortably. 'No.'

'The yawning grave that awaits us all. Nothing?'

'Certainly not.'

Mr Merry tapped his painted nails on the desk, thinking. 'Not death. But something like it. Interment, then. Loss.'

Bryant fought to remain composed, but feared the struggle was showing in his face.

'Loss? Abandonment. Some fear that only grows in darkness. Something that involves you being quite unaided, and afraid you might die alone. But at an earlier age, of course, when death still holds unknown terrors. When you were a child, perhaps.'

Bryant opened his mouth to speak but thought better of it. He tried to freeze any emotions from his face.

'You were – what, ten, eleven? And mortally afraid. Not of your parents, from what I know of your background. A stranger.' He kept watching Bryant's face carefully. 'No? Friends, then. Others the same age as you. Schoolmates you trusted. This is not fear of enclosure, not claustrophobia, not fear of the dark or even death itself. You've been in dark and enclosed places before, and it has not troubled you unduly. This is different. It's the most primal fear of all. The fear of being left alone.'

Mr Merry smiled, and the room chilled. Bryant could only watch and wait, and try to say no more. He had recalled his childhood terror just a handful of hours earlier, and the necromancer had already unpicked it from his brain.

20

CONNECTIONS

John May had returned from the Victorian undertakers to the only slightly more modern surroundings of the PCU. 'There's no question in my mind that these two "unburials" are linked,' he told Dan Banbury, drawing him along the building's wonky passageway in his wake, 'and that suggests the coffins weren't randomly targeted but that there was a common purpose the desecrations. I need you to find something for me.'

'What have I got to work on?' asked Banbury, stopping at May's office doorway. 'We'll never get permission to exhume Wallace a second time. I suppose we could try the old lady, but her next of kin will have to agree to it unless you have a watertight reason for forcing their hand and requesting an inquest.'

'There's a distant relative somewhere, that's all. We won't get an inquest without good cause.'

'I've already been sent a copy of the doctor's certificate. It's Ferguson, the same doctor who attended Thomas Wallace.'

'That's hardly surprising. Come in,' said May. He tried to close his office door behind them and failed, as the floorboards were badly warped. 'The two deaths occurred within the same catchment area. These are tight neighbourhoods. People on the older estates still know each other. You'd be surprised how many of them went to school together. Although I'm sure Arthur would read something more into the fact that they shared a doctor. What was the GP's verdict on Mrs Duncannon?'

'Lungs. She smoked herself to death. I can't see a link between the pair, beyond the fact that they were buried virtually side by side. There's one odd thing – another plot staked out next to them.'

'Yes, it's the last one to be allowed in the gardens. It belongs to the funeral director, Rummage. You think we should start keeping an eye on him?'

Banbury patted his stubbly hair, thinking. 'Not without a motive for doing so.'

'That's just it – we have nothing. The awful thing is, I keep losing sight of the boy in all of this. Romain Curtis overheard something about a star constellation, the Little Bear. And I think he died for it. Someone kept watch on his girlfriend's flat until they realized that we were staking it out. If Curtis didn't die for what he overheard, this whole thing collapses. We'd have nothing but a set of odd coincidences.'

'We need a way forward, John. It's already been nearly a working week. Banks is prowling around the place—'

'I know,' May snapped. 'Wallace and Duncannon shared the same funeral director – there might be something there, but I'm damned if I know what. Find it for me, Dan. I need forensic proof, not theories.'

His mood of frustration and annoyance had not dissipated by the time he reached the apartment of Carmelina Domínguez, in the building which overlooked the burial plots in St George's Gardens. May was ushered into a small, immaculately kept flat that could only have been owned by an old Spanish family. Inherited wardrobes, cabinets and dressers stood on a colourful tiled floor, but the focus of the home was centred on a great oval dining table covered in lace.

Mrs Domínguez explained that she had stayed on here after her husband died, and often sat by the window watching the park and its users because the green space reminded her of her old home in Cadiz, but there, she said, 'The wind, you know, it comes from every side, always the warm wind, and here it is only the rain, and the clouds so low that everything looks grey and brown.' She sighed, hobbling to her place by the window. 'How I miss my home. One day I will return and wash myself in sunlight again.' She pointed from the window. 'See, there, between the biggest trees, the graves?'

May leaned on the ledge of the open window and looked down. Beneath the dense damp branches he could see both the Wallace and Duncannon burial plots. Beyond them, a row of plants marked the plot Mr Rummage had picked out for himself. A winding gravel path steered most casual walkers away from the corner where the graves lay. Their lichen-eaten headstones were as much a feature of a London park as fountains in Madrid and squirrels in New York.

'I saw the young black man and his girlfriend on the grass late that night. I remember wishing I was their age again. Then I saw him stand and look over in this direction. I wondered what he had seen, and looked down. And there they were.'

'You say *they*?'

'Yes, two figures, standing very close together. It's silly, for a minute I thought they were dancing.'

You didn't realize one was a corpse, he thought.

'The boy ran at them, then the branches – when the wind rises they move and cut off the view. I could see someone lying on the ground, a man in a black suit, earth everywhere, and the other one had gone. A minute or two later, the boy came back.'

'What did he do?'

'I don't know. Nothing.' She tapped at the sill, trying to remember. 'I think he just stood there looking. He didn't move.'

'Why didn't you call the police?'

'You see these things and think, *It's not my business*. I know I should have.'

'And after that?'

'Your people came. There was a tent, a green one. Someone from a funeral parlour came to put the earth back. I saw the van outside. Then last night it happened all over again, only I saw less because the wind was stronger. The branches moved about a lot. But there was definitely someone down there with a shovel. And this time I called you.' She lightly crossed herself. 'It is a terrible thing when the dead can't be left in peace.'

'Do you think you'd be able to identify the person who dug up the graves?'

'My eyesight is not so good these days. A man, young, with quick movements. Beyond that, I could not say.' A look of worry crossed her features. 'Maybe – maybe there were others.'

'When?'

'The first time. Other people. I cannot really remember now. Some things you see, and it turns out you only think you see. This is another reason why I did not call you before.'

May tucked his notepad back into his jacket without writing down anything useful.

When he arrived back at the unit, he found Krishna Jhadav waiting for him. The director of Defluotech Management Systems looked as if he hadn't eaten for days, and took the offer of a seat opposite May's desk with the air of a man who might never get up again.

'I'm sorry to disturb you,' he said, twitchily checking the office's open door. 'When we spoke at my place

I wasn't really able to concentrate – my colleague wanted to use the room and . . . well, I'm used to having time to prepare, presentations and so on.'

'That's understandable,' said May, 'we get it all the time. *L'esprit d'escalier* – remembering what you should have said too late.'

'I told you Thomas Wallace was having personal problems. I think it was a bit more than that. There was a rumour going around that his wife had asked for a divorce. We heard there was some kind of money issue between them. You can understand why we started to worry about our business relationship.'

'I imagine it must have been difficult but I don't see what—'

'Mrs Wallace won't talk to me. She blames her husband's mental state on the withdrawal of our business. Believe me, I thought long and hard about the situation before reaching the decision to end our contract.'

'I don't see what I can do,' said May. Jhadav puzzled him. The man was practically shaking in his highly polished Church's. He was perched on the edge of his chair and refused to look May in the face, and nervously picked at his knuckles as if he was waiting to find out whether he had but a few days left to live. May decided to wait and let him speak.

'There's something else,' Jhadav said after unbearable moments of silence had passed between them. 'My girl-friend – she thinks we're being followed. Sometimes by car, sometimes on foot.'

'Who do you think it is?'

'I know who it is. Her, Vanessa Wallace. She drives a Renault. I recognized the vehicle registration. I think she may be unstable, and may do something, I don't know what—'

'Are you asking for police protection, Mr Jhadav?'

'No, I just thought you should know, what with all

that's been going on.' He paused, as if the words had dried in his mouth. 'I'm – Look, we're all under pressure to perform these days. The last thing I need is some crazy housewife stalking me because she thinks I caused her husband's death.'

Shirone Estanza was in the corridor of the Albany High School, drinking a strawberry McDonald's milkshake and waiting for her new friend to come out of class. Finally the doors to the art room opened and Sennen Renfield emerged. As usual, she was the last one out, and alone.

'I thought you weren't coming in today,' said Sennen, swinging her bag on to the shoulder of her navy jumper.

'I wasn't going to,' Shirone admitted, falling into step beside her. 'The cremation was at eleven, but it overran. Romain's mother had the wake in her flat. She asked me to go but I just couldn't. I didn't know any of his relatives – I wouldn't have had anything to say to them.'

'You sure you still want to go out?' Sennen asked.

'Yeah – if it'll stop me thinking about him for a while.'

'There's a rom-com on at the Brunswick. Cheer you up.'

'Not sure I'm in the mood for a film. I thought they only showed art films there. It's not subs, is it? I need something light. I can't concentrate on anything right now.'

'This is supposed to be fun. Come on, we can get some really disgusting chocolate ice-cream cake afterwards. The sugar will keep you up for, like, twenty-four hours.'

'I keep thinking about it,' said Shirone miserably. 'How things could have been so different that evening. If I hadn't pushed him to go to the club, if he hadn't got so drunk—'

'Don't even go there,' Sennen warned. 'Put it out of your mind and let the cops do their job. They'll get the guy who did it.'

'But how?'

'You're kidding, a hit-and-run? They measure tyre

tracks and match DNA and stuff, then run through all the cars on a kind of central database and – OK, I don't actually know, I've just heard Dad talk about it, but they'll soon tighten the net around him.' They swung off down the pavement towards the shopping centre.

'Someone's been hanging around the flat at night,' said Shirone.

'Who?'

'I'm not sure. The officers in your old man's unit saw him. They've added some big bloke out on the terrace all night now, just to make sure he doesn't come back.'

'That'll be Colin. I've heard all about him. He's a good guy. You should tell him you know me. My dad introduced me to someone in his unit last night. I think he's sleeping with her.'

'Oh, gross. Has he, you know, actually admitted it?'

'No, but he formally introduced her and his voice went all low and serious.'

'What's she like?'

'Big, dyed hair, loads of retro-slap.'

'What, Amy Winehouse?'

'More Monroe. She's the kind he'd go for. And she's a cop. I think she might be sort of OK. We'll see. Come on, we'll go to the movies and you can forget about Romain for a couple of hours.'

'I don't want to forget about him,' said Shirone miserably.

'Nobody's saying you have to forget him for good, just – I don't know, take your mind off it for a while.'

Shirone's voice hardened. 'Look, there's that freak who's always staring at me in the library.' She pointed at a boy in a long leather coat and skintight black jeans who was coming down the school steps. 'That's Martin Wallace. It was his father Romain saw getting dug up.' She yelled at him: 'Hey, freak!'

Martin ignored them, carrying on past.

'What, you're too stuck up to talk to us?' Shirone threw the remains of her milkshake at him. The lid came away from the cup and pink liquid splattered over the wall. She laughed. Martin hurried on, pretending he hadn't seen them.

'What are you doing?' yelled Sennen.

'I hate him,' said Shirone. 'Crazy emo freak and his crazy mother.'

'Why? What did he do to you?'

'If his father hadn't killed himself – we would never have—' But the laughter had already turned to tears and she was making no sense now, not even to herself, and all Sennen could do was put her arms around her friend and wait for her agony to die down.

21

BURYING THE LIVING

Arthur Bryant was sitting in the gloomy archive room of the Museum of London, waiting for Mr Merry to return.

'I thought you would want to see this,' said the piratical academic, setting down a pair of cardboard cartons between them. Bryant carefully moved his chair back a few inches. After Maggie's warnings he was determined to keep some neutral space between himself and his adversary.

'Tell me, Mr Bryant, what do you know about the process of apotropaic magic?'

'Not much,' Bryant admitted. 'Something to do with hiding the body of an animal to repel a malign entity.'

'It's a little more complicated than that, but we can let the definition stand. In its most extreme form, it refers to the practice of live burial. Usually it took the form of burying a mole, a dog, a chicken, a young fox or a cat alive in a building cavity to protect the home. The idea was that any evil presence attempting to enter the house would enter the body of the animal and be trapped within it. Look in the first box.' Mr Merry sat back with his ringed hands interlocked over his chest and waited.

Bryant was not keen to touch the carton that sat between them, but had no choice. He gingerly opened the lid and looked down. Stacked inside were some earthenware candlesticks, a very small pair of old leather gloves, a baby's shawl, two glass goblets and a rush mat.

'Now the second one.'

He carefully pulled up the lid and found himself looking at a stack of mummified cats, their dry grey fur and sunken eyes indicating extreme age.

'All of these items were found inside the walls of houses in Southwark and Bermondsey, together with a variety of mummified creatures.'

'Sacrifices to household gods,' said Bryant.

'Indeed. Valued items to be placed in the foundations of houses. The goblets would have held wine, and there would probably have been offerings of bread.'

'I've seen mummified cats in pubs,' said Bryant, 'in the Tiger Tavern by the Tower of London, and in Dirty Dicks, but they've all vanished in the last few years.'

'The poor dried-out creatures in Dirty Dicks were there for another reason entirely,' Mr Merry explained absently. 'The legend goes that the original owner, Nathaniel Bentley, was a dandy who neglected his personal hygiene until the day he fell in love. Alas, his lady died on the day of their engagement, and he ordered the dining room to be shut up. For fifty years he admitted no one to the upper rooms of his premises. After Bentley's death, the house was found it be uninhabitable. The dishes had rusted to the table, paintings were so thick with dirt that their subjects were no longer discernable, rats and cats had died of hunger, cemented by cobwebs to the worm-eaten furniture. It seems likely that Charles Dickens was inspired to create the character of Miss Havisham in *Great Expectations* from the story of Dirty Dick. The old wine and spirit vaults are still there in the basement, but much was torn down during the renovations of 1870 . . . this city has no respect for its past.'

Mr Merry drifted into silence, as if remembering the event, and for a brief moment Bryant sensed that here was a kindred spirit, albeit one with a very different attitude to his own.

'Where was I?' asked Merry. 'Apotropaic magic – yes, it has other uses. We have a great many apotropaic artefacts here at the museum. But some – well, they're not for public display.'

'You mean there were cases of human sacrifice?'

'We certainly have evidence of that. The practice of placing a baby in the foundation stones of a building was supposed to protect it. Conversely, there are stories of foetuses being buried on sites designated for synagogues. The Jewish faith does not permit building on unclean ground. You can appreciate that this is a subject many would find – unpalatable.'

'But not you.'

'If one is to study the practice of dark magic there is little point in being squeamish.'

'I fail to see the connection between these items and the raising of a dead body,' said Bryant, indicating the cartons with puzzlement.

'Of course, and I must apologize; there are few who keep pace with my somewhat lateral thought processes, but I suspect you may be one who will do so in the fullness of time. Let's discuss business. If I am to help you, there is something I would like in return.'

'I can't promise anything, but you can ask.'

Merry leaned forward. 'There is another matter that I believe has recently come to your attention. It involves a venerable British institution.'

'I assume you're referring to the Tower of London.'

'I am prepared to look at the facts in your case if you are willing to leave this . . . other matter alone.'

'I can't just turn a blind eye to a criminal case, Mr Merry. I work for the police, not the mafia, and I will investigate whatever I see fit.'

'Then I cannot help you.'

'I have a duty to the public that must come before every other consideration.'

'I was afraid that might be your reaction. In which case, you must ask yourself which is more important: the catching of a killer who could strike again; or the solving of a minor theft in which the items in question are already being replaced?'

'You mean the ravens.'

'I said nothing. It is a matter for your conscience.'

'If I took you up on your offer, it would only be to delay the investigation, not abandon it.'

'I need one week, that's all.'

Bryant thought carefully. If he agreed to the arrangement, he would be laying himself open to the risk of suspension and prosecution for obstruction of justice. But right now, he could imagine no one else who might be able to help him.

'One week,' he repeated. 'No longer than that.'

'Then, Mr Bryant, I think we have come to an understanding.' Mr Merry held out his hand to shake on the deal.

Bryant froze. *What have I committed myself to?* he thought, staring back at the proffered hand.

'Ah,' said Mr Merry, noting his reluctance to connect. 'We need to make our contract binding. May I suggest something?' Producing a carved ivory fountain pen from his tunic, he reached over and jabbed the back of Bryant's hand with the sharpened nib. Caught by surprise, Bryant yelped and pulled his hand back, but not before a single droplet of blood had formed. With a flick of the pen's reservoir lever, Mr Merry absorbed the scarlet bubble on Bryant's hand.

'There,' he said. 'I think we can do business now.'

Repocketing the pen inside his tunic, he now produced a card and placed it on the surface of the nearby desk, sliding it in Bryant's direction. Reading the handwritten lettering upside down, Bryant noted a title: 'The New Resurrectionists'. There was a number to call, but no address.

'These are the people you will need to contact, Mr Bryant. I warn you, though. They may seem normal, but they have extreme ideas. You can take no one with you. And remember our deal. Do not betray me. Whatever you do, be sure I will find you out.'

With the safety zone between them breached, Bryant had nothing to lose by taking the card. As he left the building and headed out into a fresh squall of rain, a chill gripped his heart. *I did the opposite of what I was instructed to do*, he thought. *I fell for his trickery. Something bad has been set in motion, and the power to stop it has been taken away from me.*

22

CITY OF THE DEAD

'I spoke to Orion Banks,' said Land, looking as if he was about to be shot. 'It didn't go well.'

'What happened?' asked May, fearing the answer.

'She's clearly of the opinion that we couldn't run a Hungarian string factory, let alone a London police unit.' Land looked around his tatty office with distaste. 'She thinks we've been wasting resources investigating this business at St George's Gardens. She doesn't give a tinker's cuss for a stoned teenager getting knocked over in a backstreet. We've been ordered to stop keeping watch on the graves, and to pull out of the surveillance on Shirone Estanza's flat.'

'But that's absurd,' said May. 'Jack, Colin and Meera are still taking turns to stake out the place. Meera went after—'

'John, they saw someone hanging around on the communal terrace. It's a block of flats; kids do that all the time.'

'What about Krishna Jhadav's assertion that he and his girlfriend have been followed by Wallace's widow?'

'It's hearsay. There's no physical proof of anything. Get

in too deep with these people and you're just going to start getting tangled up in their lives. You need to keep some distance.'

'But it's our job to—'

'Banks wants us to leak the desecration story to the press so that reporters will hang around the graveyard and do our job for us.'

'You're joking, right?' May was horrified. A journalistic circus was the last thing anyone needed right now.

'She's a media manipulator, that's what she does best. I have no say in this. I made my feelings known but she wasn't even listening.'

'And if something else happens we'll get the blame.'

'I imagine she's counting on that.'

'What do you want me to say, Raymond? That you should have stood up for us and put her in her place? Are you waiting for me to have a go at you? What I can't stand is this air of hand-wringing defeat. I'm not going to take this from her and I certainly won't from you.' He took a deep breath to calm himself down. 'I'm trying to do everything by the book. We're wading through over three thousand hours of CCTV footage from the King's Cross area, looking for a car we only have a vague description of from one unreliable witness who thinks she saw it turn into Britannia Street. Now we're going to get journalists following us around? You need to grow your gonads back and start supporting us again.'

Seething, he left Land's office before he said something he would really regret. Raymond had fought for them in the past, but there was a weakness within him that more ruthless supervisors could exploit. With Arthur out doing God knows what, he saw that he would once again have to contravene instructions and take on his bosses.

When he entered his office, he found that Arthur had pinned a map of the night sky on the teacher's blackboard behind his desk, and had taped notes over each of the constellations, including some labelled 'Not Visible to the Naked Eye'. *This is all we've got,* he thought, *a few solitary points of light, and there's no way of connecting them into something meaningful without more data.*

Thinking that there was nothing more he could do without his partner, he sat down to wait for his return. But his eye was drawn back to the constellation chart again. *Do what Arthur would do,* he thought, *find a way to connect them.* Sliding out his mobile, he checked the number he had scribbled on his pad and made a call.

Orion Banks was in a taxi opposite the offices of the PCU, stuck in traffic. She wiped the condensation from the window with a paper handkerchief and looked up. John May was standing at a first-floor window, peering out. Of the officers she had met there, she had liked him the most, but even he would have to go.

Banks had reached the top of the career ladder by playing as hard as the men. Behind a smokescreen of flirtatious mediaspeak was a calculating machine that weighed everyone's worth in terms of economic value to the company. She had a clutch of degrees that included criminal law; she smoked and drank and double-crossed with less empathy than any male in her department, and would string up her closest colleague for target practice if the need arose. It was what they had hired her to do, and she did the job well. At night she returned to an empty apartment decorated by a designer she had never met in person, to drink expensive wine alone and go over the accounts. She had no hobbies, no real friends, no family to speak of. She had work, and that was enough so long as she stayed on top. God alone knew what would happen after that.

She had been furious to discover just how little control Raymond Land had over his department. In her eyes he was worse than useless and should have been pensioned off years ago, but since the economic downturn her budget could no longer afford to make hefty payouts. The unit's senior detectives operated with wildly different methodology and appeared at odds with one another. The rest of the staff behaved like the remnants of some defunct government outpost. At least she didn't have to make them look bad; they were capable of doing that by themselves.

Within her jurisdiction, financial crime was now costing an estimated £38 billion a year. Highly organized international gangs were infiltrating the City's financial institutions at every level, committing insurance frauds on an epic scale and operating an amorphous bribery system that was proving almost impossible to stop. Down in the street, bicycles and mobiles were being stolen, and a few drunken lads got a ticking-off. Anti-social crimes, robberies and assaults had dropped away to their lowest-ever levels while the real losses occurred high above, in the City's boardrooms. There was no longer any room in the system for a bucket shop like the PCU, or any need for it.

'What is the hold-up here?' she snapped at the taxi driver.

'Roadworks,' came the reply. 'There's nothing I can do, luv.'

'I'm not your love,' said Banks angrily. 'There's always something you can do about it. Turn left here.'

'But that's a one-way street.'

'I'll take care of any consequences,' she said, sitting back. 'Just do it.'

May took a tube to Tower Hill and walked to Ensign Street, behind the Tower of London, one of those city areas that remained isolated because it was awkward to reach. He was near the once-desirable address of Wellclose Square, where so many East End Jewish intellectuals had lived. The neighbourhood was an odd mix of impoverished artists and city singles, the mysteries and scandals of the square and its cabalists consigned to footnotes of arcane London history.

Irina Cope was small and appealing, with cropped blonde hair and pretty features rendered slightly imperfect by a short chin. The late-afternoon air had grown cool, and she rubbed at her arms, underdressed for another grim London summer. 'There's a café in Wilton's Music Hall,' she said. 'We can go there, if you like. I'd take you to the flat but we have builders in.'

'I know how you feel,' said May. 'We've had builders in our office for the last eight months.'

They made their way over to the old Victorian music hall, where a few office workers sat in the soft afternoon light with coffees and iPads. Posters advertised cabaret shows by Marc Almond, Rufus Wainwright, dance troupes and various stand-up comics. The elegant building had been saved from the wrecker's ball, but still survived on barely more than the goodwill of its neighbours.

'In other countries they'd preserve a building as rare and beautiful as this,' said Cope, looking about and guessing his thoughts. 'Here they have to rely on charitable donations. I'm sorry, it winds me up. I run a small architectural practice on Cable Street, and unfortunately I know a little too much about what the council gets up to around here.'

Cope made her way to a bench and settled herself as May collected coffees. 'I don't know how much use I can be,' she said, accepting a cup. 'It started just over a week ago.'

'Can you remember exactly how?' asked May.

'Krishna came home from work and told me that Mr Wallace had been found hanged.'

So he knew, thought May. *Why did he pretend he didn't?*

'We were due to go out to dinner with someone from Berry and Rudd – Krishna collects fine wine, and wanted some advice – and on the way back from the restaurant we saw the car following us. We were on foot, coming back from Boundary – you know the restaurant?'

'I'm a police officer, Ms Cope, I don't get to eat in fancy restaurants.'

'Sorry, I suppose with your hours . . .'

'It's not the time, although we rarely finish before ten p.m. It's the pay. Please, go on.'

'Krishna saw the car first – an old blue Renault. He said he recognized it – he's got the kind of mechanical mind that remembers cars before people – there was a woman driving. He was pretty sure it was Mrs Wallace.'

'And you saw her again?'

'Outside the flat two mornings later. The woman in the flat above has lots of potted plants on her balcony – it's annoying because when she waters them the run-off gets into our bedroom window frames. Krishna had just left for work when I heard a bang. I went out to find that one of the biggest flowerpots had fallen and had just missed him. He could have been killed. You can easily get on to the balcony from the next one down, and we think she climbed on to it and waited for him.'

'You saw her?'

'Not on the balcony, but I saw her walking quickly away down the street. There have been other things: somebody chalking filth on the front door, crazy stuff.'

'You didn't report this?'

'Krishna wouldn't let me. He felt guilty about her. She'd lost her husband, and he knew the guy had been depressed over losing their account. We figured she'd stop after a while.'

'And has she?'

'I don't know. Last night I thought I saw someone out-side the window – just a shape against the street lights, but you can never be sure. Our bed's near the window and sometimes, well, it's a safe-enough area these days but even so you have to keep an eye out for suspicious behaviour.'

'I think I should talk to Mrs Wallace again,' said May. 'If I can get her to acknowledge the fact that she blames you, maybe we can move this thing on.'

'You know, I've read about your unit,' said Cope, placing his name. 'You're the guys who believe in psycho-geography, that sort of thing.'

'You're talking about the article in *Hard News*, I imagine. That's my partner. I'm not quite so easily convinced.'

'Yeah, but you know what's funny? Living in this area. Your partner must know about it.'

'Why's that?'

'All kinds of strange things have happened here. One of my neighbours is a priest and he told me that once, back in the mid-1800s, two missionaries from St Saviour's went to a dead girl's house in this street to administer the last rites. In the church there was supposed to be a relic, a sliver of the True Cross, the Cross of Golgotha, and they took it with them and laid it on the girl's chest, and she rose up from the dead. And when they built the new houses here last summer, they found hundreds of gravestones everyone had forgotten about. We're literally walking around on top of corpses.'

'London's a city of the dead, Ms Cope. They're beneath us everywhere.'

'Me, I'm easily spooked, so when this woman started following me on my way back from the shops I didn't turn and confront her like I should have, I just kept going. I should move away from this part of town but Krishna loves it here. He says when our ship comes in we'll go to the north of the city. Isn't that what the people with aspirations always do, seek higher ground?'

May was drawn to Irina Cope. She seemed so sensitive to her surroundings that he was almost fearful for her.

'I'll talk to Mrs Wallace and keep her away from you,' he promised. 'Nobody should have to be afraid of walking down their own street at night.'

He was as good as his word. Marchmont Street was on the way back to the unit, so he looked in on the off chance of finding Vanessa Wallace at home. Her son Martin answered the door with a game console glowing in one hand. 'Oh, it's you,' he said. 'I thought that creepy guy had come back again.' He sounded slightly less sullen than the first time they had met, but still refused to catch May's eye.

'Which creepy guy?' May asked.

'The fat one who giggles all the time. Rummage, the undertaker guy. I think he waits until Mum's out before ringing the doorbell.'

'Why does he come around?'

'When Dad's coffin got dug up he still didn't have a proper headstone, so Rummage says he's going to provide us with one free of charge, but he's come around twice now without calling first. I reckon he's a paedo.'

'Where's your mother?'

'At her yoga class, trying these exercises that are meant to calm her down. She's still all stressed out about Dad.'

'I'm sorry to hear that,' said May. 'I came by to see how she was.'

'She cries all the time and keeps having a go at me, that's how she is. Did you find out anything yet?'

'Honestly? No, we're not making much progress. Hopefully something will break. How are you handling it?'

'Sometimes I think he's still in the house. I'll go to the bottom of the stairs and call up, then remember. I guess I have a different way of dealing with it. I don't get depressed, I get angry. I do sports and try to burn it out.'

'Anger can be useful if you channel it,' said May. 'Has your mother been going out by herself?'

'Sometimes, yeah.'

'Will you keep an eye on her? We've had reports she's been bothering Mr Jhadav and his girlfriend, following them around.'

'Oh jeez. I wondered where she's been heading off to. She wouldn't tell me.'

'The other day she nearly killed him. I don't want to see her get into trouble. Do me a favour – call me the next time she leaves without telling you where she's going?' He handed Martin his card. 'And while you're at it, let me know if Mr Rummage calls on the house again.'

That undertaker, May thought. *He's cropping up all over the place.*

23

THE HEADSMAN

As shoppers dragged themselves back and forth to the depressing Tesco supermarket on the corner, few ever looked up at the building on Caledonian Road. If they did they would have seen a short, balding man in a rumpled grey suit with his back to the window. Of those who looked, none would have thought that the people in the room were, in their own odd ways, attempting to prevent the streets of London from descending into anarchy and chaos.

Of course, Raymond Land was an uninspiring figure-head from any angle. 'Ah, you're back,' he exclaimed, slapping his hands together with sour delight. 'So kind of you to grace us with your presence. And it's only Thursday.'

'Don't try to be funny, Raymondo. I've been working, as you well know,' said Bryant, pulling off his ancient trilby and leaving behind a frightened tonsure of white hair. Half a dozen mewling kittens followed in his wake. They appeared to have adopted Bryant as a parental figure.

'What, no snappy comeback today? After abandoning your post and leaving your partner to struggle on with an investigation that has stalled so badly that I can find nothing at all to report back on? What on earth have you been doing?'

Bryant picked up one of the kittens and scuffed it behind the ears. 'Exactly what you wanted me to do,' he replied. 'I've been staying out of the way, keeping my nose clean and trying not to bring the unit into disrepute.'

'Well, can you stop doing so?' Land demanded. 'It's getting on my nerves. I keep looking around half expecting to see you emptying your pipe into my plant pot or breaking the photocopier. Instead, everyone's just getting on with their work and nothing's getting resolved. It's most disconcerting. We're about to be removed from the case, and I don't think it's very likely that we'll be given anything else.'

'That should make you happy, surely. You'll be pensioned off to the Orkneys and you'll finally get some peace and quiet.'

'I don't want to be pensioned off,' said Land gloomily. 'Leanne isn't coming back. She won't even speak to me. The divorce is going ahead. I go home to a silent house and piles of unlaundered shirts.' He pulled at his frayed cuff. 'Look at this. I can't figure out how to work the washing machine. It seems to have hundreds of different settings, and the instruction book is in Swedish. I've run out of pants. I need some stability in my life. Without the PCU I don't know what I'd do.'

'Well, thank you for sharing that, but your pants are not my concern,' said Bryant. 'Am I to take it that you're allowing me back?'

'Yes. Oh yes.' Land practically fell on his knees.

'And I can run things as I see fit?'

'Do whatever you have to do, you can even keep your eyeball collection in the staff fridge, just give me something I can use.'

'Very well,' said Bryant. 'I shall put the kettle on, absorb a pipeful of Old Nautical Rough Cut Navy Shag and play my Gilbert and Sullivan records. Then we shall see what can be done.'

Land hated himself for being so weak. But he was glad to have Bryant on the team once more.

'I'm going to do something that could get me into serious trouble,' said Bryant, settling himself behind his desk, 'and I need your help.'

'It wouldn't be the first time,' sighed May.

'I said *me*, not all of us. I've been offered help with the Romain Curtis investigation in return for keeping away from the ravens.' He pushed aside a pile of ornithology manuals so that he could see his partner. 'But if I don't find out why the birds vanished, Matthew Condright will lose his job. He's the Raven Master of the Tower. He suffered severe post-traumatic stress disorder after fighting in the Falklands, and needs to keep his position.'

'I don't understand,' said May. 'Who's offering you this deal?'

'It's better that you don't know. I'm going to surreptitiously continue with the case, and I need you to cover my tracks.'

'How will this person even know what you're up to?' May's eyes narrowed with suspicion. 'It's that Mr Merry again, isn't it?'

Bryant glanced at the back of his hand, remembering the contract he had reluctantly signed. 'He presents himself as some kind of dark magician, but I think the reality is somewhat different. So-called necromancers keep their power by exploiting the credulity of others, but he's met his match with me. He uses the power of suggestion to undermine those around him. He wants me to think I can make no move without him seeing. But you can throw him off the scent for me.'

'How?'

'I suspect that, like the leaders of most gangs, he has a network of spies working for him, so I'll need to be careful.'

'What are you supposed to be getting in return, exactly?'

'This,' said Bryant, holding up a card. 'An invitation to meet with the New Resurrectionists.'

'I dread to ask.'

'Then don't. I'm supposed to find their representative under the tree outside St Magnus the Martyr's Church, just off Lower Thames Street. I will then be blindfolded and taken to a secret location. I need someone to follow me. Not a familiar face. Meera could do it on her motorbike.'

'What is the purpose of this, Arthur? They could be a bunch of lunatics.'

'And they could also hold the key to why Thomas Wallace was dug up and the only witness killed.'

'When is this going to happen?'

'At eleven p.m. tonight. First I have to go back to the Tower of London. You could get me there.'

'Why don't you do these things remotely? Dan can rig up CCTV feeds, video-links; there's all kinds of technology you can use.'

'There's something I have to physically check for myself. It's to do with that.' Bryant pointed back at his 1959 Dansette gramophone. A terrible wailing sound was issuing from a warped old record. 'Gilbert and Sullivan,' he said brightly, as if that explained everything.

'Keep your head down,' said May as his silver BMW turned the corner into Euston Road.

'I have a bad back, you know,' Bryant complained from halfway under the passenger seat. 'This is an undignified position for a man of my age to be in.'

'You said you couldn't risk being followed so we'll do this my way, all right?'

'This car blanket smells of perfume – have you had a lady in here?'

'I might have done. Not recently, sadly.'

'No, well, you're getting on a bit.'

'I'm always going to be three years younger than you.'

'Yes, but when the petals begin to fall from the rose—'

'I know, I know, the bees don't come round so often. Stop saying that. I can't see anyone following us.'

'That's the point, you're not supposed to.'

'Wait, there is something.' May adjusted his rear-view mirror. 'Skinny bloke on a bike in an unfeasibly tight French racing outfit.' Bryant stuck his head up. 'Stay down – he's on his mobile. I'll cut through the backstreets. Let's see if he can keep up.'

May swung the BMW left into Bloomsbury. 'It's OK,' he said, 'it looks like we've already lost him.'

'Good,' said Bryant. 'Can I come up now?'

'Well I'm damned.' May checked his mirror again. 'He must have called ahead. I think another bloke on a bicycle has taken over from him. Same red helmet and outfit. Your nemesis is a latter-day Fagin.'

As the BMW crossed the city, the cyclists followed in relay, five of them in all. Each one picked up immediately after a call from the one before.

The detectives were now passing tourists on the steps of St Paul's Cathedral. Riot-jacketed police were arguing with some anti-capitalism protestors, one of whom was carrying a placard of a giant pink pig dressed as a banker. The cyclist behind them swerved out to avoid the brawl, locking back into place behind the car.

May was amazed. 'Your contact has a very thorough network helping him. I need to get rid of this one before he realizes that we're going to the Tower. He just missed the last set of lights. Get ready to slip out. You can get into Bank station and walk through the underpass to Monument, then go one stop on the District or Circle to Tower

Hill. Can you manage without your walking stick?'

'Certainly. I use it out of affectation, nothing more.'

Liar, thought May. 'Get ready to do a stunt-roll.'

'Where's the cyclist?'

'Three or four vehicles back, but he'll have to go down the side of a bus to catch up, which gives you a few seconds. OK, now!'

May shoved open the door and Bryant all but fell on to the pavement. The entrance to the tube was just ahead. He scampered into it, much to the surprise of a woman coming up the steps.

No, it can't be, thought Orion Banks as she emerged from the station. She looked back, but the scruffy, scuttling old man had already vanished from sight.

The underpass was almost deserted. If anyone pursued him down here, he would see them. Bryant followed the arrows through the subterranean maze, heading for Monument tube station.

As soon as he emerged from Tower Hill, he called the Raven Master. 'Matthew, I need you to get me in through a discreet side entrance,' he said. 'I'll explain later.'

Within another ten minutes he was standing, out of breath, in a screened-off area of the Warders' oak-lined dining hall. 'This is the refectory you rent out to city aldermen, for mayoral functions and so on?' asked Bryant, inspecting the space.

'That's right,' said Condright. 'We have events a couple of times a week throughout the summer.'

Bryant went to the mullioned window and looked down. 'How far are we from the raven house?'

'Right next door.'

'And your annual performance of *The Yeomen of the Guard*? Is this where you hold it?'

'Well, the play is set against the backdrop of the Tower of London, so it really does become site-specific here. There are public performances held in the moat so that the White Tower is in the background, but they also put it on for privately invited audiences, and in inclement weather there's a stage that they can move into this room.'

'And I'm right in thinking that you had a production the night before you missed the ravens?'

'That's correct. Actually, there were seven performances in all, for different charity groups. But I fail to see—'

'It's not an official D'Oyly Carte production, but your own company, I understand.'

'That's right.'

'So the costumes are stored here.'

'I think so.' Condright led him behind the screen, where they found a set of clothing rails. Period outfits were numbered and hung along them in plastic bags.

'The Headsman, the man who is due to execute Colonel Fairfax with his axe, his outfit is here with all the rest?'

'I suppose so.'

'Who usually plays him?'

'Well, it's a silent role and the Headsman is masked, so as long as he's physically big we usually find one of the men to stand in.'

'And on that night, who played him?'

'I don't know. I'll have to check.'

Bryant found the garment bag he was looking for and un-zipped it. He removed a black body stocking, a black hood and mask, studded leather gloves and a long black cloak. He smelled patchouli oil and tobacco.

'What are you looking for?' asked Condright.

'I think somebody stayed behind after the tours finished and infiltrated your company. If the show began at seven he would have had less than an hour to wait. Then, after the performance, he could have made his way downstairs to the raven cage, picked the lock and gathered up the birds somehow. Which means there should be a hidden compartment here . . . Blast.' Bryant turned the cloak inside out. 'I was sure there'd be one.'

'He'd never have got seven ravens into that thing, even if he'd found a way to drug them first,' said Condright.

'You're right,' Bryant reluctantly agreed. 'But perhaps over seven nights . . .'

'No. I know some of the men who played the Headsman. There are different ones on different nights.'

'But he *was* here, I'm sure of it,' Bryant insisted. 'The theatricality – it has his touch. He came and disguised himself as the Headsman to get the lay of the land. Then he left by hiding himself among the guests. And at some point later, he must have returned.'

'I don't understand why anyone would go to so much trouble,' said Condright.

'I think I do. Oh, he was here, all right.' Bryant zipped up the bag, but the necromancer's distinctive aroma lingered. 'To nail him, I have to know how he did it.'

24

ALTRUISM

Arthur Bryant arrived at St Magnus the Martyr's Church by bus because he knew it was the last thing anyone would expect him to do. Looking down from the top deck he had seen the dark surface of the Thames buffeted by rain-squalled winds, and felt the cold hand of Mr Merry guiding him into a trap.

The necromancer was anxious not to be derailed from his purpose. But what was that? To set in motion the fall of the kingdom through apotropaic magic and the burial of live birds on some hallowed site? Even for Bryant, it was too absurd to contemplate. And, surely, Mr Merry would not wish to be entirely rid of him. Fellow travellers on London's arcane byways were increasingly rare, and their presence was to be valued. Merry would only act against him if he contravened his instructions. Of course, he had already done that by secretly continuing to investigate the theft of the ravens. The main thing now was to make sure that his nemesis did not find out.

He took shelter beneath the tree and waited, wondering where Meera had got to. Looking from the back of the bus he had failed to spot her motorbike following behind. She was usually ridiculously punctual. He surveyed the traffic waiting at the crossroads and failed to see her Kawasaki.

'Mr Bryant,' said a deep, accented voice. 'Don't turn around, please.'

Bryant froze and waited. He needed to hear more. 'I wasn't sure if this was the right place,' he said. 'Do we have to go far?'

'Not very far. I'm afraid I will need to cover your eyes.'

'Won't that look a bit suspicious to anyone passing by?' *He's Italian,* he thought, *but there's something else. It's a Resian dialect. He's Italian-Slovenian.*

'We've thought of that. Please put these on.' A hand passed him a pair of wraparound sunglasses that had been blacked out. They fitted awkwardly on his broad nose, but did the job; he could see nothing. He took the proffered hand and placed himself at the mercy of his contact.

There were a dozen steps to a car – he had not seen a vehicle pull up and had certainly not heard it; perhaps it was electric? No, just quiet; a small model, cramped in the back. Once within, the outside world was muffled.

'Can you crack the window slightly? I suffer from asthma,' Bryant lied. His driver seemed willing to comply. A hand reached over and buzzed the window down a little. The sounds of the street returned.

Bryant decided he could learn more by not speaking. Instead, he listened. There was an opening out of sound – sudden crosswinds and the squawk of seagulls: they were crossing the river. That meant they were heading over London Bridge. Depending on which way the vehicle turned, they would go right to Southwark, left towards Bermondsey or straight on to Borough.

They continued straight. The sound of traffic built up around the vehicle, trucks and buses mostly. That meant they were sticking to the main arterial road leading to the Elephant & Castle.

There were lots of halts at traffic lights. He counted

them, judging the distance between each set. The driver seemed disinclined to speak. They would have to follow the one-way system around, but then it got tricky to separate out the direction; so many roads spread out from the great roundabout.

For a while he was lost. There was nothing outside to give him a purchase on their geography. Then, a sharp left turn, a quieter road but a faster one, with a drop in sound on one side, and cooler, fresher air; it had to be Burgess Park, a wide, flat field bordered by greenery, with a new cycling track and a lake. None of the other turnings had this many trees on one side. They continued in a direct line for a few minutes, then made a turn on to a much quieter road, a left, a right, another right and a halt. They had stopped somewhere in the heart of Peckham.

Although he hadn't quite been around long enough to witness the birth of the area, it was a place he knew all too well. First mentioned in the Domesday Book as Pecheha, or 'village among the hills', Peckham was as far from an English village as one could imagine. Once it had provided a grazing pasture for farmers driving cattle to London, then it had been colonized by wealthy families in grand houses. Its greatest fame came as a breeding ground for academics and nonconformists, as colleges and meeting houses proliferated.

The Grand Surrey Canal turned the village into a town, bringing gas companies, railways and speculative builders. Soon the remaining fields were paved over. Victorian terraces were replaced by massive housing estates and gang rule. In 2000, the murder of ten-year-old Damilola Taylor led to Old Bailey trials and criticism of the criminal justice system. There were the glimmerings of regeneration in this most deprived and neglected part of the city, but some of the more unorthodox students and teachers had stayed on through the social upheavals, working in a place where few would notice them. It was likely that the New Resurrectionists would find a welcome here.

Hands reached in and lifted him out. He was led on to the pavement, up three steps, and heard a key scrabble for a lock. The street at his back was silent; where had Meera got to?

A hand pressed against his back. The air grew cooler and mustier, the smell of mouldy plaster and damp floorboards. More steps, then the murmur of voices. Light around the edges of the sunglasses now. He caught the ends of hushed sentences:

'—shouldn't be here.'

'—no choice. Someone has to—'

'—risk to ourselves.'

The glasses came off and he was given a chair. It was so cool in the stone-walled hall that he half expected to see his breath.

He found himself in a long white chapel with peeling paintwork and a half-demolished minstrels' gallery at one end. A white plastic curtain separated off the rear section on a makeshift rail. There were three young men and one woman in black cloth eye-masks watching him. Two of the males were in lab coats. The others wore jeans and sweaters and looked like students. Two were non-Caucasian. All were in their mid-twenties. The man who had driven him here indicated the others. 'You don't need to know who we are.'

'Why did you agree to meet with me at all?' Bryant asked.

'We need your help.'

'I don't see how I'll be able to help you if there's going to be all this secrecy.'

'Our identities aren't important. It's our work that counts. You are the detective who set up the Peculiar Crimes Unit, aren't you?'

Bryant shrugged. 'It was a government initiative, but yes.'

'What does it do exactly?'

'It deals with cases that represent a risk to public order and morale.'

'Kind of an old-fashioned idea in this day and age.'

'Not really. You have spin doctors now, but they can't actually solve problems, merely finesse them. If someone gets attacked in a park, we don't tell everyone parks are safe, we catch the attacker.'

'You've been doing this for a long time?'

'My partner and I were young, inexperienced students. We were employed because we were free of preconceptions and eager to learn. It was a challenge.'

'So you were free thinkers. The methods you chose to employ contravened the orthodoxy of the times.'

'Yes, and they're the methods we continue to use, despite all attempts to stop us,' said Bryant. 'Over the years we've been able to keep a handful of friends in positions of influence.'

'Then you'll appreciate our dilemma.' The speaker indicated his friends. 'We all trained in medical colleges, but our ideas were considered too advanced, too radical—'

'You mean you were all thrown out.' He looked from one masked face to the next. 'Weren't you?'

'What the medical establishment thinks of us is unimportant. Our work is what matters.'

'And what work might that be?'

'You're no stranger to the application of alternative therapies, Mr Bryant. We're taking them further, into a practical realm.'

'I don't know what that involves,' said Bryant.

'It means we're required to take steps that our paranoid nanny state finds unacceptable.'

'I assume you mean that you disinter bodies and conduct experiments on them directly, unlike your forebears, who sold them on for money.'

'We don't believe in Burking the dead, Mr Bryant,' said

another of the males. 'We've tried other methods – virtual anatomy has its uses, but even if you create an online application that factors in random flaws it still doesn't provide a realistic experience. There's the weight, mass and deterioration of organs to take into account, for a start. In a computer program you can set levels to which organs degrade according to the health of the individual, but in many major respects it's still unsatisfactory, except as a teaching tool. The human body is not a matrix of logarithms you can endlessly download and reprogram. It's a thing of meat and humours and spirit. So as educated activists, we returned to earlier methods with a proven success rate.'

'What are you talking about?' said Bryant, his sense of caution overtaken by the need to involve himself in the argument. 'Burke and Hare were corpse-robbers who sold half-rotted cadavers of no use to any real medical practitioners.' He had a sudden thought. *What if these people murdered to fulfil their quota of bodies, just like their ill-fated forebears?*

'Our work is real and important,' said the girl, who he now realized was Spanish. 'Show him.'

The others parted and pulled back the white plastic curtain. Behind it, splayed on a long wooden bench, was the naked body of an elderly man at an advanced stage of his autopsy. 'We've already found new uses for tissue to accelerate apoptosis – programmed cell death – and to encourage wound debridement,' said one of the masked boys.

'You think you can find something generations of experienced doctors overlooked?'

'Their hands are tied by the BMA.'

'Were you involved in the death of Thomas Wallace?' asked Bryant.

'Not his death. But he was disinterred by one of the group.'

'What could you have wanted with him?' Bryant demanded to know. The students' naivety was dangerous. 'Wallace committed suicide by ligature hanging. As I'm sure you know, his deoxygenated blood would have permeated his brain tissue. He'd been in the ground for over sixty hours. He wouldn't have been of much use to you.'

'We didn't want him for studies. One of our number agreed to carry out the work.'

'Why? Did he try to dig up Elspeth Duncannon as well?'

'Listen, old man, we brought you here,' said the girl. 'It's our turn to ask questions. One of the members of our group is missing.'

'The one who dug up Wallace. He did it for money, didn't he?'

'We were about to be thrown out of the building. We needed to find some cash fast. He was approached with an extremely lucrative offer. We talked it over. We weren't happy with the arrangement, but we were in a difficult position.'

'Did he know that he was being hired to disinter Wallace?'

'Yes, but he wasn't informed of the project's purpose, and he wasn't allowed to talk to any of us about it. That was part of the deal. Since then, no one's been able to get hold of him.'

'I can't find him for you unless you can assure me that you have never committed murder in order to get – material – for your research.' Bryant studied each of them in turn, demanding a promise.

They spoke together for a moment and agreed. 'We can give you our word on that.'

'But we would kill,' said the girl angrily. 'If a handful of people had to die to make an advance that could save thousands, wouldn't you do it? We don't seek to make money from what we do. The world needs cures, and somebody has to find them even though it means violating a few sensitivities.'

'Murder is more than just a violation of sensitivities, young lady. It's a boundary that cannot be crossed. If you do, you take the path that led to Josef Mengele injecting dye into children's eyes.'

The girl looked horrified. 'Such behaviour is anathema to us.'

'Then I'll do what I can for you, but I make no promises – you're operating outside the law, and I won't be able to protect you.'

'If you thought that you could change the way organ degeneration was diagnosed, and it meant bending the rules to do so, wouldn't you do it?'

'In theory, yes,' Bryant admitted. 'But in practice? What will you do without clinical trials, long-term research, published papers? You're as powerless as any homeopathy quack or scientologist peddling miracle cures to the credulous. You'll have no peer approval to back up your findings.'

'Our work will provide all the evidence we need.'

'Then you're more naive than I thought. You will never find a more willing champion for your cause than me, but I know what will happen. Every part of the establishment will unite to close its doors against you. They'll scapegoat you, and you'll go to jail. I understand how the system works. I've been an outsider all my life.'

'But things are changing. You think we're the only privately run medical society in the country? We're linked online in deep network sites, sharing our research in ways you could never imagine.'

'You still have to get it accepted, and that can't happen without social change.'

'There's not enough time to wait for that. The world is less than twenty years away from depleting food and water stocks and losing most of the species that contain the genetic make-up to save us,' said the oldest of the group. 'The only way left is to force change on to people whether they agree or not.'

'Perhaps we can argue about your altruism another time and get to the point here,' said Bryant, anxious to remind them that they were holding a police officer. 'You want me to find your chap, I need to know why he "resurrected" Wallace, and we're both running out of time. If I agree to do it, I'll have to at least know his name.'

The students discussed the matter and reached an agreement. 'Very well,' said the one who had driven him. 'We'll give you his details on the condition that you don't use him to trace a path back to us. The rest of us have to be able to keep our identities secret.'

'If I find out that he was directly involved in murder, our deal is off.'

After a moment's discussion among themselves, they folded the details into his hand. Bryant allowed himself to be blindfolded once more and was taken back out into the night streets.

25

DEATH AMONG THE GRAVESTONES

He kept the shovel wrapped in a black bin liner. It was tightly laced with brown parcel tape, but it still looked like a shovel. There were some objects you couldn't hide.

Walking along Bayswater Road towards the Victoria Gate Lodge, he felt self-conscious and stupid, like an undertaker going to work. The only people who passed him were Chinese tourists who were stopping every few yards to excitedly take photographs of lamp-posts and tobacconists'. It was raining lightly, and droplets fell from the beech leaves overhanging the railings on to his bare head. He flicked open his mobile and checked the directions once more.

It was later than he thought. He peered through the fortifying iron staves of the park's perimeter, but it was dark beneath the trees and he could not identify the site. There were supposed to be over three hundred graves in this forgotten corner of Hyde Park, but he could not see them. Worse still, he could not even find a way inside. He was nearing Lancaster Gate tube station now, but there was no break in the railing. There was only one thing for it; waiting until the pavement was clear on both sides, he scaled the spikes and dropped down into the wet grass.

He had brought a key-ring torch and flicked it on to search behind the lodge walls. His beam picked them up, rows of headstones, many of them half buried by grassy earth. Once they had been neatly ordered, but now most had been twisted by movements in the soil and were covered in moss, their ironwork inscriptions barely readable. He was looking for a grave-marker bearing the name 'Prince', with a burial date of a week ago.

He realized that finding it would take him longer than he'd expected. Crouching low among the first line of headstones, he began to decipher their dedications.

A green Jeep cruised slowly through the parklands, its lone occupant checking beneath the surrounding trees. He dropped to his stomach and lay between the plots, hoping that the branches would provide enough cover. Once he was sure that he had not been seen, he rose and continued his search. He found himself walking over stone plaques – they were everywhere.

It was a hell of a way to pay off the rent, he decided, but the money had been too good to turn down. After this they wouldn't have to worry about getting kicked out, and he could use the rest to make a dent in his student loan. The torch beam caught a name picked out in black iron: 'Ruby Heart'. Beneath ran an inscription: 'You Will Never Be Forgotten Or Replaced'. He had been told to look for fresh earth near the border of the cemetery, but the borders were unclear. Some graves had been added so that their plots thrust into and under the surrounding greenery.

The rain started falling harder. It was suddenly noisy beneath the trees. A summer night in London; he was chilled to the bone. It took him another twenty minutes to locate the plot, so small and insignificant that he realized he had passed it several times.

Unwrapping the shovel, he began to dig. Every now and

again the headlamps of a bus strobed through from the other side of the park railing, striping him in yellow light. Each time, he froze and waited for it to pass. Once he heard a noise in the bushes nearby, but decided it was just a squirrel or a fox foraging for food.

The earth came up easily beneath his spade. It had not been tamped down, and the rain had made it malleable. After he had lifted out most of the soil at the foot of the marker, he knelt in the mud and dug his hands down, feeling for the edge of the coffin. It was so small that once his fingers found purchase under the edge he was able to work it loose and easily lift it from the hole. He had brought a Swiss Army knife and a screwdriver, and set to work on the lid.

Another rustle in the bushes made him stop and listen.

He waited for a moment to see if whatever it was in the shadowed branches would move again, but now all he could hear was the rain falling hard on the leaves. Opening the knife and searching among its tools, he found a serrated blade and worked it into the seal.

The coffin burst open, releasing an appalling smell. Covering his mouth with a handkerchief he searched his pockets with his free hand, looking for his rubber gloves. That was when he became aware that there was something or someone in the bushes ahead of him. It was too big to be a fox, and appeared to be off the ground, resting on a fork in the branches.

As he set down the casket and tried to rise, there was an odd clicking sound. Moments later the air cleaved and something passed just inches from his left cheek. At first he thought someone had thrown a stick, but the object had moved too fast. Turning, he saw a silver arrow angled out of the ground a few feet behind him.

His boot slipped in the mud and he fell awkwardly as he heard the quarrel released from the crossbow stock once more. A second later he felt a searing pain more terrible than anything he could imagine. Hurled backward by the impact, his head hit the tree root behind him with a crack. He felt as if he had been pinned to it like a moth on a board.

As he began to lose consciousness, his attacker reached his side. Even as he tried to understand what was happening, he started praying that no one would come to disinter him if he died.

'Nasty,' said Dan Banbury. 'Not an accident.'

'Bloody hell, I can see that,' said May, walking around the sheeted body. It was 6.10 a.m. on Friday and already light, although the roads beyond the park were still quiet and empty.

'Just thought I should rule it out.' Banbury crouched low in the wet grass, trying to loosen the first arrow without cutting his plastic gloves. 'Lightweight steel shaft, razor-sharp tip. No wonder it did so much damage. The assailant took two shots. Didn't take the arrows away because he couldn't get them back out. The only light would have been from those street lamps back there, and given the shifting shadows from the branches overhead it couldn't have been an easy target.'

'Ah, there you are,' said Bryant, attempting to disentangle his coat from a nearby bush. 'I've been looking for you for ages.'

'Where have you been?' May asked.

'Round the back of the lodge. Very enlightening: miniature tombstones everywhere. Like a cemetery for dwarves. Where's our victim?'

Banbury lifted a corner of the green plastic sheet. Bryant winced. 'Ooh, that's nasty. Right through the left eye.'

'And almost out of the back of the skull, incredibly,' said Banbury. 'I don't suppose he suffered much. Not the sort of thing you expect to find in a London park, though.'

'You know, before the familiar image of the Grim Reaper appeared with his scythe, ready to harvest souls, he used to appear in illustrations armed with a crossbow and an arrow. Suggestive, don't you think?'

'Suggestive of your morbid imagination,' said Banbury, unimpressed.

'Who is he?' The corpse was that of a young man in a cheap dark blue anorak and jeans, his face shockingly white against the dark jade grass.

'We thought you'd know.'

Bryant added his spectacles just to make sure, but shook his head. 'I've never seen him before.'

Banbury looked around. 'What are all these little graves?'

'It's the Hyde Park pet cemetery,' Bryant explained. 'Hardly anybody is aware that it's here. It was started by accident by a Maltese terrier called Cherry. The lodge keeper had befriended his owners. When Cherry died, he allowed the creature to be buried here.'

'Why would animals be buried here of all places?'

'Dogs often got crushed under the hooves of the carriage-horses on Bayswater Road. Soon everyone was asking him if they could plant their pets here. There ended up being hundreds.'

'This is all very riveting, but right now we have a young man virtually nailed to a tree through his eye socket,' said May testily. 'And either he was one of your resurrectionists, or it's a very strange coincidence. He'd just finished digging up a dog. A Jack Russell.'

'*New* Resurrectionists,' Bryant corrected, 'and I think it's likely he was my man. He fits the description I was given.'

'The name Stephen Emes ring a bell?' asked Banbury. 'Barclaycard, back pocket.'

'That's him. Dan, get some tests run on the shovel, will you? Dabs, traces from other sites, anything you can pull off.' He squinted into the distance. 'The arrow had to come from somewhere over there, yes?'

Banbury followed Bryant's pointing finger to a gap where the bushes met the lime trees. 'I imagine so, but don't go stamping all over the earth, let me mark up a grid and do a search before this rain takes everything out.'

'And you'll need to bag up Prince here, and his little coffin,' said Bryant. 'John and I can find out who his owner is.'

'I suppose you know what he was doing here,' said May, looking down at the body skewered by the steel shaft in its skull.

'Not really, no. I just got hired to find him. I had a bit of a run-in with the rest of his crowd last night. The Bleeding Heart is pierced by five arrows. A sign of life, but not in this case, apparently.'

'I don't pretend to know what you're talking about,' said May irritably. Bryant proceeded to explain what had happened in the Peckham chapel.

'And just when were you going to inform us about this?' May asked. 'I *am* supposed to be your partner.'

'I hadn't seen you, had I? I got home, went to bed and was woken up to come here.'

'According to the emails on his phone, it looks like he disappeared from King's College a few months ago,' said Banbury. 'His friends have been worried about him. I'll let you have the call log.'

'You already had time to go through them?' asked Bryant, amazed. The PCU had no access to Metropolitan Police databanks without first acquiring permission.

'It only took me ten minutes.' Banbury tapped his jacket. 'Portable tech.'

Bryant was disgusted. 'I can't even open my emails in that time.'

May took the sheet off the body for one more look. With his head at the overgrown base of the tree and one foot curled beneath the other leg, the corpse had a distinctly Pre-Raphaelite air.

'Are you sure you want this?' Banbury lifted up the bloated body of the dead Jack Russell and lowered it into a plastic bag.

'What the hell was he doing here, digging up the corpse of a dog?' May wondered. 'This raises more questions than it answers. If he's our serial unburier, who killed him?'

'We should be able to place him at St George's Gardens,' said Bryant. 'There's one person who might be able to help us. Shirone Estanza.'

'She already signed a statement saying that Romain Curtis went back into the park by himself,' May reminded him.

'Yes, but now we have an ID, she might recognize Mr Emes as someone she'd seen hanging around outside the place on another occasion. She lives just over the road, remember?'

'I suppose it's worth a try.' May indicated the body. 'I'll get the rest of the team working on King Harold here, find out where he went, who his friends were.'

'I could tell you a little about some of those,' said Bryant, 'except that I'm sworn to secrecy.'

'Whose side are you on, exactly?'

'I sometimes wonder that myself,' Bryant muttered, looking down at the promising, wayward student now lying dead in the grass.

Shirone Estanza stood in the doorway examining the photograph for a long time, but finally shook her head.

'Hanging around outside, sitting in the gardens during the day, anything at all that might provide us with a link,' said Longbright. 'Have a think, there's no rush.'

'I don't know,' Shirone said finally. 'There are a lot of students around here because of the colleges. They all look like him, sort of ordinary. Invisible. You only notice the ones who stick out.'

'It was worth a try,' said Longbright, gathering up Banbury's photographs and putting them back in her handbag.

'Why have you got a house brick in there?' asked Shirone, peering over.

'Under British law you can't stop a suspect with a weapon but you might be allowed to hit him with something that would naturally be in your hand at the time,' Longbright explained. 'So I always carry my handbag.'

Shirone gave her something approaching a smile.

'There you go, you've got a nice smile. You should try using it more often.'

'I keep thinking what would have happened if I hadn't suggested going to the club. I could tell he wasn't really keen. I made Romain go and he got drunk. If only I hadn't . . .'

Longbright placed a placating hand on hers. 'I've heard this line of thought a million times before,' she said gently. 'It doesn't lead anywhere. You have to put it behind you and think about your own future now.'

'But it's my fault.'

'Don't think about the path you didn't take. I never do.' A sudden thought struck her. 'Do you know if Romain's funeral service was handled by a company called Wells and Sons in Lamb's Conduit Street?'

'I don't think so,' said Shirone slowly. 'It was a Co-op funeral, done on the cheap. I know because Romain's mum told my mum that some bloke came around to see her about giving him an expensive send-off. She sent him away.'

'I don't suppose you know his name?'

'Yeah, because it was a funny one, like something you'd get in an old card game. It was Gummage – no, Rummage.'

26

AFTERLIFE

By mid-morning on Friday, Arthur Bryant had violet bags under his eyes but a look of triumph on his face. 'Stephen Emes's last phone call was to the barman of the tavern at Bleeding Heart Yard,' he told May, thumping into the office and dropping papers all over the desk.

'What am I supposed to make of that? Your shirt's on inside out, by the way.'

'According to the landlord, it's where the New Resurrectionists hold their meetings. Raymond wanted us to provide physical links. If we can connect this organization with the three bodies being dug up, we're on our way to proving their involvement in the death of Romain Curtis.' He looked down at his shirt. 'I wondered why the buttons were on the inside.'

'Arthur, one of those bodies belongs to a dog. And why would they meet at a public house if they want to keep their identities hidden?'

'Like most pubs built on street corners, the tavern has an upstairs room with its own private entrance. And you'll love this part; historically, it's where the resurrectionists of old used to meet. These people wanted me to find Emes. It wasn't my fault that we got there too late.'

'They might have killed him themselves – did you think of that?'

'Then why would they have risked exposure by agreeing to meet with me, and asking me to find him?'

'I don't know.' May pushed an avalanche of notes back on to his partner's side of the joined desks. 'None of this makes any sense to me. God knows what Raymond will make of it.'

'There's something else. Mr Merry is an academic at the Museum of London, where he's making a study of apotropaic magic. To do so, he needs living creatures; specifically, birds. Even more specifically, ravens.'

'So you've got your thief.'

'It's not as simple as that, and he knows it. Both of these cases hinge on proof, and I have no evidence of what he's up to. I can't imagine how the theft was accomplished, and he knows it. Which is why he forced me to make a deal with him.'

'I'm not sure I want to hear this part,' groaned May.

'As I said, I agreed to drop the Tower investigation in return for a lead in the Romain Curtis case, but it was only for one week.' Bryant fished about in his pockets for the card. 'He gave me the contact for the New Resurrectionists, remember.'

'Why would he know they were involved?'

'He didn't. But he knew that in this great wide city they were by far the most likely candidates. Who else on the wrong side of the law knows how to dig up a body? They led me to Stephen Emes.'

May struggled to take all this in. 'Then your Mr Merry is a suspect. For all you know, he could have killed both Curtis and Emes.'

'I suppose so, but it doesn't seem likely, does it?' Bryant counted on his stubby fingers. 'Point One, he had no motive for killing them that we're aware of.'

'Romain Curtis – he saw Emes at work in St George's Gardens, yes? So Emes reported back to Merry and Merry killed him.'

'No, because Point B, the methods were entirely different. A hit-and-run and a crossbow? From the same killer? That would be a first.'

'Then Emes killed Curtis because he saw him digging up the body, and Merry killed Emes because he was exposing them all to risk.' He stopped for a moment and counted on his fingers. 'Emes. Curtis. Merry. Yes. That's what I meant.'

'Rubbish! That doesn't even make any sense to me, and I love things that make no sense. We've got five corpses, John. All right, three of them were dead to begin with and one belongs to a Jack Russell, and I don't think the ravens are connected because neat connections between two entirely separate investigations only ever happen in dreadful old detective novels. And another thing. Merry might have put me on to the New Resurrectionists to keep them in line, but why would he bother with someone like Emes?'

'I really have no idea, Arthur. I was hoping you'd tell me. I suddenly feel incredibly old and tired.' May pressed his hands against the wads of clippings and yellowed pages that were still fluttering from Bryant's desk. 'Are you going to present all this to Raymond?'

'I thought you might. He'd take it better from you.' Bryant suddenly looked contrite. 'There is something else. As you know, we've continued to investigate the thefts from the Tower, even though we were specifically warned not to.'

'*We?* I didn't agree to anything.'

'Well, I sort of agreed for you. If Merry finds out, I could be in trouble. This isn't exactly the safest building in London. The security system hasn't worked since I fixed it. I tested out that electronic face-recognition thingy by coming in with a false beard and comedy glasses, and it still let me in. Almost anyone can get through the front door. There are only the two Daves between us and oblivion.'

May was going to suggest that his partner was exaggerating the risk, then remembered that he had once succeeded in getting their old offices in Mornington Crescent blown up. 'All right,' he agreed, 'I'll have someone posted downstairs until this whole thing is over. It seems to me that we're missing the most obvious connection. Graverobbing. These "New Resurrectionists" could be digging up bodies and returning valuables to the funeral parlour. Rummage visited both Mrs Wallace and Romain Curtis's mother.'

'Rather a risky business, don't you think, graverobbing in Central London just to swipe a bit of jewellery from a suicidal man and a destitute old lady? And what about the dog? I called the owners of poor little Prince. No prizes for guessing that he was also buried by Wells and Sons, so if there's any more digging up to be done, it's there, in the funeral home.' He raised the phone and punched out an internal extension. 'Janice, I've got a job for you.'

'Miss Longbright, it's nice to see you again,' said Ron Rummage, smiling as he held out a pudgy hand. 'You remember Andy Orton, our embalmer?'

She had not spoken to Rummage's assistant on her last visit. Now Orton rose to his full height of six feet four inches to welcome her. He seemed pleasant enough until he smiled, revealing a disturbing oblong rictus of long yellow wolf-teeth.

'Andy will look after you today, as I've got some newly bereaved waiting to see me,' Rummage explained with an air of gossipy confidentiality. 'People have a tendency to die at the most inconvenient times, and I was called out last night at three a.m., so I'm not at my sharpest right now. If you have any questions specifically for me, Andy will relay them.' With a flourish of the maroon velour curtain at his back, he was gone. Longbright was reminded of a Victorian magician's set, where the mechanics were hidden behind vases of dusty fake flowers and plaster statues.

'Did you handle the burials of Mr Wallace and Mrs Duncannon?' Longbright asked, checking the notes Bryant had written out for her. He had specifically requested that she should go through the complete burial-preparation process, although he had not told her why, or why he would not attend in person. When she asked him if he wanted to partner her for the interview, he reacted strongly against the idea. It was almost as if he was becoming phobic about bereavement. She had known coppers who'd become sickened by the sight of death and had been driven to leave the force.

'Yes. Mrs Wallace wanted a fast burial,' said Andy, 'but we were dependent on the doctor's paperwork.'

'Was he buried in a suit of Mrs Wallace's choosing? How does that work?'

'She was too upset to choose his interment outfit, so Ron picked something from Mr Wallace's wardrobe. Then we filed a report on his personal belongings. He wasn't buried with any jewellery. We have to keep a note of every item. Mrs Wallace approved the outfit, and he was dressed here.'

'And once you've brought the body here, how do you prepare it?'

'We clean the skin and massage the stiffness from the muscles. Mr Wallace had a closed coffin, which makes my work simpler. In the case of Mrs Duncannon, she'd left instructions that she should be embalmed.'

'Mrs Duncannon had no relatives, is that right?'

'She did have a beneficiary, not that she left much money: a cousin in Scotland. This lady wasn't happy about the arrangement because obviously it costs more, and she had to pay for it. In the embalming process, I shave away any peach fuzz from the face that will affect the application of make-up, then I place the features for viewing.'

'What does that entail?'

'Inserting plastic caps into the eyes and closing them – they have a tendency to sink in after death. Then I add a mouth-former to stop that withdrawn look and tie the jaw with suture string, or I use a mastic gun. Then I do the arterial injection with a couple of gallons of formaldehyde solution – that's what gives the body shape. I suction out the cavity fluids, and pack cotton wool in to prevent seepage.' Orton showed appropriate enthusiasm, supplementing his explanations with hand gestures. 'There were no autopsies required in either case, but if there had been, I would have returned the viscera to the body in a plastic bag, like a supermarket chicken with giblets.' He smiled, which was a mistake. 'The rest is just styling and casketing. Mr Wallace would have been a little the worse for wear, as he was simply cleaned and emptied.'

'I wonder anybody bothers with embalming these days,' said Longbright.

'The rules of attraction remain whether you're dead or alive,' said Orton defensively. 'It's no different to ladies putting on make-up to entice a mate. Attractiveness in death brings comfort and continuity.' He gave her an appraising look. 'You've some lovely cheekbones on you. You wouldn't need much work at all, unless there was disfigurement involved.'

'What about the dog, Prince? Why did you bury him?'

'Oh, that was just a favour for someone Ron knows. I didn't do anything to him, just put him in a nice little box.'

'Was he wearing a collar?' It seemed a peculiar thing to ask, but Arthur had insisted on it.

'No, not to my recollection.'

'Has anything like this ever happened before?'

'Digging someone up? Well, there were cases a few years back in Highgate Cemetery, some kids carrying out dares, mostly. Unearthing a cadaver isn't like it is in those old horror films, you know. It's hard work getting a body back out of the ground.'

'Could you do it by yourself?'

'I'd say it would be virtually impossible. And it requires specialist knowledge to get the casket open.'

Longbright ran a crimson nail down her list. 'Can you think of any reason why someone would do this?'

'It's obvious, isn't it? Cabrini and Sons. They're down the bottom end of Marchmont Street and they've got all of that catchment area sewn up. They've been wanting to break into our territory for years. They're trying to discredit us.'

'Do you have any proof of this?'

'No, but it stands to reason. Either that, or someone's got it in for St George's Gardens. They've got a neighbourhood committee run by old dears, all very officious – nobody likes them.'

'In that case, if the purpose is merely to annoy them, why not commit a simpler act of vandalism like tearing up the flowerbeds?'

'I think you're better equipped to find that out than us.'

'There was a death last night: Stephen Emes; you're not handling him, are you?'

'Where did he die?'

'Hyde Park.'

'No, that would be Rackitt and Pembridge over in Edgware Road. Unless he was Muslim, of course.'

'Have you ever heard of organized criminal activity in cemeteries?' asked Longbright, carefully avoiding direct mention of the New Resurrectionists.

'No. But I'm sure it goes on in some areas. Medical students and such . . .'

'What makes you say that?'

'It's hard to get your hands on a body in this day and age. Students have always been ready to make a few bob.' He studied her face again, caught by the sight of her eyes in the light. 'If I were you, I should think of putting us down as your preferred representatives for afterlife care. And go for an embalming. You've far too lovely a face to waste with a closed casket. Magnificent skin tones. I'd love to get you on my slab one day.'

Longbright took her leave and headed back to report to Bryant, glad to be out of the cloying, airless room. But when she reached the PCU's offices, nobody knew where he had gone.

27

LINGUISTICS

You can't miss the British Library, on the Euston Road; it has an enormous bronze statue of Isaac Newton, bent over with a pair of compasses, in the centre of the court-yard. As much as he liked it, Bryant would have preferred some spreading trees, so that readers could sit under them with books. He felt strongly that libraries of any kind, even one this grand, should prove welcoming places.

He located his quarry up a ladder behind an immense, unsteady stack of rare books at the rear of the building. Raymond Kirkpatrick was a bear-like professor of English whose love of heavy-metal music did not endear him to library users. As a result, he worked with headphones on and had a tendency to bellow.

'*Tristram Shandy*,' said Raymond, hurling down several exquisite volumes with abandonment.

'I'm sorry?'

'Laurence Sterne, the author of *Tristram Shandy*. He was buried in St George's Fields, Hanover Square, in 1768. The site's long gone now, of course, like everything else of any bloody grace and elegance. Torn to bits by damned scumbag property developers in the 1960s. Sterne was dug up by bodysnatchers and sold to an anatomy professor. While he was lying on the slab, one of the professor's doctors recognized Sterne and had him returned to the graveyard. That sort of thing used to happen all the bloody time.' He chucked another book on to the pile on the floor.

'Should you be treating them like that?' asked Bryant.

'They're damaged. We're replacing them with better copies. Edgar Allan Poe,' Kirkpatrick volunteered, 'creepy little git, absolutely obsessed with the idea of premature burial. There's a theory that he was terrified of being buried alive, and wrote to try and effect a cure. I've got a monograph on it somewhere. Of course, we're talking about a period which was fascinated by trance states, hysteria, epilepsy, catalepsy. Look at Poe's output: positively littered with such ideas – "The Black Cat", "Morella", "Ligeia", 'Berenice", "The Fall of the House of Usher". His story "The Premature Burial" is worth a gander, although the ending's totally crap. Why do you want to know?'

Bryant expanded on the details of the case.

'Sounds like a load of old bollocks to me, but you're the boss.' Kirkpatrick bounced down from his ladder. 'Heavy metal has the same obsessions, of course, with the added frisson of Satanism chucked in. I can cue up a few tracks for you to listen to.'

'Thank you, no. I'd rather spend time on a kidney dialysis machine than have my ears tuned to one of your favourite bands. Any other advice for me?'

Kirkpatrick twiddled some food out of his beard, thinking. 'Poets' Corner.'

'What about it?

'Well, we know it's in the South Transept of Westminster Abbey, and that lots of writers are buried there, but within that space others were also tipped in. The poet Edmund Spenser died of starvation, poor bugger, and his carcass was chucked in there, but here's the interesting part. Shakespeare and his chums attended the service, and the story goes that they threw their own works into his plot in a kind of farewell salute. It was thought for many years that Shakespeare whizzed an unseen playscript into the coffin, until the grave was opened in the 1930s and it was found not to be the case. Now, if you're interested in the subject of missing folios I can—'

'As much as I enjoy talking to you, Raymond, this is starting to get irritating. How are you on astronomy?'

'Linguistics and Naming of only, not Constellations, Discovery and Exploration of. What have you got?'

Bryant attempted to fill in the rest of the missing facts without sounding as if he was going completely mad.

'Let me see if I've got this right,' said Kirkpatrick. 'Resurrectionists, a dead witness and the Little Bear. Let's not bother with the Jack Russell for now.'

'That's about the size of it, yes.'

'How old was the lad?'

'Almost sixteen.'

'Well, there's your answer. They weren't worried about him.'

'Why not? Who?'

'Well, corpses can't talk, can they?'

'I'm not with you. Thomas Wallace had a bash on his head that we think might have been caused by a misdiagnosis, so that he woke up in the coffin.'

'No no no, you silly old sod. The odds of anyone coming back to life are infinitesimal. Think about it, how does a dead body stand up? There had to be two blokes holding the corpse between them.'

'Why do you say that?'

'As much as you would like to believe that the deceased

come back to life, Arthur, try the more obvious answer. These dudes are holding up the body when a surprised kid spots them. One tells the other one not to worry. Why not?'

'Because he's only a boy,' said Bryant as the truth dawned. 'Romain Curtis looked young for his age. Everyone said so. That's what he overheard. Something like, "Don't worry – he's a minor." He was a bit doped up and had just finished naming the constellations to his girl. The stars were still in his head.'

'Exactly. But I don't understand why you're fretting over details. You say you know who's behind these exhumations, so why don't you go and bloody well arrest them?' Kirkpatrick scooped books from the floor and chucked them in an untidy pile.

'They say they didn't do it.'

'So what? People are lying, filthy, thieving pigs. Culprits proclaim their innocence all the time.'

'Perhaps,' said Bryant, 'but in this case, I happen to believe them.'

Jack Renfield was at the Bleeding Heart Tavern, talking to the head barman. 'Yeah, I took the call,' said the lad, a strapping thick-jawed thing with a strong Australian twang. 'Emes, that's the one. He's been in here a few times. He said he was looking for someone. He sounded really agitated. He had me running all over the pub, but I couldn't find him.'

'Do you remember who he was looking for?'

'Wait, it'll come to me. Something like – hang about, I had to write it down because it sounded Italian and I didn't know how to pronounce it. Let me look on the spike. We keep all the bar messages 'cause customers can get stroppy.' He headed to a cubbyhole outside the kitchen and checked through a pile of skewered notes. 'Sorry about the wait,' he said, returning with the paper. 'Here you go. Roman Conti.'

Renfield's Neanderthal brow wrinkled. 'You don't mean Romain Curtis?'

'No, mate. Just as it says here, Roman Conti. Why, is he wanted for something?'

'The chap who was looking for him was murdered last night.'

'Jeez, that's bad.' He looked past Renfield to the rain-spattered windows. 'You know, I came here because where I'm from it's all kicking off, fires, storms, the worst weather conditions imaginable. I live on the edge of a national park that's dying, mate. So I moved to London for a better life. Murders, though. Makes me wonder if I made the right choice.'

Bryant caught the tube at Euston Station and headed out towards the Seven Sisters Road, where he had arranged to meet Dan Banbury.

He realized straight away that it was a mistake to take the Victoria Line to reach Finsbury Park. London's ancient tube network could no longer cope with its one billion passengers a year, and the core of the line had become unpleasantly crowded. Nobody offered him a seat, so he was forced to stage one of his helpless-old-man-falls-into-the-lap-of-a-sturdy-young-seated-passenger routines. He went for the Oscar this time, scattering wine gums everywhere, with a beseeching look in his eyes that would have melted the heart of Genghis Khan. When he emerged from the station, he juggled his umbrella and his mobile, contacting Renfield to find out how he had got on at the Bleeding Heart.

'Roman Conti? It's too much of a coincidence,' said Renfield. 'The names are almost identical.'

'I don't know,' Bryant replied over the noise of wet tyres. 'I managed to waste two days on this investigation detouring down the wrong path, just because I wanted to believe that a corpse was naming the stars. There's no room in the force for dreamers, that's for sure. I can be a total fool sometimes.'

'According to Emes, Conti was a local. It fits; the area around Hatton Garden still has plenty of Italians,' said Renfield. 'We're coming up to the after-work rush here. Unless you've got something else you want me to do, I'm going to hang around and see if anyone's heard of this guy.'

'That sounds like a good idea, Jack. Do me a favour and check on Janice, will you? I don't trust that undertaker.'

'I just spoke to her. Apparently the embalmer wanted to lay her out – in a business sense, as I understand it.' Renfield listened to silence on the other end of the line. 'I thought you'd find that funny.'

'I don't find death amusing,' said Bryant, hanging up.

You always used to, thought Renfield, wondering what had got into the old man.

The pavements of the Seven Sisters Road were deserted. It was an area no tourist reached; Central London's backstage, chaotic and dingy. Bryant was at home in places like this. In Chelsea and Kensington there were only shuttered bankers' houses and restaurants, as oligarchs and hedge-fund managers built property portfolios, but Brixton, Tottenham, Aldgate and Walthamstow were where the real work took place.

As he passed a grocery store displaying mountains of fresh pomelos, daikons, mangoes and mandarins, Bryant thought of well-heeled professionals nibbling flavourless pea shoots in brasseries while the economically pressed families of Finsbury Park enjoyed pungent stews and curries.

There were no Starbucks here; the cafés were Moroccan, East African, Arabic. He thought about getting a Turkish shave, complete with burning-stick-up-the-nose-and-ear-holes, massage and moisturizer, but knew that Banbury was waiting for him. He checked the address he had been given for the dead resurrectionist. Banbury had installed a map application for him, but he had trouble remembering how to use it. Instead he unfolded a napkin on which he had scrawled the door number, and checked his bearings.

Emes's flat was in a grey, run-down terraced house with motorbikes in the front garden, much further from the tube station than he had realized. By the time he got there he was feeling his considerable age in every bone. Worse, the flat was on the top floor.

'I was starting to wonder if something had happened to you,' called Banbury over the landing bannisters. 'I meant to warn you it was a bit of a walk. I didn't want to come down and find you dead on the steps.'

'Why does everybody think I'm about to peg out?' said Bryant, fighting to get his breath back. He bent over and placed his hands on his knees. 'Blimey, I think I just coughed up a tube.'

'You should see a doctor.'

'No thank you. I was hoping for National Treasure status by now, not National Health. Doctors have cured old age in mice by tampering with the hypothalamus. I wish they'd get a move one. I want to be venerable, not vulnerable.'

'Come up and I'll let you walk all over my site,' said Banbury cheerfully.

'Well, you would, wouldn't you? It's not a crime scene.'

'Maybe not, but I wonder just exactly what Mr Emes was up to. You'll see what I mean.'

'My God, he's been burgled,' said Bryant as he stepped over the threshold of the flat.

'No, I think he was just incredibly untidy.' Banbury indicated the empty beer bottles piled in the sink, the stacks of magazines and dirty tea mugs left all over the floor. 'Medical chaps often live like this. It's a reaction against having to be so clinically clean during the day.

But take a look at his bookcase. I'm sure I've seen some of those volumes on your shelves.'

Bryant stepped over a partially dismantled PlayStation and read the spines of the books. *The Men Who Cheated Death, How to Avoid Resurrectionists, The Codex Extinct Animalia, Parasites that Live in Dead Flesh and Their Uses, The Diary of a Graverobber, 1811–1812.*

'You're right,' Bryant agreed. 'I do have a few of these.'

'And there are notebooks in the bedroom, dozens of them filled with his writings and drawings. He was experimenting with corpse parasites, looking at new ways to use them in medicine. It's not an original idea; they use sterile maggots to clean wounds. You should talk to Giles about it, only not over spaghetti carbonara, as he did with me.'

'Well, given what we now know about Emes, this isn't exactly outside of his academic jurisdiction.'

'Maybe not, but when you couple it with this lot – I found them under the bed.' Banbury kicked a stack of paperbacks with his boot. The top volume was Anton LaVey's *The Satanic Bible*. Beneath it were twenty other accounts, mostly memoirs and compendia dealing with the history of black magic and its rituals. 'Bit of an odd combination for a medical man, wouldn't you say?'

'The information age tempts too many students to cherry-pick from a variety of philosophies and beliefs,' said Bryant, 'even when they're mutually exclusive or even opposed.'

'I wouldn't like to find out my GP was messing about with black magic. It would be like discovering that your bank manager was also a stand-up comic. Get anything on his movements prior to Hyde Park?'

'Nothing much. He doesn't seem to have had any friends. He was seen having dinner alone in the Edgware Road. Has he got a desk?'

'Nope.'

'Bedside table, then. Let's have a nose.' Bryant picked his way through to the bedroom and started pulling open drawers.

'I was going to say it's OK to touch them now,' called Banbury with no small degree of sarcasm. When he received no reply, he went to the door. Bryant had unfolded an immense sheet of taped photocopy paper on the unmade bed. 'What's that?'

The detective looked up with concern. 'It's a map of our unit, 231 Caledonian Road,' he said in astonishment. 'The whole building, marked out floor by floor. What the hell was he planning to do?'

28

ICE IN THE HEART

London is connected.

It's wired-up, hotlinked, Wi-Fied and broadbanded to the max. So why, Orion Banks wondered, was it so hard to get hold of anyone at the PCU?

When she rang to speak to Raymond Land, her call went unanswered. All other extensions went to voice-mail, except Arthur Bryant's, which went to a horrible, squawking version of 'I Am the Monarch of the Sea' from *HMS Pinafore*. Eventually a constable from the City of London Police was dispatched to the unit to find out what was going on.

John May sent him away with a flea in his ear. The unit had gone into lockdown. Nobody else was permitted to enter the building until Emes's floor plans could be interpreted. The remaining Dave had had his mobile confiscated, and had threatened to call the police until he remembered where he was. Even the cats were secured. The PCU was to work in isolation for the rest of the day and the whole of the weekend until a breakthrough had been achieved. Although like all good plans, that wasn't what happened.

'The books,' said Bryant, when they were once more ensconced in their shared office. 'They're what worry me most. Black-magic rituals for raising the dead don't sit well with the Hippocratic oath. We need to track down the other New Resurrectionists.'

'You know you can't do that until Banks approves it,' May reminded him. 'And she's not inclined to grant any of your more unorthodox requests right now.'

'Surely she must see that since the beginning of the week we've been surrounded by superstitions concerning death? This place is covered in black cats. Did somebody smuggle them in?'

'Now you're being paranoid.'

'Something bad is insinuating its way into my life, John. I love this city but sometimes it gets on top of me. The buildings have too many histories, too many secrets. Things – collect. I knew I shouldn't have had anything to do with ravens – they're harbingers of the Grim Reaper.'

'Please, don't start infecting everyone else with your omens,' May pleaded. 'There are enough Gothic trappings in this case as it is without you adding to them.'

'Speaking of which, this turned up in the mail.' Bryant flicked a card over to May's desk.

On the front was a black panel showing a pierced human heart placed inside a pentacle. Inside it read, 'You were warned about visiting the Tower again. Prepare for the consequences.'

'A bit hokey, isn't it?' said May. 'Let's bring him in and stand on his fingers for a while.'

'What for? He knows we've got nothing on him. Dan checked the card for prints. Clean. He's trying to put the frighteners on me. It's the oldest psychological trick in the book, piling on the portents, pure M. R. James stuff. I've had worse than that in the post. Somebody mailed me a dead penguin once.'

'This sort of stuff never works, though, does it?' said

May. Bryant said nothing. 'Does it?' he tried again. 'Look, we'll get him on public nuisance, wasting police time, whatever. They got Al Capone for tax evasion.'

'What else have you got on Emes?'

May checked his notes. 'He was expelled from King's College on the advice of his senior professor, just as you said. Professor James Garrick, highly respected, has a lot of sway at the college. He's working in Ethiopia; we haven't been able to get hold of him yet. Emes's mother is in Wales, hasn't seen him in years. Dan hasn't turned up any addresses in his flat and he was found without a mobile. Maybe it was taken from him in Hyde Park. I guess you could say that's a pattern, although it's become the norm these days. There are so many people involved in this, yet it's hard to break anyone open.'

'You're right,' said Bryant, sitting back. The lights were now turned down low, and his expressive blue eyes were lost in eddying shadows. 'In the old days I would have brought everyone in and subjected them to as much mental cruelty as my twisted mind could come up with. Now I have to be more circumspect. Delay leaves room for tragedy. We're left with a trail of funeral mourners, a son without a father, a mother without a son, a wife without a husband. And that's not even counting Stephen Emes – we have no idea who might be mourning him.'

'What do you suggest?'

'Let's assume, for the sake of argument, that this is not a series of merely unfortunate events and that they're all connected: the exhumations, the hit-and-run, the harpooning of the student.

'Let's also assume that the same person is responsible in each case.

'Who do we have in the frame, really? Who has the motive, the window of opportunity, the lack of an alibi? And what if he decides to strike again? How can you stop a murder from occurring when you have no idea why it might be committed, or on whom?'

He dropped his head and spoke into his hands, so quietly that May hardly heard him. 'I keep thinking of the Bleeding Heart, and what McEvoy said: if you pierce the heart and it still bleeds, a corpse may live on. That's what all this is doing to me, don't you see? I feel as if someone is pricking me to ensure that I bleed but live on. It's the sense we all get as our lives near the end.'

'In all the time I've known you, you've never shown any fear of dying,' said May vehemently. 'Quite the reverse – you've been positively gleeful on the subject. Look at the way you tease Giles's housekeeper, and the awful way you make fun of Alma's belief in an afterlife.'

'I always felt that the receptive mind was the one you could damage most easily. Why should I be immune from the rule? I have no creed but my own, no family to put flowers on my grave. I don't have your unshakeable faith in science. I have nothing ahead but the darkness of the burial plot.'

'Oh, this is unbearable,' said May. 'For a start, I care for you. So does everyone here. And Alma is devoted to you. Now stop feeling so ridiculously sorry for yourself and get on with your work.'

Bryant did as he was told, but the image of the Bleeding Heart lodged in his mind like a frozen shard.

29

DISBELIEF

Saturday was a strange day, Sargasso-becalmed, fractious and ill at ease with itself.

The week's earlier promise had truly vanished now, and the unending summer rain thudded relentlessly across the London rooftops, testing the inhabitants. The PCU always remained open through the weekend when it had an active investigation, and did so this weekend as well, although a lockdown was meant to be in place. Longbright arranged a roster so that the staff could get a few spare hours to themselves. Most of the time she was able to provide cover with three or four officers, but occasionally the shifts went out of synchronization so that she was left with an imbalance. When that occurred she became a Jill-of-all-trades, doing everyone's jobs.

This was what happened on Saturday morning. Normal life had got in the way of work: Bimsley was due a check-up at UCH to see if he had damaged his back falling down the stairs at the drugs clinic, Land had been forced to meet with a divorce lawyer and Renfield had promised to pick up his daughter from the dentist.

Longbright knew that nobody had had time to double-check the sets of phone records Banbury had requested, so she prepared for the arduous job of running down the call columns, highlighting each in turn. The Met had specialist software for this, but it wasn't licensed to the City of London, and certainly not to the PCU. She checked each message against a set of half a dozen phone addresses, hoping that something would jump out at her.

When it did, she very nearly missed it. Making a note of the call, she went through to the detectives' office, where she found John May at work.

'I've got something,' she said. 'Mrs Wallace rang Krishna Jhadav on the morning of her husband's death. Eleven thirty-five a.m., little more than three hours after he died. Why would she have done that? And the doctor, Iain Ferguson, he called the funeral parlour several times, which I suppose is to be expected, but there were an awful lot of calls between them. I think about seven in all.'

'Let's find out about Mrs Wallace first.' May took the number and rang Jhadav's mobile.

Jhadav sounded out of breath. He was at the gym burning off more corporate anger. 'It wasn't exactly a phone call,' said Jhadav. 'Hang on, let me get off this thing.'

May answered Longbright's quizzical look. 'He's on a running machine.'

'You still there? Yeah, Mrs Wallace – she called me to scream a load of abuse, said her husband had killed himself because of me. She said it was because I took the account away from him.'

'So you lied to us when you said you didn't know that Wallace had died.'

'Come *on*, man. You come breezing into my office in front of my colleagues, putting me on the spot like that, what am I supposed to say?'

'What did you tell Mrs Wallace?'

'Nothing – I couldn't get a word in edgeways. I let her rant on for a while. I knew she was being irrational and needed someone to blame. Finally I said I was sorry for her loss and rang off as quickly as I could. She was obviously very upset about what had just happened and I was in her firing line. She probably rang all her husband's ex-clients.'

'No,' said May, glancing up at Longbright again, 'it seems she just rang you.'

'Do you have any more information about why he killed himself?' asked Jhadav.

'His wife said he'd been very agitated since he lost your account. He wasn't expecting to keep his job, and didn't think he'd get another one at his age.'

'I'm sorry to sound callous, mate, but we aren't in charge of ensuring the mental health of our suppliers. He started doing his work badly, and no amount of advice from me could put him back on track. I must stress that it was just our business arrangement that suffered. I still valued him as a friend.'

'Hold on one sec.' May had become aware that Longbright was trying to attract his attention. He looked over and saw her holding up a piece of paper: 'DID WALLACE RETURN ALL WORK FILES?'

'Do you know if Thomas Wallace gave you back all your work files?' said May.

There was a pause on the other end of the line. 'No, not everything. Thomas ceased to handle our company contract but continued to deal with my personal affairs.'

'I may have to take this further with you, Mr Jhadav. It depends on the direction of the investigation.' He rang off. 'Janice, where did you get that?'

'Arthur left me a note yesterday. Why would he need to know if there were any files left behind?'

'I don't know, but you got your answer. Wallace continued to handle Jhadav's personal affairs, which I imagine involved retaining private financial documents. Arthur clearly knows something we don't. I hate it when he does this. What's the old buzzard got up his sleeve? For that matter, where is he? It's like sharing an office with the Scarlet Pimpernel.'

'He's gone to a shooting range in Harrow on the Hill to learn how to fire a crossbow,' said Longbright matter-of-factly. 'He'll be back this afternoon.'

'Of course he has,' said May. 'I suppose we're lucky he didn't buy a shovel and head off to Highgate Cemetery for a practical lesson in bodysnatching. Now what?' Longbright was staring at her phone.

'Oh, a text from Jack. His car's broken down. Would I go and collect his daughter.'

'Go on, off you go. I can look after things here.'

After Longbright had gone, May turned his attention to the board behind his desk and studied it. Everyone they had interviewed to date featured somewhere on there, their timelines drawn with blue and green Pentels in a nightmarish maze of connections. One thing he noticed when he stepped back and studied it from a distance was how the living and the dead were all geographically linked. Every single one of them had connections inside Bloomsbury.

Broadly speaking, the area was bordered by four main thoroughfares: Euston Road, Tottenham Court Road, High Holborn and Grays Inn Road. The first two exhumation sites, Wallace's legal practice, Curtis's flat and the funeral parlour: all fell within the jurisdiction.

He wrote: 'All 3 burials handled by Wells & Sons.' In red he added the only three locations that were outside of the area: the site of Stephen Emes's death at the north edge of Hyde Park, Jhadav's Threadneedle Street office and the headquarters of the New Resurrectionists somewhere in Peckham.

What particularly annoyed him was the lack of contradictory information in the case. Usually participants failed to agree on timings and alibis, but here everything fitted seamlessly – too much so for his liking.

That could only mean one thing. Someone was collaborating in the creation of a lie. But with Banks still sitting on the file of requests for forensic tests and search warrants put in by various members of staff, there was nothing more that could be done. She had restricted their access to the tools they most needed.

'Is there anything to eat?' asked Bryant when he returned. 'I'm starving. It's a Saturday, we're supposed to get a sandwich allowance.'

'You were gone a long time.'

'Are you surprised? Harrow on the Hill is a pain in the arse to get to, out past Wembley on the Metropolitan Line. That's where my Freedom pass comes in handy. Saves me having to jump over the barrier.'

'Couldn't you have gone somewhere nearer?'

'No, because of Deirdre Cornholt.'

'Who—'

'She owns a fish shop. She sells them. I mean for aquariums – do we say aquaria? Do you remember I took a week off in 1982 to go to Majorca?'

'Very, very vaguely, by which I mean no.'

'I gave her my Siamese fighting fish to look after and she accidentally boiled them.'

'I'm not entirely sure where this is going, but pray continue,' said May patiently.

'Well, she still feels guilty, and she always said if there was anything she could do for me – and then I remembered that her son is a sports master at Harrow, so she arranged for me to be taught how to use a crossbow.'

'And how was that for you?'

'Interesting. It wasn't as heavy as I thought it would be. The new ones are made of lightweight compound materials, all very state of the art. I had a bit of trouble with my cocking. But you can use a cocking rope or a winch to take the effort out of loading it. There are plenty of full-sized models but there's also a pistol crossbow that's incredibly portable and light. They're virtually silent, too. The shocking part is how readily available they are. You can pick one up for as little as twenty quid, and that's brand new. They go up to five hundred pounds, though, and then there are hundreds of accessories. You have to be eighteen to purchase one, but you can buy them virtually anywhere because they count as hobbyist items. I'm amazed we don't find them being used on the street more often.'

'You think it was easy for someone to pick off Emes even in the dark like that?'

'I think so, if you'd had a little practice. Accuracy proved to be my problem. I was aiming at a target but one of my arrows went into an ice-cream van and quite a few simply shot up into the air and vanished. Dan got some forensic feedback from the shaft that went through Emes and reckons we're looking for something called a Trueflight carbon-tipped bolt. Unfortunately, almost all crossbow specialists sell them online. How have you been getting on?'

May indicated the board. 'See if anything on that makes any sense. I've been staring at it for ages.'

'Yes, I did the same thing last night until I felt one of my heads coming on. I had to hang a eucalyptus-oil-soaked tea towel over the standard lamp. The odd thing is, I don't get the feeling that we're missing something obvious. It's all right here, if only we could put it together in the correct order.'

May rose and stretched his back. 'Why did you want Janice to find out about Jhadav's files?'

'Oh, you know, talismans,' said Bryant, his off-handedness making him sound all the more mysterious. He followed May's eyes to the board. 'Do you notice something?' he asked. 'The funeral parlour is at the centre of everything on that rather spidery map you've drawn.'

May looked, and realized his partner was right. Wells

and Sons sat in the middle of a circle that included Jhadav's and Wallace's offices at its southern base, the homes of Romain Curtis, Elspeth Duncannon, and even the owners of the dead Jack Russell, Prince, at its east and west sides. Just below the northern edge were the Scala nightclub and St George's Gardens.

Bryant pulled an old-fashioned tailor's tape measure from his pocket and slapped it on the board.

'It's an area no more than a mile wide,' he said finally. 'They all know each other. Everyone's involved somehow – we just have to prove it.' He avoided looking at the neighbourhood that lay immediately below. Bleeding Heart Yard was marked in red, and had a question mark scrawled above it. Instead he went to the eastern edge of the area he had marked and tapped his pen on the roundabout at London Wall. 'And there,' he said, 'overlooking all of us, sits Mr Merry, planning our demise.'

'Arthur, your crazy warlock-academic or whatever he calls himself is *not* involved in this.'

'You don't know that,' said Bryant. 'This could all be part of his grand design.'

'There are only three motives for murder,' said May. 'Sex, money and revenge.'

'That's not true. He has a fourth, the oldest motive of all. Power. I think he wants control of the city.'

'What, you reckon he's behind all this, manipulating everyone for the sole purpose of destroying you? I don't even know how to respond to that, although the phrase "paranoid delusion" springs to mind.'

'He doesn't want to destroy us, merely bypass us. He's after something bigger.'

May shook the idea from his head. 'I can't listen to you any more, Arthur. This is arrant nonsense. Don't you see? He's wormed his way inside your brain with all these phone calls and notes and predictions. You can make people believe in all kinds of rubbish just by nagging away at them and undermining their confidence.' He leaned forward and looked hard into Bryant's eyes. 'You know what I understand least about you? You don't believe in God, yet you're always ready to believe in the Devil. Well, you can't have one without the other. Belief or disbelief, which is it to be?'

'Disbelief,' said Bryant softly, but he didn't sound as if he meant it.

30

STRESS FRACTURE

Longbright sat in the waiting room of the dental surgery in Cowcross Street reading a two-month-old copy of *Hello!* magazine. When Sennen Renfield emerged she hooked her finger in her mouth to reveal a neat white filling, then waited patiently for Longbright's explanation.

'He's always got an excuse,' she huffed. 'He shouldn't have offered if he wasn't going to come. I didn't need to be collected. I can get home by myself; I'm not useless.'

'Nobody's saying you are, Sennen. Jack needed to take his car battery to a garage. We have to take time off in turns. Your father has a very demanding job, and he's having to put in very long hours.'

'Yeah, I know all about it. Can we go and get noodles?'

'What do you mean, you know all about it?'

'I go to Albany, don't I? Shirone Estanza is in my class and Martin Wallace is in the same year but only just, because of his birthday. Romain was as well.'

It hadn't occurred to Longbright that the children of those involved might all know each other, but it was hardly surprising, considering there were probably only two secondary schools in the neighbourhood.

'Are you all friends, then?' she asked.

'Not really. I'm mates with Shirone. We see Martin around. He doesn't notice me but I think he likes her. He always seems to turn up at break time. He asked her out once but Shirone unfriended him on Facebook because he posted a photo of her; she liked Romain a lot. She's been very upset since he died.'

As they headed down into the street, an idea occurred to Longbright. Bryant had a habit of using outsiders to help him gather information in investigations. 'Do you know Martin Wallace well enough to talk to him?'

'I guess so.'

'Could you find out how his mother is?'

'Why?'

'If I tell you something, how do I know you'll keep it to yourself?'

Sennen gave her an old-fashioned look. 'I'm my father's daughter,' she said. 'You know what he's like, right?'

Longbright was all too aware of Jack's clam-like qualities. She decided to take a chance. 'Mrs Wallace went around to one of her husband's old clients and threatened him. And we think she might have followed Shirone Estanza home and stayed outside her flat one evening, keeping a watch on her.'

'I've met her at school – she's a miserable cow. But why would she act like a stalker?'

'I don't know. Perhaps she blames Shirone for what happened to her husband in some way. It occurred to me that she might think Shirone was involved in what happened at St George's Gardens that night.'

'Shirone definitely encouraged Romain to go to the Scala club. He didn't want to because he knew her brothers were going to be there.'

'So,' said Longbright. 'Could you do a little undercover work for me?'

'You want me to spy on my friends?'

'No, not at all. I'm not looking to get anyone in trouble. It's just that sometimes young people don't feel comfortable talking to older people. There might be things they don't want to mention to us because they're worried we'll get the wrong idea or it'll make them look silly. That's the last thing we want to do. No one would know the information came from you. Your friends would be protected, and it could help us get a handle on this whole thing, because frankly we're not getting on too well by ourselves.'

Sennen was clearly excited by the prospect of helping. 'What do you want to know?'

They stopped at the kerb, and Longbright turned to Sennen. 'I want to know what Martin Wallace thinks his mother was doing. Just keep your ear to the ground. You may find out things I never could.'

'I'd only do it to help them, not hurt them.'

'I give you my word, Sennen, I only want to get them cleared from our inquiries so that we can concentrate on getting to the truth.'

After a minute of silence, Sennen looked at her and gave an almost imperceptible nod.

Later, Longbright realized it was one of the biggest mistakes she'd ever made.

'That crazy woman is outside again,' said Irina Cope. 'Take a look.'

Krishna Jhadav pulled back the kitchen curtain of the house on Ensign Street. There at the kerb, with the engine idling, he could plainly see the old blue Renault, and Mrs Wallace seated behind the wheel, staring straight ahead. Her features were expressionless. She looked as bored as a taxi driver waiting for a passenger to sort out change.

'She's not well,' said Jhadav. 'What am I supposed to do?'

'You have to go and say something to her. She can't just hang around outside all day. Last week she nearly dropped a planter on you. God knows what she'll try to do next.'

'You don't know that,' said Jhadav. 'You didn't see anyone up on the balcony.'

Irina was really angry now; why did he always refuse to believe her? She snatched back the curtain. 'Look at her, Krishna. You've met her socially, you know what she looks like, and that's the woman who followed me from the shops three days running, swearing at me under her breath. She thinks her husband killed himself because of you!'

'Maybe he did,' said Jhadav. 'I took the account away because he started crying in a board meeting, can you believe that? He told me his bank was refusing to extend his credit lines, but is that my fault? It obviously all got too much for him.'

'What matters is that she's decided you're culpable, and you don't know what she might do next. She's under the kind of stress that makes people act crazy. And I'm just as much at risk as you.'

'All right, I'll go down and talk to her.'

'Be careful, Krishna.'

Jhadav turned back and kissed her on the forehead. 'She's in a weird place right now, but what is she really going to do? You think she's packing a shotgun?' It was still raining, so he put on a jacket and ran downstairs.

Mrs Wallace remained motionless as she watched him approach. Jhadav knocked on her window and made a turning motion. Eventually she let the glass down an inch. She was wearing the kind of clothes you slipped into on a rainy Sunday when you had no intention of going out. Looking in he could see that her feet were encased in tartan slippers.

'What are you doing here, Mrs Wallace?' he asked.

She glanced at him briefly, then stared ahead through the windscreen once more. 'You know very well.'

'You can't stay outside the house. My girlfriend's up-stairs and she's very upset with you. She's taken pictures of your car. She'll take them to the police if you don't go away and leave her alone.'

'I'm the one who's been left alone,' she said finally. 'I'm the one whose husband is dead because of you.'

'I don't know how many times I have to tell you this. Your husband lost our account because he was unstable, he was a nightmare in meetings and he reeked of alcohol first thing in the morning. He couldn't do his job, so we didn't renew his contract.'

'That's not true, and you know it. It was you who put him under so much pressure in the first place.'

'I think you need to see a doctor,' said Jhadav, lean-ing down to the window to address her directly. 'If you don't get help, and if you don't stay away from us, I'll get someone to take care of you. But right now you need to get away from outside my house before I call the police.'

It happened in the blink of an eye. She grabbed his tie, twisting it around her fist, and put her foot on the accelerator, swinging the wheel with her free hand, tearing away from the kerb.

Caught by surprise, Jhadav was pulled to his knees and dragged along the tarmac. The knot on his tie slipped tighter and her grip on the fabric remained fierce, so that he could not breathe or free himself.

A van was approaching from the opposite direction and she swung the vehicle to the right. Jhadav was caught between the driver's door of the Renault and the cars parked at the kerb. Door handles and wheel arches tore at his clothes. His legs swung wide. One shoe lost its sole. He tried to get his fingers under the tie.

He realized that she wasn't going to stop, and fought back. The tarmac burned through his jeans and bit into the flesh on his kneecaps. He knew that if she swerved hard again he would be crushed to death by the parked vehicles.

As he screamed, she seemed to snap out of her trance and suddenly released the tie. Her car shot forward, slewed to the right and collided with a Mercedes parked on the other side of the road.

As Jhadav yelled and rolled across the wet tarmac, bloodied and torn, Mrs Wallace collapsed on the steering wheel and began to sob.

31

CONTAMINATION

'I'm not going to press charges,' said Jhadav, examining the white square of tape on his elbow. 'I wouldn't mind some new clothes, though.'

He was seated with Longbright in the busy coffee shop of St Bart's Hospital. The knees of his jeans and both elbows of his blue suit jacket were torn open. Both his kneecaps had been bandaged. There was a livid scarlet cut across the bridge of his nose that gave him an aura of toughness.

He had been kept in until the examining doctor could ensure that there was nothing seriously wrong with him. After making his rounds and prodding his patient in the ribs a few times, the doctor had handed him a release form and told him to report any severe headaches or sudden changes in his condition.

'I mean, what's the point?' said Jhadav. 'She's clearly unbalanced. I'd only be making matters worse for everyone.'

'Did you talk to Miss Cope about your decision?'

'No, she been upset enough in the last few days.'

'Very well,' said Longbright, 'but I have to advise you

that as a police case number was issued, Mrs Wallace will be required to undergo psychiatric assessment and charges arising from the assault may still stand.'

'She lost her husband,' said Jhadav heatedly, 'she has every right to be angry. She looked around for someone to blame and found me, and that's the end of it. Just so long as you keep her away from us.'

'There's no question of the situation arising again,' said Longbright. 'I'm just sorry it got this far. We should have acted earlier.' Jhadav's attitude puzzled her. He didn't seem the easily forgiving type. His girlfriend had been threatened and he had nearly been killed, yet he just wanted the police to leave him alone. She saw this kind of behaviour all the time when villains were involved, but Jhadav was a white-collar worker with only a tangential connection to the case.

As she took her leave, she decided to dig a little more deeply into his background. But first, she needed to summon Vanessa Wallace and threaten her with the spectre of a jail sentence. While she did so, the lads could check her vehicle for signs of any other contact with pedestrians. After all, someone had run down Romain Curtis in what could have been a similar fit of road rage.

Bryant sat in on the interview but left the questions to Longbright, knowing that women always responded better to the detective sergeant. Mrs Wallace looked as if she was still in shock.

'Have you been seen by a doctor?' Longbright asked.

'Yes. He gave me some of these.' Mrs Wallace looked tired and resigned. She took a foil panel of small blue pills from her handbag and held them up. 'Diazepam. I think they're meant to reduce anxiety.'

'You understand the seriousness of what you did?' asked Longbright.

'I understand that I lost my temper, yes. I obviously

don't know my own strength.' She held Longbright's gaze in defiance.

'You could have killed him.'

'Then we'd be equal, wouldn't we?'

'Krishna Jhadav was not responsible for your husband's suicide, Mrs Wallace.'

'Of course I'd expect you to say that. He's Indian. You have to be seen to be taking his side. Political correctness.' She turned her head aside and stared angrily at the wall.

'There's a difference between political correctness and racism,' Bryant interrupted. 'His background has nothing to do with Detective Sergeant Longbright's question.'

'Mr Jhadav's girlfriend says you followed her,' Longbright pointed out, 'and that you dropped a plant pot on him.'

'I didn't mean for the plant pot to fall. That was an accident. My arm caught it.'

'What were you doing on the upstairs balcony? How did you get up there?'

'I rang the doorbell and they let me in. A couple of Chinese students. They didn't seem to speak any English so I just walked past them.'

'I don't understand. What on earth did you expect to achieve?'

'I wanted to hear him say it. That he was guilty. I wanted to force the words out of his mouth.' She looked off into the distance, as if wishing she was far away and all this was long over.

That was the point at which Bryant would have allowed his impatience to get the better of him. Luckily, Longbright was made of sterner stuff. 'Mr Jhadav was doing a job that required him to keep his company's best interests at heart,' she said. 'He acted within his rights.'

'It wasn't my husband's job to be the reluctant keeper of all his dirty little secrets,' said Mrs Wallace furiously. 'When you're next called upon to champion Mr Jhadav,

take a look into his company and see what Defluotech
Management Systems get up to. Don't bother searching
their website, though, that's just full of jargon. Oh, and I
seem to remember there's a nice picture of children playing
in a field of daisies. Google the company name instead
and follow a few of the links back to his factories outside
Mumbai. See what the brokering of toxic chemicals and
rotting animal parts actually involves. Then ask yourself:
If I became the unwilling repository of illegal information,
how would I ever live with myself?'

'You're saying that your husband was forced into an
untenable position because he was made privy to details
of Defluotech's business practices?' asked Bryant.

'I'm saying they filled rivers with dead pigs in India and
poisoned an entire town,' said Mrs Wallace, as if talking
to a child. 'They told my husband to help them hide the
evidence and bury the legal problems. And when he said
he wasn't prepared to become part of a cover-up, they
snatched the account away overnight, and took all their
files back.'

'You think there was evidence of irregularities in those
files?'

Mrs Wallace suddenly appeared less certain. 'I don't
know. Probably. There must have been. I never read them.
You have to understand that there were contracts that ran
to hundreds of pages. They're designed not to be understood by a layman.'

'And your husband returned everything that pertained
to the company?'

'Every last damned thing, and he was glad to be rid of
it all.'

Longbright tapped her notes with a pen. 'But Mr Jhadav
says your husband retained his private account.'

'Not any more. I returned that, too, when I cleared out
Thomas's personal effects. I wanted nothing from that
man contaminating my house.' Her voice hardened. 'How

do you think I felt when I saw my husband being torn up inside because of his job? When I watched him night after night, sitting at his desk in tears? Knowing that there was nothing I could do to help?'

'But if your husband felt that strongly, surely he would have—' Bryant began.

'I think we'll leave it there for today,' said Longbright, throwing him a warning glance. 'Thank you, Mrs Wallace, we'll be in touch.'

'Contamination,' said Bryant that evening. He was sitting in his favourite armchair, an overstuffed Victorian horror of maroon and lime brocade that he had been carting from one London home to another for most of his life.

'You'll get lost in that dreadful old thing,' said Alma, looking up from her knitting.

'Yes, I'm shrinking.'

'I'm going to come in one evening and find you've slipped down the back of it and suffocated to death.'

'Why is everybody talking about my imminent demise all of a sudden?' Bryant exclaimed.

'You're the one who's usually talking about death. Anyway, what do you mean, contamination? Have you been mixing up chemicals in your bedroom again?'

'No, I'm talking about spiritual harm. Do you believe there is such a thing?'

'Most certainly. Hold out your hands.' Bryant did as he was told, and Alma started winding some kind of hairy blue wool around them. 'And it happens to the most vulnerable people of all: the young. Think of those young girls and boys entrusted into the care of priests who then abuse them. You can get rid of the physical effects, but it's harder to heal the mind.'

'It's not just the young, Alma. Suppose someone wanted to make me believe I was about to die – do you think I could die because of it?'

'What, you mean take your own life?'

'In a way. Allow myself to be damaged.'

'It's possible.' Alma unspooled the wool with practised ease. 'If you're feeling vulnerable. Is that how you feel at the moment?'

'I'm not going to say yes, because then you're going to tell me to come to church with you. I just feel – susceptible.'

'You have to find more strength of will than the person who's doing it to you,' she said, watching her knots.

'As ever the voice of reason,' Bryant marvelled. 'What if I'm not feeling strong?'

'Then you need to talk to someone who'll make you stronger.'

'Why didn't I think of that?' Bryant asked himself. 'I don't know what I'd do without you.'

'You'd have to darn your own jumpers, for a start.'

'Get this stuff off me.' Bryant shook himself free from half a mile of unpicked angora and attempted to get out of the armchair. 'I have to make a phone call.'

'But I wanted to get this back in one piece tonight,' Alma complained.

'Perhaps you should give it back to the rabbit.' Climbing to his feet, he searched around for his hat and coat, forgetting that he was still in his slippers. 'Leave my dinner in the oven,' he instructed, 'and don't wait up.'

32

THE UNHAUNTING

The Ladykillers Café was an amusing post-modern re-creation of a 1950s English tearoom, with the added horror of the new century's prices. Tea was served in witty pots, and the fairy cakes came with inverted commas around them. It had been started as an ironic pop-up but had settled down to become a neighbourhood institution, springing fresh-minted from the wreckage of the old, nicotine-stained King's Cross. And it provided a pleasant respite from the surrounding bellicose pubs, especially as North London's resident Grade II white witch rarely touched alcohol. 'It dims my psychic abilities,' she explained. 'And it gets me plastered.'

Maggie Armitage favoured the colours of spring and tended to wear them all together at once, so that she looked like an upended flowerbed draped in costume jewellery. It was a look few women outside the witchcraft world could pull off. While queuing to pay for the teas she broke a necklace of gold beads, scattering them across the floor and down the stairs, which woke up a couple of the sleepier patrons and caught one unsteady old dear completely by surprise.

'I can't tell John about this, Maggie, he'll think I've lost the plot even more than usual,' said Bryant, ignoring the crash of china and examining the pastries. 'Death is stalking me. I can hear his dry bones clicking in my shadow. I can feel him brushing against my heart.'

'Are you sure your jumper's not too tight?'

'No, this is the pale horseman himself, charging up behind me with dirty great hooves.'

'I can see the problem,' Maggie agreed, peering up at the cake counter. 'You're haunted. I don't mean by supernatural forces – it's more of an infection in your soul. We simply have to unhaunt you. Do they have Battenberg?'

'Over there, by the macaroons. How do you intend to do that?'

'What, eat marzipan?'

'No, unhaunt me. Is there a standard procedure?'

She thought for a moment. 'We need to start in a place that has special resonance for you.' They found a 1940s drop-leaf table and seated themselves.

'We could go to the Nun & Broken Compass,' Bryant decided. 'I do some of my best thinking over a pint of Bishop's Wellington.'

Maggie leaned forward on patched purple elbows. 'I meant somewhere you've left your spiritual imprint. You haven't been in your new flat for long enough to imbue it with psychic resonance.'

'I wouldn't say that. I've already blocked my bathroom sink. I was shaving the bobbly bits off my scarf.'

'Be serious for a moment. You have been polluted with bad karma. Your mind can make you sick, Arthur. If you're easily susceptible – and you are – you won't just die from cancer, say, but from believing that you're dying of cancer. You turn your cells against themselves. If everyone treats you as if you are dying, you buy into it. Everything in your whole being becomes about dying.'

Bryant took a sip of his tea and grimaced at its

weakness. 'If this is about curing yourself with positive energy, you've got the wrong mug.'

'Listen to me. I took part in a clinical trial in which around a quarter of patients in control groups – those given supposedly inert therapies – experienced powerful negative side effects. The severity of those side effects matched those associated with real drugs. Human suggestion is a powerful weapon, Arthur. Our lot suffered from something called "anticipatory nausea" because they were told they would. Around sixty per cent of patients undergoing chemotherapy start feeling sick before their treatment because they've been warned that's what will happen.'

He pointed a finger at her. 'It was you who told me to be careful of Mr Merry in the first place. You set me up to be wary of him.'

'I know, and I blame myself for that. Whether he genuinely possesses powers or just uses various auto-suggestive techniques, I believe he can do real harm. I should never have told you so much about him. Clearly, he managed to get to you. What is it he made you fear the most?'

Bryant thought back. 'He knew about something that happened when I was a child, something I never told anyone. I was locked inside a corrugated-iron air-raid shelter. I thought I was going to die.'

'Narrow houses,' said Maggie, nodding knowingly. 'That's what they used to call coffins. I presume he met you at the museum.'

'Yes, in the restoration room for the undisplayed items.'

'At the back of the ground floor? But don't you see? It's a coffin-shaped room! And I bet he was surrounded by crates.'

'Yes, great oblong ones large enough to put a man in. The World War Two exhibition was playing next door. I could hear the fall of bombs and – and bricks collapsing. He offered me a cigarette from his case, which I thought was odd because there's no smoking anywhere in the building.'

'The crates, the cigarette case,' she said, 'more coffins. He's done his research on you. Arthur, you understand how magicians use the power of suggestion and you still didn't see what he was doing? Parlour tricks, that's all they are, although in the right hands they can work astoundingly well. We have to counteract this. Where do you spend the most time?'

'At the unit.'

'Then we'll go there and get you comfortable. I'll put you into a light hypnotic state, make you a bit more pre-disposed to my treatment. It's all right, I'm qualified. I took Magic and Psychology at Keeble College.'

'I didn't know you went to Oxford.'

'No, this was Keeble Technical College in the Shetland Islands, but it still counts. I also came back with a degree in woodwork.'

They demolished the last of the cake and headed for the PCU.

'We mustn't tell Raymond you're in the building,' said Bryant. 'He'll have kittens. Actually, that's an unfortunate phrase.' He halted on the landing as several mewling black balls of fur trotted past. 'Where are we going to do this? We can't use my office, someone will find us.'

'Even at this hour?' asked Maggie.

'There's usually someone here until midnight when we have a case on.'

'What about the attic?' She looked up the darkened stairwell. 'Isn't that full of the stuff you couldn't move into your new flat?'

'I had nowhere else to store my automata, my bar billiards table or any of my Tibetan prayer wheels.'

'Perfect,' said Maggie, leading the way. 'I've got every-thing I need in my carpet bag.'

'We haven't wired any lights up there yet,' said Bryant, taking the stairs. 'We're not going to hold a séance, are we?'

'No, I went off those after Daphne sent my mother's Wedgwood out of the window during a table-tapping session. She doesn't know her own strength.'

Armed with torches, they entered the attic and cleared an area next to Madame Blavatsky, her waxen features looming out of her glass case like a turbaned housewife. There were several other display cabinets, a group of dandified hedgehogs arranged in a cotillion, some coconut penis sheaths from the Watabili tribe and a stuffed weasel in a little bowler hat. 'I've been meaning to throw those out,' said Bryant, eyeing them from a safe distance.

'We have to block the entrance to the room,' Maggie explained. 'So that nothing bad gets in. Or gets out.' The pair shifted an old Welsh dresser over the floorboards until it stood across the attic entrance. Bryant was wiping his dusty hands on his waistcoat when he caught a strange look in the white witch's eyes. She nodded silently at the wall.

In the space behind where the dresser had stood was revealed a large crimson heart, its flesh pierced by five silver arrows. Droplets of painted blood fell from the blades to the floor. Their torch-beams revealed other gore-drenched hearts and arrows painted all around the attic.

'The Bleeding Heart,' said Bryant, awed. 'He's been here. He's marked his territory.' He dabbed his forefinger at the wall and licked it. 'Poster paint.'

'It's a way of making sure you do his bidding,' said Maggie.

'How would he know I'd come up here and see them?'

'Oh, Arthur, *everyone* knows you come up here. There's no time to lose.' She withdrew a set of coloured chalks and began scratching a design on the floor that eventually resembled the sea-monster drawings from old marine maps.

'Right, make yourself comfy.' She found him a small folding stool and sat herself on a sparkly Moroccan cushion. 'What we're going to do tonight is very serious,' she explained. 'I have to make you confront the spectre of your own death. I'm not going to pretend it won't be traumatic.'

'So is this psychology or witchcraft?'

'A bit of both, I hope.'

They began breathing exercises, then visualization techniques. Over the next two hours Maggie took her old friend back to that day on the bomb-site and reordered the event until it resulted in a different outcome. She used every mind trick in the book: neuro-linguistic programming, targeted rapport, unconscious communication, meditation, cold-reading, psychic transference and confirmation bias, with a hefty dose of auto-suggestion. She also tried regressive hypnosis to try and find out what he had done with her deep-fat fryer, which he had borrowed and never returned.

The experience was emotionally draining, and by the time it was over Maggie had turned quite pale and was experiencing the familiar gnaw of stomach cramps. She brought Bryant out of his trance, then rose unsteadily to her feet and crunched down two Nurofens.

'People don't understand what it takes out of you to do this,' she said. 'You probably won't sleep tonight. Well, the proof's in the pudding. How do you feel? Try to recall your childhood fears now.'

Bryant rubbed his face about, as if moulding his features into a new setting. His limbs felt curiously light, as if he was ready to run off down the road. 'Do you know, I can still remember the whole thing,' he said, 'but why was I ever afraid? Nothing happened. I survived.' He shook his head in wonder. 'I came out of that iron coffin and was taken home by the policeman. Home – that's where the real troubles were for me.'

'And what do you feel when you look down into that hole in the earth and think about the terrors of the night grave?'

Bryant closed his eyes, then snapped them open. 'Nothing. Either a man is dead or he's not. Premature burial is just a bogeyman used to frighten children.'

She permitted herself a smile of triumph. 'Then I think you can consider yourself unhaunted.'

'Maggie, you're a genius. I don't know why you didn't do this for me years ago.'

'Because you never told me about your past.'

'There are things I don't tell anyone, not even John. I feel sorry for those born into the information generation; they'll never have any real privacy unless they choose to disappear completely. Me, I've half disappeared already. What a relief. But you should sit down, you look terrible.'

Maggie gave an uncertain smile. 'No, Arthur, I'll stay on my feet. If I sit, I'll sleep for at least six hours.'

'Is there anything I can I do for you?'

'No, I'll be all right once I get home.'

'At least let me pay for a taxi.'

'Darling, I've never taken a penny for my services. Although I do sometimes allow clients to provide hot tea and chocolate digestives.'

'Then that's what you shall have. And tomorrow, I'm going to take that charlatan Merry to pieces.'

'You'll have to be very careful,' Maggie warned as they negotiated the narrow staircase down. 'He's still danger-ous. I think that list of rules I gave you still holds, in spite of what you've told me. Mr Merry is a cold-reader. He can convince total strangers that he knows all about them. You mentioned apotropaic magic. I assume from this that Mr Merry thinks he's creating some kind of occult master plan. He believes the raven's wing can cast the shadow of death across the land. Whether it's real or imagined, he's still trying to bring about the fall of England, but from

what you've told me about the new set-up you'll need concrete proof to arrest him, and that's rather hard to come
by in our game. People have been searching for the truth
for hundreds of years.'

'I'll find it,' said Bryant. 'But he can wait. The priority
now is to find out if Romain Curtis was deliberately
killed, and who shot Stephen Emes.'

'So the cases are linked?'

'Certainly. At some point they brushed against each
other. One thinks of London as too vast for such connections, but it's not, of course. Overlaid on the tube map are
thousands of other maps joining people from every walk
of life. At the interchanges are those who inhabit a dozen
different worlds. Mr Merry is one such man.' He grinned.
'But I think he's met his match in me.'

33

INFILTRATION

Early on Monday morning both investigations were restarted in earnest, but first Bryant wanted to find out how the Bleeding Heart had been painted in the PCU's attic, and he had a pretty good idea.

'I told you, I don't bloody know what happened to him,' said Dave, the remaining builder. Like most Turks Bryant had met, he seemed to get much better value out of the word 'bloody' than the English, flattening it into a properly foul cuss word.

'Well, what happened to the other Dave?' asked May.

'He put his back out lifting some tellies off a lorry in Southend – nothing illegal – so the agency sent a replacement.'

'And you can't even remember his name?'

'No, I don't remember names without vowels, so I just called him Dave. He was going to sort out the electrics. He made some diagrams, then carried out some work. He was only here for the morning. Went for lunch; I didn't see him again after that. The towel rail in the second-floor toilet is still live.'

'What kind of work did he carry out?'

'How would I know? He didn't fix the electrics, but he was a bloody good artist. Showed me this painting he'd done and said he was going to make it into a mural. *He* signed off on it.' The remaining Dave stabbed a hairy finger at a startled Raymond Land.

'Some scruffy Herbert thrust a piece of paper in front of me,' Land complained. 'I sign things all the time.'

'So you let a stranger walk in here and – God, what else did he do?' asked May. Armed with the map Bryant had taken from Emes's flat, the detectives headed for the second-floor staircase, closely followed by a contrite, hand-wringing Land.

They began their search in the bathroom with the live towel rail. Bryant couldn't resist testing it – the way one does when a waiter tells you not to touch a hot plate – and got a few volts up his fillings. May tapped the wall. 'This plaster's fresh. Hang on a minute.' He lifted a dreadful, dust-caked reproduction of Fragonard's *Les Hasards heureux de l'escarpolette* from the wall and peered under it. At the centre was a tiny black dot.

'I think we've been infiltrated,' said May.

Land squinted at the device. 'What is it, a camera?'

'Of course not, you clothhead,' said Bryant. 'If it was a camera all it would see is the back of the picture. It's a microphone.'

'Why stick it in the bathroom?'

'Because when the door's open you can hear anything that's being said in the corridor,' said May. 'And the door won't shut properly. There are bound to be others.'

They split up and started examining the building room by room. Longbright found one under her desk. Bryant found one on his bookcase. Land found one glued to the back of the framed photo of his soon-to-be-ex wife. 'She's still betraying me even though she's gone,' he said miserably. 'I'm lost. I don't understand what's going on at all. Why would this—'

'Ne-cro-man-cer,' said Bryant helpfully, breaking the word into easy syllables.

'Why does he want to listen in on us?'

'Because he knows we're investigating him?' May suggested.

'Can we trace these things back to him and nail him that way?'

'We can pinpoint their manufacture but not who they're transmitting to,' May replied. 'Did you find anything that looked like a listening device in Emes's flat?'

'Nothing that I saw,' said Bryant, 'but I'll check with Dan.'

Land couldn't have looked more confused if he'd been blindfolded and turned around three times. 'Then why were the building plans there?'

'The obvious answer is that Merry knew Emes. He never seems to do his own dirty work, so he put someone else on to it. When you operate in a particular field, you soon get to know who else is around. We know that Emes was available for hire.'

'Could somebody draw me a diagram showing how all these people are connected?' Land pleaded. 'I'm lost.'

'You do understand the nature of our work, don't you?' asked Bryant. 'It's wool-carding. Kept apart, people are fundamentally decent and mean well, but when they're put together they get themselves into terrible knots. Our job is to disentangle, clean and re-weave the fibres of social life to produce a continuous cord suitable for processing.' He slapped the chaotic paperwork he had abandoned on Land's desk. 'Just assume for now that all the suspects in this case know each other, and that one of them is a murderer.'

'Star Building Maintenance,' May told his partner back in their office. 'The other Dave was arrested over in Essex for transporting stolen televisions. He was replaced by a Latvian builder called Pavils who is currently being sought by the authorities in Riga for failing to report to his probation officer.'

'And they sent him to a unit that requires security clearance?' asked Bryant, incredulous. 'How did he get through the system?'

'That's what I asked. Recommendations, apparently.'

'From whom?'

'Have a look at this.' He chucked a page across the joined desks while Bryant fumbled for his bifocals. 'He was cleared for maintenance work in the new rare-documents gallery at the Museum of London. There's a sign-off on the bottom.'

Bryant found himself looking at the signature of one of the museum's assistant heads of department, Dr S. Emes. 'It's a forgery,' he said. 'Emes was kicked out of King's College and went to work with the New Resurrectionists. Look at the name of the department head at the foot of the letter. Prof. P. W. Merry, PhD, DMS. You realize what this is,' he added excitedly. 'It's proof.'

'Of what?'

'That Merry's a charlatan and perhaps something much worse. Now we have links in a chain of command. Merry uses his New Resurrectionist pal Emes, and gets a workman replaced here. He provides clearance so that Pavils can bug the building. And while he's here, Pavils is under instruction to paint the Bleeding Heart in the attic. Merry's not clairvoyant. He sent me to the New Resurrectionists in exchange for a promise that I wouldn't pursue the Tower of London thefts, so we know he has a connection with them. What we need to find out now is who else was connected with Emes. One of these people hired him.' He stabbed his finger at the names on the board behind him. 'And after he did their dirty work, they got rid of him. Who's going to hate a resurrectionist most? How about a funeral director?'

'You have absolutely no empirical data that would allow you to assume that,' May complained.

'No,' Bryant agreed, pointing out of the window. 'It's called blue-sky thinking. I learned it from the online manual Orion Banks sent everyone. I was going to bin it but then I decided to print it out as there was nothing to read in the staff toilet.' He grinned. 'So you see, it turns out I've always been ahead of my time. I was just waiting for everyone else to catch up.'

'We're raiding a funeral parlour?' Dan Banbury repeated. 'That's nice, isn't it? Perhaps we should follow it with a spot of go-karting round the local crematorium. Talk about no respect for the dead. Bloody hell.'

'I don't like it any more than you,' said May, 'but Arthur seems convinced of their involvement in the death of Stephen Emes, so we now have a search warrant. Let's get cracking.'

Ron Rummage was waiting outside when they arrived. His jolliness had dissipated with the news that his premises were to be searched. 'This is really too much,' he complained, anxiously wiping his spectacles. 'This company buried William Gladstone in 1898 and Stanley Baldwin in 1947. We've earned the good faith of monarchies and governments, we've been entrusted with the final state secrets, and now we're being treated as common criminals. We have a reputation to maintain. What do you expect to find?'

'We're hoping to eliminate you from the investigation,' said Bryant truthfully. 'You have to look at it from our point of view: a man who attempts to bodysnatch your clients must be regarded as an enemy, no? A respected lawyer, a much-loved local figure and even a dog, all of whom had been planted by you . . .'

Rummage winced. 'Must you say "planted"? We are funeral arrangers, morticians, mourning specialists—'

'I'm sorry, but at some point you do put people who are brown bread into boxes and shovel wet dirt on them,' said Bryant maliciously. 'If we could get started?'

'Do you have a faith, Mr Bryant?' asked Rummage as he unlocked the front door.

'No, Mr Rummage, I decided to forgo that particular emotional crutch a very long time ago.'

'But perhaps you could still find it in your heart to have a little respect for those who still need religion in their lives, and prefer not to think of their departed loved ones as "brown bread", as you so distastefully put it. And nor are they "pushing up daisies", "dropping off perches" or "hitting room temperature", as I've also heard you policeman say behind my back. It's utterly indecent. We try to provide the emotionally traumatized with a little inner peace, not upset them further by conjuring up the image of a corpse with a faceful of mud. Your abrasive attitude is very far from helpful.'

May fought to suppress a smile. It was a long time since he had heard someone put Arthur in his place. 'We'll try to keep this as brief and undisruptive as possible,' he promised, allowing Banbury to take over. Rummage sat and watched in dismay as the rooms were systematically searched. Bryant stayed silent and thoughtful until his mobile produced an alarming chorus of 'When the Buds Are Blossoming' from *Ruddigore*. After taking the call, he appeared to have lost interest in the search he had initiated.

He rose, suddenly eager to be away. 'You two can handle this. I'm going to bring in Mrs Wallace.' He raised his hat. 'Mr Rummage.'

May found himself frowning as he watched Bryant take his leave. Something in his partner's manner unsettled him. Instead of being relieved that Mr Merry was not about to rain down plagues of frogs on his head, he seemed keen to put the entire matter behind him. Reading

Bryant's motives required, at the very least, expertise and prescience, but this time May felt himself being firmly deflected.

He always does this before he announces a breakthrough, he thought hopefully.

34

A DEAL

During mid-morning break, Sennen Renfield went look-ing for Martin Wallace. She found the boy disconsolately kicking a plastic football against the playground wall in the sifting rain. She hadn't figured him for the football type, being an indie, or whichever tribe it was that he belonged to now. None of the pupils came here any more – on days like today most stayed inside playing online games of escalating complexity.

'Hey,' he said, concentrating on the ball. 'What are you doing out here?'

'It's too hot inside. There's a fight going on over game controllers. The new Call of Duty maps are out – like I care. I can't be doing with all that testosterone. How are you?'

'Getting there. It'll all be over soon.'

'What do you mean?'

He kicked the ball harder. 'I'll soon be out of school and away from here. Far away, like South-East Asia or something.'

'You don't mean yet – you mean after your exam results?'

'Not necessarily,' he said sulkily.

'I guess I'll have to go to any college that will take me,' she said. 'I don't think my grades are going to be that great.'

'I'm not going to college.' Another, angrier kick. 'My old man spent half his life studying. What was the point of that? He ended up hanging from his own school tie off the back of a bedroom door. What a pussy.'

'Are you getting counselling?'

'No. Why would I want to do that?'

Sennen remembered Longbright's request. 'Well, what with everything your mother's going through—'

Martin gave her a sharp look. 'What about my mother?'

'I heard she was outside Shirone Estanza's flat, just hanging around watching her.'

'Not true. She was hanging around outside the flat of the guy who killed my father. They had a fight in the street; like that could have been any more embarrassing. My mother did something really stupid and the guy ended up in hospital.'

'What did she do?'

He slammed the ball again. 'Only tried to strangle him with his tie. Just like my old man.'

'Wow. You really think he killed your dad?'

'He didn't hold a gun to his head, but yeah, I'd say he killed him.'

'How did he do that?'

'He works for some sleazy waste-disposal company that sells dead animals to the Third World. He dumped all the details of his scummy working practices on my old man, and when Dad told him he was having moral issues with them, he made him go broke.' Martin stopped the ball at his foot.

'Why didn't your dad talk it over with your mum?'

'He didn't tell her anything about his work. All she cared about was how much money he was making. He told me.'

'But your mum was upset enough to—'

'I don't want to talk about her any more, OK?'

'I was just interested, that's all.'

Martin eyed her suspiciously. 'You're good friends with Shirone, right?'

'Yeah, we hang out together.'

'I'll do a deal with you. You can ask me anything you want if you arrange for me to talk to her.'

'I can try. But she's not looking for a boyfriend.'

'I didn't say I wanted to go on a *date*.' He used the grandma-word with heavy irony.

'You don't say much at all, do you? Anyway, why would she go out with someone she's never going to see again? You're going to South-East Asia.'

'I didn't say I was going alone.' He dismissed her, returning his concentration to the ball. 'So, is it a deal?'

Sennen sighed. She liked Martin, but Martin was interested in someone else; it was the story of her life so far. 'Yeah,' she said, 'it's a deal.'

35

MR BRYANT EXPATIATES

If there was one thing Raymond Land liked more than a tidy office it was a bar graph showing that crime statistics were down, preferably one in nice bright primary colours, clearly labelled in a neat sans-serif typeface, inserted into a congratulatory email from the Home Office.

Instead he found himself reading a barely comprehensible barrage of invective from Orion Banks and her department of language-manglers, complaining about the sheer pointlessness of attempting any communication with him. His face fell as his eyes skimmed the screen – *disincentivized macromanaging* – *public/private paradigm loss* – *unleveraged core competency* – *skill ecosystem malfunction* – *market-facing personnel deficits* . . . He couldn't bear to read any further.

Right, he thought, *it's time somebody put their foot down around here. Cometh the hour, cometh the man.* It was five o'clock on Monday evening, over a week since the investigations at the Tower of London and St George's Gardens had started, and what had they to show for it? Bugger all. He called Longbright, who summoned the rest of the team to the common room, including Giles

Kershaw, who was over at St Pancras Mortuary, in the middle of autopsying a workman who had fallen under an earth-mover.

Last autumn, Land had watched Orion Banks give a presentation at an awayday entitled 'Pathfinder Projects In Policing'. He particularly recalled her intuitive use of body language, the nape of her bare neck and the way in which her tight blue skirt stretched fetchingly across her thighs. People listened to her, not just because she was attractive but because she was in command. He felt sure that if he could just prove he was cut from the same executive cloth, someone would finally notice him and would have him moved to a department where his talents could be better used. It was time to start being a little more ambitious rather than just hoping for a transfer to the kind of town where a lottery win made local headlines.

Today's email was a setback, certainly, but he felt sure he could turn the situation around. He wasn't the most decisive executive officer, but he was a thorough communicator – there had been many occasions when Bryant and May had announced he was giving them 'way too much information', for example – and he felt sure he still had much to offer the force. Although part of him still thought it would be quite nice if his next unit was situated somewhere like the Scilly Isles.

He peered out of his office, listening to make sure that everyone was assembled. Then he took a deep breath and went into the room.

He immediately stumbled over, his right foot entangled in a length of purple wool that led around Bryant's chair leg and up to the detective's partially unravelled scarf, which had been knotted around the coat-stand.

Dusting himself down, Land found himself looking at more cats than members of staff. He had a team of eight, PC Fraternity DuCaine currently being on secondment to a Met unit, and ten cats, or strictly speaking one overweight mother cat and nine kittens. Bryant was smoking a pipe and reading an old copy of *Fortean Times*. Mangeshkar was texting. Bimsley and Banbury were comparing phone apps. Renfield and Longbright were having some kind of domestic, and Kershaw appeared to be holding a dead mouse. May quickly rose, hushed everyone and sat back down again, turning to face him. By doing so, he unconsciously established where the real authority lay in the room.

'Eight officers working on two simple cases,' Land began, 'over a period of one week consisting of twelve-hour days, and where are we?'

'Technically there're nine staff,' said Bryant, looking over the top of his newspaper, 'if you count yourself.'

'And there's the intern,' said Bimsley.

'And most of us worked over the weekend,' said Renfield.

'So saying that it's sixty hours, or thirty per case, you'd be wrong because you'd need to factor in another, what, fourteen or sixteen weekend hours,' added Banbury. 'That's assuming the cases were equally weighted, which they're not.'

'Just shut up, all of you, you're all bloody useless,' yelled Land, breaking his own personal record for losing the room.

'I don't think that's fair,' snapped Mangeshkar. 'We've carried out CCTV checks, phone checks, surveillances and door-to-doors and we've conducted over two hundred personal interviews so far. I've got plasters all over my feet.'

'We moved the case further on than it would ever have gone under the Met,' said Bimsley. 'It's not our fault if it doesn't make any sense.'

'You still don't get it, do you?' said Land, searching the confused faces before him. 'Even after all this time. *It doesn't have to make sense.* You can't make sense of human nature. A loving husband and wife share a house together for ten years, then one day he batters her to death with a golf club. Moments after he's arrested, he bursts into tears and says he loves her. Does that make any sense? A selfish woman leaves a kind, caring husband for a smarmy little creep who teaches flamenco to pensioners and has been living in a converted railway carriage in Wales for the last decade. Does that make any sense? Don't talk to me about sense. I've been alive for forty-seven years and I have absolutely no understanding of human nature whatsoever. I might as well be living with a completely different species, giant squids or perhaps some kind of insect colony.'

'I thought you were older,' said Bryant.

'What I need is a result,' said Land. 'I don't give a fiddler's fart whether a thief broke into the Tower of London and stole a bunch of pets or whether he machine-gunned all the Warders and blew up the armoury. In fact I'd prefer that because then the case would fall under the Prevention of Terrorism Act and would be taken away from us, and I'd be able to tear up the paperwork. And if someone wants to go around digging up the city's corpses and then decides to tie rockets to them and fire them across the street at oncoming vehicles I really wouldn't give a tinker's toss, so long as there was something I could write in the blank section of the form that's currently sitting on my desk. But no, I have nothing at all except a chain of events that couldn't be more random if you painted them on ping-pong balls and dropped them into a bingo machine.'

Land was surprised to find himself sweating, and sat down with a thump on an orange bendy chair.

Bryant gave May one of his meaningful looks. 'Thank you for that,' he said, removing his pipe and folding his paper into his lap in the silence that followed. 'If you've quite got everything out of your system, I'll endeavour to link together some of your bingo balls.'

He rose to his feet, digging painfully about in his waist-coat for his bifocals and then a minuscule scrap of paper. Land could not help but notice that everyone in the room had turned to look at him.

'Let's start with ravens, shall we? Native to these isles, birds of great mystical significance, harbingers of death, progenitors of superstitious power. They disappear from their most famous, most ancient home and we're asked to investigate not because of any real belief in the idea that when they vanish England falls, but because it will keep us occupied with a piece of pointless PR while the City of London gets on with the serious business of keeping the Square Mile banks secure during a massive fraud cyber-attack.'

There was a murmur around the room.

'We're palmed off with some guff about placating the English Tourist Board and preventing the confidence of overseas visitors from being dented, despite the fact that this ridiculous fable has been repeatedly discredited and laid at the feet of late-Victorian fantasists. In other words, my dear Raymondo, the case is there to keep us out of the way.

'But then an entirely unwarranted intrusion occurs: a bizarre event that actually fits our remit and gets passed to us too quickly for the City of London to do anything about it – you remember it was put on the incident log by a local PC who contacted this unit because we were the only ones in the vicinity who were still open. The event – an interrupted exhumation – is compounded almost immediately by the death of its only witness.' He addressed the others like a lawyer during his summing-up. 'Now, one would think that's something to get your teeth into. First directive: to decide whether Romain Curtis was killed as the result of what he had seen or heard. Well, we knew he'd heard something – a phrase that turned out to be "He's a minor". The culprits are saying, "Ignore him, he doesn't matter." Corpses don't talk, so the person who's holding Wallace up is talking to – who? Two people, then, not one. Which explains Wallace's right arm. Curtis stated that he saw it rise. What he saw, I imagine, is a pair of idiots trying to stop a corpse from falling over by holding it under the arms. Wallace had been in the ground since Friday morning. Rigor mortis had worn off.

'Curtis doesn't see that the corpse is being held up. He's been smoking dope, for a start, it's very dark beneath the trees by the rear wall of the gardens, and if the act was premeditated, his graverobbers are presumably wearing dark clothes. What he gets is a nice little puppet-show, rather like the Black Theatre of Prague. And what he sees makes such an impact on him that he leaves his girlfriend on the street and goes back for another look. Whatever happens then is what decides his fate.'

Bryant played the room, hooking a thumb into his waistcoat. 'Does Curtis take a photo? We don't know, because there's nothing on his phone, so if he did, he deleted it. The next evening he is followed to a local club by one of the perpetrators, who spikes his drink. Curtis collapses in a backstreet and is dispatched. The question remains, did he go back to take a photograph in the gardens? He's a teenager; that and texting is virtually all they do. Of course he did. But at this point a new mystery surfaces: during the course of the evening Curtis's shirt mysteriously changes colour. Why? What happened to it?

'Now our so-called bingo balls of fate start to line up in quick succession. Other bodies are disinterred, and it transpires that all were buried by the same undertaker. Yet despite this, the senior funeral services director of Wells and Sons comes up clean. But there has to be a link, no matter how unlikely: a suicide, a sickly old lady, a dog, none of whom knew each other. What were they buried with?' He checked his notes. 'A pair of silver cufflinks, a paste brooch, a diamanté collar, nothing to get excited about there. I thought perhaps there was something else in one of the coffins, but Prince's little casket didn't even have a lining, so no luck on that front.

'Now we turn our attention to a group of disgruntled medical students frustrated by the limitations of the pharmaceutical industry – the New Resurrectionists. They've followed the path of their forebears and taken to supplying themselves with cadavers. I'm sent there by my only real suspect in the raven-theft case. Why do I say he's a suspect? Because Mr Merry, a so-called "academic necromancer", is in fact a gargantuan fraud in a pirate hat whom I have been convinced to take seriously. He, however, takes himself very seriously indeed, which makes him dangerous, especially after he sends me into the clutches of a paramedical splinter group with an illegal agenda.

'The obvious question is, why would he do such a thing?' Bryant looked about the room. 'Let's go back to the reason why I suspect him of being a birdnapper in the first place. He's a believer in apotropaic magic: the power of animals to bring about great psychic change. Ravens are right up there among the most powerful mythological fauna of all, and ravens from the Bloody Tower are enfolded into the very fabric of England's mythology. OK, we know that to be a load of old cobblers, but Merry's clients don't and will doubtless pay top dollar to see him conduct a ceremony that is intended to initiate the fall of the nation. When does a man stop being a harmless crank? When others are prepared to believe in him and back it up with cash.

'Merry may be a charlatan but he's an astute reader of human nature, what we might call a sensitive. After our interview he instinctively knows that I suspect him. So he sends me into the lions' den. Even if he doesn't know the specifics of the New Resurrectionists' involvement in my case, he's pretty sure of two things: one, that they *were* involved somehow; and two, that they'll want to see their enemy up close.'

He raised a finger at them. '*But* . . . Mr Merry has made a mistake. It transpires that one of his employees was hired to conduct the exhumations, because they're all but impossible to manage alone. This, then, is the crossing point between the two cases. But we still come back to the fundamental question: why remove the bodies from the coffins at all? And why dig up a dog?'

Land thought he had finished and stood up, but Bryant continued. 'Meanwhile, there are other undercurrents. Mrs Wallace starts attacking her husband's client, first verbally, then physically, blaming him for the death of her husband. Her son Martin confirms that his father became privy to information that he found morally compromising, and did not know what to do about it. Wallace's performance at work suffered, so his client Krishna Jhadav removed the account and ruined his livelihood, which arguably led to his depression and suicide. By the way, it was Janice here who discovered that Thomas Wallace had a history of treatment for depression.

'During the third exhumation, which, as it's a very small canine, we can assume only takes one person this time, the resurrectionist is shot dead with an arrow from a crossbow. Even though the choice of weapon is bizarre, we do have a suspect. Unfortunately Mrs Wallace turns out to have been at home with her son that night, and we even have confirmation from our own team, because she goes out to the local corner shop, walking past the front terrace where Shirone Estanza lives. We know someone was keeping a watchful eye on the girl, and presumed it was Mrs Wallace because she thinks Estanza knows more than she's letting on.

'Which leaves one other main suspect in the frame for the death of Stephen Emes, and that would be someone in the New Resurrectionists who knew what he was up to and felt that his actions compromised the safety of the group, which is why I want their headquarters turned over with an electron microscope and mint surgical tweezers until we get some hard forensic evidence. And if that isn't an advance on a random collection of bingo balls I'm Shirley Bassey.'

Having completely run out of breath, Bryant seated himself and looked about for his smouldering pipe while a kitten peed on Raymond Land's shoe.

36

WASTE MANAGEMENT

Krishna Jhadav's left arm and hip still ached on Tuesday morning. As he walked down to the service corridor in the building's basement, he shrugged his shoulders and twisted his head from side to side, trying to loosen his tender muscles. He cursed himself for having made the appointment today.

He was still angry with Wallace's crazy bitch wife for trying to drag him off down the street, but what hurt more was seeing how upset Irina had become after he'd returned from the hospital. He had carefully avoided any detailed explanation of what he did for a living, knowing that she would not be able to handle some of the hard realities of his job. They were virtually living together these days. If the relationship got any more serious he knew he would have to find a way of broaching the subject with her, and he had a bad feeling about how she would react.

His swipe card got him into the restricted area, but there was no one to meet him on the other side. This was not unusual; most of the system was automated now. He was heading to the back of the building, where he followed the directions marked 'Primary Basin'.

He had not wanted to come here this morning, but he was desperate. The factory was owned by one of his most loyal clients, but it had been fined half a dozen times in the last five years for Health and Safety infractions. This time it was more than likely that there would be a government investigation, but he couldn't afford to turn down the money. Inspect the consignment, approve the paperwork, ship it out; he had been through the procedure a hundred times before. This was his third trip, and the last, but three was the minimum he could get away with. After tonight he could sign and deliver, paid up front.

Reaching the last of the signs warning that all non-site personnel needed to be accompanied, he pushed open the brushed-metal door to the primary sedimentation treatment tanks.

The grey concrete bowls set in the basement floor were dry and empty. Galvanized-steel walkways criss-crossed them, and at the far side a bank of digital monitors recorded the system's activity. The tanks were used to settle sludge, allowing grease and oil to float to the surface. This was skimmed off by rotating mechanical scrapers that drove the collected scum towards a hopper in the base of the tank, whence it could be pumped to sludge-treatment facilities. Fats and oils from the floating material could then be recovered for a rendering process called saponification.

Jhadav looked around for a technician, but found no one. As the factory was largely unoccupied today the tanks were still unused, although the sewage lines were open for clearing waste. Usually, all active areas of the site were required to be manned throughout the working day, but his client had managed to reduce on-site personnel to just two managers.

Jhadav crossed the diamond-patterned walkway to the monitors and checked the back office. Neon striplights were on everywhere, the equipment was functioning, but there were no members of staff on duty.

He stared impatiently at the monitors, the diagrammatic mazes of pipes and tanks, most of them blank, a couple marked in red to indicate that they held waste in containment. Four empty office swivel chairs stood in a row. He wondered why people got so squeamish about waste. Everyone produced it but nobody wanted to know where it went. He was always surprised by the level of hysteria that accompanied the siting of factories: neighbourhoods up in arms, local petitions, council protests; if there was one thing in which Britain led the world it was overreaction. So there was a little horseflesh in supermarket beefburgers: wasn't that a small price to pay for cheap convenient food? Waste was the same. You were prepared to produce it, but you didn't want it anywhere near you.

Jhadav had seen enough. Everything seemed to be in order. He was glad the managers had received instructions to make themselves scarce for the final visit. He was about to leave when he heard movement somewhere below him. Looking over into the nearest basin he saw something come to rest near the shallow indentation at the centre of the basin.

The object looked familiar. There in the centre, sliding to a stop over the drainage grille, was a black leather Bulgari wallet. It was definitely his, because several credit cards had come loose and lay scattered on the basin floor. Irina had talked him into choosing the damned thing but it fitted euros, not pounds, and he had regretted buying it ever since. It had been in one of his pockets when he had arrived – he'd taken it out to get at his entry card – but the pockets were too shallow and it had a habit of falling out.

The basin was around four metres deep, but a short retractable steel ladder was fitted over the side. Jhadav slipped through the railing and climbed quickly down, retrieving the wallet and repacking it with his cards. He couldn't quite see how it had ended up here.

He was about to climb back up when he heard a noise in the vent set in the side of the basin, about one and a half metres up from the angled base. Bringing his ear closer to the outlet, he heard it more clearly. A mechanical calibration, dividing off the seconds.

He did not see the arrow until it was right in front of his face. A tintinnabulation filled his head as he reeled back under its impact, trying to understand what had happened. He raised his right hand to his cheek and brought it away wet. His fingers looked as if they had been dipped in red wine. His neck started to burn.

Jhadav turned and was horrified to see the smooth steel shaft jutting out of his collarbone. He tried to maintain his balance but dropped to his knees in shock.

The ringing continued, driving out his ability to think clearly. He looked up at the blackened opening of the outlet, watching in horror as an explosion of dense brown effluent lolloped from the gaping vent.

The smell was unbelievable, something solid and overwhelming that blinded his senses. It spattered from the unsealed pipe, blasting in every direction, spraying his eyes, removing the grip from the soles of his shoes. He slid heavily on to his back, scrabbling at the floor.

The pipe was in full flow now, discharging the backed-up waste of the tank above in a great arc, which was forced out by pressure alone. It had already covered the base of the tank. The effluent comprised a lethal combination of liquids, solids and gases. The reek of methane burned his sinuses. Jhadav felt himself losing consciousness, and knew that if he did not reach the ladder he was doomed to die in here.

He had seen enough accidents on silage projects – workers were frequently overcome by the fumes and hardly ever managed to get out alive. Slipping and sliding in the raw waste, he fought to reach the bottom rung of the ladder, but a fresh blast of sewage hit him in the middle of his chest, throwing him from his feet. He twisted as he fell, punching the arrow deeper into his shoulder. His skull cracked against the base of the steel ladder, and he landed face down in the untreated sewage that was flooding into the basin.

Held in place by the run-off, he floundered weakly, but now his arm was caught behind the conduit ladder and he was unable to move in any direction.

Flopping like a seabird trapped in tar, Jhadav's movements grew fainter, finally stilling as his body was subsumed within the cloacal deluge.

37

SHAFTED

On Tuesday morning at 9.35 a.m. all hell broke loose. News of Krishna Jhadav's death reached the PCU. Orion Banks immediately called Raymond Land with a torrent of furious questions. Land deflected her call with a rare demonstration of spine, and the unit was divided into two work-teams. Meanwhile, yet another request for a search warrant was entered against the premises of the New Resurrectionists, although this was only in principle, as Banks had still not approved Bryant's earlier written argument for locating it.

'Jhadav was found in a factory called CaroFrend Processing,' Bryant pointed out. 'Interesting derivation, abbreviated Latin for "to crush meat". Funny how companies always think that it'll sound better if they translate their purpose into something vaguely classical.'

'Banks is having a meltdown,' Land warned. 'She's blocking all of our documentation, refusing to process anything. I don't think the CoL has any idea what she's up to. I asked her why and she told me, and I quote, "This isn't an investigation, it's a David Lynch cheese dream." I don't even know what that means.'

'I wouldn't worry about her, old sock,' said Bryant. 'Her phone call to you was more an act of self-preservation than genuine concern. Banks is arse-covering against a future inquiry. I've seen the type before. Her eye's more on the clock than the mantelpiece, if you know what I mean.'

'No, I don't know what you mean,' Land admitted. 'I never know what you mean. If you knew all of that – what you said in the meeting last night – why on earth didn't you foresee what was going to happen to this fellow Jugdish?'

'Jhadav,' Bryant corrected. 'If I'd have foreseen that I'd have been a clairvoyant, not a copper. It doesn't fit the pattern. I had him down as an outsider. This puts him at the centre now, where I should have kept him all along.'

'It's a bit late for that, isn't it, considering he's dead?'

Bryant shot him a jaundiced look. 'You don't have to remind me. Make sure someone's with his girlfriend at all times until this is over. Is Banks going to approve the bloody search warrant or not?'

'I told you, she won't commit until she's been through your paperwork,' Land explained. 'You don't even know where this building is.'

'Then we go ahead without her.' Bryant turned to the immense London map book on his desk.

'You can't do that!'

'No? Watch me.'

'Anyway, why didn't Meera follow you?' Land asked. 'I thought she was going to keep tabs on your movements.'

'She ran out of petrol,' said Bryant. 'You hadn't signed off on her petty cash. Now, we're looking for a small chapel set back from the road, disused, probably Wesleyan.'

'How could you possibly tell it was Wesleyan from beneath a blindfold?' asked May.

'I imagine the Wesleyans formed a reasonable fit with our students' beliefs. Evangelical, anti-slavery, pro-women's rights, believers in free will and moral responsibility – OK, some dreadful stuff too – but more importantly, there were a lot of chapels in South London that were closed down after the war. They're generally Grade II listed and leased out for private use on the condition that the building fabric isn't tampered with. They're simply constructed and quite bare inside, and don't have the huge windows you associate with Anglican churches. I've pinpointed the three most likely properties.' Bryant tapped the page with the end of a rubber fish containing a biro, the only pen he'd been able to find.

'Here, you'll be able to see the actual buildings,' said May, reaching across to his computer and opening Google Maps. He typed in the co-ordinates and went to Street View. 'Tell me if you think any of these is right.'

'Wait, go back a bit,' Bryant commanded. 'That's the one.'

'Are you sure?'

'Gravel drive, *Griselinia littoralis*. London privet. I found a bit stuck to my sleeve. That's the place.'

'Good enough for me,' said May. 'You'll have to lead a team there. I'm heading over to Battersea with Giles and Jack, to check out Jhadav's body. I can't say I'm looking forward to it.'

Only Longbright and Land stayed behind. The remaining Dave offered to come along, but it was decided that he would be more useful mending the lavatory. Bryant drove in Victor, his bashed-up primrose-yellow Mini Minor, despite the protestations of Banbury and Bimsley, while Mangeshkar followed behind on her Kawasaki.

'My brake lights aren't working, so you might go into the back of me a few times,' Bryant warned as they set off.

Meanwhile, May drove the others to the headquarters of CaroFrend Processing, where Krishna Jhadav's body had been found.

'Apparently he was there running an assessment of their

waste-disposal requirements for his brokerage report,' he told the others. 'He didn't take an assistant and didn't put it in his diary, and only the guard signed him in. Sounds like it might have been a dodgy deal.'

They crossed the Thames, passed under a railway bridge and into the grey hinterlands of Battersea. 'After all those grand plans for the power station they're ending up with six hundred million quid's worth of absentee-owner flats,' said May disgustedly, 'just like all the other apartment blocks around here. London's going to be a millionaires' wasteland soon. Keep an eye out on your left, we should be coming up to the place.'

They halted before a windowless building of dull grey steel, set back behind a row of run-down betting shops and discount housewares stores. 'Couldn't be more invisible if it tried,' said May, looking up. 'This is the sort of place where the stench of rendered fat would once have turned the surrounding area into rookeries. The reaches of the city beyond Chelsea, Albert and Battersea Bridges still have these invisible industries. I guess new technology has rendered them safe.'

'Not for Jhadav,' said Renfield. They were checked at the gate and admitted to a small car park, where two men were waiting for them.

'Thank God,' said the older of the pair, a robustly over-weight man in his late fifties. 'We were starting to think you weren't coming.'

'Traffic,' said May, making the introductions. David Callow was the site manager. Nobody caught his side-kick's name, or needed it. They were led into an office so devoid of features that it might have belonged to an MOT centre or a chartered accountancy firm. There they were issued with swipe cards and led along a series of down-sloping corridors.

'Ninety-eight per cent of the system is automated,' Callow explained. 'There are just four full-time employees.

Everything else is operated remotely, either preset or programmed from another unit.'

'What was Mr Jhadav doing here by himself?' asked May.

'It was just a formality, required by law before he could sign off on our contract,' said Callow dismissively. 'We have a security guard who checks the monitors every two hours. It's not strictly necessary as they're regulated elsewhere, but it's good to have, you know, actual visual registration.' He said this as if the idea of using one's eyes was a faint absurdity. 'What we don't understand is why he went down into one of the tanks. It's not difficult but you do have to climb a ladder. There's no way you could wander into one by mistake. We had to drain the tank, which meant pulling his body out and hosing it down.'

'You realize you've probably destroyed any forensic evidence by doing so,' said Kershaw.

'We had no choice – health-and-safety emergency regulations. We had to store him somewhere until you arrived, and the only vented areas are in the basin rooms. There's no real biohazard risk because the effluent is partially treated, but the methane . . .' He let that sentence hang in the air, aware of how unappealing it was starting to sound. 'The room next door was empty so we took him there. Here's where he was found. The guard realized that someone had opened the outlet discharging effluent into the tank. In that kind of situation the tank has to be immediately blown and its contents annulled.'

'Do you have any idea who opened the outlet?'

'To our knowledge there was only Mr Jhadav in the building. The guard was meant to be up here but – well, he wasn't at his post at that point.'

'Where was he?'

Callow looked embarrassed. 'He'd gone for breakfast. We don't have an on-site canteen so he went to the café over the road.'

'Leaving Jhadav here by himself.'

'Yes, but nothing could have gone wrong because Mr Jhadav was not in the control area.'

'Clearly something did go wrong because someone came in with Jhadav and killed him,' said Renfield sharply. 'So you've got a security breach, for a start.'

'How easy would it be for an outsider to gain entry?' asked May.

'They'd need a registered swipe card.'

'And apart from that?'

Callow looked blankly at him. 'Well, nothing. Most people wouldn't know what to do unless they were pretty good with computers.'

'How good?' asked Renfield.

'I don't know. I'm not very good with them myself.'

He pushed open a grey steel door and stepped into the dimly lit monitor room. 'You see, three screens for the basins. There's very little that can be controlled from here beyond shifting the CCTV cameras and filling and clearing the tanks, and those controls are purely included here as a safety measure.'

May examined the primary-coloured touch screen. 'You mean you just have to swipe these two panels? If I can work it out, anyone can.'

'There's a bit more to it than that,' Callow assured him, unable to conceal his uneasiness. 'We conform to all national safety standards.'

'The barest minimum, I imagine. At least you have footage of this on your hard drive.'

'Well, yes, we'll have footage of the tanks filling, but not the platforms above them. The primary purpose of recording the basin area is to make sure that the grilles are functioning correctly.'

'So in the event of a terrorist attack, say, you'd have no footage of the culprits?'

Callow halted in his tracks. 'Mr May, you have to

understand that there would be absolutely no danger to anyone outside. Even if all three tanks were filled and blown, their contents would remain contained on site in dampers beneath the building. There's no physical connection between the internal pipework and the outside water and sewer systems. Waste is reduced and removed in solid form.'

May sighed. 'Let's go and see the body.'

Jhadav was in a room next to the walkway, lying sprawled on a pair of bath-towels, as if arranged for sunbathing. Although his skin and clothes had been hosed clean, he reeked. A stump of steel protruded from the right side of his collarbone. Only Kershaw didn't seem to notice the smell. He crouched close to Jhadav's neck. 'It looks like the same type of arrow to me. See the crosscut end? Deeper than the other one, probably knocked further in when he fell.'

Kershaw dug out a pair of plastic gloves and felt in Jhadav's jacket pockets. He carefully lifted some wet pages and unfolded them. Raising his eyebrows at May, he indicated the type.

'I hope this isn't going to take very long,' said Callow. 'We need to get back on schedule.'

'You left Jhadav here unsupervised, and you let someone else into the building,' May pointed out. 'That's just the start of your problems, because the attention this attracts is going to bring down an incredibly rigorous inspection of your work practices. So right now you probably want to return to your office, lock your door and hide until we've gone.'

'This isn't going to get out,' Callow warned. 'I've already briefed our PR department.'

'Of course you have,' said May, 'but guess what? Your publicity agent has no power against the weight of the British legal system when it decides you're in the wrong, despite what you may think.'

'Then you'll be dealing with our lawyers.'

'No,' said May, 'we'll be dealing with *you*. Your lawyers will be dealing with the court.'

'I hate people like that,' said May as they walked away from CaroFrend. 'There's something very shady going on there. Jhadav turns up for an inspection with nobody present and the tanks cleaned out so there's nothing to see, and his certification document is already filled out in his pocket with yesterday's date? Let's have a look at his company accounts and see if there are any large amounts going in the wrong direction.'

'What are you looking for?' asked Kershaw.

'Payments in the form of incentives or bonuses, made from the company that's supposed to be doing the paying out. I'm willing to bet that Jhadav was cutting deals with his clients, bending the H and S regs for a fee on the side. That in itself may have nothing to do with his death, but it'll give us leverage to investigate.'

'You don't suspect that guy Callow of being involved?' Renfield asked.

'I think there are easier ways of ending a difficult business relationship than firing a crossbow bolt through your client's neck,' said May.

38

RUNNER

'This is the right street,' said Bryant. 'I heard the brushes operating in the car wash on the corner. My hearing aid always picks up sounds like that. I just have trouble following conversations sometimes. Particularly if they're with people I don't like. We turn here.'

He pointed through the car windscreen at the small cream-painted chapel set back from the road. 'There you go,' he said. 'The New Resurrectionists.' Swinging Victor into the drive without indicating, he almost caused Mangeshkar to shoot straight past. As Meera guided her Kawasaki in, Bimsley jumped out and pulled the iron gates shut as a precaution.

The four of them headed up the chapel steps and rang the bell. 'I didn't have high hopes for anyone being here during daylight hours,' said Bryant. 'Colin, you and Meera go and see if there's another way in. Dan and I will be here.'

'Surely the uses of dead tissue must be fairly limited?' said Banbury while they waited.

'Giles thinks not, especially if they're looking at bacterial DNA. There are more base pairs making up the genes, and you can use them as templates for proteins and enzymes. The problem is, any findings made from bodies that weren't registered on the national database wouldn't be medically permissible, and would leave them liable to public prosecution. That's why they couldn't simply make arrangements with relatives to take away the dead. They had to disinter them after registration with a funeral home.'

Bimsley opened the door. 'It's the right place but there's no one here,' he said, stepping aside. 'Nobody living, anyway. There's a cadaver in a chiller cabinet in the back room.'

The chapel was much as Bryant remembered it, except that there were signs that the society had moved out in a hurry. In the main hall beyond the vestry the floor was covered in fistfuls of white packing pellets that drifted about like fat maggots, as well as rolls of brown plastic tape and staple guns. A blackened biscuit tin showed evidence of having held burned paperwork.

'They probably disappeared over the weekend,' said Banbury, crouching down and rubbing the ashes in between his fingers. 'There are no open windows, and the smell of burning is hard to get rid of.'

'Dan, can you come here?' called Bimsley. They all went. Propped up outside the back door, beneath the overhanging eaves, was a state-of-the-art Predator Elite crossbow, matt black, elegant and lethal. 'Looks like our murder weapon.'

'They wouldn't have done a runner if they weren't as guilty as hell,' said Meera.

'No,' said Bryant, waving his stick about. 'This just proves they ran from someone, not us. They wanted my help in finding Stephen Emes, remember?'

'Did you call them after we found his body?' asked Banbury.

'No. I didn't want to set off any alarm bells.' He looked

down at the crossbow as Banbury unwrapped a clear plastic bag, preparing to move it. 'This doesn't look right, leaving it outside, even under the eaves where it wouldn't get wet.'

'Maybe they put it out here and forgot it in the rush to go.'

'They had no motive, Dan. As far as we know, Stephen Emes was one of them.'

'Who knows what was going on between them? They probably lied to you,' said Banbury. 'It seems to me everyone in this whole case is lying.'

'Take this place apart, will you, and find out where they got the cadaver. Meera, you stay here and give Dan a hand. I can take the crossbow back for you.'

'Oh no you don't,' said Banbury. 'You'll get dinner all over it or shoot yourself in the foot or something. It stays with me. Go on, I'll see you back at the unit.'

Bryant and Bimsley left just as the rain started again. 'The way I see it,' said Bimsley, 'this lot already chose to operate beyond the law. It's a small step from digging up corpses to committing murder.'

'They were doctors, Colin. They were trying to do something for the betterment of mankind, even if they were going about it the wrong way. Jhadav was running deals with waste-disposal managers – it makes me wonder if he was dealing in something more than animal by-products and crossed their path in that capacity. But killing Emes and hiring me to find him doesn't make sense.'

'OK, but whether the crossbow is theirs or somebody left it there, it's pretty incriminating.'

Bryant climbed behind the wheel of Victor and dug around for his keys as rain began to lash the windscreen. 'I agree,' he said, 'but we're being sidetracked. That's what's been happening all through this investigation. Every time I start to pursue a through-line, it diverts. Or rather, someone deliberately diverts me. Here's a trick you can try. Take any single participant in the case, dead or alive, and assume they're guilty, then follow their story back to its roots and try to work out what happened.'

'Does it work?' Bimsley asked, folding himself up into the car.

'Very often. But not in this case.'

'Isn't it too late now?'

'What do you mean?'

'Of all the things they could have taken, they left the crossbow behind, Whatever plan they had, it's finished. They won. It's over.'

'No, Colin. Anyone who's found it possible to commit at least two murders in the same week will think they can get away with it again. They're lost and dangerous, and may not be able to stop.'

Back in the shadowed chapel, Banbury was measuring muddy bootprints and lifting tracks, narrating his findings while Meera kicked about, bored, listening to the rain on the roof. It sounded as if some of the slates were missing. She looked up, trying to trace the sound of falling water, and found a young man staring back at her half-way through the open skylight. Caucasian, long-haired and scrubbily bearded, he looked like a surprised student.

'Dan!' she called, running for the back door. Outside, she tried to understand how anyone could have climbed up to the edge of the roof, then saw the scaffolding stack in the corner. Sliding down the tiles, the boy dropped hard on to the scaffold boards and scrambled down as Meera threw herself at the poles above her head and tried to pull herself up. He stamped hard on her left hand, causing her to yell out and fall back. She landed badly on the gravel below.

Banbury appeared at the door just as the student dropped from the scaffold frame. 'Stop him!' Meera called.

'I don't – *apprehend* – people, Meera,' said Banbury. 'Isn't that your, um—'

'Ankle,' Meera gasped. 'Don't lose him.'

Banbury sized up his opponent, around twenty-three and fit, easily identifiable in a red Carhartt hooded sweatshirt and black jeans, making for the drive. John May had always said they should be ready to cover each other's jobs, but surely this wasn't what he'd had in mind?

His target had already opened the gate and gone into the street, so Banbury followed. He kept a steady pace behind the student, but had trouble gaining ground. He had quite short legs, that was the trouble, and—

A moment's loss of concentration and the young man had gone. He could only have swung into the nearest side street. Banbury reached the corner and looked in. *Just great*, he thought, *a farmers' market, I might as well be in a Bruce Willis film*. There, ahead, the red hooded sweatshirt was pushing between the shoppers.

Banbury ran into the crowd with more force than he intended, but had underestimated the stopping power of large African ladies armed with shopping bags. They blocked him in a solid wall. He found it easier to get ahead of the red hood by running behind the stalls.

He had to judge the moment carefully, waiting until he was drawing parallel, then dived between two stalls, barrelling into the young man hard from the side. They fell together on to a fruit stall, splattering peaches and scattering apples as the crowd fell back around them.

The lad's recovery time was impressive; he was back on his feet while Banbury was still scrabbling around in the smashed fruit, being berated by a fearsome-looking stallholder waving a large pair of scissors.

Banbury managed to throw out a fist and grab a handful of the red sweatshirt, which was enough to lever him upright. The student pulled free and dropped back behind the stalls, into the draper's at their rear, with Banbury following, now seized with a determination to bring him in.

Through the linen shop – very good prices on poly-cotton sheets, pink candlewick bedspreads and baby-blue pedestal mats – up the darkened back stairs to its first-floor showroom, valences and pelmets, then through a fire door leading to a hallway, with the lad remaining tantalizingly beyond reach.

Banging through the door ahead into a blazingly bright room, Banbury realized they were now on the top floor of the lighting shop next door. The properties were connected.

The student was a deft mover, manoeuvring himself between the glass pendant lights and standard lamps without breaking a thing. Banbury stopped a low-slung chandelier with his head, scattering crystals in every direction, but retained enough balance to continue forward propulsion across the room. They headed through another linking doorway.

Now he found himself in the warm perfumed air of an Afro-Caribbean hair salon and nail bar. None of the clients were frightened, but one of the girls yelled and threw pink spiky rollers at him as he passed. The student looked back and saw that Banbury, deficient in all tracking skills but tenacity, was still behind him.

The entire terrace appeared to be connected, like market buildings in Morocco and India. A further door took them through to the upper floor of a homewares store, its shelves filled with saucepans and knives of every imaginable shape and size. *I'm going to die here,* Banbury thought, catching his breath as he searched among the overcrowded stands.

He thought of arming himself with a carving knife, but they were sealed in plastic packs. A flash of red at the far end set him off again. Turning on his heel, he grabbed the largest utensil he could find by its handle. He beat Red

Hood to the end of the next shelf and swung as hard as he could, catching the student's head a glancing blow with a wok.

Red Hood threw a punch back that connected with Banbury's collarbone and sent him sprawling into a stack of smashing, clattering teapots. *A hand on the shelf, another on the door jamb, he's leaving spoor everywhere,* Banbury could not help thinking. This time there was no further exit available. Red Hood spun around, looking for a way out, then started moving to the open window at the front of the room.

No, Banbury thought, looking down at the red-and-white-striped awning of the stall twelve feet below, *I thought we agreed, no Bruce Willis moments.*

He could not see what it sold, but for all he knew it was garden shears and bread knives, all pointing upwards. Red Hood jumped without thinking twice, and Banbury, having come this far, could only follow.

The stall sold pillows and duvet sets. The awning split when his quarry hit it, and Banbury followed, landing among the quilts and comforters. Unfortunately one of the wooden top-struts fractured and a shard pierced Banbury's left thigh. On the other hand, he'd landed directly on top of Red Hood and would have now been able to cuff him, if he had been carrying handcuffs. His wallet was in his jacket, which was still hanging on the back of the chair in the chapel – it had his Met and PCU ID cards in it.

'I'm a copper, call my unit if you don't believe me,' he yelled at the horrified stallholder as the man beneath his boots started to revive. 'I'm not getting off him. Write the number down. Have you got a pen? This guy is under arrest. My God, I'm out of condition.'

39

WIVES AND MOTHERS

'It's not a hook-up,' said Sennen Renfield as they headed down the steps of Albany High School on Tuesday evening. 'She has some study questions, and I told her you could help her. On one condition.'

'What's that?' Martin asked.

'I'm there too. I'm looking out for her interests, OK? She's been through a lot and I don't want you upsetting her.'

'Why would I agree to that?'

'Because you like her.' Sennen knew she had won the argument. She was greatly enjoying her new covert role among her classmates. It felt as if she had the upper hand for once. She was in control.

'OK, let's go.' Martin slung his bag over his shoulder, not waiting for her to catch up.

'She's in a coffee shop in King's Cross Station,' Sennen called. They walked together through the rain, slipping between stalled cars, dodging the tourists who dragged their cases between terminals wondering what on earth had possessed them to come to London in the summer. 'She's scared to go anywhere by herself. First she had your mum stalking her—'

'I told you it wasn't her. Why are you always going on about my mum?'

'There's a lot of weird stuff happening. My dad says there's someone going around wiping out, like, *everyone* to do with Romain Curtis.' She'd made that last part up, but it sounded feasible.

'What would your dad know about it?'

'He's only in charge of the entire case, isn't he? He's a police officer, yeah?'

'You never properly explained what he did. I thought he was, like, behind a desk or something.'

'You didn't ask. Anyway, my dad says they're getting ready to make an arrest any moment now.'

Martin suddenly seemed interested in her. Now she was *really* loving the new level of attention, and decided to take it further. 'And you know something else? He already knows who the killer is and why they did it and everything. Only he's not allowed to say until they make the arrest.'

She could tell she had impressed him. 'Wow,' he said, clearly seeing her in a new light. 'So the investigation's right in our 'hood.'

'Yeah,' said Sennen. 'But I can't say any more.'

'What do you mean?'

She decided to extemporize. 'He told me who did it. He needed to share what he knew with someone 'cause it was eating him up.'

'Jesus, Sennen, don't tell anyone else; something like that could be really dangerous,' Martin warned. 'Suppose they found out that you knew something? They could come after you.'

'That's why I'm friendly with Shirone's brothers,' said Sennen. 'Nobody's going to mess with them 'cause they're really hard.'

'OK, but maybe you should carry a blade or something, just in case.'

'I'm not walking around tooled up,' said Sennen indignantly. 'Hello? School's got a knife arch?'

'Fair enough.' They had turned into Euston Road and crossed over to the station. Martin caught sight of Shirone sitting by the rain-streaked window in the coffee shop and held up his hand. 'There she is. You coming in or what?'

'Try and stop me,' said Sennen with new confidence.

Vanessa Wallace had barely been able to stop crying in days. She couldn't bring herself to look in a mirror – she was sure that her swollen face added years. She supposed she was lucky that Krishna Jhadav had refused to press charges on the condition that she stayed away from him. Could nobody else see the truth? The police were useless; she could trust no one. God, and the embarrassment of a restraining order, or at least the threat of one, on top of everything else. She hadn't been happy for a long time, but now she was living a nightmare.

She had cleaned everything in the house ten times over, and there was finally nothing left to do. She had wanted to clean inside Martin's room but he kept the door locked, jealously guarding his private space. She wanted to get him to open up about his father, but nothing would make him talk to her. All he ever said was that he hated Thomas for being so weak. They had never been a demonstrative family, never been able to discuss their feelings without embarrassment, and hatred was such an unlikely emotion for Martin. There was no violence in him, just undirected pain.

Her behaviour in the aftermath of Thomas's suicide had distanced them even further from each other, and nothing could ever be put back together. Thomas had been a decent man, a moral man, in spite of their differences. He'd loved her and his son but he'd never found his proper place in the world. Now she had lost her place too, and wondered if Martin would ever regain his equilibrium.

He was refusing counselling, and she feared he was falling behind in his studies. The old *M*A*S*H* song was wrong; suicides weren't painless, they were horribly selfish.

But Martin – he was her only hope, and perhaps he would be all right. In the last twenty-four hours he had changed somehow, brightening up a little, taking calls in his room, talking to one of the girls at school. She knew he was sweet on the tarty-looking one who'd been out with the boy who died – a name like Shirley, but one of those made-up names girls had these days. Perhaps she would be able to reach him, if anyone could.

Irina Cope found herself standing in the middle of the aisle in Sainsbury's, not knowing what she was doing there. After hearing how Krishna had died, she had called the agency and been instructed to take off as much time as she needed. Her appalled disbelief at being told the news had already given way to a stranger, more dislocated feeling. She felt cheated out of something indefinable. Krishna had never confided in her, never opened up to her. She had always assumed that one day they would talk, sharing their pasts and thoughts for the future, but now that opportunity had been lost. How could you mourn someone you had never really got to know?

She thought, *Either I have to get a basket and buy something, or I need to leave. What did I come in here for? Yoghurt? Tea?*

Janice Longbright, the detective sergeant who had been so kind towards her, had called with the news that Jhadav's death was not accidental. She had immediately thought of Vanessa Wallace, but had then wondered, was it remotely likely that someone who had already been cautioned by the police would take Krishna's life?

Her partner, the man she had hoped to marry, had made money buying and selling waste for a living, and he had drowned in it – was anything more bizarre ever likely to happen? She wanted to run home and lock the doors, to get under the covers and never leave the flat again. They'd had a baby-faced local constable posted outside the house since Mrs Wallace attacked Krishna, and now Longbright had told her he would stay until the case was closed. She looked about her, at the mothers and children doing their weekly shopping, living lives where nothing too strange or disturbing ever happened, and could not understand why she had been singled out for this torment.

Romain's mother, Louisa Curtis, returned from the church in Finsbury with Alma Sorrowbridge. They walked slowly together through the rain with their red and yellow umbrellas touching, talking of God's plans for the world. They didn't reach any firm conclusions, but Mrs Curtis appreciated the walk back even though her shoes were letting in water. It was good to have someone with whom she could share her troubles.

'Mr Bryant isn't what you'd call a believer in the traditional sense,' said Alma, somewhat euphemistically. 'He's always picking holes in the Bible and making fun of it.'

'Well, it *is* contradictory,' said Mrs Curtis. 'Doesn't Elijah get taken up to heaven in Kings, when it says that no man can rise up to heaven in John? There are a lot of passages like that. I don't think you should take it literally.'

'Mr Bryant certainly believes in something,' Alma decided, 'but I think it's linked to an inner spirit rather than a greater power. Police officers have a very black-and-white sense of morality. He reckons people should suffer what they make others suffer. I'm never quite sure whether he doesn't like people at all, or loves them too much.'

'It helped to be with other people today,' said Mrs Curtis. 'The children have been wonderful. So many of them have written to me about Romain. I didn't realize he was quite so well liked. There are flowers tied to the lamp-post on the street where it happened. The class wanted to hold a candlelit vigil there, but Camden Council wouldn't let them. Something to do with Health and Safety. It's all so confusing. They talk about closure, don't they? I'm not sure I know what that is. I mean he's gone and I'll never really find out why, so I just have to let him go without knowing.'

Alma looked over and saw her sniffing, and dug out a packet of paper handkerchiefs. 'You can't start crying now, not after you got all the way through the service.'

'He was my light,' Mrs Curtis said miserably. 'He was the one who would have changed us all.'

'Then you have to make sure he still does,' said Alma firmly. 'We have to put our trust in Mr Bryant. Even though he doesn't believe in God, perhaps God has belief in him.'

The bereaved women of London walked in the rain and shopped and looked from their windows, and tried to imagine a world where their tragedies had not happened. They knew that the city had rolled on through plagues and wars and bombings and fires, and its families had survived by transmuting into strange new forms. London was cold and hard, but could, when the occasion called for it, rise, warm itself and provide succour, so the one thing none of them did was wallow in self-pity. To live here required the ability to change and evolve.

Death came suddenly, but life on these streets was never truly over.

40

BETWEEN THE LINES

'Where the bloody hell have you been?' asked Raymond Land as Bryant swept in, scattering rain and paperwork everywhere.

'Don't be cross – I hate it when you're cross.' He waved at the intern. 'You, Lavinia or whatever your name is, could I have a cup of tea? I'm gagging.'

'I don't do tea,' said Amanda Roseberry sweetly. 'I'm Radio Operation and Driving Skills, not Teabags, and so far I haven't had a chance to use any of my training.'

'Look, I'll try to think of a way of using you if on this occasion you whip up a brew, how about that? Raymondo, I urgently need to talk to John so you'll forgive me if we forgo the lighthearted banter for a while.'

'You don't wriggle away that easily,' said Land. 'Orion Banks has put my direct line on speed-dial since we found Jhadav's body. She won't be put off any longer.'

'What is she going to do, Raymond? Close us down? That was Oskar Kasavian's job, and look how far that got him. She's the one who's been delaying us all this time. Banks is a summer rain; she drifts in and gives everything a good soaking before dissipating and re-forming over some other poor sod's department. Don't worry about the small things. We're so close now.'

Land's ears pricked up. 'What do you mean, close? Do you have something?'

'Yes, I do, as it happens.'

'Then tell me, just this once tell me first. Arthur – may I call you Arthur?'

'Absolutely not.' Bryant shrugged apologetically. 'I have to see John. You know he's the other half of my brain.'

'Well, what am I?'

'You're sort of like the control part of any experiment.'

Land looked stumped. 'What is that supposed to mean?'

'I talk to you and I always know what not to do,' Bryant replied.

Land was crestfallen. He had really tried of late, but this was the last straw. 'I go out on a limb for you,' he warned. 'Everyone out there thinks you're mad.'

'Good. So long as they continue to underestimate us, the more we'll surprise them.'

'But I don't want to surprise anyone!' shouted Land. He found himself arguing with an empty room.

Bryant discovered his partner at his computer, attempting to spear rolls of congealed spaghetti carbonara on to a bending plastic fork.

'When was the last time you had a home-cooked meal?' Bryant asked.

May thought for a minute. 'I think it was just before Brigitte gave up on me and returned to Paris,' he said. 'I'm used to eating with a keyboard in front of me now.'

'After this is over I'll have Alma cook us a beef and ale pie. We've got ourselves a New Resurrectionist. Our Dan managed to land him, or rather, land *on* him. Meera's quite put out about it. She doesn't like to be upstaged when it comes to duffing up suspects. She sprained her ankle falling off some scaffolding. Dan's got a bandaged leg but he's really making a fuss over what was effectively a splinter, the big baby.'

'Who is this person he's caught?' asked May through a mouthful of cold pasta.

'One of the men who was there the night I was taken to the chapel. I recognize his voice.'

'Is he here?'

'He's waiting in the interview room. Thought you'd like to sit in.'

They headed upstairs together. 'You're going to be sensible with him, aren't you?' asked May. 'I know you're probably on his side but I don't want you blithely waving everything he says through the logic checkpoint just because his ideals match yours.'

'I resent your insinuations about my impartiality,' Bryant replied. 'Just for that, you can ask the questions.'

'Resurrectionists? Oh no you don't, this is your baby.'

As Bryant seated himself in the interview room, he checked the charge sheet. 'Addison Court? Sounds like a council block. Are you sure that's your name?'

'I was born in America.' Despite being sat on and arrested, Court was impossibly fresh-faced. He had the Midwestern milk-fed look of a college kid. London had yet to leave its grubby scuffmarks on him.

'Ah, so you are. Well, let's not remove the remaining scraps of dignity from the proceedings by pretending that you don't know why you're here. The question is: why did you run?'

'We left behind a body,' said Court. 'There wasn't time to take it with us.'

'Why did you all feel the need to vacate the premises with such celerity?'

'I'm sorry?'

'Why did you bugger off?'

'We heard about Stephen getting shot in Hyde Park. We thought you'd decide that one of us did it.'

'How?'

'How what?'

'How did you hear about him getting shot?'

'We had a phone call.'

'A man with a deep, slightly Eastern European voice?'

'Yeah.'

'Mr Merry picked up the news from the mics,' Bryant told his partner. He turned his attention back to the student. 'Why would I think that one of you was guilty? You asked me to find him, remember?'

'It meant you'd come looking for us, whether you thought we were guilty or not. Our security had been compromised. We needed to relocate. Kinda sad, seeing as Stephen went to all the effort of securing our rent.'

'Fair enough, I'll buy that. Do you have any idea who shot him?'

'I think we all assume it was the person who hired him.'

'Why do you think that?'

'Because he's taking care of business, man. He went to Stephen because he needed someone who knew how to dig up a grave and open a casket. He'd have had to let Stephen know what he was planning, and once Stephen knew, he was a risk.'

'Which brings us to this mysterious client,' said Bryant, leaning forward. 'What do you think he wanted?'

'I figured maybe it was part of some ritual. An occultist, a harmless crazy with too much money.'

'Any clue to his identity?'

'Only that he went to the Bleeding Heart. Stephen had to go there to meet up with his client. It's where we—'

'Hold your meetings, yes, I know. Right, you stay here,' Bryant instructed. 'John, book Mr Court for, oh I don't know, tampering with dead bodies or breaking and entering a hairdresser's or something. There must be a statute that will cover it. I'll be back shortly.'

On the way out, he asked Renfield to remind him of

the name of Emes's contact at the Bleeding Heart Tavern, then headed off to the tube.

Bleeding Heart Yard was a tiring uphill walk from Chancery Lane, but at least it was close by. As he emerged from the station he realized he had forgotten his umbrella, and it was still hammering with rain. The gutters had turned to racing streams.

By the time he reached the pub, even his vest was soaked. He found the barman of the Bleeding Heart just starting his evening shift. The pub was surprisingly quiet. 'Where is everyone?' asked Bryant, shaking out his overcoat and hanging it on a chair.

'The power's off in Hatton Garden,' said the Australian. 'A road drill went through a cable.'

Bryant understood the implications. It meant that the electronic security grilles protecting the diamond quarter might not be working properly, so the local merchants would be staying inside their offices until the fault was repaired.

'You spoke to my sergeant about a man called Stephen Emes,' said Bryant. 'You rented the upstairs room out to him.'

'I told him all I knew,' said the barman, turning his counter diary around. 'Here's the booking. First Thursday of every month.'

'Did you know who they were, what they were doing?'

'That's not our business. There're groups all over London meeting in the upstairs rooms of pubs.'

'Don't remind me,' said Bryant. 'A private members' event, yes?'

'Apparently so.'

In an act of generosity that acknowledged Bryant's hopeless Luddism, Banbury had laminated the faces of everyone involved with the case on to oblongs of cardboard the size of old-fashioned cigarette cards like a suspects' Top Trumps set. Bryant pulled out the set now and began thumbing through it. He set down three: Romain Curtis, Stephen Emes and Krishna Jhadav. 'Now,' he said, 'did you ever see any of these people in here on the same night?'

'I don't see the members,' said the barman. 'They use the side entrance. But this one made the bookings.' He tapped Stephen Emes's card. 'And I remember this one.' He singled out Krishna Jhadav's card.

'Any particular reason why you remember him?'

'Yeah, the pair of them must have first met in here, 'cause I remember when the Indian guy came in the other one stood up to shake his hand, and I thought that was so English, you know? We're not that formal where I come from.'

'When did this happen?'

'Around a week ago, maybe longer. It might have been early on the evening of the Friday before last. We're not open on Saturdays.'

'Did he speak to you?'

'I don't think so. The younger guy ordered the drinks. He was sort of nervous. I figured he was here for some kind of job interview. I watch everything from behind the bar.'

'Thank you,' said Bryant. 'If you ever decide on a career change, you have the makings of a fine policeman.'

By the time Bryant got back, the lights were low in the PCU, and only May remained at his desk.

'It's fantastic,' said Bryant, hurling off his sodden coat and throwing himself into his ratty overstuffed armchair. 'Do you realize what's been going on? No one has told us the truth. Oh, they've told us to the best of their abilities, but whether they've meant to or not, they've all left something crucial out. What are we supposed to do? We can't torture them for answers, more's the pity. It's a matter of reading between the lines. Once you do that, you start to get a more complete picture. Is there anything to eat? I don't seem to be getting any meals at the moment.'

'I can offer you half of Janice's crayfish and rocket sandwich left over from lunchtime,' said May.

'That'll do.' Bryant accepted the sandwich and took a huge bite from the centre of the bread. 'Where was I? Yes, we have to reassemble everything into a cohesive time-line. What did you say was in this? Crayfish? It tastes like bathroom grout. Let's start back at the beginning, be-fore Romain Curtis took his girl to St George's Gardens. God, I can't get through this, it's gone under my dental plate.' He dug out the mashed sandwich with an index finger and lobbed it into the wastepaper bin. 'The very first thing we know is that Krishna Jhadav arranged to meet Stephen Emes at the Bleeding Heart Tavern. Why? Because he needed to dig up a dead body.'

'Why did he want to do that?'

'I don't know yet but I have a very good idea. Please try not to interrupt. Emes agrees to carry out the work, but says it will take two of them to do it. I'm guessing Jhadav reluctantly agrees to help him. So, on Sunday night they head for St George's Gardens with their equipment, and Romain Curtis sees them. Emes – or Jhadav – says, "There's someone watching." The other one looks over and sees a skinny stoned kid, whom he dismisses, saying, "He's a minor." Which the starstruck Curtis hears as "Ursa Minor". He leaves with Shirone Estanza, but decides to go back and take another look out of curiosity. This upsets our pair of gravediggers, and somehow they manage to keep tabs on the boy. The next night, they follow him to the Scala club and spike his drink, running him over in a backstreet.'

'Why did they change his shirt?'

'Who says they did? Maybe he changed it because he'd spilled booze on the old one. So, the only real witness is dead, but whatever business Jhadav has is unfinished.

Something has gone wrong, and he needs to dig up another body, then another. He *must* have been looking for something left in one of the coffins.'

'But Rummage was absolutely sure the caskets were empty, both before and after disinterment.'

'Fine, we'll have to fill in that piece later. Meanwhile, Mrs Wallace has been following Krishna Jhadav about because she blames him for her husband's death. Unfortunately she has no proof, having returned any incriminating documentation *on Jhadav's instruction* to her husband's ex-client. No wonder she's so upset.'

'Does she know Jhadav was responsible for digging up her husband?'

'I don't see how she could; she just feels that if he hadn't acted as he did, Thomas Wallace would still be alive.' He thumped the board at his back. 'Now we come to the events in Hyde Park. Stephen Emes is still working for Jhadav, and this time we have to assume he finds whatever Jhadav has been looking for, because Jhadav no longer has any need for him, and shoots him dead.'

May held up a hand. 'Stop, stop, you've gone wrong somewhere. Jhadav was able to send Emes alone because it was only a pet cemetery this time, and he could manage by himself. It's hardly likely to have been Jhadav who shot him, because he died by the same method.'

'Yes, there is that. The man at the centre of all this, one Ronald Rummage, is adamant that nothing was buried with his clients, human or non-human, so we have another problem there. I felt sure we'd find something on his premises. What are we missing?'

'It's as you said,' said May. 'Someone knows more than they're telling. The trouble is, the only person who can really help us has been murdered.'

'It doesn't mean he can't help us just because he'd dead,' said Bryant reasonably. 'Think about it. He was shot in the shoulder. The arrow probably wouldn't have killed him but the waste did. I think somebody wanted him to drown in the very by-products he was illicitly brokering. That sounds like a extremely Jacobean form of revenge to me.'

'Jacobean,' May repeated. 'I can't wait to hear the rest of this.'

'Oh, I think you can,' said Bryant, 'at least until tomorrow.'

But in a moment just technically this side of tomorrow, at half a minute before midnight, events began to cascade.

It started because of a split shoe. PC Julie Biggs was ending her shift when the sole of her right boot began letting in water. She had intended to march along King's Cross Road and down towards Mount Pleasant, but instead she cut down Handel Street towards Hunter Street, because she wanted to reassure herself that the little heel-repair bar she sometimes used still existed, in which case she would visit it tomorrow. As she detoured past the fern-filled burial ground of St George's Gardens, she heard a clumsy rustle of branches, and turned to see an overweight man wrestling with a garden spade.

'Blimey, mate, it's a bit late for playing silly buggers, isn't it?' she said, climbing nimbly over the railings and heading towards him, only stopping when she realized he was attempting to dig up a grave.

'It's not how it looks,' Ron Rummage began lamely, theatrically setting the shovel to one side as if he had just discovered it in his hand and now wished to distance himself from its acquaintance.

'How do you think it looks?' PC Biggs was intrigued to know.

'Like I'm digging up a coffin.'

'Funny, 'cause that's pretty much what it looks like to me an' all. Wanna talk me through this before I run you in?'

'I'm a funeral director,' said Rummage.

'A bit late to be working, isn't it? Do you need the over-time?'

'This is one of my burials.'

'You must be a perfectionist if you came back at mid-night to give it another bash.'

'My good woman, you don't understand—'

'I'm not your good woman,' said Biggs, 'I'm an officer of the law and what you're doing is illegal.'

'I would question that,' Rummage promised, looking as furtive as a priest. 'This plot is within the gift of my company, and I am charged with its upkeep. If I think there's something wrong, I'm within my rights to attend to the problem.'

PC Biggs folded her arms. No honest citizen should ever do anything that makes a police officer stand back and fold their arms. 'At midnight,' she said slowly. 'All by yourself. You're nicked, mate. Bring the shovel.'

41

CASCADE

On Wednesday morning, Janice Longbright stepped into a nightmare of her own making.

She did not become aware that something was wrong until Jack Renfield called her moments after she arrived at the PCU. 'My daughter's missing,' he said. 'Her mother dropped her off on the way to school but she never got there. I tried calling you but you must have been in the tube. I don't know what to do. I need your help.'

'How do you know she's missing? Where are you?'

'I'm outside the school gates right now. She wanted to walk here even though it was raining, I don't know why. She was very insistent. Her mother thought it was odd, but you know how teenage girls can be.'

'Sounds to me like she was meeting someone. You need to check her class register and see if there's anyone else who's not turned up.'

'I just did that. Some of the boys have gone to football practice and part of the class is on a trip to the Tower of London, so they won't be able to marry up the registers until they do the return head-counts.'

'OK, don't move, I'll be there as soon as I can.' She grabbed her wet coat and put it back on.

'Where are *you* going?' Land looked surprised as she rushed past without answering his question. 'And where are my detectives?' he asked anyone who might be within earshot.

Half a dozen kittens shot across the corridor. 'They've gone out,' said the remaining Dave, sticking his head around the door frame. 'Something about a shovel.'

'Get on with your work,' said Land, annoyed at having to rely on a decorator for information on the whereabouts of his staff. 'Is there anything else I should know?'

'Yeah,' said Dave. 'Don't try to flush the toilet. We've got a blowback problem.'

Land found Meera in the common room. 'What are you doing here?' he asked. 'I thought you'd hurt yourself.'

'I've sprained my ankle,' she said, 'not my brain. I've got a crutch. I don't need anyone's help.'

'Yes, we all know you don't need anyone's help,' said Land testily. 'Where's Colin?'

'He's gone with John and Mr Bryant to the undertakers. Rummage got released on bail after a PC spotted him trying to dig Thomas Wallace up again.'

'I knew he was dodgy. Didn't I say so all along?'

'No.'

'I was being rhetorical.'

'No you weren't. Rhetoric implies the incontrovertible certainty of the answer.'

'Don't get smart with me, young lady. It's time I got some respect around here. I'm all that stands between you lot and the infinite darkness of the City of London Police Authority.' Land stormed out and would have slammed the door for effect if the remaining Dave hadn't taken it off its hinges.

*

Longbright called her boss as soon as she got outside. 'Arthur, I have a favour to ask,' she said. 'I wouldn't normally do this but it's important. You know your way around the Tower of London, don't you? Jack's daughter might be there on a school trip. Is there any way you can check on her?'

'You know I have strange operating methods, but we are actually in the middle of a murder investigation. The school run is a bit off my beat.'

'That's the problem. She's gone missing and I think it might have something to do with the investigation. I did something I shouldn't have done.' She explained the situation.

Bryant was horrified. 'My God, Janice, after that terrible business with John's daughter? You know what happened to Elizabeth, the sting that went wrong! God, we used her example as a warning to others for years. What the hell were you thinking? Leave it to me. I'll drive there in Victor. John and Colin can handle Rummage.'

Longbright met Renfield outside the school gates, where he stood in the shelter of a plane tree making calls. She approached him with trepidation, knowing that she would have to tell him the truth, no matter how painful it would be for them both.

'I can't get hold of anyone,' Renfield complained. 'We're supposed to be living in the twenty-first century. I found a few of her friends but nobody's seen her, and most aren't answering their mobiles because they're in class. I've left a message for Shirone Estanza; I'm hoping she's going to call me back. Martin Wallace is on some kind of sports trip. That just leaves my daughter unaccounted for. It's not like her to do this. Her mother's still stuck in a meeting. She's going to go mental when she gets out of it.'

'Listen, Jack,' Longbright began awkwardly, 'this may be my fault. I talked to Sennen about helping us out.'

Renfield closed his mobile and looked at her. 'What do you mean?'

'Well, she was so difficult at the outset. I thought there might be a way that we could bond, so I sort of enrolled her.'

'Christ, Janice, what did you say?'

'I suggested that she could check among her friends for information. Just keep her ear to the ground and report back, especially if she heard anything about Mrs Wallace.'

'But what if she spoke to someone who actually knew something? You could have put her directly in the line of fire. Didn't you think that through? She's impressionable and easily led. All that confidence she exudes is fake. You must be able to see that.'

'I'm sorry, Jack, I just wanted her to like me, and I'm so used to the job that I guess I didn't think about the dangers.'

'You told a fifteen-year-old girl to go and pick the brains of a possible murderer. If anything's happened to her—'

'Don't say it,' warned Longbright. 'I know I screwed up but I won't let any harm come to her. Arthur is on his way to the Tower right now to check on the school bus. He's a London tour guide in his spare time, he knows everyone on the gates there. He'll find her and bring her back. And if she's not there, I'll find her myself, I swear it.'

Renfield was looking over her shoulder. Shirone Estanza was walking across the playground towards them with her bag clutched to her chest, in tears.

'What did you think you were doing?' May asked Ron Rummage. 'Going to St George's Gardens at midnight?' The funeral director had been released and allowed back to his place of work, pending an interview.

'I know how it looks,' said the flustered Rummage. 'I know it makes me a suspect. I just wanted to see for myself.'

'See what?'

'The three coffins,' he said, as if it was evident. 'Professional curiosity on my part. Thomas Wallace, Elspeth Duncannon and Prince, they were all prepared right here at the same time. I was sitting here last night and the thought struck me: I must have missed something.'

'What do you mean?'

Rummage pushed his glasses up his nose. 'I checked the caskets when they were empty, and again when they were filled. It's as I told you, neither Duncannon nor Wallace were buried with anything other than what their relatives had given me, cufflinks in the case of Wallace, and a cheap little brooch in the case of Mrs Duncannon. There was nothing hidden in any of the caskets. But there can't have been any other reason for digging them up.'

'There can,' said May, 'because we know that one of the two men involved belonged to a medical society that believes in disinterring corpses for experiments. We've identified another body they were using: Edward Simmons, fifty-three, a railway worker who died of a heart attack ten days ago. He was buried in St Mary's Cemetery, Battersea, by a branch of the Co-operative Funeral Services. So he's not one of yours. He was disinterred two nights after he was buried. Do you know what I think? You thought Thomas Wallace must have been buried with money on him somehow, and you wanted it for yourself.' It certainly wasn't what May thought, but it was important to keep Rummage's blood pressure up so that his defences stayed down.

'No, that's not true!' the funeral director insisted. 'You have no idea what this sort of scandal could do to our business. I know you've managed to keep it out of the national press somehow, but people in the neighbourhood are talking. We're a family firm that's survived for two hundred years – we can't allow ourselves to be destroyed by this.'

'Did you believe him?' asked Colin as they left the funeral parlour.

'I think he panicked himself into believing that he'd done something stupid and accidentally buried Wallace with a valuable item on him. And he had to find out what he'd done,' said May.

'But surely when he had to re-inter the body, he'd have had a good look then?'

'You heard what he said. It didn't occur to him before then that he could have made a mistake. He had to make sure the company wasn't at fault, and instead of going through the proper channels he decided to check at a time that wouldn't draw attention.'

'In a graveyard in the middle of the night.'

'It's an unpoliced garden that's usually deserted. And it's a place where he feels completely at home. But I agree, he was an idiot. I think we should lay this one to rest. It's not Rummage. Besides, there's something more important we need to do. We have to take Krishna Jhadav's flat and office apart.'

'Why?'

'Because his company is going to be under investigation, and we need evidence of what he was up to.'

'I don't see how that's going to help the case,' said Bimsley. 'Anyway, that would be down to the CoL's financial mob.'

May was adamant. 'Digging up his former client was an act of desperation. And so was killing Romain Curtis. We have to know what drove him to such measures.'

Bryant had no trouble finding the bus arriving from Albany High School; it nearly ran him over as he backed out of Victor. He spoke to the two supervising teachers and checked the crowd of rowdy Bloomsbury children, but there was no sign of Sennen Renfield.

He was about to call Longbright with the bad news

when he saw a familiar rotund figure passing through the Warders' gate of the Tower. The entrance was being manned by Matthew Condright, the Raven Master.

'That man you just let in,' said Bryant, breathlessly waving his stick in the direction of the retreating visitor. He had recognized Mr Merry instantly, even without his pirate boots and tricorn hat. 'You know him?'

'Of course,' said Condright. 'That's Mr Pettigrew; he's the Tower menagerie's veterinary surgeon.'

It was all Bryant could do to stop from slapping himself on the forehead. 'I've been a complete fool,' he told the Raven Master. 'Of course – Matthew, I have to place him under arrest. Is there a way we can keep him locked up somewhere?'

'This is the Tower of London,' said Condright with an evil smile. 'Incarceration is what we do best.'

42

MEETING MERRY

Bryant peered through the mullioned window of the Yeoman Warders' Keep House and wondered what Mr Merry was thinking as he sat at his table sipping tea and going through some kind of order book. The Tudor room was hung with bric-a-brac: pewter goblets, horse-brasses and china. 'It's all right, Matthew, you can leave the two of us alone,' said Bryant cheerfully. 'I'll be quite safe.'

'Well, if you're sure . . .' Condright scratched doubt-fully at his spade beard. 'I'll just be in the next room if you need me.'

Bryant took a deep breath and threw open the door, entering, not without a certain theatricality, in a blast of wind and rainwater. He headed for the Warders' tea urn, then took in the room, making a grand point of noticing the only other occupant.

'Well well well,' he said, 'look who's here.' Battering out the sleeves of his coat and making his way between the chairs, he seized the shocked necromancer's large hand and shook it vigorously. 'How the devil are you?'

'Rather an odd coincidence to find you here, particularly after our last conversation,' said Merry, taken aback and clearly displeased.

'Oh, not at all, I've known all the Warders socially for donkeys' years. We have lots of things to talk about other than those blasted missing birds, you know. Many, many years ago my beautiful wife Nathalie worked for the Tower of London Trust. People always seem surprised that a dry old stick like me could have had a spouse. Gosh, it *is* good to see you.' He kept touching Merry, on the shoulder and sleeve, patting his arm and slapping his back, until his opponent was nettled by the invasion of his personal space. Finally he sat down in the opposite chair, staring and smiling in a most disconcerting fashion. Merry was quite unsettled.

'Forgive my cynicism, Mr Bryant,' he said at last, 'but I refuse to believe that your arrival here today is coincidental.'

'Oh, but it really is. You're the last fellow I expected to see, honestly you are. But I'm glad you're here, as I quite miss our little chats about . . . apotropaic magic, wasn't it? Where did you get the cats?'

Merry appeared nonplussed. 'What cats?'

'Black ones, presumably. They're bad omens, aren't they? Although lucky in some cultures, I suppose. But it's not just cats that bring maledictions, is it? Owls, they're dreadfully dangerous. Rats, goats, pigs, magpies, bats, snakes – all signs of impending death. Not necessarily permanent, of course; after all, things have to die to be reborn so we're looking at – what? The end of empire and its economic rebirth, perhaps? A lot of people would pay good money to see that. Weren't we talking about Dirty Dicks, the East End pub, last time? It turns out somebody swiped their collection of mummified cats. And it appears someone also snaffled a bunch of bats – I forget the collective noun – from the London Zoo. A colony, isn't it, or a cloud?'

'Where is all this leading?' asked Merry, increasingly impatient and uncomfortable.

Bryant rose and paced about behind his adversary, forcing him to turn around. 'Well, let's just pretend for a moment that you are a dishonest man.'

Mr Merry narrowed his eyes. 'Assume away.'

'Very well. I imagine a syndicate of like-minded individuals, wealthy, old and European, buying up grand houses. I take it you've heard about these Russian gentlemen in Knightsbridge, building down many floors beneath their Edwardian properties? So-called 'iceberg houses'? Adding cinemas, swimming pools, garages, bowling alleys and whatnot? As rich as Croesus – such an apt phrase. Herodotus tells us that Croesus was so rich, he had every house guest take away as much gold as he could carry upon leaving. I think that's a tale with which you might be familiar. I imagine these oligarchs are wealthy but not terribly sophisticated. Some say they passed from barbarism to decadence without going through civilization. Apparently many of them still believe in the old religions, and in particular apotropaic magic. They need to ward off harm, and want to do something more than just cross their fingers, knock on wood and light a Hallowe'en pumpkin. And there you are, ready with the perfect solution. Expensive ceremonies with the highest-end ingredients, complex rites that involve the burial of specific birds and animals.'

Bryant pounced forward alarmingly. 'And one very special, very wealthy client who paid you to bring the ravens to him alive, so that he could keep them underground in his new house. But not just any ravens – the very ones that supposedly protect the empire. This is where superstition meets vanity and wealth.'

He paused for effect, expecting Merry to protest, but the academic sat there in silence, stone-faced.

'The question that must have vexed you most, I suppose, was how on earth to provide provenance?' Bryant continued. 'I mean, you could have tried to palm off your client with any old ravens, and simply explained that the Warders had replaced the stolen ones. But no, I can't imagine your sense of pride would have allowed you to do that. The ravens had to be *seen* to be stolen. Besides, your benefactor might have checked up on you. That's why you masqueraded as the Tower's veterinary surgeon.'

'There was no masquerade involved,' said Mr Merry. 'I am qualified to adopt the title.'

'I'm impressed,' said Bryant. 'I underestimated you. At first – you'll forgive me – I thought I was dealing with a charlatan, but you're smarter than I thought. You made sure that your reputation as a necromancer preceded you. And you're adept at building a sense of dread. Like many who believe in the outer reaches of the corporeal world, Maggie Armitage is rather too open to suggestion. Her warnings about your abilities would unnerve the hardiest non-believer. A very clever move, that, recruiting innocent, harmless people like her to spread the word about you. It's all just PR, of course, but of a superior kind.' He playfully punched Mr Merry on the shoulder.

'Yes, you certainly know how to get the best out of your staff. You planted a workman in our unit to bug the place and give you inside information. Getting him to paint the bleeding hearts on the wall was a nice added touch, because you knew I had knowledge that the New Resurrectionists were meeting at the Bleeding Heart Tavern. You thought you'd hand me over to them, never expecting that they would ask for my help. It was a bit lazy of you, getting Stephen Emes to pick up a copy of the PCU building's floor plans from the London Metropolitan Archives, just because it was round the corner from the Bleeding Heart. Too easy to check. So now let's behave like adults and not bother with the tiresome rigmarole of denial. After all, you do have the satisfaction of achievement, despite subsequent discovery.'

'You still don't know how I did it, do you?' Mr Merry sat back and folded his arms, waiting patiently. He seemed more relaxed now that the truth was out.

'Well of course I do,' said Bryant dismissively. 'What set me thinking was this: how do you tell one raven from another? If somebody wanted them, how would he know he was actually getting the ravens from the Tower? The answer, of course, was that he wouldn't unless you gave him proof that the originals had gone. Your solution was to make sure they vanished – where they went was no concern of yours, because you simply got some more. And your client never knew otherwise. Once I realized that vanishing a bird was different to stealing it, everything became clearer. And the vet thing was a bit of a giveaway. A vet doesn't just come here to check on the health of the menagerie's occupants. Matthew Condright told me that the birds were allowed out into the grounds during the day, and that they stayed because they had their wings clipped. How long have you been the vet here? Between a year and eighteen months?'

'Something like that.'

'The mistake I made was in misunderstanding the terminology. I honestly thought "clipping" was just that, the severing of tendons that allow the birds to fly. I should have realized when I saw them hopping about on the lawn that they could easily lift their wings. Clipping involves regularly trimming the actual ends of the flight feathers, doesn't it? And the feathers grow out, just as human hair does, needing to be cut. Although you were careful to make the ravens' wings appear clipped, what you actually did was hobble them with . . . some kind of clear gum, was it?'

'Exactly so. Quite harmless to the birds, and invisible.'

'They probably tried to peck it off, so you kept an eye

on them, got them used to it, reapplied the stuff as their lifting feathers grew out – the amount of clipping that makes the difference between being airborne and remaining grounded is pretty negligible, I understand, so Matthew didn't notice, especially as it was night by the time the ravens came back to their cage. And when you're around something unusual all the time you barely see it any more. Matthew didn't need to examine the birds, just count them.

'On your last visit you ascertained that the feathers had fully grown back and cleaned off the gum. You arrived early, probably picking one of those misty mornings one often gets down here at the river's edge, The birds left their cage and simply flew out one by one, before the Warders had started duty, before the public started turning up for the day. And because they all went at once, it looked as if someone had stolen them in a single audacious act of treason. Because it *is* treason, Mr Merry. High treason is the crime of disloyalty to the Crown, and it's still considered to be the most serious of all offences in the United Kingdom. Mr Condright, would you come in for a moment?'

Matthew, the Raven Master, appeared in the connecting doorway.

'Remind me, what are the crimes covered under the charge of high treason?'

Condright watched Mr Merry as he replied. 'I think they include plotting the murder of a monarch, committing adultery with members of the royal family, waging war against them or helping their enemies, or attempting to undermine the line of succession, Mr Bryant.'

'There you are. It used to be met with extraordinary punishment, because it threatened the security of the State. Luckily for you, hanging, drawing and quartering has fallen out of popularity, although I can't think why. I'm sure some cable channel would broadcast it. Tell me, Mr Condright, when was the last treason trial?'

'The last one that ended in a death sentence was 1946, sir. William Joyce, the fascist broadcaster from Brooklyn, New York, also known as Lord Haw-Haw. We shot him in the bum and hung him.'

'Luckily for you, though, since the Crime and Disorder Act of 1998 became law, the maximum sentence for treason in the UK is now life imprisonment.' Bryant chuckled to himself. 'And ravens – well, it's not like trying to cop off with a princess, is it?'

For the first time, Mr Merry looked as if the ground had shifted beneath him.

'Mr Condright, will you do me a favour and keep Mr Merry locked up in the Tower while we send over a team to take his statement and formally charge him?' Bryant turned to the necromancer and grinned. 'Lock him up in the Tower – forgive me, but I've always wanted to say that.'

43

UNDERNEATH

'She kept telling everyone that she knew how Romain died, and who the killer was, and now she's gone,' said Shirone Estanza, wiping her eyes. 'But she couldn't have known.'

'Why not?' asked Renfield. The three of them were standing in the only dry spot they could find, beneath the school playground's bicycle shelter, a British summer triptych.

'You're her father: you wouldn't have told her, not if you thought it was someone close to her. Would you?'

Longbright noticed Renfield looking at her, and wished the ground would swallow her up. 'Do you have any idea where else she's likely to have gone?' she asked. 'Or who she might have been planning to see?'

'I don't know,' said Shirone despairingly. 'Maybe Mrs Wallace.'

'Why her?'

'She knows what's going on. She must do. She's been at the centre of all this right from the start.'

'What makes you say that?'

'Everyone talks around here. We know more than you

think. She knew about that guy Jhadav, didn't she?'

'Knew what? That he was in St George's Gardens the night you and Romain were there?'

'She must have known about it, or at least guessed, like I did. Why else would she have started stalking him?'

'What about her son, Martin? Has anyone seen him?'

'Not yet. He usually has archery practice on a Wednesday—'

'Archery?' Renfield repeated.

Longbright realized that Estanza had not known about the murder method, because in the end Orion Banks had decided not to fully raise the press blackout. 'Where does he go for practice?' she asked.

'The school doesn't have a range and nobody else takes it to his level, so he has a pass to some place in Hatton Garden,' Shirone explained. 'He's allowed to go without supervision. Mr Tarrant is the teacher, you can ask him where—'

Longbright and Renfield were already on their way.

The confrontation with Mr Merry had thrown Bryant off-track for a while. As he fruitlessly searched for a taxi in the rain, he called his partner and tried to explain himself. 'I told you something was wrong, and now I think I know what it is,' he said. 'The contract Krishna Jhadav cancelled with Thomas Wallace. Wallace was under a lot of stress. His company was going bust, he'd lost his biggest account, but he'd been there before. He'd suffered bouts of depression for years. Who knows what other factors were involved in his decision to take his life? Are people fundamentally truthful or do they always instinctively lie to protect themselves?'

'What are you getting at?' asked May impatiently.

'Just this,' he shouted above the noise of wet traffic. 'Mrs Wallace returned Jhadav's private financial files. I think she definitely had something on him. But that's no reason for stalking and attacking him. If she really believed that Jhadav was responsible for her husband's death, wouldn't she have gone to the police? She didn't, because she didn't need to.'

'I still don't see what you're saying.'

'She wasn't going after him, *he* was going after *her*, don't you see?'

'No, frankly I don't.'

'Listen, I have to find her right now. I'll explain everything when I get back.'

'You probably want to know how Jack's daughter is,' May prompted.

'Oh, good point, is she all right?'

'No, we haven't found her. Turns out she shot her mouth off about her father's involvement in the case, and may have suggested she knew who was responsible. We think she took the morning off school to go to an archery range with Martin Wallace. Apparently she has a crush on him. We're on our way there now.'

'Archery—'

'Don't worry, we're ahead of you.'

'I'll come and find you as soon as I'm done,' said Bryant. 'We're getting close, John – I'm sorry about Jack's daughter.'

May was about to reply, but Bryant had already terminated the call.

Bryant found Vanessa Wallace exactly where her neighbour said she would be, standing at the foot of her husband's grave. Rain rattled loudly in the leaves overhead. The plane trees provided a dry bower for them.

'I wish you had confided in me from the outset,' he said, standing beside her and looking down at the grave-marker. 'It would have prevented so much tragedy.'

'Would it have changed anything?' When she raised her eyes to his, he saw that she had been crying. She wore a drab beige raincoat, like an early presage of autumn. 'You don't understand, Mr Bryant. We're a typical London family. We take care of problems without help from others. Oh, we'll talk to the neighbours over a cup of tea, but we don't share, not really. We're not emotional people. We try to make things right. If we fail, we simply don't discuss the problem again. We were all supposed to have become more open after Princess Diana's death, but all that "sharing" – it never really took hold. It's just not us.'

Bryant stepped closer. He could see the tiredness in her features, how anxious she was to tell someone what had happened, but even now he knew she would not admit the truth without further encouragement.

'It must have been very difficult for you,' he said gently, pushing at the wet earth with his walking stick. 'Seeing the grave repeatedly dug up. You can't have had much sleep lately.'

'You have no idea how awful it's been,' she said, still studying the freshly turned turf at her feet. 'To know what I know and not be able to . . .'

'Let me see if I can help. Krishna Jhadav bullied and compromised your husband. He told him about Defluo-tech's working practices because he honestly thought your husband wouldn't have a problem with them. But he was wrong, wasn't he?'

'Thomas hated having to know,' she said. 'Every filthy little trick, every backhander and bribe. "All part of the game" – that was what Mr Jhadav told him. Is money laundering just a part of the game? Is paying off safety officials? Thomas lay awake at night thinking about what the company was doing. He thought of going to the police. Finally he told Mr Jhadav that he couldn't handle the account any more. It was he who gave it up, not the other way around. But you can't take back knowledge, can you? Not once it's been shared. It preyed on his mind.

I think he thought back over his life and decided it hadn't amounted to very much.'

'You called Jhadav on the morning of your husband's death.'

'No, Mr Bryant, I called him back. He had already tried to call me.'

'Do you think they were money laundering? Is that what your husband told you?'

'As far as I can tell they were quite open about it. They made a lot of cash they couldn't bank, and needed Thomas to hold it somewhere for them.'

'Do you know where?'

'No. Mr Jhadav kept asking about the rest of his files. Then on the morning of the funeral – I was already dressed in black, ready for the service, and to keep my mind occupied I started sorting through the last of the folders. I put them in a box and left it out for collection. In the bag containing the contract-termination papers there was a small envelope addressed to Thomas, so I thought nothing of opening it. I was within my rights as a widow, surely?

'Inside was a little plastic memory stick. Nothing else. I tried it in Martin's laptop but I couldn't open it. But I knew it had to be important if Mr Jhadav had left it with Thomas for safekeeping. It was still in my hand when the car arrived. It was raining. It only rains at funerals in films, doesn't it? But there we were, standing in St George's Gardens, just me and Martin and an aunt we hadn't seen for years in the falling drizzle.'

She looked at the trampled grassy space between the burial plot and the trees, remembering. 'Mr Orton and Mr Rummage were here from the funeral parlour. There was no vicar; we're not a religious family. We were waiting for the coffin to be moved into place, but Mr Rummage said they'd take care of it immediately after the service. Apparently that's what they do in these circumstances. So

I said a few words, and threw a handful of earth into the grave. I don't know what made me do it – but I threw the memory stick in as well. It seemed like the appropriate thing to do. I just wanted to be rid of it all. Martin went home, but I stayed to watch them lower the coffin. And whatever nasty little secret Mr Jhadav had left on his flash drive stayed with my husband in his grave, under the casket.'

'Did you tell him what you'd done, taunt him with the knowledge?'

'No. Not in so many words. I just said I'd buried the evidence.'

'Did he ask what you meant by that?'

'No, but when I heard about the plot being dug up, it was obvious he understood.'

'You could have simply denounced him,' said Bryant.

Vanessa Wallace looked him in the eye. 'I'd have had to explain why I knew. And that would have made Martin hate me even more. Instead I let Jhadav hound me, and I baited him. Then it all just got out of hand, and there was nothing I could do to stop it.'

44

THE ROSE GARDEN BOFFIN

It took Orton and Rummage just over an hour to remove the coffin again. The wet earth had not been tamped down, and was easy to remove. 'Third time lucky,' Rummage chuckled. 'I'm not being funny, Mr Bryant, but I've never had a client move about so much. In the grave, out of the grave, I think he'll be glad of a lie-down after this. Where's Mrs Wallace?'

'I sent her home,' said Bryant, relighting his pipe. 'I need you to sift the earth immediately beneath the centre of the casket. We're looking for a small piece of black plastic. One of those computer thingies. A dingle.'

'A dongle,' said Mr Rummage. 'Right you are.' He stopped for a moment. 'Is that what all this has been about?'

'You probably want to mind your own business at this point.' Bryant puffed contentedly at his pipe and stood back. There was nothing he enjoyed more than watching others work.

It was Orton who found it. Rising in the grave like Hamlet fishing for Yorick's skull, he held the muddy black stick aloft. Bryant gingerly took it from his fingers but didn't offer to give him a hand out.

'I'll leave you chaps to tidy up,' he said. 'I think it's safe to say that Mr Wallace will be staying at home from now on.'

Herbert Constable was not Bryant's first choice for cracking the flash drive, but none of his other expert freelancers seemed to be available. He was a former MI6 cryptography expert based at the original 'Station X' in Bletchley Park, who had retired at the age of seventy-six to tend the rose garden in Regent's Park. He met Bryant in his shed, tucked behind the piddling fountains and crisply clipped walkways of the park's Inner Circle.

Constable reminded Bryant of a grey stick insect, a Giacometti-like figure of a man, awkwardly folded up in a little hut filled with manure bags, pitchforks and plant pots. A whistling kettle and a large brown china teapot sat atop a small stove next to an incredibly filthy computer. Constable blew some dead leaves off the keyboard and gave it a bash to get the dirt out.

'It's about time you upgraded that thing, isn't it?' asked Bryant.

'A computer doesn't require a new OS every six months just so I can play a new level of *Angry Birds* on it, Arthur. Actually I've stripped this little bugger out and given it some oomph. It may look like a Ford Prefect but it's a Ferrari under the bonnet. Anyway, I'm waiting until quantum computation is perfected, then I'll do some serious upgrading. These youngsters wandering about with voice-activated mobiles think they're so modern, but once retinal tasking and D-Wave System technology is up and running it'll look like they're carrying baked-bean cans attached to bits of string. How have you been keeping? I heard you were down at Bletchley recently with Angela – not rekindling an old flame, surely?'

'That's classified information,' huffed Bryant. 'She was helping me with an investigation.[1] Just as I hope you will. I've got a dangle.' He produced the mud-encrusted flash drive and gave it a wipe with his hankie.

'A dongle. Right, give it here. God, did you have to bury it first?'

'I didn't bury it, someone else did. I thought you might be able to open it. I'm as technical as a Tunisian.' He explained as much of the situation as he knew himself, but in such a Bryantian way that it made virtually no sense.

At some point Constable gave up listening and inserted the drive into a port on his Mac, wiping a clean patch on his screen. Underneath the dirt was a picture of the rose garden in full glorious bloom. When the folder appeared he double-clicked and waited again. Half a dozen blue-grey files popped up in two lines. Bryant was now at the limit of his technical knowledge, and looked wistfully at the teapot.

'Odd,' said Constable, running a wrinkled hand through his long grey hair. 'What's supposed to be in these things?'

'I'm not sure,' Bryant admitted. 'Hopefully something damning about the financial practices of a waste-management company. Why?'

'I can't open the files. They're not password-protected, they're just empty.'

'Why would someone keep empty files on one of those things? Can I make some tea?'

'It's already brewed,' said Constable. 'I know what you're like. Give me a minute to think. Whatever's on this stick, it's not in the files.'

Bryant poured thick brown tea into white enamel mugs. 'But there's nothing else on it, is there?'

---

[1] See *Bryant & May and the Invisible Code*

'Perhaps,' said Constable. He fiddled about for a few minutes, trying various combinations of keys to no avail.

'It wouldn't have to be the information itself,' said Bryant. 'It could just be the key to where it is.'

'That makes more sense,' said Constable. 'The system abbreviates file names for the sake of space. But if I click and hold – as if I was going to rename them – I can read the full titles, yes?' He gave a low whistle. 'Well I'm damned. You're right. The information isn't in the files themselves, it's in their names. Look at this.'

Bryant leaned forward and read the full titles of the little folders. 'Romanée-Conti'. 'DRC 1990'. 'Code 1536'. 'Palace of Whitehall'. 'DSQ45106'.

The first line rang a bell with Bryant; Jhadav had used the pseudonym 'Roman Conti' when meeting Stephen Emes at the Bleeding Heart.

'Whitehall Palace,' Constable said. 'Funny how the word "Whitehall" has become a metonym for all things governmental. The original building's gone now, hasn't it?'

'It burned down in 1698,' said Bryant absently. 'The MoD now stands in its place.'

'Do you know what this means?'

'I've a pretty good idea,' said Bryant. 'Henry the Eighth. He was an inveterate collector of precious objects, you know. In 1536 he had a wine cellar built in the basement of the Whitehall Palace. I imagine that when the directors of a company go into the money-laundering business, the biggest problem they face is how to invest their provenance-free cash into something that will continue to appreciate in value. Run those first two titles together and Google them, will you?'

Constable did as instructed and read from the screen. '"Romanée-Conti. In 1996, eight bottles of Romanée-Conti DRC 1990 fetched $224,900 at auction at Sotheby's London. Seven of the bottles were subsequently lost during exportation. The single remaining bottle instantly became one of the world's rarest and most valuable wines, commanding many times the original valuation." It says here, "One of the prime reasons for the high price of this wine is the low soil yield in the area of France where it is produced. It takes the produce of three Pinot Noir grape vines to make one bottle. The average age of the vines is fifty-three years . . ." There's a lot of guff about that year having below-average rainfall followed by rain, which staved off vine rot, but you get the general idea.'

'I certainly do,' murmured Bryant. 'I don't suppose Jhadav could be trusted to keep the director's ill-gotten gains under his own name somewhere, so he invested it. The only part of the Whitehall Palace that survived was Henry the Eighth's wine vault. It's now in the basement of the Ministry of Defence.'

'Then what we've got here is a key to where he left the wine, its label, location, pass-code and item number,' said Constable, ejecting the flash drive and handing it back.

'Hang on, can you write it down for me on, you know, a proper bit of paper?'

'I already have.' He handed Bryant a yellow slip.

'Thanks, Herbert. This has been most enlightening,' said Bryant. 'Can I take a buttonhole on the way out? Nothing rare, something red with a bit of scent will do. We must see a bit more of each other.'

'You could come by and give me a hand in the rose garden sometime,' said Constable. 'It's a lot more therapeutic than digging up dead bodies.'

45

ONE FROM THE VAULT

Martin Wallace led the way down the wet stone steps cut
into the side of the building. There were few passers-by in
this dingy corner of Clerkenwell. 'I've only got an hour's
practice booked and I'm already fifteen minutes late,' he
said. 'You didn't have to come with me.'

'I wanted to,' Sennen told him. 'I had a private study
double period anyway. Martin, do you think your mother
knows more than she's letting on? Is that why she started
following people?'

'My mother . . . All I can tell you is that since my old
man died, she's had some kind of weird persecution
complex. We don't have much to do with one another.
Nothing she says or does ever makes much sense to me.
Dad was the only one I cared about.'

'I thought you didn't like him, the way you talked.'

'You don't know much about males, do you?' He pushed
open a red fire-escape door and held it open. 'It's quicker
this way. Mind the puddle.'

They were standing in a steel and concrete basement
below one of the larger jewellery stores in Hatton
Garden. 'This used to be a storage vault for diamonds,'

Martin explained. 'A lot of the older Jewish companies have moved out now, but they still own the buildings, so they rent out the spaces. It's perfect as an archery court. Hardly anybody ever uses it so I can practise whenever I want.'

He led the way to a grey steel locker at the rear of the room, and changed his sweatshirt for a tight black vest. Sennen could not help noticing the muscles in his upper arms.

'How's your dad getting on with the case?' he called back, removing an aluminium case from the shelf and opening it.

'They're going to make an arrest any time now,' she said. 'He tells me everything. Sometimes I help him out on investigations.'

'Like this one? They interviewed my mother like she was a criminal.'

'They have to talk to everyone, so they can eliminate suspects.'

'So she's a suspect?'

'Of course. And so are you.'

'Me? Why?'

She pointed to the crossbow in his hands. 'I think you know why. How good are you with that thing?'

'I'll show you,' he said slowly. 'Have you got an apple or something in that bag of yours?'

'No – I've got an orange.'

'Take it over to the target and put it on your head.'

Sennen gave a nervous laugh. 'No. That's how William Burroughs killed his wife.'

'He used a handgun and a glass of water. And he was off his face. What? Don't you think I can do it?'

'It's not that.'

'Then what?'

'I know you were involved, Martin.' She made it sound like common knowledge.

Martin shook his head and smiled at the ground. 'How do you know that?'

'I told you. My father is working on the case.'

'They don't know the truth.'

'Ah, but I do.' Her eyes were knowing, her smile flirtatious.

'I don't see how that's possible. You don't even know me.'

'I do. I know everything about you,' she said confidently. 'I've watched—'

He cut her short, pointing. 'Go to the target.'

'What?'

He indicated the straw board at the other end of the range. 'Now.'

'Why?' It was dawning on Sennen that she was no longer in control of the situation.

'Just do what you're told.'

'No, Martin.'

'Go to the target, Sennen.'

Picking up her rucksack, he gripped her hand and led her across the concrete floor to the far end of the room, which was divided off with chicken wire. 'All you have to do is forget what I'm doing and stand very, very still.'

He pulled down a fresh white paper target and placed her in front of it, carefully arranging her so that she was facing him beneath the spotlights. Then he took the orange from her bag and balanced it on her hair. At first it wouldn't stay in one place, so he flattened it slightly and tried again.

'Martin, please don't do this.'

'Don't move. If the orange falls off, I'll shoot you in the head. Do you understand?' He turned and marked out his paces.

She found herself shaking involuntarily. At any minute it seemed her legs might collapse from under her. She needed to find a bathroom very badly.

The orange was starting to slip. Tilting her head, she fought to keep it from falling. She could hear water trickling in a steady, mournful stream somewhere behind her. The floor around her shoes looked wet. Even though it was cold in the basement, sweat trickled down to the small of her back. She realized she had behaved like an idiot. Nobody knew she was there. She had even turned off her mobile so that they wouldn't be interrupted.

Martin stood with his feet apart and hefted the crossbow on to his arm. 'Do you still think I killed them, Sennen?' he called.

She was terrified now. 'No. I didn't say that. I just said you were involved.'

'Why would you say such a thing?'

'I wanted you to – to—'

'Go on.'

'I thought you'd notice me.'

'Why would you want that?'

'Because I like you. I thought you'd like me more—'

'If you called me a murderer?' There was a click as he loaded the shaft into the crossbow. 'That's an interesting seduction technique.'

'They wanted me to find out about your mother. The police think she knows more than she told them.'

'My mother and I don't talk to each other,' he called back, carefully taking aim. 'Nobody in our family ever talked to anyone else. I'm going to be completely honest with you, Sennen. Seeing as you've been honest with me.'

'Martin,' she pleaded. 'No. Don't say it. Let me leave and we'll pretend this never happened.'

'No, I think you need to know.'

'Please don't.'

'I managed to kill Krishna Jhadav eventually. The first time, I hit the man who was helping him. I didn't mean to. But I got Jhadav in the end. He died as he lived, drowning in shit.'

'I won't tell anyone, Martin. I promise. I'd never tell.'

Martin lowered his eyeline along the shaft and prepared to fire.

'I may not look it, but I am a policeman,' said Bryant vehemently. He held his place on the steps of the Ministry of Defence as the rain pelted down, wishing he didn't have to justify his position so often.

'The MoD is a separate jurisdiction,' the security guard explained. 'I can't let you inside, Mr Bryant. We know all about the Peculiar Crimes Unit. A right bloody thorn in the side, you've been.'

'Then I have to inform you that you're obstructing the course of an ongoing City of London Police investigation. I just need access to the wine vault for a few minutes.'

'The vault's run by a separate private company, but I still can't let you in. We have no spare personnel at the moment, and the rules say that all visitors must apply in advance and be accompanied by one MoD official. Private individuals are all issued with their own personal security codes.'

'Wait a minute,' said Bryant. 'Private individuals? Why are they using the vault?'

'Because as soon as the bloody Tories got back in, they flogged off the cellar and let their rich pals store wine there,' the guard confided. 'It's all prestige and privilege.'

'I thought you civil servants were supposed to remain impartial,' said Bryant.

'You believe that and you work in the public-service sector?' scoffed the guard. 'Are you sure you're a copper?'

'No,' said Bryant, brandishing his code. 'I'm just an incredibly wealthy and well-connected man with a private security number for the vault. And I need to get access to what's mine.'

'Fair enough,' said the guard, stepping aside. 'You could

have said that in the first place. It would help if you didn't dress like a tramp.'

Bryant was taken to an immense brushed-steel lift that looked as if it was used to move bullion, and the guard swiped him in. 'I can't take you down,' he said, reaching in and punching the –3 button. 'The vault's on a timer. You've got exactly ten minutes from when you input your code, then the area shuts down again. So you'd better get a move on.'

'A bit restrictive, isn't it?' said Bryant as the doors slid shut.

'This is the Ministry of Defence, not a bingo hall,' muttered the guard, returning to his post. 'My shift's just about to change over, pal. You'll have to sign out with my relief.'

Bryant found himself in a concrete corridor lined on one side with clear plastic panels, behind which was broken brickwork belonging to a much more venerable building. The far end opened out into the wine cellars. The entrances to the original individual vaults were lined in Portland stone and stood four feet off the ground at ten-foot intervals along the floor. At this depth the walls were stained with black streaks of damp, a reminder that the Thames ran like an artery through the heart of the city, and always found its way through the cracks.

The floor had been raised and replaced with polished red bricks. Iron-framed lamps hung at intervals, releasing a warm, low light. At the farthest end, near a dozen old wine barrels laid on their sides, was a blank steel door. Narrow and coffin-shaped, it had been set deep in the thick wall. Beside it was a small metal box, its plastic lid covering a code panel of letters and numbers.

Bryant consulted his slip of paper and, praying silently, punched in *DSQ45106*. There was a faint hiss of pressurized air escaping, and the door popped open by two or three centimetres.

Welcome to the world of the super-rich, Bryant thought. *No fuss, no noise, no questions asked.* He opened the door and stepped inside. Motion-sensor light panels were already flickering on overhead. The room was tiny, barely higher than the top of his hat, and narrow. It was lined with small square glass panels. An electronic gauge set in the brickwork told him that it was 10 degrees centigrade. It clicked into life, rebalancing the temperature to allow for the fact that he had opened the door.

This time he needed a four-digit code, *1536.*

Entering it, he was just able to open the door by standing to one side. Carefully, he eased out a polished black wooden box, vaguely recalling that you had to store vintage wine horizontally to keep the cork moist. The cold air was already starting to dig into his bones. When his mobile suddenly started barking out 'Come Friends and Plough the Seas' he jumped and almost dropped his cargo. Cradling the case in the crook of his left arm, he dug out his mobile with his right.

'Where are you?' asked Land. 'I really need to know what you're up to. Why did you go and visit a retired code-breaker? Jack and Janice aren't answering their phones. Colin and Dan are taking the Wallace house apart without authorization and your partner has simply gone missing. And some beardy-weirdie called Mr Merry has just been brought here in handcuffs.'

'So what's the problem?'

'The problem?' Land all but shrieked. 'The problem is that none of this was approved by Orion Banks. She's threatening to—'

'Let her threaten,' said Bryant. 'I'll be back in a few minutes to close the case.'

He could hear Land still complaining as he turned off his mobile, noting its miniscule red bar of power. Unclipping the wooden lid of the case, he examined the final green bottle of Romanée-Conti DRC 1990, nestled in thick straw.

So this was how Krishna Jhadav and his co-conspirators had spirited away their bribe money. They had not been prepared to entrust the details of its location to any one director. Instead, in an act of chutzpah, Jhadav had handed it to his legal representative along with all of his other sensitive documents, simply because he knew that Thomas Wallace was too honest to ever plug in the flash drive and see what they were up to.

But in a twist Jhadav could not have foreseen, the depressed executive had killed himself and the flash drive had gone missing.

Bryant wondered if Mrs Wallace had openly blamed Jhadav for Thomas's suicide when she called him. Certainly she had taken her revenge, throwing the flash drive into her husband's burial plot. And when she'd heard that his body had been dug up, how quickly did she realize what must have happened? Bryant knew that if you had two facts, A and C, say, but no B, it was fairly easy to build a bridge between the ones you were absolutely sure of.

He stood with the bottle balanced in his hand, thinking quietly.

Krishna Jhadav had received his files back from Mrs Wallace, but there had been no envelope containing a flash drive. Mrs Wallace had hinted that it had been buried. Jhadav had gone to see Ron Rummage to ask if anything could have been placed with the corpse. Rummage wouldn't have known the answer, but he hadn't been able to guarantee that it hadn't, either.

Jhadav had enlisted Stephen Emes to help him dig up the casket, but had not thought of looking underneath it. He had returned to Rummage – or possibly Orton – and bullied the only other possibility out of one of them; that perhaps the flash drive had accidentally gone into one of the other two caskets buried that week, those of Elspeth Duncannon and the terrier, Prince.

But he didn't find it.

Worse, someone shot his helper. Jhadav was trapped. The police had visited him. He couldn't go to the wine vault and make a fuss without drawing attention to himself and giving the game away.

Bryant was angry. Everyone had kept something from him. Rummage had missed out the detail of his visits from Jhadav because, as he put it, 'We've been entrusted with the final state secrets.' There was no way that he was ever going to fully disclose what happened in his chapel of rest.

Mrs Wallace knew all too well why her husband's coffin had been broken open, but had refused to explain because she wanted to keep her revenge intact. The only power she had over the man she held responsible for the death of her husband was knowing that she had literally buried his lifeline to the future.

But, of course, Jhadav knew that she knew, and threatened her. She avoided admitting that she was being intimidated by cleverly reversing what everyone thought, and making it look as if she was stalking him. She hadn't meant to kill him with a falling plant pot, she had simply done it to draw attention to her behaviour. So long as she appeared to be the aggrieved party, her secret remained safe.

Only one part of the story made no sense. What had happened to Romain Curtis on the night he'd gone to the club? And why did he change his shirt?

Bryant was still pondering the question when the lights snapped off and the steel door swung shut, sealing him inside the chill walls of the vault.

46

SEALED FATES

Sennen Renfield's tears were making her face itch. She wanted to raise a hand to her cheek, but was frightened that Martin would release the trigger of the crossbow. His right arm was out of the shadows and quivering, as if he was fighting to control his own nervous system. She knew he was too good a shot to miss.

'You can't do this, Martin. You can't hurt anyone else.'

'I only meant to take out Jhadav,' he replied. 'Romain told me he'd seen two of them. I didn't know they were the same height. I just saw an outline against the trees. I should have waited until I was sure.'

'You have to tell the police exactly what happened. You have to tell them about your father. They'll listen to you.' She was shaking so violently now that she could feel the orange starting to roll from her head.

'If I give myself up, my life will be over,' Martin called back. 'How old will I be when I get out of prison? How will I get a job? Stephen Emes had a wife and a kid before he joined the New Resurrectionists. I found his family on Facebook. They changed their names to avoid being associated with him. People will do the same thing to me.

I was always the stupid indie kid you all made fun of.'

'Not me, Martin, I would never—'

'I have to finish it, Sennen. You know—'

'No, my father—'

'Your father doesn't know anything.'

'All right,' she cried. 'You're right. I made it up.'

'Why would you do that?'

'Because . . .' She could hardly say, *Because I think about you every waking second of the day and I'd do anything for you, anything*, because he barely knew she existed. It was so cruel; she wanted Martin but he wanted Shirone, and Shirone had only ever wanted Romain. '. . . I like you,' she finished lamely. She wished he would fire and end the agony.

'You're the only one who knows what really happened, the only one who'll ever know,' Martin said slowly. She knew then that she would not leave the basement alive.

She felt the shot lift strands of her hair. The arrow skimmed her skull and knocked the orange aside, but didn't pierce it. She screamed and dropped to the floor, scuttling across the room as he came running after her.

Outside, Renfield and Longbright were looking for the entrance, but the building's basement was unmarked.

Longbright held up her hand. 'Wait, I heard someone. They've got to be in the old car park.' A ramp curved below, but the shutters at its base were closed. 'We must be able to go down from inside the building.'

They ran back to the main entrance and headed for the lobby.

If he hadn't been so very cold, Bryant might have laughed at the circumstances which had resulted in him being shut inside a glass tomb beneath the Ministry of Defence.

And now, for some unfathomable reason, he had no signal on his mobile. He'd had one a minute ago. Where had it gone? That was the trouble with technology, it was just so *random*. There had definitely been a tiny red bar. Red was good, wasn't it?

Overhead, a thin emergency light flickered on, buzzing faintly.

Nobody at the PCU knew he was down here. Even the MoD security guards had switched shifts. The temperature was not so low that it could kill him, although at his age one never knew. But the tiny corridor of cabinets was sealed at tightly as any coffin, and the air would not last long.

It's not fair, he thought, *Thomas Wallace gets disinterred on a regular basis, and I have to get buried alive.* He fancied that it was already getting hard to breathe.

Running his free hand along the wall, he searched for a release catch or an emergency button that would bring help. The smooth concrete yielded nothing. He tried the edges of the door to see if there was any way he could prise it open, but had no fingernails to speak of. He could discern the narrow lip of an orange rubber seal around the steel frame, but had nothing to cut it with. Usually his coat pockets were filled with sharp and potentially dangerous objects, but not today; Alma had made him empty out everything that was pointed and incendiary when she went to the dry cleaner's, and he had yet to put it all back.

He turned about in the narrow space, feeling the walls close in on him. He was determined not to panic. Maggie had cured him of his past terrors. He would not allow them to come rushing back.

All the wine cabinets were sealed tight and locked with codes, except for the one that Jhadav had rented.

He set the box containing the rare vintage down on the concrete floor and studied it thoughtfully. He tried his phone again. Nothing. Now even the fine red bar wasn't showing.

With a heavy heart, he realized he had no other choice.

Lifting out the bottle, he swung it experimentally by the neck. He decided to take one final proper look at one of the rarest red wines in the world before smashing it.

His brow creased. Instead of it reading 'Romanée-Conti DRC 1990' on a neat white countersigned label, he found that it said 'Tesco Blossom Hill Merlot Blend California 2014'. The bottle had a screw top, and there was even a price sticker: £4.99.

'What the bloody hell?' For a moment he stared at the thing, wondering if he could have made a mistake. Then he began to laugh. Of course. He almost felt like congratulating Jhadav.

Unscrewing the lid, he allowed the wine to pour out through his fingers. Then he dropped the bottle on to the stone floor. The first time, it bounced. He tried again from a greater height, and this time it split into lethal shards. Picking up the longest sliver, he set about cutting the door seal.

Longbright found the stairs to the diamond merchant's basement first and called Renfield over, heading down. The main fire door operated from a London bolt, and was quickly kicked open by Renfield's mighty nailed boot.

They heard Sennen cry out from somewhere deep inside. There was no point in trying to be quiet now. Renfield also kicked open the inner red metal door and allowed it to slam back against the wall. It was best that they made as much noise as possible.

The great grey concrete bunker that stretched before them was in virtual darkness, except for a spotlit archery run at its far side. The corridor was lined with chicken wire. Longbright quickly took in the scene: the target, the crying girl, the boy with the crossbow raised, the distance between them. Everybody froze.

'Put it down, son,' said Renfield. 'Let her go. I'm her father. You can still stop this.'

Martin turned fractionally to study them. It was the split second Sennen needed. She screamed and ran for cover. Martin released a second bolt from the crossbow. From this distance it was hard to tell if he had meant to or not.

Cleaving the air, the arrow buried itself into the breeze-block wall beside the schoolgirl's head, spraying dust and granules of brick.

Renfield was a beast unleashed. He threw himself at the boy before he had a chance to reload, slamming him on to his back.

Sennen ran to Longbright and buried her head in the DS's shoulder. Their apologies cancelled each other's out.

47

COOL

At a little after eight thirty that evening, Orion Banks sat at the head table in the PCU common room and checked her Cartier watch, waiting for everyone to settle down.

'Well,' she said finally, 'as Mr Bryant has seen fit not to grace us with his presence, I think we should press on. First item, this business of the ravens appears to have settled itself without any help from us and we now have someone in custody, although there's no accompanying documentation – why is that?'

'This was Mr Bryant's initiative,' Land explained. 'He doesn't do paperwork.'

'Then there is no case,' said Banks loudly and clearly. 'Do you understand? It has no value stream. Do you understand what I mean when I talk about malicious obedience? It's the process of following a superior's instructions while hoping for failure, and I think it's something you're all guilty of.'

'We get results,' said May hotly. 'We've just brought in the killer of Krishna Jhadav and Stephen Emes.'

'You cannot say that sort of thing out loud,' warned Banks. 'This is simply not how you are meant to operate.

And the case is unfinished. Your organizational hierarchy entirely prevents risk closure.' She looked up to the ceiling and blew at her fringe. 'How can I explain this any more exactly? There is no causal through-line.'

Bryant appeared in the doorway and made his way wearily to the only spare seat. He looked even more dishevelled than usual, and reeked of alcohol. There were red wine stains down the front of his shirt.

'Have you been drinking?' asked Banks, her eyes widening in horror.

'No, but I plan to after the debrief,' said Bryant, plonking himself down. 'Where are we up to?'

'Miss Banks is tearing us off a strip for not producing a casual landmine,' said Raymond.

'I don't need a landline,' said Bryant, 'I've got my mobile. Not that it worked today, just when I needed it most.'

'Whose fault is that?' asked May.

'Henry the Eighth's,' Bryant replied obtusely.

'Can we please keep this meeting on track?' asked the exasperated Banks. 'I'm not here to judge, just to point out the flaws in your systemization techniques and try to rectify them. Mr Bryant, it seems to me that most of the problems here arise from your continued refusal to share information.'

'Then let me share some information with you right now,' said Bryant. 'First of all, let's trace back your causal through-line, as I just heard you call it.'

'So you *did* understand.'

Bryant smiled slyly. '"When the wind is southerly, I know a hawk from a handsaw." Indulge me for a minute or two, please.' He gathered his wits and presented himself to the room. This was the part he liked best. 'John, shall I do the honours?'

May held out his hand. 'Please, be my guest.'

'This started with a company that took bribes for matching up the buyers and sellers of industrial waste.

And before you say anything, they're registered in Threadneedle Street, which makes it a City of London case. The directors of Defluotech needed to bury some illegal profit, and Krishna Jhadav, wine buff and *bon viveur*, decided to invest in something that had a fantastic resale value. As the directors didn't entirely trust each other, they left the arrangements to Jhadav and his corporate lawyer, one Thomas Wallace, a small-time operator with a failing business, someone operating below the radar of the Serious Fraud Office.

'What they hadn't bargained for was that Mr Wallace couldn't handle the burden of knowledge, and decided he'd had enough of life. Revenge is a dish best prepared earlier, a lesson that Vanessa Wallace failed to heed. In a moment of spontaneous anger and grief, she threw away something she hoped was of value to Mr Jhadav and his partners; she chucked a flash drive that had been left in her husband's care into his grave.

'Her son was devastated by the loss. Martin Wallace barely spoke to his mother. For an emo or an indie or whatever he's supposed to be, he wasn't very good at expressing emotion. All he knew was that, in addition to being responsible for his father's death, Jhadav and Emes were now desecrating his memory by trying to disinter him.'

'Wait, how did he know it was them?' asked Land.

'He was friends with Romain Curtis,' Bryant replied.

'We'll get to that,' said May, who knew that his partner liked to take things in order.

'Martin Wallace mistakenly shot Emes dead,' Bryant continued, 'but it had the positive effect of making Jhadav fearful for his life. Martin left a crossbow at the chapel to make sure that Emes was blamed. He did a lot of crazy things. It was he who watched Shirone Estanza's flat, not his mother. If only the pair of them had been able to talk to one another, all this might have been avoided. Instead, the boy avenged his father, but he also lost his reason. He'll be tried under the Youth Justice System for the murders of Stephen Emes and Krishna Jhadav, and for the attempted murder of Sennen Renfield.

'Now we come to the saddest part of this story, the death of Romain Curtis. There was one anomaly that struck both John and myself early on in the case. Curtis had changed his shirt between the time he went out to the Scala nightclub and the time he was found in Britannia Street two and three-quarter hours later. Why? Shirone Estanza, who accompanied him, couldn't recall how he was dressed, but his mother was sure he left the flat in some kind of black T-shirt. However, he was found in a pale blue Superdry shirt, a brand he hated.

'We know that Curtis was a fashion student and wanted to study at St Martins. We know he liked to design his own clothes. On Sunday night, when he went back into St George's Gardens to take another look at what he had seen, it seems likely that he did so to take a photograph. Not because he wanted to identify the vandals caught digging up a grave, but because it looked cool. The kid loved horror films! His photo showed two men and an upended open coffin. What Romain Curtis did next only makes sense in the light of his age and the way he was treated. He printed the picture he'd taken on to a T-shirt. Although neither Emes nor Jhadav considered the boy to be a threat – he was, after all, only a minor, and a stoned one at that – they decided to be on the safe side and keep an eye on him. It couldn't have been difficult; Curtis was well known in the neighbourhood where Shirone Estanza's brothers hung out and kept a watchful eye on everyone.

'But much to Jhadav's horror, he found that Curtis was wearing a shirt with his face on it, as if he was daring him to do something about it. Curtis wasn't, of course, he just thought it looked neat. It's likely he didn't even realize his photo had caught two men dressed in black on either side of the corpse when he took it, because he didn't mention it to me or to the officious Community Support Officer. I imagine that later on Monday afternoon when he uploaded the shot, he saw them revealed and thought the composition would make a good design. He didn't have his own computer at home; he used his mother's. We searched the computer he shared at school. Our oversight was to fail to search *her* hard drive. I think we'll find the shot there.

'Jhadav knew he'd had his picture taken, but hadn't been able to go after Curtis – he and Emes had an unearthed body to contend with, and they still hadn't found what they were looking for. Instead he asked around the next day, following Curtis, taking Emes along with him, trying to figure a way of finding out what the boy had seen. They probably saw him talk to friends – Martin Wallace, for one. And there they all were that night, arranged in a classic death-metal scene, Jhadav and Emes and a corpse and a coffin, displayed on the boy's chest for all the world to see, with a band logo underneath that read "The Bodysnatchers". Did Martin Wallace recognize his father in the picture? We'll have to ask him about that.

'One of them – probably Emes, who had access to medical supplies – spiked Curtis's drink at the bar so that they could get him into a stairwell and take his shirt. But they lost him in the crowd. Shirone Estanza's brothers heard what was going on – they missed very little – and warned by them, Shirone ran out to find him.

'When I met Shirone Estanza, I realized something else. She's very short. She has a penchant for wearing absurdly high heels. She wore them to the graveyard, and she was wearing them to the club that night. She couldn't run around the backstreets trying to find Romain, so she got hold of the keys to her brother's van. She didn't know where to look and she hadn't passed her test, but she had a good idea which route he would take, the one he always took, through the backstreets.

'She wasn't to know that he'd been drugged; she just thought he was drunk. And there he was, falling into the road right in front of her. She couldn't find the brake in time and hit him, and to make matters worse, in her panic she managed to reverse into him. Terrified and tearful, the poor girl fled the scene. She had no idea she'd killed him.' He shook his head sadly. 'In all of this, she and Romain were the real victims. Moments after she'd gone, Jhadav turned up and was able to remove the offending shirt.

'Jhadav thought he'd cleared everything up, but like so many guilty parties, he couldn't leave well enough alone. When I interviewed him he clumsily tried to tell me that Wallace had a fear of being buried alive.

'Shirone Estanza wasn't stalked by Mrs Wallace but by her son. Because he cared for her; because she was at risk. And there's one last matter to clear up.' Bryant dug a piece of pink toilet paper from his coat pocket and held it in his fist. Banks gave a grimace of puzzlement.

'What did the laundered money from Defluotech Management Systems buy? I assumed Jhadav had invested it in a bottle of rare vintage wine, but then I thought it seemed a lot of effort to go to for something that was still valued at under a million pounds. These were big boys. What if Jhadav's company had made a lot more money than that? Here's what was inside the bottle: the North Star diamond, not especially large but astoundingly well cut. It vanished from the Congo in 1997 and turned up here in a secret sale last year. It would have lost its provenance but maintained its black-market value. Jhadav consigned its security to Thomas Wallace, who was an Old Harrovian. If there's one thing Old Harrovians know about it's wine, and Wallace knew the location of London's most secure vault.

'Wines of an exceptional vintage appeared in the years

when a comet was seen in the sky, like the legendary Château d'Yquem of 1811. So you see, there really was a connection between the stars, the wine, and – the diamond.'

He unwrapped the flawless pink diamond and raised it high so that everyone could see. Unfortunately the toilet paper was torn and it fell out from between his fingers, bouncing along the warped floorboards and dropping straight down between them.

'Don't anybody move,' said Raymond Land.

48

STARS, WINE AND DIAMONDS

On Thursday afternoon, Janice Longbright found the final item she needed to add to the report: a Facebook photograph posted by a girl in the Scala nightclub showing Romain Curtis, Shirone Estanza and some of her friends standing at the edge of the dance floor. In it, Curtis's shirt was clearly visible. It showed what appeared to be a scene from a horror film: two clearly identifiable men and an opened coffin.

Longbright studied the picture for a while, her chin resting lightly on her knuckles, then emailed it to Louisa Curtis. It was Romain Curtis's final photograph. She hated the pictures of victims more than anything, those cheerful shots of people who had no inkling that they were about to lose so much. She still had a picture of her mother in just such a pose. And Sennen Renfield had come close to joining that tragic group. Longbright sniffed and closed down her computer screen.

Next door, Colin Bimsley closed his locker and went over to the window where Amanda Roseberry was standing.

'I know you're going to think this is forward of me, and

probably inappropriate, seeing as we're in the workplace and everything,' he said, 'but now that the case is wrapping up I wondered if you'd like to maybe have a drink with me.'

When she turned around, he realized she was on her mobile. Placing her hand over it, she looked at him enquiringly. 'Sorry, what?' she said. 'I'm on the phone to my boyfriend. He's stranded in Zurich and asking me for a decent hotel. I can only think of the Baur au Lac. Have you any ideas?'

'Oh.' Colin looked down at his shoes. 'I've never been to Europe. Except Marbella, with some mates, on a stag weekend. I was sick in a pedalo.'

'Sorry.' Roseberry turned back and listened to her phone. 'Well, try them first, darling, and if not head for the Hyatt.' She rang off and returned her attention to Bimsley. 'You're terribly sweet, Colin,' she said, looking into his eyes. 'But—'

'It's OK, you don't have to say it.' He gave an apologetic smile. 'I'm not on your level. I should have known better. Good job there's still a class system, eh? It protects you from blokes like me.'

'There's someone here who likes you very much, you know,' Roseberry whispered, discreetly pointing across the room. 'She just pretends she doesn't.'

Colin looked over and saw Meera staring at her computer screen with intense concentration, chewing the end of a Pepperami stick.

Bimsley wasn't sure. 'You really think so?' he asked. 'She looks kind of angry.'

'You just have to be patient.' Roseberry squeezed his arm. 'Go on, go over there. Say something nice and make her unscrunch her face.'

At the end of the hall, Longbright took Renfield to the cluttered evidence room, one of the few places in the building where she was sure they could not be overheard.

'I need to tell you this, Jack,' she said, taking his arm. 'Years ago there was an unsolved case, a man preying on young girls in the streets behind Leicester Square. There was incredible pressure on us to close the file. We realized that John's daughter Elizabeth bore a strong resemblance to the last victim, and she volunteered to re-enact the attack. The operation went very badly wrong. We all swore that such a situation would never arise again. So what did I do? I put your own daughter in the firing line. It's always going to stand between us, and it's something I can't ever put right. I'm sorry.'

'You're right,' said Renfield. 'I know you did it to get closer to her, but it was a serious error of judgement.'

'I don't expect either of you to forgive me. And I understand if you want to let things go between us.'

'It's not my decision, it's hers. Sennen's back with her mother. I talked to her this morning.'

'How was she?'

'Still pretty upset, although not as much as I thought she'd be. My ex-wife now thinks you're the Antichrist, of course. But it's safe to say that you've had a profound effect on my daughter.'

'Why?'

Renfield screwed up one eye, stuck his finger in his ear and wiggled it. The gesture was more endearing than it sounds. 'Well,' he said, 'she's decided she wants to join the police force.'

In the building's corner office, Raymond Land sat hiding behind his computer screen as Orion Banks paced before his desk. 'Extraordinary,' she said for the third time. 'I don't know how they did it. No methodology, no planning, nothing but organizational chaos. And out of it comes lightning in a bottle. Literally. I've been to every seminar, every presentation, but they never explained anything like this.'

'It's just the way they are,' Land ventured. 'The way

they've always been, right from the start. They attract the unusual. You wouldn't believe some of the people who've helped them.' He ticked them off on his fingers. 'A professor who finds missing people by analysing newspaper cuttings. A forensic expert who thinks he's a werewolf. A biochemist who impersonates his dead wife. A gang of counter-culture hippy types called the Southwark Supernaturals. Witches, conspiracy theorists, lefties, fascists, criminals on the run. Sane, intelligent people who believe they're reincarnated Vikings or characters from Gilbert and Sullivan operettas. We've had things going on here I could never put in official reports. You know they always say there's a fine line between genius and madness? Well, here the line gets rubbed out.'

Banks was incredulous. 'And they've used these methods for years and got away with it?'

'Barely. It feels like we've done nothing but fight closure for the last couple of decades. The government has taken everything else away, but they'd be wrong to shut this unit down. Bryant will tell you that England has a long history of hiring such people. He says that during the war Winston Churchill employed the horror writer Dennis Wheatley to work out what the Germans were up to. Churchill also got Royal Academy artists to camouflage battleships. And, indirectly, he founded this unit. The people who were hired then would never have passed modern-day psychometric tests. But the culture of taking on innovative outsiders survived. In the 1950s, the development of the microchip came from people who could barely take the top off a boiled egg without help.'

'So you must still have a few friends in high places.'

'A very few,' Land conceded, 'but those friends are even older than Bryant. Sometimes it feels like I'm working in a Victorian magic shop when everything around me is Starbucks. It's a different world now, your world, all financial forecasts and PowerPoint presentations and target-driven results. This place can't last much longer. We need some new allies.'

Banks picked a speck of fluff from her pink and black tunic. 'Yesterday I was ready to write you off myself,' she said. 'But two things interest me. The first is this.' She reached into her case and pulled out a spread-sheet. 'You get results. I conducted some research of my own. You've closed eighty-four per cent of the major cases you've been involved with. You have the right idea, you've just been going about it the wrong way, fighting with everyone.'

'You said two things.'

She tucked a curl of hair back behind her ear. 'The second is – less tangible. These days detection has given way to prevention. It's about crunching the numbers. At least, it is over in Head Office. But here – I look back at the last ten days and what do I find? Stars, wine, diamonds, bodysnatchers. You're not normal, any of you. People don't like what's not normal, and try to crush it. As you say, you badly need an ally. Perhaps that person is me.'

Land looked like someone had jumped out of a bush to surprise him. 'Really?'

'It's not an entirely altruistic thought, Raymond. I have a small department and limited resources. I need to make a name for myself, but the big budgets are awarded to the fraud boys. Some parts of the City of London have weak stats that drag us all down, but with the right handling your unit might be able to make a difference and push the figures up for me.'

'So we'd be a team,' said Land.

'No, I'd still be your boss.'

'Oh.'

'May I speak confidentially?'

'Of course.'

'When we found out that you were under our jurisdiction, we downscaled you. Actually, we wrote you off. I think it was a mistake. I might be able to guarantee that you get the things you need to tackle bigger cases.'

'Tell me what I have to do,' said Land.

49

WATERLOO BRIDGE

On Friday morning the sun put in a surprise appearance, catching everyone unawares. Sweaters were slung over shoulders, coats were draped across arms, umbrellas were sheathed, scarves vanished and even a few pale knobbly knees protruded from pairs of shorts. On the South Bank, strollers, cyclists and a couple of mimes (the Duke of Wellington and a man dressed as a talking dog in a kennel) crept cautiously out into the light. Joggers appeared among the commuters crossing Waterloo Bridge. It felt almost pleasant to be outside.

This was particularly true for Arthur Bryant, who had just discovered (not for the first time, but he was prone to forgetfulness) that escaping your own death instantly repaints the world in vibrant hues.

He stood in the middle of Waterloo Bridge with John May, just as he'd done on the lunchtime of the day they had first met all those centuries ago, and looked down into the fast-flowing river. At these reaches the Thames does not break into waves but appears to mushroom and blossom from beneath, a warning sign of the lethal currents that pulse below its surface.

Bryant leaned over the railings and breathed the rich damp air. He was the only one on the bridge dressed in an overcoat, scarf, jumper, shirt, braces, undershirt, vest and mittens. 'Do you think there's an element of truth in all legends?' he asked.

'I imagine so. Some small grain around which the stories accumulate, yes,' replied May.

'I was thinking about the legend of the Bleeding Heart,' he said, 'and the death of Alice Hatton. I could find no evidence that she ever existed.'

'Didn't that story involve dancing with the Devil?' said May. 'I'm not surprised you didn't find anything.'

'It's just that there's a condition – Giles was telling me – it's called takotsubo cardiomyopathy, or stress-induced cardiomyopathy. It's a sudden weakening of the heart muscles caused by temporary stress. And because it could be brought on by news of the death of a loved one, it became known as broken heart syndrome, or bleeding heart. I wonder if that's how the yard got its name. And I wonder if it's why Martin Wallace chose to kill with a crossbow. He had to pass the yard and the tavern sign every time he went to archery practice.'

'I think you're romancing again, Arthur. He shot Stephen Emes through the eye.'

'Only because it was dark and he made a mistake. And those youngsters, infatuated with one another, but all with the wrong partners: more bleeding hearts. I think if things had been different, Martin Wallace and Romain Curtis would have been friends. None of this would have happened if Vanessa Wallace hadn't acted impulsively. The whole thing was a house of cards that would have collapsed if just one person had been completely honest.'

'I feel sorriest for Shirone Estanza. In the law's eyes her crime starts with not having a driving licence and goes on to manslaughter.'

'Youth and mitigating circumstances are on her side,' said Bryant.

'She might be lucky. You have to hope for compassion. We have to put in a recommendation.'

'One thing still puzzles me, John. Why did Mr Merry tip his hand by showing me the evidence of apotropaic magic? It's almost as if he was testing me, to see if I could work it out.'

'I think he was arrogant enough to think that you wouldn't. I suspect such men set tests of strength for themselves. So,' said May, 'taphophobia, fear of being buried alive. Necrophobia, fear of death. Isolophobia, fear of being alone. I looked them up. Which one were you suffering from?'

'What do you mean?'

'For most of the week you avoided me and behaved like you'd seen your own ghost.'

'Perhaps I had,' said Bryant. 'For years I've had this strange feeling: when I'm alone it's as though I cease to exist. I thought to myself, what am I? A repository of useless knowledge. A walking history book. I've no social skills, nothing to offer anyone. London's rushing past me to a brave new future. I'm just an obstacle.'

'No, said May, 'you're a touchstone. If others can't see that, it's their loss.'

The seagull that dived past them was a piercing white against the olivine water. Its feral shriek broke the mood. Bryant threw it a piece of sausage sandwich he'd been saving in his pocket.

'Look at the Thames,' May said. 'It's the only thing in this city that doesn't change.'

'Oh, it changes,' Bryant replied, happy to be back on solid conversational ground. 'The composition alters from Teddington to Tilbury, from the Roman occupation to the sovereignty of bankers. There are no more frost fairs, no more carcasses of cows and cats, fewer pollutants, fewer ships. It was once wider at the Tower of London and harder to cross. There were nineteen arches supporting London Bridge, and the current was so strong that it pulled boats under. Can you imagine? Severed heads dipped in tar and placed on spikes, the stench of the tanneries, plague and cholera and everywhere, every day, the most astonishing, wonderful sights. They said when London laughed, the world laughed.' He turned away. 'I was born in the wrong time.'

'That's not it,' said May. 'The trouble with you is that you want to see it all, the entire two-thousand-year history. And you'd quite like to stay with it into the distant future. But you can't. None of us can. We each get our own particular slice of London life, and that's all. You have to make the most of it, Arthur. And you weren't born in the wrong time. When you were a baby there were still horses on this bridge. There was war and malnourishment and capital punishment. You've seen the greatest changes in the city's entire history. And it's a better place now, even though it's getting a little too crowded for my tastes.'

'I'm not complaining,' said Bryant, loosening his scarf a little. 'Did you know, after the Blitz, the city employed two PCs full time to take pictures of the burned-out buildings? Arthur Cross and Fred Tibb – they built up a complete record of what needed to be reconstructed. There have always been people in London who care and make a difference. That's all I ever wanted to be, one of those people, like the copper who freed me from my childhood prison. I don't know if I've managed it.'

'I think you know the answer to that,' said May, leading him away by the arm. 'Come on, I'll buy you a pint and you can tell me some more implausible legends.'

'Is it me, or is it getting hot?' Bryant asked suddenly.

'It can't be you,' said May. 'You're never hot.'

'Well, I feel it today.' He untangled his scarf and pulled

off his mittens, turning his hands cautiously to feel the summer breeze. 'My goodness, that's rather nice.'

'Oh, this is priceless,' said May, pulling out his mobile. 'Hang on.'

'What are you doing?' Bryant demanded to know.

'Putting this online.' May took the shot before Bryant could stop him.

The photograph shows a funny old man with too-large false teeth, standing in the middle of a bridge, grinning into the camera and wiggling his fingers.

Christopher Fowler is the multi-award-winning author of many novels and short-story collections, including *Roofworld*, *Spanky*, *Psychoville*, *Hell Train*, *Plastic* and eleven Bryant & May mystery novels. His memoir, *Paperboy*, won the Green Carnation Prize, and he recently published a second acclaimed autobiographical volume, *Film Freak*. Chris writes a weekly column in the *Independent on Sunday* and lives in King's Cross in London. To find out more, visit www.christopherfowler.co.uk.